Much lo

To Vi

MW01233363

*I really am real!

WHY DIDN'T SHE JUST LEAVE AND COME ON BACK HOME?

A Patsy Waters

PS: I like you because
you are - - -

Why Didn't She Just Leave and Come On Back Home?

A NOVEL

Allice Patsy Davis Waters

iUniverse, Inc.
New York Lincoln Shanghai

Why Didn't She Just Leave and Come On Back Home?

iUniverse books may be ordered through booksellers or by contacting:

iUniverse
2021 Pine Lake Road, Suite 100
Lincoln, NE 68512
www.iuniverse.com
1-800-Authors (1-800-288-4677)

ISBN: 978-0-595-42934-9 (pbk)
ISBN: 978-0-595-87274-9 (ebk)

Printed in the United States of America

DEDICATED TO MY DAUGHTERS, AND THEIR FAMILIES

Caddie sat in a rocking chair on the front porch of the Victorian boarding house, where she lived on Peachtree Street. She removed a crumpled letter from her sweater pocket, and smoothed its edges.

"Morning, Caddie. You all right? I missed you at breakfast." Caddie looked up and smiled.

Mrs. Meredith stood at the bottom of the front door steps, holding a gallon bucket filled with freshly cut red roses.

"I'm fine. Just wanted to sleep late." Caddie walked down the door steps, and reached for the bucket. "You grow the most beautiful roses, Miz Meredith. Let me help you."

"Thanks, Caddie. Don't spill water on yourself, now."

"I'll be careful."

"You got a new letter from your sister?"

"No. It's the same."

"She ever call your office or write and say when to meet her?"

"No," Caddie sighed.

Mrs. Meredith wiped her face on a blue, cotton apron and smoothed her short, gray hair. "Bless, Pat! If that don't beat everything! She knows you need to ask off from work and all. Go in the house right now, and call her neighbor's number again. What's her name? Miz Mitchells?"

"I've called several times. Believe Miz Mitchells is away from home."

"I see you reading the letter over and over again. Something about it bothers you, doesn't it?"

"Yes. It's different from all the other letters I've ever received from her."

"Caddie, when you let me read Macie's words, it seemed to me like she might be leaving her husband. You take it that way?"

"Oh! No! Macie and her little girls are just going to Three-Mile Crossing for a visit. Why would you think she might be leaving her husband?"

"Don't take me the wrong way. I've noticed a lot of people come and go through this boarding house. Don't worry about me thinking out loud. I'm sorry."

"That's okay, Miz Meredith, but why would you think she's leaving Dan?"

"Well, since you asked, she wrote you for the money for the train tickets, instead of getting the money from her husband, and the most important thing I noticed is the fact that she doesn't mention her husband's name in her letter one way or the other."

"Oh! I see what you mean." Caddie frowned.

Mrs. Meredith smiled and reached for the bucket. "See you at dinner."

Caddie sat back down in her chair, and re-examined her sister's long message. *Usually, Macie writes short messages on picture postcards that depict the place where they live. She always mentions how happy she and Dan and the little girls are.* Caddie smoothed the wrinkles off the coffee-stained letter with her long fingers. *But, this letter is written differently. Parts of it are formal. Macie wrote it slowly, neatly, deliberately, and poetically. She complained about how homesick she is, and wants to come home.*

_________, Tennessee
_________, 194__

Dearest Caddie,

You're a wonderful sister! Thanks so much for the loan, and sending the extra money. It'll be good to have a little left over after I buy the train tickets for Penny, Kathryn and myself. Am very homesick and can't wait to see you. I can just close my eyes, and picture us when you, and Jake and I were all living at home with Aunt Mae and Uncle Hume.

I remember so many fulfilling and happy moments about our childhood—so many things that I miss now. Those little things have become very important. Remember when Aunt Mae stood before her dresser mirror and brushed her soft, white hair and created a queenly bun? Remember how her reflection smiled back in the mirror, and her face crinkled in all the right places? She'd touch one of her front teeth which hung slightly longer in front, with her pointy finger, and rear back with her hands on her hips, and analyze herself. When she'd notice us watching her with those amazing eyes that could see into our soul, she'd reach out and hug us to her large and billowy breasts.

I remember the time when her white teeth were lightly shaded with a film of snuff, and she smiled and said it was her secret "vice."

Sometimes she smelled like pine trees or sweet gum bark, octagon soap or home-made starch. Sometimes she smelled like apple pies and herbs or strawberries, and sometimes she smelled like the sweetness of "bought" perfume. What did she smell like to you?

How marvelous it was to have Aunt Mae teach us the love for all nature—the love for all creatures, the birds, the flowers, the chickens that occasionally walked into her kitchen, and the dogs that lounged on the porch. I especially loved our walks in the woods, along the pine-needle strewn paths, down to the mossy lawn at the spring! I miss the rocks and the hills. Don't you?

A N D

Wasn't it great when she'd say, 'Come on! Let's go and see something no one has ever seen before!'

Remember, Caddie, how we'd walk hand-in-hand, along a winding trail across a log, over a brook and sometimes to one of the springs, and stop along the way? We'd kneel down, quietly, as she gently lifted a leaf, a limb from a tree, or maybe a rock. Right in front of our eyes was something no other human being had ever seen! Sometimes it was new life developing from the oak, or a compound of ants, termites or maybe an earthworm!

It was so special to see something no one had ever seen since God placed it there.

Sometimes we whispered at that altar where we knelt. Sometimes we laughed. Remember?

I loved the way she caressed our hair when we were little girls, and say, 'If you feel lonely, remember you're not alone. All you have to do is look around you. Look under a leaf, under a rock, in a tree, in the sand, at the sky or in a creek. Just take time to look and you will find some of God's other creatures, just waiting for you to come around.' She would laugh, reach down, pick us up and swing us around and around. I want to be a mama like that.

I miss our long walks and talks with Uncle Hume. The crinkles around his twinkling eyes speak love in itself. Remember when we were little girls, and he held us on his lap, and he'd say, 'Everything is gonna be all right.' I can't wait to hear him say that again.

I want Penny and Kathryn to experience that love we experienced as little girls when we were their age. Being so far away from home is causing us to 'miss out' on many important/meaningful things in life. Thanks for giving the girls—for giving me that chance by sending the train fare.

Much, much love,
Macie

P.S. I'll repay you just the moment I can. Can't wait to catch up on all the news. Have you found anyone special?

* * * *

Caddie walked to her room, and laid Macie's letter on her desk. *I'm homesick, too, and miss everyone at home, especially Jake.* She pulled paper, pen and ink from her desk, but placed it back when she realized that the ink was dried in the bottle.

* * * *

Atlanta, Georgia
At the Law Office
*_______, 194_*
Dearest Macie,
You failed to give an arrival date in your last letter. I tried to call Miz Mitchell's number but got no answer. Please call me or write fast! I'll need to do the usual stuff to be off from work and meet you at Three-Mile Crossing.
I can't imagine how much Penny and Kathryn must have grown Can't wait to see y'all.
I'm on my lunch hour, and I need to finish this note fast. Have a deadline—typing a legal brief. I like my job, but it can get hectic—sometimes awfully stressful.
Find a telephone somewhere and call me at my boarding house or here at the office, and let me know when you plan to arrive at Three-Mile Crossing? My telephone numbers are: ______________ and _____________, just in case you lost them.
I'll try to call you again, when I get home this evening. I love you and miss you! Give Dan and the baby girls a hug from me.

Love! Love!
Caddie

P.S. Your letter or should I say your dissertation (ha! ha!) made me very homesick and made me want to go back to Three-Mile Crossing. Call me ASAP! To answer your question, about me being interested in someone special—I still date a guy that lives at the rooming house, but it's nothing serious—just friends. I'll fill you in when I see you.

* * * *

Aunt Mae poured Uncle Hume another cup of coffee. "I had a terrible dream last night, Hume."

"What was it about, Mae?" Uncle Hume covered his mouth, and yawned. He stretched his long and lean arms over his head. When he shifted his weight, the oak chair creaked.

"I dreamed I was somewhere upstairs—believe it was in this very house. I was just a sitting, and gazing out a tall, tall, narrow window, and looking down into a chicken lot.

"I saw a Dominecker hen and three baby chicks feeding on corn, and one of the little chicks stood all alone a little distance from the rest of the brood. Suddenly, a huge, black shadow of an over-sized bird passed over the mama hen and chicks. The elongated shadow circled.

"I looked up thinking it was a chicken hawk, but instead, it was a giant, white dove. All of a sudden, right before my eyes that gorgeous giant, white dove turned black. It flapped its wings hard and screeched a deafening screech! It swept down to where that baby chick was standing all alone, and clutched it in its ugly claws and ascended, soared upward, and came zooming towards my upstairs bedroom window! It turned its large feathered head to one side, and one of its shiny, dark black eyes covered the entire window, and formed a mirror. I glanced briefly at my frightened reflection in the bird's eye. That bird swooped before me so fast, it was unbelievable! I stood helplessly in a bright, bright light, in a vacuum of spiraling energy that caused my white night gown to billow, and my long, scraggly, white hair to stand on-end! That giant bird flew straight up and away with the chick dangling in its scabby claws. Its wide wingspan clouded the sun!"

"That's a terrible dream, Mae." He took a sip of black coffee, sat his cup upon his saucer, and exaggerated a shiver. "Don't dwell on it."

She opened her eyes widely. "It was such a nightmare!" She sat down at the table across from Uncle Hume, and twisted a corner of her red and white checked cotton apron in, out and around her hands and fingers.

Uncle Hume reached over and cupped his hands over hers until she calmed.

"Hume, that gigantic black dove made a big swoop and snatched that little chick up in its bare claws and flew away! Far, far and away."

"Not a pretty dream, huh, Mae?"

"No! It was frightful. When I woke up, I thought *I'll never see that baby chick again!* The dream was so vivid in my mind, I went outside this morning and looked on the side of the house to see if that giant bird left scratch marks on the side of the house or window-sill."

He shook his head sympathetically. "Try to forget it, Mae."

"I keep seeing those ugly claws. It's a bad omen, Hume." She pulled her navy, woolen sweater tighter around her neck and shoulders.

"No such thing, Mae. It's just a dream. Not a bad omen."

"I hope so, Hume."

Uncle Hume took a deep swallow of black coffee. "Why are you so upset, Mae? What could the dream mean? That we need to watch out for our baby chicks? We can do that."

"I suppose."

"Mae, you're such a religious woman, why are you so superstitious? You're giving me the willies."

"You've got the willies? I didn't mean to—"

"I just had a shiver run down my spine." He smiled and released her hands. "Remember what they say. Dreams won't come true if you wait and tell them after breakfast, and you made sure that you told the dream after breakfast," he smiled.

Aunt Mae stared back at him and gave a weak smile. "You're superstitious, too."

"Not like you." He rubbed his stomach. "Great biscuits!"

"Dreaming about this giant, black, shadowy bird is a bad omen, Hume."

"Good biscuits and ham, Mae," he said, emphatically, and to end the subject, he arose from the table. "After I milk and feed, we can talk about it again, if it'll make you feel better." He pulled on his red and black checkered, woolen jacket, and reached for a milk-pail. "Where's my hat?"

"On the rack at the front door. I'll get it for you."

He observed her closely when she walked slowly across the room.

"It's bad luck to dream about black birds. Sorry to bother you with my terrible dream." She stood at the back door and held the screen door for him.

No bother, a 'tall, darling. Always tell me your dreams." He squeezed her elbow, consolingly.

* * * *

Aunt Mae dressed in her black-voile dress, black straw hat, trimmed in a black grosgrain ribbon, and admired herself in the mirror. Uncle Hume came into the room, waving a small blue and black checkered tie and hung it around his neck.

"Please help me with my tie, darling."

As Aunt Mae attempted to straighten the tie, he held her so closely, so tightly she could hardly move her arms. "Gotcha!" He said, and kissed her on the lips.

They laughed, as they always did.

The spell was broken when the dogs barked and the guineas sounded an alarm.

"Who can that be this early in the morning?"

They rushed to the front porch, and recognized Sheriff Olliff's county vehicle approaching.

"Something's wrong! George-West Myers is with Sheriff Olliff. They wouldn't be coming down here, now, if they could wait till church time to see us." Aunt Mae crossed her arms over her breasts, and held her shoulders tightly, dreading to hear what they had to say.

Sheriff Olliff and George-West Myers got out of the automobile slowly. They both removed their gray felt hats.

George-West held his arms towards them and began to speak before he reached the porch. "There's no easy way to break this news."

"Oh! No! What is it?"

"I've already called Caddie in Atlanta at her boarding house. She's waiting to hear from you."

"What is it, George-West? What is it, Sheriff?"

"What? What?"

Sheriff Olliff guided Aunt Mae to a chair. "I agree, George-West—there's no easy way—Dan Zanderneff called from Tennessee. Said to tell y'all that 'Macie is dead.'"

"Oh, no! How can she be dead? What happened?" Aunt Mae screamed. Uncle Hume reached towards her.

"Dan just blurted out that Macie killed herself."

"Killed herself!" screamed Aunt Mae.

"No! No!" Uncle Hume groaned. "She couldn't have! She wouldn't—couldn't kill herself!"

"Dan found Macie dead in the bathroom. Dan said that she slit both her wrists."

"We just got a letter from Macie saying she's coming home! Tell me whatcha say is not true—it's not true!"

"Macie's not the type to kill herself! She loved life! Where's Jake? Does Jake know?" Uncle Hume's voice cracked.

"Jake's helping transport some prisoners from our jail to Atlanta and Alabama," Sheriff Olliff replied softly.

"Please try to find him! We need Jake."

"We'll do what we can," said George-West. "Caddie's waiting to hear from you," he whispered. "I telephoned her about Macie, just as soon as I heard this tragic news."

"I sent Deputy Jones to fetch Laughing Eyes and John McIntosh to come and be with y'all. I knew you'd want your best friends to be here with you."

* * * *

When the cabdriver stopped at a ramshackle house in a downtrodden neighborhood, Aunt Mae and Uncle Hume looked at each other.

"This is not '327,' is it?" Uncle Hume asked the cabdriver.

The cabdriver rested his arm upon the back of the front seat, and turned around to face them. "Yes, such as it is."

Uncle Hume paid the man.

A wreath of white cotton roses, with black leaves, tied with a black grosgrain bow, hung on the wooden front door of the run-down house. An elderly, short and overweight lady opened the door to a dingy, darkened hallway.

"Good afternoon. We're Mae and Hume Brown."

"I'm Betty Sue Mitchells. I live next door." She smiled nervously and timidly, and moved aside to make room for them to enter the small hallway. "I'll show you to the coffin in the parlor."

"Where's Dan?" asked Aunt Mae.

Dan rushed forward and threw his arms around Aunt Mae and sobbed, "You know how much I love Macie! I love her! I love her!"

"We know. We know," Aunt Mae hugged him, patted him on the back, and attempted to calm him.

They wept together.

Dan turned around to greet Uncle Hume and held him tightly around the neck. "I love Macie!"

"Yes! Yes!" Uncle Hume's lips trembled. "We all did. We all loved her."

"Your maw and paw are so sorry they couldn't come," Aunt Mae consoled.

"I want to see my mother," Dan lamented.

"Your mother's upset she couldn't be here with you. Wants you to come home as soon as you can. She said to tell you to hurry on home."

"And, my dad?"

"Had to stay and take care of your mama and the farm."

Dan continued to sob. "Caddie's in the front room."

"We know you loved Macie! Let's go see Caddie."

"Here I am." Caddie stood in the doorway, still holding her suitcase. She placed it on the floor and the three of them hugged. "I just got here a few minutes ago. It's not real!"

"Yes, a shock!"

"Did anyone ever get in touch with Jake?" Caddie pushed her long, platinum-blond hair away from her shoulders. It cascaded to her small waist and hips.

"He's still in Atlanta or Alabama. He'll be mighty sad," Aunt Mae sighed.

"Yeah, he'll be mighty shook up," said Uncle Hume.

"He worshipped Macie," Caddie murmured. She rubbed her nose and her full red lips with trembling hands.

"Loves you too, Caddie."

"Not the way he does her. He worships Macie," she said more emphatically.

"I know, Chile." Aunt Mae noticed the emphasis Caddie made on how Jake felt about Macie. "He loves you too, Caddie. Take us to Macie."

* * * *

Aunt Mae looked around the dimly lit room and noticed Penny and Kathryn huddling together and hiding behind a straight-back chair. When she took them into her arms, they trembled.

"Penny, do you remember me and Aunt Caddie?" asked Aunt Mae.

Caddie picked up the adorable blue-eyed, blond little girl, who looked a lot like herself. "Hi, Penny."

Kathryn flinched when Aunt Mae lifted her into her arms, and stroked her long, black hair. She observed Aunt Mae with watchful hazel-green eyes. "You and Penny are beautiful little girls, just like your mother." Kathryn stared at Uncle Hume with wide open, frightened eyes, and hugged Aunt Mae tightly around the neck, as if she'd never let her go.

* * * *

"I'll stay with Penny and Kathryn while y'all talk to Dan," Caddie whispered. "We'll probably go outside and play."

Uncle Hume and Aunt Mae turned away from the coffin, and walked around the small, sparsely furnished house until they found Dan Zanderneff, sitting at the kitchen table.

"Dan, where did Macie die?" asked Uncle Hume.

"I keep seeing her lying on the floor." His voice cracked.

"What happened? Macie wrote us she was coming home."

Dan's puffy and blood-shot eyes were distorted beyond recognition. His sorrowful countenance made it harder to ask about Macie's death, but they had to hear how Macie died.

"Where did it happen, Dan?"

"Can't believe this is happening. I loved Macie!" Dan slumped lower in his chair and placed his hands on top of his head.

"We know you loved her," Aunt Mae insisted. "She's our daughter, and we have to know what happened!"

"Y'all come on. I'll show you where Dan found Macie. It happened in the water closet," Betty Sue Mitchells whispered.

Aunt Mae and Uncle Hume walked hesitantly into a small and immaculately clean bathroom. Nothing appeared to be out of place. Nothing in that small place indicated why Macie would want to kill herself!

Betty Sue Mitchells whispered, "After the undertaker came and got her body, some of us church folks came over here and straightened up the place, and I cleaned the blood up, right here in the water-closet. All by myself."

"Oh, my Lord! Lord have mercy!" Aunt Mae placed her hand over her heart, and held onto the door-jam. Uncle Hume placed his arm around Aunt Mae, and searched her ashen face.

Betty Sue Mitchells stood in front of the blotched, wall mirror, where the silver had flecked, and pointed her chubby index finger while she spoke. "Blood was all over the sink. A little bit of the blood was on the walls just above the sink and right here behind me." She pointed. "Some was on the ceiling and the wall. Some of the blood was on the floor and baseboard, right over in that area where Macie fell." Miz Mitchells placed her hand over her mouth, pointed under the sink, and closed her eyes, as she re-lived the scene.

"You're a wonderful person to be able clean this up, Miz Mitchells," Uncle Hume said, appreciatively.

"Dan couldn't clean it up. He was just beside himself! It was hard to do, but I managed to do it because I liked Macie and the little girls.

Aunt Mae shook her head in amazement.

"Miz Mitchells, we appreciate everything," said Uncle Hume.

"Yes, touching her blood was a hard thing to do, but wish I could have done more to help her."

"You have done more than enough," said Aunt Mae.

"Thank you, Miz Mitchells. Thank you," Caddie whispered.

"You've been a great friend. I'm sure Macie loved you," said Aunt Mae.

"Macie was one of the sweetest and one of the most beautiful ladies that I've ever seen. She had the most luxurious, long, black hair and the biggest blue eyes that I've ever seen. She was a lovely person."

"Yes," Aunt Mae agreed.

"I have a couple of beds at my house. You're welcome to spend the night."

"Thank you, Miz Mitchells. You are a very nice lady."

"Hume, I thought Macie was happy—except for being homesick. Why would Macie want to kill herself? What drove her to do this horrible thing?" Aunt Mae twisted her white cotton handkerchief, in and out and around her fingers.

"Miz Mitchells, what was Macie's state of mind? Was she sad the day she died?" Uncle Hume asked gently.

"Her state of mind?" asked Miz Mitchells. "I'm not sure what you mean—"

"Yes, what was she doing—thinking? Feeling? Saying?"

"I didn't see Macie the day she killed herself. The last time I saw her, she told me she was going home for a visit to see y'all, and she seemed happier than I've ever seen her."

"Yes. Yes. We were looking forward to her visit."

"—but, to answer your question, as to how well did I know Macie and her feelings, no one knew her too well, but I know she was a sweet girl. Tended to Penny and Kathryn, and was a very good mother."

"Yes, she certainly was," said Aunt Mae.

"I wish I could tell you more, but Macie stayed to herself mostly. Hasn't been living here long, you know."

"Yes, Macie and Dan moved quite a bit," said Aunt Mae.

"She was very excited about going home. She told me y'all adopted her and Caddie, and a boy named Jake. I could tell she thought a lot of every one of y'all."

"Macie and Caddie are adopted—not Jake. He's our foster-son."

"It's so sad Jake couldn't come," Betty Sue Mitchells whispered. "Macie sure did like Jake, but, then, she loved everyone!"

"Yes. We dread seeing Jake when we get back home." Aunt Mae pushed white ringlets of hair from her forehead and wiped her eyes with her handkerchief.

"Miz Mitchell, do you know if anyone at all talked to Macie the day she died?" asked Uncle Hume.

"Just Dan. That's all."

"Miz Mitchells, another thing. When did you first learn Macie was dead?"

"Dan ran over to my place justa crying out that Macie had killed herself. I called the ambulance on my telephone, and, then, I ran over here to Dan's and Macie's house, as fast as I could, and ran up on the porch and through the front door! Dan pointed to where Macie's body was justa laying on the water-closet floor. I figured she was dead when I saw her. I knelt down and took her pulse on her neck, and checked her eyes. I could tell she'd gone on to glory."

"Nothing makes sense, does it Miz Mitchells?"

"No, Sir. Not a 'tall." Miz Mitchells wiped sweat from her brow, behind her neck, and across her thin lips with a white, lace handkerchief.

Aunt Mae and Uncle Hume found Dan in the front room sitting beside Macie's coffin.

"Dan, I hate to make you think about what happened, but why do you think Macie wanted to kill herself?" Aunt Mae whispered.

"I had no inkling she wanted to kill herself, but I did know she was depressed." He avoided her eyes. "I didn't know she was this bad." He raked one of his hands over his brownish hair with blondish, sun-bleached streaks, and leaned back.

"Depressed?" Her voice faltered.

"Yes. Macie acted depressed." Dan rubbed his eyes. His usually handsome face was blotched and distorted.

"Dan, why didn't you let us know Macie was depressed—especially bad enough to kill herself? I would have come out here to be with her. I would have let her rest—I could have cooked and taken care of y'all." Aunt Mae hesitated. "Hume and I would have stopped everything at our house to come and help y'all in some way. I can't believe you didn't ask us," she retorted curtly, sharply.

"I didn't know she felt so bad, myself." He closed his eyes, and leaned back in a straight-back chair. He stretched his six-foot frame restlessly, and covered his face with his long, right arm. "I really didn't know how bad she felt."

"Dan, just the other day, we received a very sweet letter from Macie telling us that she was coming home! She was anxious to see us. She missed us! What happened? It was a happy and pleasant letter. No depression—no mystery."

Dan arose abruptly from his chair.

Aunt Mae followed Dan onto the front porch, where he fell into a rickety slat-backed chair, and held his head in his hands. "Yes, she looked forward to going home to Three-Mile Crossing, but, then—but then she did this horrible thing!" He snubbed. "I loved Macie. I don't know what the girls and I will do without her. Beautiful, beautiful Macie!"

"Now, now, Dan," Aunt Mae soothed. She stood behind him and stroked his shoulder.

"Let's go back inside the house, Mae," said Uncle Hume.

They walked back into the front room and stood beside Macie's coffin.

"She's put up real purty. Real purty!" said Betty Sue Mitchells.

"I'll miss her—" Caddie rearranged one of Macie's dress-cuffs and caressed her long, black hair.

"Hume—"

Uncle Hume looked down into Aunt Mae's sad, blue eyes. "Yes, Mae?"

"Why did Macie leave us like this? I want to ask her why she killed herself and why didn't she know how much we'll miss her? She knew we loved her! And, how could she leave Penny and Kathryn?" Aunt Mae whispered. "How could she leave everyone?"

"I've never known anyone that committed suicide." He took a long breath, and placed a strong arm around her shoulders.

"Me either. If only Macie could speak to us!"

A knock sounded at the front door.

"That will be the church people bringing y'all some supper." Betty Sue Mitchells straightened her black taffeta dress, and walked slowly towards the front door.

* * * *

After a funeral service at Macie's church, the family sat around the kitchen table. "How can we help you, Dan?" asked Aunt Mae.

Dan nodded his head in the direction of the bedroom door. "Aunt Mae, you'll find a couple of suitcases in the bedroom closet. Would y'all please pack up Macie's and the girls' stuff, and take those things with you? Macie had drawings, paintings and stories that she wrote for Penny and Kathryn? I'll have to ship the furniture."

"We'll be glad to take it, Dan. We'll take everything we can."

"Please tell Maw and Paw I'll see 'em in a couple of weeks."

"We'll give Joanie and Mr. Zanderneff your message, Dan, but we want you to go with us. You need to be with us at the burial. You'll never forgive yourself if you don't go," Aunt Mae begged.

"I can't—I don't have the money to go to Three-Mile Crossing, and then turn right around and come back here."

"I'll give you the money for a train ticket, Dan."

"Can't accept it, Uncle Hume. I don't even have money for the burial."

"Then, I'll loan it to you. Whatcha say?"

"I can't accept. No telling when I could pay you back."

Aunt Mae stared at Dan, not understanding his reasoning for turning down the money. She wondered how he could say he loved Macie very much but not travel with her body to Three-Mile Crossing for her burial.

"Pay me anytime, Dan," said Uncle Hume

"I can't, Uncle Hume."

"Well, then, we'll take the babies with us and see you in a couple of weeks." Uncle Hume arose from his chair and went to the front porch.

Betty Sue Mitchells assisted in the care of Kathryn and Penny, while Aunt Mae and Caddie placed Macie's few belongings in one of the cardboard suitcases: A few dresses, three pairs of shoes, drawings, small water-color paintings, several small packets of letters, and one large brown paper packet tied neatly with white cotton string, marked *Manuscript.*

The little girls' belongings were just as meager.

Aunt Mae walked through the house and made a mental note of where her daughter spent her last hours. She reverently caressed the highly polished carved roses on Macie's antique oak bed, and those other items she knew Macie might have touched. She stopped at one of the kitchen windows and looked out. "Caddie, tell Hume to come here a moment." Aunt Mae observed four fence posts surrounding an herb garden, and each post held a small birdhouse. Running red and pink roses clung to the fence on each side of the garden.

Uncle Hume stood between Aunt Mae and Caddie in front of the kitchen window, and looked out into the backyard.

"What does that remind you of?" asked Aunt Mae.

"Well, I'll declare." Uncle Hume blew his nose on his handkerchief, folded it and replaced it in his back pocket. "Can you believe it?"

"It's exactly like your herb garden, Aunt Mae, with herbs, and flowers. The birdhouses Uncle Hume made for Macie are sitting on the four corners of the fence-posts just like yours," Caddie whispered. "Can we take the birdhouses with us, Uncle Hume?"

"We'll place the birdhouses on four fence posts, around a garden that we'll dedicate to Macie. Penny and Kathryn should like that.

"I need to gather some of her herbs to place in our special garden," said Aunt Mae.

*　*　*　*

At the railroad depot, Dan gave everyone a hug and a promise to be at Three-Mile Crossing within a couple of weeks.

"Change your mind, please, Dan—" Caddie begged. "Come and be with us."

"I would if I could. But—" He squatted down in front of Penny and Kathryn. "Give me a little hug to last me 'til I see you in a few days. I love you."

"We'll take good care of Penny and Kathryn. Don't you worry."

"As I've already said, I just don't have the money to go to Three Mile Crossing, and then turn around and come right back here to handle things," Dan apologized. "Tell Maw and Paw I love 'em! Tell 'em."

"Take good care of yourself," said Aunt Mae.

They waved at Dan, and the train pulled out of the station.

"Dan's mighty sad. I sure hate to leave him."

"I know it, Caddie. His ma and pa won't understand why he's not coming back with us. But, Caddie, I'm glad you're with us," said Aunt Mae.

"Me, too. Think Jake's already back home and waiting for us?" Caddie asked.

"Jake told Hume on the telephone he'd pick us up at the Southern Depot in Gainesville."

*　*　*　*

"There's Jake!" Uncle Hume pointed to Jake standing on the depot platform.

Caddie stretched her neck to see him.

"Where's Dan?" Jake asked, as he clung to them. His tall and muscular frame towered over Aunt Mae, but he stood evenly with Uncle Hume.

"Dan's not coming to the burial. He'll be here in a couple of weeks."

"Not coming! Why not?" He patted his hands through his curly, blond hair, hurriedly and exasperatedly. "That ass! Why did he not take care of Macie? And, now, there is no good excuse for him not traveling with her body, and attending the graveside service!"

"Didn't have the money. I offered him the money but he refused."

"What man who loves his wife would miss her burial service?" Jake spoke harshly. His blue eyes filled with tears.

"We're trying not to think about it."

"It's too upsetting."

"Jake, remember, this is Penny and this is Kathryn." The little girls held Aunt Mae's skirt and hid behind her.

"A little dark-headed Macie and a little blond-headed Caddie!" Jake exclaimed. He held his arms out towards the little girls. "Aren't y'all gorgeous! How old? Never can remember."

"Penny's three and Kathryn's four."

Jake hugged the little girls and placed them on the ground as gently as if they were china dolls. "Now, let me look at you! Y'all are so precious!" he exclaimed.

"They certainly are," Caddie said softly. An awareness and shyness overcame her. She stood and waited for him to acknowledge her.

Jake turned to Caddie and smiled. "You're looking gorgeous, as usual." He hugged her tightly. "I missed you, Caddie."

She reveled in the sensation of his touch—the scrub of his whiskers on her cheek—the aroma of "Old Spice." "Missed you too, Jake."

He released Caddie and reached for Aunt Mae.

Aunt Mae sniffed. "Jake, you been in the bottle?"

"I'm sober, Aunt Mae. Very sober. You know I worked too hard two years ago to shake the booze habit to get back into the bottle," he smiled sadly. "Stay here and I'll pull the car around." He held Caddie's arm with one hand and her suitcase in the other, and they walked towards his black Ford.

Aunt Mae looked after him with suspicious eyes. She knew the smell of moonshine when she smelled it.

"Mae, stay out of it. Jake's not your little boy anymore."

* * * *

The bell in the belfry of the small, red-brick church at Three-Mile Crossing rang throughout the hills, and mourned the death of one of its own.

At the crest of the hill, and overlooking the cemetery, stood an exquisitely carved, six-foot tall marble angel, with long and slender outstretched arms. She looked upward and toward the east. The funeral procession moved slowly along the red clay road, among the giant, age's old red oak and black oak trees, until they came to rest at the feet of the angel.

Caddie stood beside Jake and looked up and into the face of "Jake's angel." She realized that the angel had been a comfort to Jake—ever since he placed her there.

The words of Psalm 123 drifted on the cool breeze, and echoed in the valley.

Aunt Mae observed the handsome contour of Reverend Buker Webster's face while he read familiar scriptures. He held a small, black notebook with his left hand. His glasses slipped down his nose, and he pushed them back upon his face with his right middle finger, held his elbows at the waist of his pants, and gave a jerk on the waist with his wrist and elbows to pull them up. *Where is the preacher's bible? Doesn't he need a bible to preach a funeral!* She felt the pressure of Uncle Hume's arm around her shoulder. *I can hardly remember the funeral services in Tennessee and the train ride back home.* She sighed in frustration and despair, and looked around the graveyard for Dan's parents. She observed the Zanderneff's standing at their family gravesite. *Standing way over across the cemetery—does that mean the Zanderneffs thought Macie should have been buried at the Zanderneff's gravesite and not beside Macie's mother and father? Why are they not standing here beside all of us? Beside their granddaughters? Are they embarrassed because Dan didn't come to the burial? What? Good! The Zanderneff's are moving over here to be closer to us.*

Grandmaw Taylor and Uncle Albert Taylor sat nearby on a wrought-iron bench, and leaned forward on their walking canes.

Camellia shrubbery planted in front of the headstones of Macie's mother and father shed their red blossom tears upon their graves, and spilled over onto the disturbed, red clay at Macie's grave.

When Aunt Mae bent down to place a wild, white daisy on the top of Macie's coffin, she felt the presence of God, and the love of their many friends who stood closely beside them. Her hands trembled. She pulled her homemade, black velvet shawl a little closer around her shoulders. She strained to hear the words of Reverend Webster, "For what is your life? It is even a vapor that appears for a little time, and then vanishes away."

When the thud of red clay sounded upon Macie's coffin, she and Uncle Hume reached out in front of them and placed their hands upon Penny's and Kathryn's shoulders.

At the Taylor gravesite, a gentle breeze caught the fresh, white and pink wild flowers, tied with baby blue ribbons and delicately intertwined in the ropes of an extra small, wood-seat swing that hung from a gigantic limb of a black oak tree. The ghost of three year old Billy Taylor began to glide the swing gently, back and forth—back and forth.

* * * *

Jake gave Kathryn and Penny each a small, cherry-flavored, penny sucker. He hugged them tightly, and placed them on the front door steps. Their feet dangled and barely touched the next step-rung. He searched their little faces seeking Macie's face in theirs, and gave them an affectionate pat on their heads. "Know your daddy thinks the world of his pretty little girls." He slouched on the steps beside them, combed his hands through his unruly and curly blond hair, and looked into the distance.

His mind wandered and relived the hours he spent with Macie. He envisioned her walking towards him. She looked the same, but her always evident smile was replaced by closed lips and a frown. *Macie, I can't believe you killed yourself! Always believed we would settle down here together at Three Mile Crossing. Believed I'd be a Deputy Sheriff or the Sheriff and you'd be my wife. Dan's a handsome guy, and has a way with words. Never could figure it out. He was like someone just too good to be true—doing everything just right. His poor upbringing and mine were about alike, so how'd he ever learn to sweet-talk? Dan won you over and married you, but why didn't he take care of you? Why are you dead?*

Unspilled tears in Jake's wide apart, round, blue eyes became glassy, and reflected the nightmare.

* * * *

Friends and neighbors filled the Brown's kitchen tables with food and drink, took over the care of the livestock, the food preparation for the family, and the total care of Penny and Kathryn for several days.

Caddie felt guilty for staying in bed and having no energy to work with the family. She pulled a quilt, "The Yellow Star of Texas," closer to her shoulders and turned over. Macie's last letter played over and over in her head, causing her head to ache.

Someone knocked on the door.

"Come in, please," said Caddie.

"Brought you some tea." Laughing Eyes placed a cup on the bedside table, touched Caddie's forehead, and attempted a smile. "Hope you'll enjoy it."

"I feel so useless, so tired and listless, but most of all, my heart is aching. Thanks for helping us, Laughing Eyes."

"You're welcome, Caddie." Laughing Eyes straightened her black hair, pinned at the nape of her neck and smoothed her blue apron. "It's a great privilege to help out."

Caddie heaved a sigh. "What would all of us do without you and John?"

"Yes—our families go back a long ways." Concern for Caddie showed in Laughing Eyes' dark, brown eyes and the furrow on her brow deepened. "All the times your family has done so much for us, this is nothing. Just glad to help."

"Is Jake still here?"

"Not sure where he is. You know he's taking Macie's death mighty hard."

"Yes, I know."

"I called Pem to tell him what's going on, but he's in the middle of a quarter at law school and couldn't come. Said to tell you he'll see you just as soon as he can."

"Thanks. I miss Ole Pem."

"Misses you, too."

"Laughing Eyes, please comfort Aunt Mae all that you can."

"Someone will be here to help as long as this family needs us."

"Thanks, Laughing Eyes."

"Grandmaw Taylor and I are taking care of Penny and Kathryn. We're trying to do things for Aunt Mae, but she's still plugging along trying to do for the family."

"And, Uncle Hume?"

"He's walking in the woods."

"I feel guilty just lying here."

Laughing Eyes plumped a pillow on the bed and straightened the bed covers.

"What kind of tea is this?" Caddie licked her lips.

"A refreshing tea for a special girl." Laughing Eyes smiled. "Take this time to sort it all out. I'll check on you later." The door closed behind her.

Sort out things, huh? Macie, how could you be so selfish? I'm MAD at you, but I feel guilty about feeling so angry. Caddie whispered. She tried to "picture" Macie's actions at the very moment she slit one wrist and then the other one, but she couldn't visualize the act. *Macie! Speak to me and tell me why you took this way 'out.' Why did you kill yourself?*

Caddie held her breath, and listened—listened for the voice of Macie, but all she could hear was the beat of her own guilty heart.

Birds chirped a happy song outside her window, but their sweet sounds didn't console her.

* * * *

Aunt Mae covered her yeast bread dough with a white muslin cloth, and placed the bowl on the kitchen cupboard to rise. She thought of Jake and how depressed he appeared when he returned from the spring that afternoon. She knew his strengths and failures when he was a child, as a man, and as one who loved Macie. She thought of the day Macie and Dan married, and how cowered and dejected Jake had appeared. A great change came over him that day and he began to drink.

She drained pickled green beans, cooked with fat-back, from a black iron Dutch oven. Dipped them into a yellow ceramic serving bowl trimmed with royal blue stripes, and placed slices of fried sugar-cured ham upon a white, stoneware platter. Her thoughts dissected Macie's make-up: *Where was the quirk I've never seen—that unidentified link which allowed Macie to kill herself? What motivated her towards death? Did she have to be weak to commit suicide or strong enough to carry it through? Which was it?*

She found no answers.

* * * *

After Jake went home that evening, Aunt Mae prepared the little girls for bed. When she removed Kathryn's and Penny's dresses, their flinches and the fear in their eyes startled her, but she was more startled to find the slight discoloration of old bruises and scars upon both their small, and skinny bodies. *No one told me the little girls were injured! Betty Sue Mitchells bathed and dressed Penny and Kathryn for the funeral and the train ride home. Since we arrived home, Grandmaw Taylor and Laughing Eyes and other friends bathed, dressed and took care of the little girls. No one mentioned the bruises! Were they not concerned?* She showed the bruises and scars to Uncle Hume. She showed the bruises to Uncle Hume.

"Who did this terrible thing!" he demanded.

"I've already asked Penny and Kathryn, and they just hold on to each other and stare at me. Won't say a word. Bless their little hearts!"

She prayed for their healing while she placed her own special blends of healing balms and ointments upon their backs, and touched the fading outline of the whelps.

She removed red flannel healing blankets from her healing basket and warmed them beside the wood-stove in the kitchen, wrapped a blanket around each of the little girls, and placed them in Uncle Hume's lap. They snuggled to him, and stared at her.

Uncle Hume wrapped his long arms around them. "Everything's gonna be all right," he soothed. "Henny-Penny and Kackie are gonna be all right." Uncle Hume gave them their nicknames that day and they were called those loving words ever since.

Aunt Mae went outside, stood in the front yard, searched the starry sky, and prayed for guidance and peace of heart.

Much later, she entered the cabin and found the little girls asleep in Uncle Hume's lap.

Aunt Mae and Uncle Hume placed Henny-Penny and Kackie in their bed, and sat before the fireplace. Aunt Mae poked the fire, and sparks flew.

"Who do you think did this horrible thing? Who beat them? And beat them hard enough to bruise them and scar them?" Uncle Hume squeezed his eyes shut and closed his hands into fists.

"Dan and Macie are kind and sweet people. Who did this? We'll have to ask Dan."

"Dan and Macie would never mistreat the little girls, but if they didn't mistreat them, who did?" Uncle Hume questioned.

"I'd hate to think that Macie was a child beater?"

"How could she be a child beater? I know she loved them!" Uncle Hume exclaimed.

"What about Dan?"

"No. Neither of them could do such a thing."

"Do you think Macie really wanted to come home when she wrote and told us she did?"

"Of course, she did, Mae."

"If so, why didn't she just come on home. Macie knew how much we loved her. I don't understand."

"Mae, I don't know why and I don't want to think about Dan or Macie beating Henny-Penny and Kackie. When Dan gets here, do we show him their bruises first, and ask for an explanation or do we lecture him for his neglect in not writing, and hate him for not coming to Macie's burial and not showing up later?"

"Hume, I don't know what we'll do first, but Dan'll get a piece of my mind!"

"I'm going to bed, Mae." Uncle Hume yawned.

"Hope you can sleep."

"Sleep? What's that?" He searched her tender blue eyes. He stretched his long, muscular arms over his head and hobbled stiff-legged to their bedroom.

* * * *

Aunt Mae placed her pine-straw mending basket in her lap, and threaded a needle. *Hume's hair was as black as a crow when I first met him but now he has a full head of white hair. He's as handsome as the day we got married. I know he misses working on that ole G& NW train, crossing the Chattahoochee River, and stopping at Brookton, Clermont, Cleveland, and near the Indian Mound at Old Nacoochee Valley. Things sure have changed! We need to get in touch with his friends from the sawmills that took those logs out of the mountains down to Helen, and loaded them on the train. I know he misses his railroad buddies. Might help him feel better to get in touch with them.*

Uncle Hume dropped his boots on the floor, and the noise startled her back to reality. *Lord, it's good to have Hume and his great strength right here beside me. What if Hume and I learn that Dan did beat those little girls? What would we do? What would we say to Dan? Oh! My! What a mess!*

* * * *

The small community held folk of every monetary level: a few wealthy, some middle-class, some poor and a lot of very poor, but being poor did not change pride, dignity nor poise.

Since the mountains didn't hold enough jobs for its people, many of them left their homes to seek a livelihood elsewhere through necessity. The close-knit community grieved for family and friends, when one of its own left home to "seek his fortune." Most of those who left remained forever homesick for the red clay of its hills.

"Wish you could stay here with us and not have to go back to Atlanta." Aunt Mae held Caddie a little longer than usual.

"Me too," Caddie whispered. She pulled a short-brimmed, black hat on her head. Smoothed her hands over the black taffeta bodice, and small waist, and brushed specks of dust from her long, black skirt.

"We'll tighten our belts a little tighter, if you want to stay. I've already told you that," Uncle Hume whispered.

"Thanks, but I need to make my own way," she sighed with disappointment. "Ms. Meredith and my bosses are expecting me back in Atlanta."

Henny-Penny and Kackie held on to Caddie's skirt. "Be good little girls. Be sweet," Caddie bent down and smiled, showing her even, white teeth. "I'll miss you." She kissed them, and they clung to her.

"Jake, you be extra careful driving Caddie back to Atlanta, you hear?" Aunt Mae bossed.

Uncle Hume laughed and pointed at Aunt Mae. "A back-seat driver and she's not even riding."

"You know I'll drive carefully," Jake smiled. "We'll be talking about Macie along the way, and I'll take Caddie right to the door of her boarding house. Don't you worry none."

* * * *

"Hi, Jake. How are you getting along?"

"Getting along pretty well, Reverend."

"I see you park here at the church lots of times, and I presume you walk to Mae and Hume Brown's home. Why not drive?"

"Road's narrow and bumpy, but I do drive to their house, occasionally? Thought I'd walk today, since I have the day off from work," Jake smiled.

"Heard Uncle Hume's folks named this place *Three-Mile Crossing*. Wonder why?"

"They say Grandpa Brown named the place many years ago. He'd say, 'I need to go to The Three-Mile Crossing,' and then he'd walk from his cabin three miles to the main road—up here to the crossing to get the mail or catch a ride into town."

"Is that a fact? This place is not really a town, but just a beautiful place in the middle of nowhere to get somewhere."

"Yes, a beautiful spot in God's country. The nickname of 'Three-Mile Crossing' just caught on. If you'll notice all the stores are built on each side of that four-way crossing, but most everyone calls it *Three Mile Crossing.*"

"Interesting how we nickname things. Let's go to the parsonage and get a couple of horses, and I'll ride with you to their house. That okay with you?" Reverend Webster pulled his white collar higher around his neckline.

"Sure. I'd love to ride. You've got some handsome horse-flesh!" said Jake.

They rounded up a couple of horses.

The Blue Ridge Mountains were a hazy, sky-blue. Cattle lowed and watered at the edge of a lake near the parsonage.

They left the main road and took a narrow trail towards Mae and Hume Brown's home. Heavy vegetation held back the direct sunlight and cast spidery webbed shadows on the decayed leaves. A gentle breeze brushed their faces, and a drone of insects filled the air. As they went deeper into the woods, birds called and squirrels scampered playfully in the trees.

Suddenly, Reverend Webster yelled out when he rode into a circular spider-web. "Dad-burn-it!" He knocked the spider-web off his head and face, wadded it up in his hands, and wiped his hands on his shirt. "I'm going to kill that spider!"

"Let that spider be." Jake scolded. "It's not doing any harm."

"No! Just look! It messed up my glasses." He held his hand out and showed the remains of the crumpled cobweb hanging to the rim of his glasses, and began to reach towards the spider.

"Let that spider alone!" Jake raised his voice. His face turned red and he frowned, thinking the preacher of all people, should be protective of God's creatures.

Reverend Webster placed his glasses back on his face, but took them off immediately and cleaned them. "That makes me so angry!"

Suddenly, a wind infiltrated the pine trees and the trees began sighing and moaning.

"We better hurry 'fore we get wet. It's a coming up a cloud!"

"Jake, I've never heard anybody say *It's a-coming-up-a-cloud*," Reverend Buker Webster laughed.

"It's a good southern term," Jake responded without smiling. "Thought you were from the south."

The wind died down as quickly as it had begun.

Reverend Webster slowed his horse's gait. "Yeah—I'm southern born. Sure am. I know you are also, and I also know that you're lucky to have Aunt Mae and Uncle Hume as your friends!"

"Been more than friends."

"I like them. How old are they?"

"Aunt Mae's sixty-five and Uncle Hume's seventy-five."

"Tell me about Macie Zanderneff. Did you know her well?"

"Of course, I knew her better than anybody—except Dan, I guess. I was already living with Aunt Mae and Uncle Hume, when Macie and Caddie came to live with us."

"Oh! You're adopted?"

"No."

"Which one did you like the best—Macie or Caddie?"

Jake didn't say anything for a few minutes.

"Both."

"Cute girls?"

"Yes, of course." Jake took on a far-away expression. "Both are very cute girls, and I like them both, but I'm closer to Macie in age. Mostly, Caddie was a chatterbox and pestered and aggravated us older kids, looking for attention. Macie was real little—had dark-hair, blue eyes and freckles on her nose. Cutest little thing you ever saw. We walked to school, and studied together. One time for school work she had to write a poem, and she'd write a line of poetry, and I'd write the next line to rhyme hers." Jake smiled. "You know stuff like that. Caddie would say, 'Let me do it, too,' and made up a funny limerick. We laughed at her, but I took more patience with Macie. She was quieter and more serious than Caddie." Jake stopped talking and became reflective. "I don't know if you know it or not, but Caddie's always been able to outplay all of us boys whether it was playing pool or board games. She can pitch and hit a ball, too."

"Sounds like a nice childhood, Jake. I envy you."

"Yes, it was. Did you have a good childhood, Reverend?"

"Nothing like yours, Jake," he frowned. "Tell me more about your growing up."

"It was nice. Macie and I would run away from Caddie sometimes and she'd yell that she'd get even with us. She did, too. Caddie would do something silly to make us laugh. She'd put June-bugs down the back of my shirt and things like that, and one day she put a little bit of flour in my hat, and hung it back on the hat rack, and it dumped all over me when I put it on my head, just the minute we were going out the door for church. Boy, I was a mess! Aunt Mae was upset cause I missed church, but Uncle Hume just laughed and laughed until he cried—just wiped tears from his eyes. Caddie stayed away from me all that day, fearing what I might do to get even, but she was so afraid Aunt Mae would be mad. Aunt Mae was the one who had to clean up my wool hat and suit. But, it took a lot to make Aunt Mae mad." Jake hesitated and smiled at his fond memories.

"Did Aunt Mae punish Macie or Caddie? Or you?"

"Just made us go to bed early. That was a horrible punishment we thought."

"Noticed Caddie at the funeral. She's a pretty young lady."

"Yes, Caddie is beautiful. Caddie was always just a little ole Tomboy." Jake clucked to his horse. "She's such a good friend, I'm sorry she had to leave Three-Mile Crossing."

"So, you liked Macie a lot, huh?"

"Yeah, I liked Macie a lot.

"Work is scarce here, isn't it?" asked Reverend Webster.

"Scarce as hen's teeth!"

"Think Caddie will move back here from Atlanta?"

"No jobs are here. I doubt she'll ever move back."

"So, the three of you were foster children?" Reverend Webster inquired.

They dismounted at a small waterfall and watered the horses at the creek.

Jake raised his voice in order to be heard over the sound of the waterfall. "Caddie and Macie were adopted."

"It seems like the Browns would have wanted to adopt you, too." Reverend Webster attempted to console.

"Complications kept me from getting adopted. When my mother died, my father just up and left and never came back, but deep in my heart I always thought he'd be back someday."

They mounted.

Jake galloped ahead, and flushed a covey of quail.

Reverend Buker Webster caught up with Jake, "Anymore foster children?"

"No, but we played with a lot of children. Played with Ole Pem, Dan Zanderneff, the Clements boys, the Daniels boys, the Donahoo boys, the Meyers and the Taylors to name a few. Have you met Ole Pem?"

"No, I haven't had the pleasure."

"Pemrick McIntosh—we call him *Ole Pem* for short, is one of my best friends. We hunted, fished, played football and softball, all over these mountains. Laughing Eyes and John McIntosh are his parents."

"So, Laughing Eyes—I meant to say Monica—and John are the parents of this guy I keep hearing people talking about. The rumor is he's handsome and smart, too."

"He does all right. Ole Pem's studying law in Mississippi. Gonna work for Judge Pewter, when he passes the bar."

"I'd like to know more about Macie. Where did she meet her husband?"

"Oh, her husband—uh—" Jake's words stumbled. "Dan grew up about five miles up the road—came to our house a lot. Even though he grew up here, he's different.

"Different? How?"

"Well, he more or less isolated himself, and stayed in the books all the time, when he wasn't working on his dad's farm. Dan quoted scriptures and Shakespeare, had the voice of a radio announcer, and could 'sell snow to an Eskimo'."

"Interesting man, huh?"

"I guess you could say that—"

"So, he and Macie fell in love, and got married?"

"During Macie's senior year in high school, she skipped into the house one day and said she was marrying Dan. I have never been more surprised and disappointed." Jake hesitated, and looked ahead.

"Guess you were more than surprised, huh?

"Yes, her courtship and marriage to Dan was a surprise," Jake uttered indistinctly. "They married right after they graduated from high school." He spoke so low, Reverend Buker strained to hear his words.

"Weren't you aware that Macie's and Dan's relationship was serious?" Reverend Webster observed Jake closely.

"No. I only knew that they did a few socials together. Right after they married, they moved—no way for them to make a living here."

"Lots of people have to leave Three-Mile Crossing, huh?"

"Macie and Dan made it back home to visit one time, after they left."

"Did Macie and Dan get along, okay?" asked Reverend Webster.

"Yes, they did as far as we know."

"So, you say Dan hasn't been in touch with the family at all, lately?"

"We don't know where he is," said Jake.

"Usually a prompt person?"

"Always on time. That's why we're so worried."

"It is puzzling," Reverend Webster said thoughtfully.

"Tell me about yourself, Reverend."

Reverend Buker Webster pulled his white collar a little higher about his neck. "Not much to tell about me, Jake."

"Bet you have a lot of stories to tell."

"Not really. I moved a lot before my wife—Locket—and I got married and came to Three-Mile Crossing. Can't believe we've been here six months already."

"Where you from originally?"

"Born in South Georgia; grew up in Louisiana, and I spent a number of years in Europe. Then I came back to Louisiana where I met Locket at a Christian retreat."

"Glad y'all enjoy living here. I don't want to ever leave this place again, myself," said Jake.

"You left to go to work?"

"No, I went to college. Was lucky that I could come back to Three-Mile Crossing, and work at the Sheriff's office after I graduated."

* * * *

Jake and Reverend Webster rode into a large clearing. "There's the cabin." Jake pointed.

A waft of smoke curled from a chimney at the back of a two-story log cabin, snuggled in the valley at the foot of the blue mountain range.

They passed a very small log cabin, smaller than most. Cherokee roses grew on each side of its front stoop. "What is that quaint little cabin?" Reverend Webster pointed.

"A quilting house."

"What is a quilting house?"

"Some of the ladies in the community meet here with Aunt Mae to piece and quilt. It has lots of shelves for folded material and cloth scraps. Tables and chairs surround a large table, and quilting racks hang from the ceiling."

When they neared the two-story log cabin with a high-pitched roof, all of the dogs began to bark at a stranger, except Ole Jeb.

Ole Jeb raised his head, stretched slowly, and wagged his tail when he saw Jake.

Aunt Mae stood motionless on the front porch, holding a whisk broom, as she watched the men approach.

Uncle Hume waved from the barn.

"Jake, you're a sight for sore eyes!" Aunt Mae exclaimed. "Howdy, Reverend Webster. Mighty fine horses." Aunt Mae removed her apron and motioned for him to sit down on the front porch, all with one big swoop of the hand.

"Thank you, Aunt Mae."

"My great-grandmother used to rock me in this chair when I was a baby." Aunt Mae caressed the back of the chair lovingly.

"Got anything good to eat, Aunt Mae?" asked Jake.

"You were born hungry, Jake! Pound cake is in the pie safe."

"Where you say the little girls are, Aunt Mae?"

"On the back porch playing with Spooky and Shadows," she smiled.

"Spooky? Shadows? Is that a game?" asked Reverend Webster.

"No. Baby kittens," she laughed.

"I like your place, Aunt Mae." Reverend Webster made himself comfortable in the rocking chair.

A chicken climbed the stairwell, walked across the front porch, and into the open doorway.

"Thank you, Reverend. You've never had any of my special herb tea, have you?"

"I'd love to try some. Locket said it's delicious. By the way, a chicken went inside your house."

"That ole chicken won't hurt a thing. Where's Locket?"

"At church practicing the piano."

"Next time bring her with you."

"I ran into Jake at the church, and invited myself to come along," he smiled broadly and his yellowish-gray eyes twinkled.

"Glad you did. Glad you did."

"It was the first time Jake and I have really carried on a conversation." Reverend Webster held his hands in his lap, stretched his long legs, and cleared his throat.

"Jake's a fine young man," she smiled.

"He told me about Macie, Caddie and a little about his friend, Pemrick McIntosh. I've heard his name over and over again since I arrived at Three-Mile Crossing. Does he ever come home for a visit?"

"Ole Pem comes home when he can. He's in law school."

"Hope to meet him sometime."

"You'll see Ole Pem at the church house the next time he's here. He always goes to church."

"You're calling him *Ole Pem* and he's just a young man, isn't he?"

"Just a nick-name. We use the word *ole* like it's a word of endearment."

"I've noticed in these parts that the word *ole* is used before the names of dogs and other animals, as well as people."

"Yes," she laughed, "but *Ole Pem* just suits him better than *Pemrick. Old* in this instance is another word for *wise.*

"Wise Pem—Ole Pem. So quaint!"

"No. Suitable. Wonderful!"

"Like *Laughing Eyes* suits Monica better than *Monica,*" he said facetiously and laughed.

She frowned and studied his demeanor. "Yes, I call people names that I think fits their personality." She searched his eyes. *Surely, this preacher's not being sarcastic!*

"It seems like you are the foster mother of many children."

Aunt Mae's eyes welled up and her voice cracked. "Hume and I adopted Macie. God rest her sweet soul, and Caddie! But we claim Jake as our son, too."

She wiped the tears from her eyes on the corner of her blue and white checkered apron.

The wind flapped the clothes on the clothes-line a short distance from the house, and the clouds became overcast.

"That's what Jake told me."

"Please make yourself at home while I prepare a special tea." She handed him a week-old Sunday newspaper, and observed him intensely. *He's married and he's a preacher, too, but just too curious about my Macie! I wonder why*? She stepped over Ole Jeb and walked into the house.

When she arrived in the kitchen, Jake was finishing a piece of pound-cake.

"Cake's really yummy," he grinned. "I revived the fire in the stove for you."

"Thanks. Listen, Jake, I've been so worried about you—about everything."

"Didn't mean to worry you none. Been out of town."

"Been in the bottle?"

"No, not that. Just working. Really. I've been out of town," he responded agitatedly.

"I'm glad you've come to see us today, so you can check on these sweet baby girls, and their father."

"Dan?" Jake stopped eating, and looked puzzled.

"Of course, Dan! Who else? It's been weeks, since we left him in Tennessee. Wish I'd asked him more questions and noticed his reactions, when we were with him."

"Wonder where he is?" Jake stopped eating, and placed the remainder of the cake upon the plate. He picked up his cup and drank a large swallow of cold coffee.

"Said he needed to take care of business before coming here! That's all I remember."

"What do you mean for me to *check* on these baby girls?" He drew his eyebrows into a furrow.

"They have the slight discolorations of many bruises and scars all over their little bodies!"

"I haven't seen any bruises or scars!" He shook his head and frowned.

"Miz Mitchells and the church ladies got Henny-Penny and Kackie ready for the train ride. Then, you'll probably recall that Grandmaw Taylor and Laughing Eyes took care of them when we first got home. Caddie and I didn't dress the little girls at all for several days. So, I didn't know about the bruises until everyone went home that week after the burial, and I undressed them."

"Sure, I remember seeing the neighbors here taking care of Hen-Penn and Kackie, right after the burial."

"How can all those ladies bathe and take care of Henny-Penny and Kackie, and not say a word to us about finding bruises and scars on them?"

"Aunt Mae, I'm sure they have a lot of questions, too, and they're probably waiting for you to speak to them about it."

"I do plan to ask my friends the reason why."

"Does Caddie know about the bruises?"

"Not yet."

Jake raised his voice. "Well, you need to tell me about these things!" he banged his hand on the table. "Do you think Macie or Dan beat them?"

"We don't know."

"Hume and I went to Judge Pewter's office and tried to call Dan, but he still has no phone. We also tried to call Betty Sue Mitchells' number and got no answer. Dan's parents haven't heard a word from him, either!"

"Can't figure it out, unless Dan had something to do with Macie's death and ran off somewhere. Did y'all call the Sheriff's office in Tennessee, and see what the Sheriff had to say about Dan?"

"Yes. The Sheriff told Judge Pewter the case was closed. Listen, Jake, surely, you don't think Dan had anything to do with Macie's death!"

Uncle Hume came in and placed a wire basket of eggs on a small table. "Howdy, Jake, how you been?"

"Not too good, Uncle Hume. You said the Sheriff told y'all the case is closed, huh?" At first Jake's face turned pale, and then a bright reddish hue. His hands turned into tight fists.

Uncle Hume frowned. "That's right. The sheriff told Judge Pewter that the case is closed."

Jake stood up. "I need to see Henn-Penn and Kackie." The screen door banged, banged, banged three times, when he went out the screen door to the porch.

"Hume, you do remember that Reverend Webster's still waiting on the front porch. Please see about him, won't you?" Aunt Mae frowned. She removed the tea kettle from the stove, set it onto a pot-holder on the counter, and followed Jake.

Jake squatted down in front of the little girls. "Henn-Penn, you and Kackie stop chasing the cats long enough to see Uncle Jake." He took the little girls into his arms. "I'm gonna be gone a few days, but I'll see you when I get back, okay?"

He reached into his bulging shirt pocket and pulled out two small, brown, paper sacks.

"That candy, Jake?" asked Uncle Hume.

"Yes, little penny-suckers. Bet my baby girls are gonna like these."

"Thanks, Uncle Jake."

"Thanks! Orange! My favorite!"

Henny-Penny placed a solid black cat with yellowish-green eyes on the floor. "I drew a picture, Uncle Jake. Wanna see?" She held her colored drawing towards him.

"Of course, I do—"

"It's not very good." Henny-Penny sighed, and sat down on the door-steps.

"Henny-Penny's flower is taller than her tree." Kackie pointed at the flower, and shook her head, critically.

"Maybe she's putting emphasis on the flower," Jake smiled. "Henn-Penn, if I were your art teacher, I'd give you a good grade."

"I drew it for my mother. My mother is gone to heaven."

"Your mother would have loved it. You did a fantastic job," Jake said emotionally.

"She's my mother, too," said Kackie.

"Her name is *Macie*," sighed Henny-Penny.

"Yes, I know. *Macie* is a lovely name for a lovely lady."

"Will you take my picture that I drew to my mother in heaven?"

Jake looked helplessly at Aunt Mae. "What can I say? That I'll take it to heaven?"

Aunt Mae nodded.

"Yes," he answered helplessly.

"Thank you, Uncle Jake."

He lifted both of them at the same time and hugged them tightly.

Aunt Mae gently pulled up the back of Henny-Penny's and Kackie's dresses, so Jake could see the ugly scars and the yellowish cast of the bruises."

"Jake, do you see what I've been trying to tell you?"

"You should have already told me. I'm leaving now!"

"Where to, Jake?"

"Tennessee."

You going to Dan's house?"

"Yes, I am. By the way, that's the nosiest preacher I ever saw. Asked me a million questions, mostly about Macie."

"Just curious, I suppose. Since he preached her funeral, maybe he wonders what she was like when she was alive."

"And, you know what, Aunt Mae? Once I started talking about Macie and our childhood, it was like I just couldn't stop talking. I talked and talked, and talked. Since Macie died, I just can't stop talking about her."

"You need to talk everything out, Jake. Don't be hard on yourself."

"Why would he want to know about Macie, her being dead and all?" asked Jake.

"Beats me?"

"This preacher does act kinda strange, sometimes," Uncle Hume responded so loudly that Aunt Mae cringed.

"Listen, the preacher's still on the front porch. You two go on back out on the front porch and be with him. Lower your voices," Aunt Mae scolded. "I'll bring the tea."

"What you gonna do, Jake?" asked Uncle Hume.

"Going to Dan's house and then to the Sheriff's Office?"

"You'll find some smoked meat out in the smokehouse."

"Thanks. Don't worry if you don't hear from me for a few days."

"Check the cellar for apples and the kitchen for some dried fruit."

"Thanks."

"You're more than welcome."

"Jake, take the rest of this cake and some pie." Aunt Mae pointed towards the pie safe. "Here's a shoe box to put it all in."

Jake ran towards the smokehouse.

Aunt Mae, Uncle Hume, and the little girls joined Reverend Webster on the front porch. He frowned, and arose from the rocking chair. "I'm afraid I've come at a bad time." He smoothed his mud-spattered, tan pants.

"Sorry to keep you waiting, Reverend. We had to attend to some personal matters out in the kitchen." Aunt Mae poured the hot mint tea into cups and handed him a cup and saucer.

He sniffed the aroma of the tea. "That's understandable, since I just came by for a visit unannounced."

"Glad you came to see us. Jake said tell you he won't be staying."

"That a fact? Hoped to talk to Jake some more," said Reverend Webster.

"Thought I heard you talking sometime ago, when I came to the front door, Reverend," said Uncle Hume.

"Just practicing one of my sermons." He sipped the tea.

"At least you didn't waste your time waiting for us slow pokes."

"I was just enjoying the mountain view. You have a lovely place."

Aunt Mae followed his gaze to the sky-blue mountain range.

Henny-Penny and Kackie ate pound cake and drank mint tea from miniature-sized teacups. A small teapot sat in the middle of their small, oak table, along with the small, brown paper sacks, which still remained unopened.

"More tea, Reverend?"

"No, thank you. The cake and herb-tea were delicious. What herbs do you use?"

"This is just some mint that I got out of my herb garden. I added a little bit of grated orange peel and a mixture of several other herbs to get that extra flavor. I grow herbs in my garden, but I also forage for a lot of them in the woods when I need them."

"Very refreshing tea. Foraging, you say. I've never been."

"Most folks say it's woman's work."

"Woman's work?" questioned Reverend Webster.

"Yes, but it's not all work. It's fun gathering berries, pulling leaves, cutting bark, and digging roots for cures."

"You must excuse me. I have a lot of work to finish" Uncle Hume glanced at Aunt Mae for approval, as he shook hands with Reverend Webster and left the porch.

"But, of course, Uncle Hume. I'll see you later."

"Don't push yourself, Hume. Don't overdo."

"I'll be all right, Mae.

"Aunt Mae, one of the main reasons I came today is—hopefully—to purchase some of your special healing ointment. Hear it'll cure anything," Reverend Webster smiled, nervously.

"It's good stuff for healing, all right."

"I nicked my neck really bad with my razor." He briefly pulled down his collar, uncovered a bandage, and released the collar so fast, he hardly gave her time to observe the worst razor-burn she had ever seen. He held one hand around his throat to keep the bandage from slipping, and pulled his black turtle-neck sweater higher around the neck. He pushed his black, premature gray hair from his forehead and smoothed his almost white sideburns.

"When I first saw you ride up today, I thought that you were wearing a priest's collar. Then, I noticed it was a bandage."

"Yes, a bandage."

"I have just one batch of my special ointment left. It's in my healing basket out at the quilting house."

"How much you charge?" Reverend Webster inquired.

She sized him up. "Fifty cents."

Reverend Webster smiled when Aunt Mae returned from the quilting house with a snuff-box which held her sacred ointment. He paid her with a half-dollar.

"Glad to get the money, Reverend. Most of the time, everyone barters with me."

"Hear your ointment has mystical powers—cures—healing abilities."

"Oh? You heard that?" she laughed.

Jake ran from the backyard and waved. "I'll leave your horse back at the barn, Reverend! Okay?"

"Sure, Jake. I'll rub her down. Just leave her at the stable!" Reverend Webster stroked his smooth, tanned face, and gently pulled the bandage higher around his neck. "You're a remarkable woman, Aunt Mae. The people in these parts call you *The Healing Woman.* You're highly respected. What else could a person ask for?"

She met his intense, well-controlled yellow-gray eyes, fringed by dark black eyelashes and smiled. "I have my good points, I suppose, but the title *Healing Woman* scares me."

"Why?"

"Always need to give God the credit for any healing that's done." She searched Reverend Webster's face for reaction.

"Yes, Yes! True. So true, Aunt Mae. I didn't mean to take anything away from God, of course." He pulled his six foot two frame from the rocking chair, and smoothed the bandage on his neck.

"Reverend Webster, you said you don't want to 'take anything away from God?' You can't take anything away from God, unless He allows it."

"That could be debatable, huh?" He smiled shyly, and lowered his eyes.

He gave Henny-Penny and Kackie a little pat on their heads. "Have fun with Spooky and Shadows. You hear? See you Sunday."

"Goodbye, preacher," said Kackie.

Henny-Penny just stared at him.

Aunt Mae observed his mud-spattered boots and unkempt person, and tuned into his affected tone of voice, when he bid the little girls goodbye.

You are a gracious hostess, Aunt Mae." He shook her hand and walked away rapidly.

The feel of his soft and clammy hand lingered a moment.

"Come again, and bring Locket," she called. Her bright blue eyes narrowed into two slits as she observed him mount.

Uncle Hume returned to the front porch. "Preacher's gone, huh?"

"Yes, he's gone. The real reason he came was to buy some of my special healing ointment."

"Did he pay or want to swap something?"

"He gave me a fifty-cent piece.

"That's good."

"I wasn't thinking of the consequences when I showed Jake the little girls' bruises!"

"Jake had to know about the bruises, Mae. He's family. It's gonna be all right."

She glanced into Penny's and Kathryn's startled eyes, staring back at her, and wondered how much they understood. They sucked on their penny-suckers and held their little brown paper sacks tightly.

Henny-Penny stuck her sucker out for Ole Jeb to have a lick.

"Henny-Penny, don't let Ole Jeb lick on your sucker, please."

Aunt Mae smoothed her hair back on each side, re-pinned the queenly bun, and sat in her grandmother's rocking chair. "Come sit with me, babies." She held her arms out and the little girls climbed into her lap.

"Sing, Aunt Mae! Sing!"

She rocked the rocking chair over the rickety, rough boards, patted her feet, and crooned:

Grasshopper Green is a funny hopper.
Hoppity, skip and jump!
He wears funny little clothes of green, and brown.
Such a clown!
He tips his little red hat as he passes our way.
Did you ever see such a sight?
A dressed up hopper saying, "Have a nice day!"
Hoppity, skip and jump!

The little girls snuggled closer.

* * * *

Jake took a leave of absence from the Sheriff's office.

He drove fast and recklessly along the crooked and narrow mountain roads until he reached Gainesville, Georgia, and scheduled the next trains to Tennessee.

The dirty, smutty windows blocked his view and the sound of the train clanking down the tracks and the desolate hoot of its whistle added to his misery. *Did*

Macie kill herself, and beat her children, too? Surely not! Who, then? Dan? Macie? No! No!

An elderly lady sat beside him fanning herself with a palm-leaf fan. From time to time he glanced her way, and marveled at how her wrist never ceased moving. Mile after mile she flitted her wrist and stirred the stale air. *I just can't imagine that Dan would leave his little girls, and not ever inquire about their welfare. To think they still have feint, yellowish bruises on their bodies. They've been through some hard times and must have had some mighty hard licks! Many licks! And the scars! How did they get on their little bodies!*

* * * *

When Jake arrived at Dan Zanderneff's house, he found it abandoned.

Betty Sue Mitchells and some of the other neighbors told him Dan moved all of his goods and furniture out of his house the day after Macie's funeral into Miz Mitchell's woodshed. They thought he went to Three-Mile Crossing to see about Penny and Kathryn, and his parents.

"I understand that you saw Dan that evening before the Sheriff got here, Miz Mitchells?" asked Jake.

"Yes, I was the first one to see him. Dan ran over here to my place. He was justa crying out that Macie had killed herself. Then, I ran over to Dan's and Macie's house just as fast as I could and ran up on the porch and through the front door! I nearly tripped over a heavy suitcase in the front hallway, and I just opened the closet door, that was right there beside the front door, and shoved the suitcase in the closet to get it out of the way. Then, when I saw Macie, she was justa lying crumpled up on the floor and blood had shot out of her wrists onto the floor, the walls, the ceiling, and everywhere. It was horrible!"

"Miz Mitchells, you stumbled over a suitcase?" Jake gasped with surprise, and held his open hands towards her, beseechingly, seeking more information.

"I sure did stumble over that suitcase," she nodded affirmatively.

"Was it packed? Did it look and feel like a packed suitcase or was it empty?" Jake searched her face intently.

"It was heavy—it felt very heavy, like it was packed," said Betty Sue Mitchells.

"And, you showed the suitcase to the Sheriff when he arrived?" Jake continued, cautiously.

"No, I didn't tell the Sheriff."

"Didn't tell him? Why?" asked Jake.

"It slipped my mind. In all the excitement, I didn't mention it. Was it important?"

Jake stammered, "Miz Mitchells, do you have a key to Dan's house?"

"No, Jake. Sure don't. But, he's gone, anyhow. Dan left town," said Betty Sue Mitchells. "His furniture is in my shed."

"This is very personal, Miz Mitchells. But, did you ever hear the little girls crying at any time?"

"From time to time all babies cry."

"And Macie? Did you ever hear her cry?"

"That is personal, I'll admit, Jake. But, to tell you the truth, I never heard her cry and I never saw her cry. Jake, I didn't want to mention it, but I did see bruises on both Penny and Kathryn on the day I bathed them, and got them dressed for the train ride. That was right after Macie's funeral."

"That's why I'm here. We found the bruises."

"I figured you would."

"Miz Mitchells, I'd like to pay you for the storage of the furniture up to this time and I'd like to ship Macie's furniture back to Three-Mile Crossing. I have room for it at my house. I can keep it in the back room for Henny-Penny and Kackie."

Miz Mitchells nodded her head in agreement. "Well, since Dan never paid anything in the first place, and I also need my storage shed, you can have it. If Dan comes back wanting the furniture, then I'll tell him where it is."

* * * *

Jake went to the undertaker's establishment that handled the embalming arrangements for Macie's body. He knocked.

A young man appeared at the door, and identified himself as the undertaker's assistant.

After some informal chit-chat, Jake asked the assistant several troubling and pertinent questions. "Did Macie Zanderneff have bruises on her body at the time her body was brought in? Were you at the autopsy?"

"I shouldn't say anything about it, but some bruises were on her," the assistant stated, sadly.

"So, you were at the autopsy?" asked Jake.

"Yes, but all I did was mostly observe."

Jake yelled, "That's all?"

The assistant held his fingers over his mouth, as if to hush himself, and shook his head. "Sir, I am so sorry. I shouldn't have said anything. These are questions for the family. I can't answer any more questions. I could lose my job!" He stepped back and closed the door.

Defiantly, Jake kicked the closed door. "I am family!" he screamed.

Since he knew that most people in positions such as undertakers or their assistants are usually more close-mouthed, Jake wondered if the young man had volunteered as much information as he did because he might have had his own suspicions about Macie's death.

* * * *

Jake went to the Sheriff's office and asked for the Sheriff's help.

"What really happened to Macie?"

The Sheriff spoke sternly. "Jake, listen to what I'm saying. Macie Zanderneff committed suicide. The case is closed. Let it be. Let it be."

"Let it be! Let it be! How can I do that? How can a person do that?" asked Jake.

"Jake," the Sheriff reiterated, "I was present at the time, and saw her body in the bathroom. I saw her body at the undertaker's place. I know the case. She killed herself. She slit her wrists. As hard as that is to swallow, she did it herself. Now, do like I suggest. Let it be." He patted Jake on the back, and went behind his desk and sat down.

"Dan must have killed her!" Jake exclaimed. "Otherwise, why would he leave so abruptly, and with no one knowing where he went?"

"Let it be!" the sheriff said gruffly and stood up.

Jake knew in his heart that he could not leave it alone—just "let it be." "I knew Macie well enough to know she'd never kill herself!"

"But, Macie did kill herself, Jake," the Sheriff said a little softer.

"Sheriff, I talked to Dan's and Macie's next door neighbor, Miz Betty Sue Mitchells. She said when Dan ran over to her house and told her that Macie had killed herself, she ran back with Dan to his house, and as she went into the front door—into the hallway, she tripped over a heavy suitcase just inside the door." Jake stopped talking long enough to catch his breath.

"Tripped over a suitcase?" said the astonished Sheriff.

"Yes, Miz Mitchells said she opened the hall closet, and shoved it in a corner of the closet just to get it out of the way, and, then, she followed Dan to the bathroom, where she saw Macie slumped on the floor."

"Jake, are you telling me that Betty Sue Mitchells told you that she moved a suitcase out of the middle of the front hallway and it was at the front door?"

"That's what she said. Did you know about this, Sheriff?" Jake asked angrily.

The sheriff held up his hand to quiet Jake. "Wait! Hold your horses just a dad-gum minute! This is the first I've heard anything about a suitcase. Did Betty Sue tell you the suitcase was packed?" asked the Sheriff.

"Said it was very heavy, just like if it was packed. You see, Macie was supposed to be on her way home to Three Mile Crossing. It's a little town in Georgia—in the mountains. None of us ever knew Macie to be depressed. She would not kill herself."

"Macie's home town?"

"That's right."

"Dan told me about Three-Mile Crossing, when I interviewed him about Macie's suicide."

"Her sister, Caddie, sent Macie the money to buy train tickets for her and the two baby girls—Henny-Penny and Kackie!" Jake said heatedly. "She probably had the packed suitcase in one hand and leading Henny-Penny and Kackie out the door with the other when Dan stopped her from leaving. That's what I think—"

"Why did Betty Sue Mitchells shove the suitcase in the closet?" The Sheriff sat back down. He pulled on his lips and curled the bottom lip between his fingers.

"Because she tripped. Because it was in the middle of the hallway—it was in the walking path and in the way." Jake's chin trembled. "Please listen to me!"

The sheriff tapped his pen on the desk. "The suitcase was sitting in the door-way and Betty Sue Mitchells moved it?"

"That's what Miz Mitchells said."

"Jake let's go over to Betty Sue Mitchells home, and talk to her." The sheriff reached for his hat. "I can't believe she didn't tell any of us about the suitcase, Jake. It puts a different light on things."

"Yeah and Dan's left town—don't know where."

"You say that Dan's not at Three Mile Crossing? Do you know where he went?" The sheriff frowned.

"No, he's high-tailed it off somewhere," Jake spoke a little too loudly. "Sheriff, the house is not rented yet. Can you show me the place where you found Macie? I'd like to see the bathroom for myself."

"I'll do it only as a fellow law officer. I'll get the keys from the landlord and take you over to the house so you can walk through, if you think it'll help you feel better about it all."

"Thank you, Sheriff. I want to see the closet where Betty Sue Mitchells put that packed suitcase she tripped over, when she went into the house with Dan and found Macie on the floor."

"Jake, get this straight," the sheriff said, firmly, and wagged his finger to verify he meant *business*. "I talked to Betty Sue Mitchells about Macie's death and she didn't tell me anything about tripping over a suitcase in the hallway—packed or unpacked. I can't believe I haven't been told that Miz Mitchells might have moved evidence," he repeated again.

"Evidently, Macie was packed to come home—going back home to Three-Mile Crossing."

"Macie meant to go home, huh?" The sheriff rubbed his chin and became more pensive. "What happened to the money her sister sent Macie for the tickets?"

"Maybe Dan didn't want her to leave and he stopped her! Maybe he cashed in the tickets!"

"Wonder where Dan went?" asked the Sheriff.

"No one seems to know, Sheriff. He moved the furniture out of his house and into Miz Mitchell's woodshed."

*   *   *   *

The Sheriff opened the door. "Come on in, Jake. I just hope you can feel better after coming in and looking around, and see everything for yourself." Their careful and slow footsteps made dusty tracks on the wooden oak floors and their whispers echoed throughout the small rooms.

"Thanks, Sheriff."

Dan's house was too quiet.

The musty, chalky and stuffy odors of the past lingered in the house. Their voices echoed throughout the small rooms. Everyone whispered reverently, and Jake became spell-bound when they neared the all-white bathroom, and entered the last place that Macie breathed her last breath.

Jake knelt on the white linoleum floor, and inspected a baseboard near the sink. "This looks like a little speck of blood." He reached towards the baseboard.

The sheriff tugged at Jake's hand before he touched the sacred blood of the one he loved. "Get up, son. Come on and I'll buy you a cup of coffee. Come on, yuh hear?"

"I hear," Jake whispered.

"Jake, I'll talk to Betty Sue Mitchells and see if I can learn a little more. It does look strange that Dan just left—just disappeared. I thought he followed his little girls to your home at Three-Mile Crossing, just like everyone else thought. We'll ask the neighbors some questions and look into this matter a little closer. Come on, Buddy. Let's go talk about it."

* * * *

It was late when Jake returned to his cabin at Three-Mile Crossing. How he dreaded telling Aunt Mae and Uncle Hume that Dan Zanderneff had skipped the country! He placed one of his scrapbooks on the kitchen table and sat down. He removed a twig of Rosemary herb from his pocket, held it to his nose and drew in a deep dredge of its pleasing odor. The fragrant oils caused an itch. He rubbed his nose. He spread the herb to dry between the pages of his scrapbook that held years of memories. He smoothed birthday and Christmas cards from Macie, and removed wrinkles from faded and stained sketches of woodsy plants that Macie drew when she was a young girl. He caressed the dear, coffee-stained pages and closed the book. *Macie, I'll never forget your herb garden in the back yard of that lonely place—back there at that God forsaken hole where you died in Tennessee. It was so typical of you to carry your love of plants and nature with you wherever you went.*

He opened the scrapbook to a clean page. Removed a piece of Blue Horse note book paper from his pocket, unfolded it, and smoothed it out on the kitchen table. He stared at the hand-drawn picture of the flower that Macie's beloved daughter, Penny, drew for her. The child had said, "Take it to heaven and give it to my mother." He picked up a blue drawing pencil and wrote, *HEAVEN* on the top of a page in his scrapbook, glued the back of the child's drawing and pressed it lovingly onto the record of *HEAVEN.*

He removed a brown paper sack from his jacket, dumped the herbs he'd gathered from Macie's herb garden onto his kitchen table, and stared at the crumbled remains.

He removed a crock jug from his cabinet, poured two fingers of moonshine into a pint jelly glass, and began to sip the strong drink. He winced when the fumes saturated his nostrils.

He slumped forward in a burgundy, comfortable over-stuffed chair, and stared into the blazing fire, as it licked and devoured the resins on the smutty walls of the fireplace.

The more he drank, the more elongated, distorted and twisted the images of Macie's face illuminated in the flames. *Macie! You hear me? Dan ran away! I know he must have killed you and made it look like suicide!*

He quenched his eyes shut, and tried to squeeze the distorted fiery images of Macie out of his head—his mind—his soul.

And, then, he thought of his mother and father.

When I was just six years old, and mama got real sick, I don't remember who told me that she had contracted tuberculosis. I can't believe that on the day she died, daddy just dug a grave in the backyard, buried her, and staked a wooden cross to mark her grave. That cross is still in the backyard—right where daddy put it. He said, 'Sorry, Son. Won't be no funeral. It's just you and me, now." He prayed the Lord's Prayer, and ended the prayer with 'Oh, Jesus!' And held me, tightly. He took me inside the house, filled a left-over biscuit with butter and blackberry jelly and handed it to me. After I ate the biscuit, he said, 'Jake wash up these dishes here on the kitchen table. I'll get us a squirrel for supper.' He just reached his long, muscular arms up to the gunrack right here over this fireplace and removed one of the shot-guns. 'See you later, Son,' he said to me, and then, he walked out the back door and into the woods—to never ever see me again.

Dear God, where did daddy go? How could he leave me? Abandon me? I was just a little boy!

His heart panged with anger and rejection. When he poked the smoldering coals, sparks flew about and bounced on the dusty hearth.

Days and days passed and daddy didn't come back. I was very afraid—afraid to go to sleep at night. I ate all of the cold, hard biscuits and preserves that were in the pie safe, drank all the buttermilk in the churn, and picked blackberries from the vines in the backyard. I ate the vegetables and preserves from the fruit-jars that I could open.

I remember those jars that I could not open, I smashed the lid off with a hammer, and ate what was in the jars.

Even now, if I close my eyes really hard, I can almost feel the fine pieces of glass in my mouth.

He wiped his tongue with his long, pinched fingers.

I'm not sure how many days passed after daddy left to go squirrel hunting, but I sure was glad to see Aunt Mae when she came to nurse mama. She found me sitting at mama's grave. I was holding Pretty Kitty. I still miss Pretty Kitty.

From that day forward, Aunt Mae, Uncle Hume and Pretty Kitty were the only family I've ever known, until Macie and Caddie came to live with us.

He struggled to arise from his bulky, stuffed chair and went to the kitchen. He poured another finger of moonshine into the glass jar and sipped. He picked up a handful of the fresh but crushed rosemary, basil, dill and chives from the table, and stuck his nose into their fragrance.

Macie, how could you leave me—leave all of us?

He broke a stem of Rosemary from the cluster, carried it back to the fireplace and sat down. He sneezed when the sticky oils of the herb entered his sinus.

The fire "died-down," but he lingered before the warm hearth and hated his father for abandoning him.

Uncle Hume and Aunt Mae are so sweet—so amazing! They did their best to console me: 'Your father loved you. Something happened out yonder in the woods to keep your daddy from coming back home to you.'

He closed his eyes.

I can still see the dear, dear faces of all the neighborhood men I know and even those men I didn't know that came in and took charge; formed a search party, and searched for days and days. But, they found no trace of daddy. Deaver Clements and Uncle Hume kept on looking, long after everyone else went home. I owe them a lot.

Aunt Mae and Uncle Hume excused daddy for burying mama in the backyard and wanted me to forgive him too. 'Forgive him! Your father knew how afraid the neighbors were of tuberculosis! Your daddy was very upset and had problems with their friends abandoning your mother, him and even you. He probably felt like no one would show up for a formal funeral, so he prepared a family burial for her. He did the best he could.'

Are you dead, daddy? Are you alive? Aunt Mae wants me to forgive you, daddy, for not coming back to me, but I just can not do it.

He threw his jelly-glass into the fireplace as hard as he could. The fire caught the remainder of the alcohol, and blazed brightly! The blaze died down as quickly as it flashed.

He held his aching head, which throbbed with anger and rejection.

Uncle Hume made arrangements to have mother's body placed in a polished, pine coffin, and buried at Three-Mile Crossing on the Brown's gravesite, under those old, old oak trees.

The fire smoldered. He threw a log in the fireplace at the thought of his father's abandonment, scattering smoldering embers. He poked the fire and it blazed brightly and came alive.

Purchasing my exquisitely carved, marble angel is the best thing I ever bought when I got out of college. I still owe some money to the tombstone company. Let's see—how much? He held his temples tightly.

I just love my angel watching over mama. It makes me feel better knowing that I have taken care of mama in her death, even if you didn't do it, daddy. Just think—my angel not only looks over mama but she looks over Macie, too.

You hear me, Macie?

His thoughts jumped and jumbled. He pressed his right temple tightly with his index finger, held a long stem of the rosemary herb so close to his nose that its sticky substance irritated his nostrils, eyes and face. He rubbed his hands on his shirt and stared into the fire.

Macie's distorted face flickered in the flames.

Macie! What happened? he whispered. *Tell me what happened.*

He dozed and nodded. In the distance, a bob-cat cried out, and suddenly he became cold—chilled to the bone, and the soul.

He staggered to his wrought-iron bed-stead, wrapped his tall, muscular body in a tightly woven, cotton flannel "Indian" blanket, and fell upon the unmade bed, being oblivious to the slats under the mattress, which fell to the floor.

* * * *

It was around midnight. An owl hooted. Reverend Buker Webster pulled the curtains back from his study window and looked out, hoping to catch a glimpse of the hooting owl that persisted in its call. Upon searching the moonlit, dark-silhouetted back yard, and seeing nothing out of the ordinary, he sat at a desk in his meticulously clean study.

He rubbed his tired eyes and stared at particles of dust not visible to the naked eye, and raked the particles from his desk into his hand. He removed a wooden box from his right bottom drawer and sat it in the middle of his desk.

He removed a bottle of bourbon and a shot glass from the left bottom desk drawer and set the items upon his desk. After wiping the rim of the shot glass with his long fingers, he poured. He thrust the strong liquid into his mouth. It burned his throat, but it didn't keep him from having another, and another.

He rocked back and forth against the high back of his chair for several moments. His heart filled with love and happy emotion when he stroked his sacred box of letters. He walked over to his well-stocked library and removed a book named, "The Insect—The Bug—The World." He removed a drawing pad and colored pencils from one of the shelves and returned to his desk. He opened the book to a page depicting the eye of one of the insects and copied the eye. His rendition of the many faceted sections of the insect's eye appeared in good proportion. He colored each facet different colors—red, green, blue and yellow. He admired his finished product and placed the drawing in a cardboard portfolio.

He stared at an original oil painting of his mother which hung on the wall directly in front of his desk. She had exquisite features: perfectly coiffed black hair, high cheek bones, and blue eyes. Her slender body was exaggerated in the long white dress with blue sash. The high, white-lace collar, pearl broach and pearl earrings emphasized the loveliness of the face.

I want to be perfect for you mother, and I strive for "perfection," but a great yearning calls out to me and this inexplicable burning urge and desire to do otherwise takes over some part of my existence deep within myself. Please try to understand.

He removed a hand-mirror from his desk drawer and reflected his intense yellow-gray eyes, and handsome, tanned face. As he pulled at the black, curly locks of hair clipped close to his head and examined the sprinkles of pre-mature gray, and the almost white sideburns, he knew his mother would not approve of its short length. He sighed loudly, and laid the mirror down.

He removed gold-embossed, initialed stationery from a teakwood stationery box and wrote a letter. He placed the letter, along with a photograph in an envelope, licked and sealed the flap. He hugged the letter to his muscular chest, leaned his head back onto the high back, wine velvet stuffed chair with gold trim, and sighed heavily.

"Dear Mother,

I saw the beautiful lady at the lake today. I know I told you that I wouldn't follow her again, but I just had no other choice. She looked exactly like the day we saw her sitting on the veranda. You remember how beautiful she was? Well, she's still just as magnificent—just as beautiful—"

"Buker, you going to bed?" Locket called.

He held the letter tightly, and listened intently.

"Buker, am I interrupting your prayers?"

"Yes, I'm still praying!" He frowned at his wife's interruption.

"Want some cocoa or tea?"

"No. I'll be along soon." He swallowed the strong liquid in his shot glass, and poured again.

Long into the night, he prayed to his mother for deliverance of his aching soul, and asked her to comfort, and protect him during the haunting of the night, which usually interrupted his sleep.

* * * *

Locket Webster looked into her oval shaped dresser mirror, smoothed her short, bobbed, blond hair, adjusted the straps on her pink satin gown and got into one of the twin beds in hers and Buker Webster's bedroom. B*eing a preacher's wife is such a lonesome life. It should be exciting! I can't get used to Buker's Saturday night rituals. His studying and getting ready to "preach" on Sunday is quite an ordeal. When he closes himself away from the "world" to pray and prepare his Sunday message, he blocks everything else out, including me.*

Why does Buker appear to be so distant, particularly since we got married.

What could I have done to provoke him?

When he isn't in his study or dark room developing photographs, he goes fishing in the lake nearby, hiking or horse-back riding. He wants all of his clothes ironed, with neat pleats and creases. And, that's okay, but if his fishing clothes aren't pressed exactly right, he pitches a fit, and the simplest things set him off. I try to make sure everything is done his way—everything!

I can't imagine someone dressed so neatly when he leaves home can come back later with such disheveled clothes and muddied and scratched boots. His nervous gestures are unbearable, and he seems to have a black cloud of depression hovering him. He doesn't talk to me and doesn't want me to talk to him and as time passes, he becomes more and more aloof. He just answers my questions, in a curt, touchy and overly sensitive manner. He is so exasperating when he finishes my sentences before I can express my train of thought!

How much longer can I go on pretending? Teaching school satisfies most of my mental needs, but Buker is a failure as a husband. To just think—we've never slept together! Why? I'm attractive. Why has this marriage never been consummated, and we are husband and wife in name only. What would a good psychiatrist say? If I talked to an expert, I'd say, 'Mr. Psychiatrist, the physical side of this marriage being nil, I wonder if Buker might be seeing another woman. I've belittled myself for being so suspicious, and I've determined it's my lack of experience, and lack of self-confidence. It's hard to ignore our having no more hand-in-hand strolls, no more lovely notes and poems, no more movies, no more bouquets of flowers, no more plays to attend, and no more boxes of candy, after we got married. What happened to the attentive, gallant, handsome, and romantic man I fell in love with? I don't want to admit failure, and admit my mistake in marrying someone so uncaring. Why was I so attracted to Buker, when so many other eligible suitors were available? How could a piece of paper—a marriage certificate change the way Buker treats me?'

And, the psychiatrist would probably shake his head and say, "How do you feel? *What do you think? Maybe you should go on home, and try a little harder."*

And, I would say, 'Mr. Psychiatrist, I don't need your services. I need a divorce.'

What did I see in Buker? I yearned to be a preacher's wife, but why did I want to be a preacher's wife so badly that I'm accepting this bad treatment? Why did Buker marry me? I want children, and he does not.

I feel the failure and the disillusionment, but, most of all, I feel trapped. I made a big mistake the day I married Buker Webster. The very Reverend Buker Webster. How can he pretend to be so pleasant in public and totally indifferent in private? He is a selfish man who lives in a different world from me—a separate place. I need to get a divorce, but would my career, as well as Buker's be over? Oh! What a stigma!

Right now, I just exist. I want to be happy! Dear God, please help me! Please do something! Please intervene! Please!

* * * *

He moved quietly into the bedroom, trying not to disturb Locket. He laid down upon a companion twin bed, and prayed for a peaceful sleep to encompass him, but, instead, a fitful sleep came upon his conscious and unconscious.

Giant, golden brown and black Monarch butterflies, and Pea-green Luna (Moon) Moths, with multi-colored eyes, chased him. He flapped his red spotted muscular insect wings to their best advantage and flew in and out of a dark forest of many trees. Wispy green-black shadows enveloped him and he hid in a green fog.

Giant lightning bugs with reddish-colored spot-light eyes, as well as yellow-bodied moths with blue wings joined in the chase to find him—to destroy him. He was defenseless against their numbers and electrifying colors.

They caught him! They jabbed and pierced his scaly insect body with long and unexpectedly sharp antennae, and pulled off his black and red spotted wings! His body fell hard to the ground, first. He stared upwards and watched his bloody, red-spotted wings drift down towards nothingness.

He moaned, moved restlessly on his bed, turned over and drifted into a deeper sleep.

* * * *

It was a cold morning. Aunt Mae pulled on a light, blue wool sweater and lit the wood-stove in the kitchen. "Get up and start getting ready for breakfast," she called.

The aroma of cinnamon and yeast rolls filled Uncle Hume's nostrils. He came into the kitchen, hooking the gallowses of his overalls. "Smells delicious and wonderful in here."

Aunt Mae set the table.

Uncle Hume poked the fire in the fireplace. "Gonna let Henny-Penny and Kackie sleep?"

"Yes, do them good," she said.

"Hume, I'm kinda worried about Jake. Been days and days since he left. You worried?"

"Well, considering the miles he had to go, and the kind of investigation he had to make, I believe it'll take awhile. I'm not worried about the length of time, just what he might do to Dan, if he finds out he had anything to do with beating Henny-Penny and Kackie. I'm anxious to know what he found out."

"Me, too. I do hope everything is all right," she said. "Changing the subject, I was a little surprised Reverend Webster purchased some more of my special ointment for his razor-burn yesterday. Still had a bandage around his neck."

"I musta been in the field, when he came." Uncle Hume sat down at the table, and smoothed a corner of the red and white checkered oil-cloth tablecloth with his long fingers.

"I asked him if he wanted me to check his razor-burn for him, but the Reverend pulled the bandage up higher around his neck. Made him look like he had on a priest's collar, it came so far up on the neck."

"Well, he's not a priest."

"Hume, I hate to say this, but I can't explain how I feel about that preacher, except disappointment."

"Now, Mae, don't get too disappointed if you can't get close to the preacher."

"Reverend Webster wanted to know if Macie had a good personality and stuff like that. Wants to know all about her."

"Jake said the preacher asked him about Macie, too," said Uncle Hume.

"Wish Brother McClure was still here."

"Listen, Mae. Dan will be coming in here one day, soon. That's what worries me. You thought about that haven't you, Mae? If he wants to take Henny-Penny and Kackie, you know you'll have to give them up. And, listen to this, too. If Dan's folks come a' wanting them babies—you might have to give them up to them. That's what worries me, Mae. I'm not worried about Buker Webster, and his lack of personality. I'm worried about Dan. You know that Dan's folks are Penny's and Kathryn's flesh-'n-blood." Uncle Hume picked up a milk-pail and started to the door. He saw the disbelief and horror on her face. "Surely you realized you may not get to keep Macie's babies."

"But Macie is our legal daughter. We adopted her."

He placed his arm around her shoulder consolingly. "We'll fight for Henny-Penny and Kackie—go to the court if we have to. Let's talk to Judge Pewter."

A pig began to squeal.

Uncle Hume ran to a kitchen window and looked out. "Confound it! One of Joseph Daniel's dogs is in our pig-pen again!" He grabbed a shot-gun from the gun rack which hung over the back door, and ran outside.

* * * *

After he milked the cow, and fed the animals, Uncle Hume spent the morning walking, and rambling in the woods.

He stopped at a sweet-gum tree, which fanned out into a golden-yellow canopy, nestled himself into the dry leaves at the base of the tree, and leaned back. He pulled a pack of chewing tobacco from his shirt pocket, unfolded his pocket knife and cut a chaw.

Ole Jeb snuggled his head against Uncle Hume's knee.

"Ole Jeb, "I wish I could wake up out of this nightmare, and have things back like they used to be!" The dog snuggled a little closer.

Uncle Hume observed the soft, golden, green hue of Yellow Meadow against the blue mountain range, and wondered why the mosses and grasses were so yellow in that small area.

He closed his eyes and reflected upon what he and Aunt Mae should do about Henny-Penny and Kackie. *Dan has always been a very good boy. Even though the odds are stacked against him, I want to give him the benefit of the doubt.*

Uncle Hume arose and stretched his long arms. "Yeah, Ole Jeb, something's happened to Dan, or he'd be here! Lets walk." Ole Jeb stood up, stared at Uncle Hume, and wagged his tail.

* * * *

Later in the day, Uncle Hume sat on the front porch reading the family bible, and enjoyed the aromas of fried chicken cooking and hot yeast bread baking in the kitchen.

From the wavering sound of the "hill-billy" music on the radio, screeching and squawking, he knew the battery was weak.

He removed his wire-rimmed glasses, leaned the Bible against his chest and observed Henny-Penny and Kackie playing with Ole Jeb in the front yard. He propped his feet on a small, wooden stool, and looked into the distance. *Thank you, God, for your Goodness. How do I get answers to these hellish happenings that are so foreign to my way of thinking? How?*

* * * *

While the chicken was frying, Aunt Mae prepared a banana-pudding for the Saturday night square dance and box-supper, and hummed along with the radio. She and Uncle Hume took much delight in out-dancing the young and old, alike, and in particular, buck-dancing. They had blue-ribbons galore, to prove it. She glanced at the colorful array of many award ribbons attached to the pie-safe with straight pins, filling one side of the cabinet from top to bottom: Blue, Blue, Blue, Red, White, Red, Blue, Blue, and Blue—she counted 25 ribbons, and smiled.

She placed a white, cotton napkin in a shoe-box, which was decorated with red and yellow paper hearts and flowers. Green leaves flowed across its lid and around the edges.

As she packed her box-supper, Uncle Hume came into the kitchen and sniffed loudly. He placed his thumbs in imaginary gallowses, stuck his tongue in his cheek and raised his eyebrows. "I wonder what handsome fella will bid on your box-supper."

She laughed and thumped her hand on her heart.

* * * *

The Meeting-House, once a two-story barn, sat directly behind the church. It was a meeting place for one and all—a place where they held church meetings;

town hall meetings, political meetings, square-dances, parties, weddings, box-suppers, reunions and used it as headquarters for dinner-on-the-ground.

Brother George-West Meyers made an announcement. "A lot of the white-wash chinking is missing between the logs of the meeting-house, so we need a committee to replace the chinking and do some other repairs, as soon as possible. Also, we'll need to do some white-washing on the wooden boards on the back side of the church-house and the meeting-house."

Some of the Elders of the church met after the short meeting.

"Reverend Buker Webster is not a God called preacher because he reads every word of all his sermons and he doesn't know how to respond properly to misery and everyday problems," one of the Elders grumbled.

"George-West Meyers musta been out of his mind on the day *he picked* Reverend Buker Webster for our preacher!"

"Don't ever ask the preacher a question about the bible. He avoids all the questions I've asked about creation and salvation! He'll just say, 'What do you think'?"

"Mixes it up with science, and stuff."

"So, what are we gonna do? George-West Meyers brought him here."

"We need George-West Meyers' tithes and offerings. He runs this church."

"Yeah. Can't upset George-West, don't you know."

"I guess we do nothing, as usual."

"The Reverend is a handsome man, but he doesn't act like other preachers."

"He's aloof."

"My daughter says he's real good looking. She likes to come to church because she likes to look at him."

"Yeah! My wife thinks so, too."

"He'll be gone one of these days."

"And, this, too, shall pass."

"Some of the preachers have been good."

"Some have been great."

"And, then, we come to The Reverend Buker Webster!"

* * * *

Henny-Penny and Kackie played in the backyard under a Weeping Willow Tree. It's long swooping, seaweed-like branches formed an intricate shelter—a private playhouse. Aunt Mae retrieved them from their play. "Let's go to the spring, and get a bucket of water." She tousled Penny's and Kathryn's hair, and made them laugh. Each child carried an empty lard bucket along the narrow and winding path to the spring. As she observed the little girls walking along the path, she thought about Dan. *Why does he not write? Why has he not contacted his parents? Why have his parents not visited Henny-Penny and Kackie or asked to keep them? Why?*

Why, churned in her head.

"Can we run ahead to the tree-house, Aunt Mae?" asked Penny.

"Best you wait for Aunt Mae." She pointed towards a quaint little building, with mosses growing on its top and hovering over the creek. "I'm going to the spring house. Need a churn of buttermilk."

"Can we go to the tree-house while you get the churn?"

"Just a reminder—don't be dangling your feet over the side of the tree-house."

The little girls threw their lard buckets down on the ground and ran happily towards the tree-house. It was like re-living the past, having Macie's babies run ahead of her, as fast as their little legs could carry them.

She stopped, stretched her upper torso, and held her lower back. She remembered young, unwed Hannah Anderson, who lived down the road, and would be ready to give birth any day. *Lord, please be with Hannah's folks in their embarrassment, with her young'un not having a legitimate paw. I'm looking to You to help me when Hannah's time comes, like You've always helped me, and I thank You, now, and I'll thank You, then. Lord, please give me the physical and mental strength I need to teach Henny-Penny and Kackie Your ways. Amen.*

* * * *

It was late in the evening when Aunt Mae and James Anderson arrived at a ramshackle, wood-framed, two-story house, which sat on flat-rock pillars.

Two little boys ran in the yard playing tag. Dogs barked wildly; guineas, and geese ran loose in the red-clay yard, and squawked loudly.

Aunt Mae laughed. "Nobody could ever sneak up on this house! Those guineas and geese make good watch-dogs!" She waved to the little boys, "Hey Bobby! Hey Tommy!"

"Don't need a real watch-dog. We've got watch-birds!" James Anderson laughed, but, then his smile turned into a frown.

The stale smells of urine, and sweat, mixed with the musky odor of turnip greens cooking, permeated the air, making a pungent odor. Aunt Mae spoke briefly to Uncle Albert, and walked upstairs to Hannah's room.

"Hello, Hannah, I'm here!" Aunt Mae opened all the windows in the bedroom. "Let's get some good breathing air in here."

"I'm glad you're here, Aunt Mae." Hannah smiled weakly. "I was worried."

Grandmaw Taylor sat in an oak chair near a fireplace in Hannah's room, and leaned forward on her cane, "Mae, I'm not much help. My leg is giving me problems again." Grandmaw Taylor wore her snow white hair in a plaited bun pulled to the nape of her neck. The bun was held by large, yellowish celluloid hair pins. She smoothed a navy blue, floor-length dress and regardless of the time of day or the event, a starched white apron covered her dress. Her tanned and wrinkled face held piercing bright green eyes that usually twinkled mischievously, but that day her never ending smile turned to a frown of frustration and fear for her beloved granddaughter, and it showed in her worried eyes.

Aunt Mae set her medicine basket on the floor next to the fireplace.

"Just give me your moral support." She kissed Grandmaw Taylor on the cheek.

Aunt Mae caught the mother's nervous glance, and comforted her. "Oh, Missy, don't worry about the windows being open just for a little while. Do you have the cloths sterilized?"

Missy nodded her head, as she walked to a dresser drawer, removed a brown paper packet, and handed it to Aunt Mae. "I hope it suits you. I worked hard to fix everything up, just right. I took them ole sheets and bleached them in lye soap, rinsed them out good, and dried them in the sun, and then I put them in the hot oven, hot enough to kill any kind of germs, and, then, I wrapped the cloths in that brown paper, just like you said."

"I'm sure it's all fine. You always do a good job in everything you do, Missy." She removed the white adhesive tape from the package and handed the brown wrapper back to Missy. "Keep this paper for something else. Might come in handy."

"Heavy brown paper like that's hard to come-by," volunteered Grandmaw Taylor.

"Everything looks good. Thanks for the pan of water." She washed her hands and dried them thoroughly on one of the sterilized cloths.

Aunt Mae pushed sprigs of carrot-red, curly hair from Hannah's brow and wiped it with one of the wet cloths. She patted her on the shoulder and smiled. "How are you feeling, Chile?"

Hannah grabbed her stomach. "I'm in terrible pain, Aunt Mae. I didn't know the pains would be so hurtful." Her wide open green eyes caught and held Aunt Mae's as a pain began its execution throughout her body.

"I put an ax under Hannah's mattress right when the pains started, Mae." Grandmaw Taylor hobbled over to the bedside and took one of Hannah's hands. "You'll be just fine, Hannah. You're in mighty good hands." She shuffled towards the door, and turned back to speak. "Mae, let me know what I can do. Don't want to get in the way."

When Aunt Mae examined Hannah, and pulled the bed covers back over her, she noticed an expensive watch on Hannah's wrist. She raised Hannah's arm to observe the watch closer: *Bulova.* Hannah stiffened her arm. She laid Hannah's hand down gently, and walked over to a rocking chair and lifted a "store-bought" baby shawl. It was luxurious and soft to the touch.

Aunt Mae walked to the open window, stuck her head out and breathed-in deeply. "Come over here, Missy, and see God's promise of a fair day tomorrow, in that absolutely gorgeous, red sunset."

When Missy came to her, Aunt Mae put her arm around her waist. "Lie down awhile. We'll be working here probably all night."

Missy's shoulders slumped and she sighed heavily with frustration. "I'm nervous," she whispered, and left the room.

Hannah's watchful eyes never left Aunt Mae's face. She didn't want the disapproval of anyone, especially Aunt Mae, a person who was always good to her, always bragging about her beauty and her achievements.

Aunt Mae returned to Hannah's bed, sat down and took her hand, just as pain rushed Hannah's body. Tears flowed from her eyes and her chin trembled, "Aunt Mae, I am sorry to disappoint you!"

"I love you regardless of what you do. Only our Creator dare judge you. But, Hannah," she said, as she picked up her wrist and tapped the new Bulova watch, "I ask of you this one thing—don't sell yourself short. Sometimes we make a choice and our soul—our whole being is left to deal with that choice. In the end, it's our choice."

"Aunt Mae, I love him," she whispered. Another pain wretched her body, and she muffled a cry in her pillow.

"I know you do. I know you do." She patted Hannah's hand, and kissed her on the brow.

"I love him! I love him! He loves me, too!" Hannah whispered, frantically.

"Try to relax," Aunt Mae soothed. She held Hannah's hand tightly, as she pondered over who the father could be. *Who? He had to have enough money to buy expensive things for Hannah, and for the baby.* Her eyes rested upon the very expensive and lovely baby shawl, on a dresser nearby. *The baby's father probably has some money. So, what young man has money?*

It was close to daylight, when Missy returned to Hannah's room with another knife and placed it under the mattress to "cut" down the pain—a superstition which passed from generation to generation. She opened a trunk and removed one of the quilts, "God's Eye," and spread it over Hannah's feet. Then, she added a couple of logs to the fire in the fireplace.

Aunt Mae pulled the bed covers away, but kept "God's Eye" close to Hannah's upper body. She touched the crown of the head of the new soul in spasm to be born, and prayed for a healthy baby. "God's will be done."

The delivery went smoothly. "Hannah, it's a darling little boy! Look, Missy! You have a handsome grandson!" Aunt Mae held the baby up high in the air and examined his reaction as she brought him down into her cuddling arms. He kicked excitedly and examined his new world with wide open eyes.

"Is he okay? He's not crying? I was afraid that I marked him when I saw a turtle." Hannah whispered timidly. She breathed deeply, and held her breath.

The baby began to cry.

"He's perfect!" Aunt Mae exclaimed.

Missy smiled through misty eyes and wiped Hannah's brow. "Thank you, Jesus!" she laughed.

After she bathed the baby and wrapped him in sterilized cloths, Aunt Mae handed him to Hannah. "Here is one of the most handsome baby boys, I've ever seen. I've never seen so much blond hair on a newborn in all my days." The thick hair on the baby's blond head stood straight up and his dark blue eyes searched his surroundings. He sought the face that belonged to the voice he'd heard for nine months.

"Thank you, Aunt Mae. He is beautiful, isn't he?" she said weakly. The baby snuggled and wriggled to be close to her. "Aunt Mae, will you name him for me?"

Aunt Mae glanced at Missy, and she smiled and nodded.

"Why, I'd be pleased to give a pretty baby boy a real nice name." She thought for a moment. "Let's call him Benjamin!"

"Benjamin," Hannah whispered. She smiled, snuggled the baby close to her breast, and dozed.

Aunt Mae continued to pray as she pushed and guided the afterbirth onto a strip of a red flannel healing cloth. She bound the cloth around the remains tightly and placed it in a man's shoebox. "Here, Missy, have James bury this bloody issue."

* * * *

Even though this "country" family could afford expensive, tangible possessions, Aunt Mae was always surprised they had so few personal items. The Taylors and the Williams had enough money to loan to their neighbors. She examined the meager luxuries: silver candlesticks, a carved antique clock on the mantel, and a highly polished antique round oak table with matching chairs, sitting in front of the fireplace.

Grandmaw Taylor and Uncle Albert spoke in unison, "Good morning, Aunt Mae. Please join us for breakfast."

"Good morning! Hannah's got the cutest little baby boy you ever saw. She let me name him."

"Come again—what did you name him?" asked Uncle Albert.

"Benjamin," said Aunt Mae

"Benjamin! I like it. Thank you for all the things you've done for us, Mae!"

"You're welcome! Hannah did real well," she replied.

"Don't get around too good anymore, or I would have worked with you." Grandmaw Taylor brushed tears of joy from her eyes with the back of her hand.

Steaming coffee, fried eggs and ham, browned, buttered biscuits, and fig preserves awaited her. "If you prefer tea, we can oblige with some real good, Red Sassafras."

"Red Sassafras? That would hit the spot, if the tea is already made," said Aunt Mae. "I noticed the leaves are changing, when I rode over yesterday. The yellows of the sweet-gum trees and the reds of the dogwood and sumac are vivid colors this year." She smiled, and pushed the white, fuzzy ringlets of hair from her forehead.

"Wish I could get out and see for myself, Mae. Don't get further than the porch much anymore," lamented Uncle Albert Taylor. "You know, the thing I notice more about getting old is this: I remember trivial things that happened long time ago—those things that didn't mean much at the time. Now, I try to figure out why those trivialities have become so important." He chuckled.

"That's an interesting thought, Uncle Albert," said Aunt Mae. "Wish I had something to give you for your ailments."

She rummaged in her medicine basket. "In the meantime, let's talk about trivialities. I don't believe anything is trivial. What about you?"

"Guess I believe everything has some reason for taking place in our lives, except rheumatiz," Uncle Albert laughed, and showed his tobacco stained teeth.

"When ole rheumatiz set in, I ain't been much good for nothin' since," he sighed. "Got anything in that herb-basket of yours that might help me?" He leaned forward, and stared at her basket filled with neatly folded paper packets. His shoulder-length, white hair fell forward into his eyes. He sat back and shoved it behind his ears.

"I'll give you some herb powders before I leave." She lifted her cup to her lips, and relished the Red Sassafras tea.

"So, you think everything is important—that it's pre-ordained, Mae?" asked Uncle Albert.

"Uncle Albert, we should believe nothing is left to chance. Sometimes we have to make our own luck. I've noticed you never leave things to chance. You're a successful business man."

"Aw, Shaw! Mae, I just use my head," he laughed at her compliment, and touched his head.

"Yes, your head and your money to make money."

Uncle Albert chuckled and wiped his white mustache between his fingers. "Aw, Shaw."

"James is getting several things gathered to take with you, Aunt Mae. Our way of thanking you for your help with Hannah," said Missy, as she re-entered the room.

"Glad to help!"

"You are nice, Mae. Very nice." Uncle Albert's kind, pale, blue eyes, hooded with shaggy white brows, searched her eyes and face intently. "Yes, you're a very unique person."

When the meal was finished, Aunt Mae removed the dishes, made the room orderly, and sat back down for a visit.

Two little boys peeked in the doorway from to time and ran away each time Aunt Mae looked up. "Come here and see me, Tommy and Bobby. Come and see me," Aunt Mae called. "What happened to those sweet little boys who used to hug and kiss me every time I saw them?" They peeked around the door-facing.

"Mae, I'll bet they're jealous. You always take so much time with them. Yesterday, when you got here, you went directly to Hannah's room. Guess they noticed that. Now they have a little competition with Hannah's baby. What's his name again? Benjamin?" asked Uncle Albert.

"Yes, I'll bet they are jealous of Benjamin," Aunt Mae said softly and philosophically. "It was an honor to get to name him."

"A good, strong name, I'd say," Uncle Albert arose from his chair. "Thanks for having breakfast with us, Mae." He was tall, and slightly stooped. He shuffled slowly towards the front porch. "Heard about Hume's 'Lectric Lights Fund. Tell him I'll loan him the money, so he can get the wires strung down to your house. Won't charge him as much interest as I do other folks, since y'all are always helping us out." He patted the bulge of his wallet in the bib of his well-worn overalls.

"That's mighty nice of you, Uncle Albert. I'll tell him."

No one would ever guess Uncle Albert made a living collecting interest on the money he loaned. His white hair and mustache were always neatly trimmed, but he wore patched overalls and a sweaty, brown felt hat, giving the illusion of one who was poor.

The front screen door squeaked and slammed and she heard Uncle Albert sigh loudly when he sat down heavily in a chair on the porch.

"Mae, I bumped that ole bum leg of mine again and messed it up good. Got fever in it. Did you bring any of your special ointment with you?" Grandmaw Taylor squirmed in her chair. She pulled her dress up to her knees and looked down to examine her swollen legs.

Aunt Mae removed several packets of papers from her medicine basket, and a snuff-box containing her special ointment. "Grandmaw Taylor, I'd like to make my usual swap—the ointment, and some herbs, for your empty snuff cans to put my special ointment in."

"That's a good swap for me, Mae," she laughed. "But, like I always tell you, you're getting the short and the raw end of the deal."

"Glad to make the swap. I need the snuff cans to hold my special ointment."

Grandmaw Taylor yelled, "Bobby! Tommy! Come to Grandmaw Taylor."

The little boys peeked around the doorway. "Come in here, Bobby and Tommy. Grandmaw needs you to bring all of her empty snuff cans." The little boys ran to the back porch, ran back to Grandmaw Taylor, dropped several snuff cans into her lap, and kept running.

"Thank you, Bobby. Thank you, Tommy," Aunt Mae called.

"Now, Mae, tell me the truth about Hannah. Is she and that little baby okay?"

"Couldn't ask for a more perfectly formed child! He has a head full of blond hair, and lots of it!" The antique clock struck nine. "You'll see how precious he is when Missy brings the baby downstairs."

"Blond hair? Well I'll be! Billy Joe had the thickest, blondish hair I ever saw! God rest his baby-soul."

"Yes, I remember—"

"It seems like yesterday he had pneumonia and died."

Mae, I know you're weary. Want to lie down awhile?"

"No, Grandmaw Taylor, but thanks for asking."

"Heard in the grapevine no one's seen Dan since the funeral. Not even his maw and paw? Is that right, Mae?"

"You heard it right. Joanie and Mr. Zanderneff are worried, and so are we."

"That's hard to believe. Wonder if something happened to Dan?"

"I ask the Zanderneffs all the time if they've heard from Dan and they just say, 'Sure haven't,' and look sad. Can't figure them out. Joanie acts afraid to pet the girls, and Mr. Zanderneff just stands off at a distance and stares at Henny-Penny and Kackie."

"Well, I'll be jiggered. Wonder why?"

"Maybe embarrassed about Dan abandoning the children. Who knows? Since no one has heard from Dan, Jake went to Tennessee to see what he can find out. He's probably still in Tennessee."

"Sure hope Jake learns something."

"Yeah," said Aunt Mae. "Me, too."

"Henny-Penny and Kackie are adorable—just the spit image of Macie and Caddie when they were the same age—same color of hair and all. I'm worried about the bruises and scars Laughing Eyes and I found on the children." Grandmaw Taylor raised her scraggly, gray eyebrows, leaned forward, and rested both her hands on her walking cane, awaiting reaction.

"You and Laughing Eyes never mentioned that you found bruises and scars on Henny-Penny and Kackie! Tell me why?" She leaned towards Grandmaw Taylor with one hand on her hip, waiting indignantly for her answer.

"Knew you'd be upset, but knew you would see the bruises the first time you bathed and dressed the girls. We treated them with liniment, and Lord only knows what Laughing Eyes went out in the woods and brought back to put on them. She made a good salve and I'm sure that helped. We also showed the bruises to Doc Stowe. Didn't Doc tell you?"

"No, he did not. I haven't seen him. Jake and Hume said you probably didn't tell me because you didn't want me to worry and agonize over the situation any sooner than I had to."

"Hume's right, God love him! Don't want to hurt you, Mae, by asking you this, but did Dan or Macie beat their little girls?"

"Don't know. But I can't believe they would ever do such a thing," said Aunt Mae.

"Listen, Mae, don't you and Hume ever worry about whether Dan will be coming back and take them away, or his maw and paw will try to take the little girls away from you?"

The clock ticked loudly.

"That's exactly what Hume asked me! Why have Joanie and Mr. Zanderneff not even been over to our home to see them. Grandmaw Taylor, it just doesn't make any sense!"

"That's a fact. Makes no sense a 'tall. I can't imagine Joanie Zanderneff not wanting to be with her little grandbabies! But—let me change the subject."

"Sure, Grandmaw Taylor. What is it?" Aunt Mae could tell something else preyed strongly on her mind.

"You know, that preacher-man, Reverend Buker Webster. He came over here to check on my health the other day. Sat right there in that chair where you're a sittin'. His boots were muddy and all scratched. Now, that's a strange man. He hem-hawed and hem-hawed and finally, I said, 'Preacher, you got something on your mind?' And he said, 'As a matter of fact, I do have something on my mind.' That preacher proceeds to ask me if I tell fortunes and read cards, and I looked at him, long and hard, and I asked him who told him that I just might read cards, and he said he got it pretty straight. So, I looked him over and decided I didn't want to read cards for no preacher-man. Mae, it kinda bothers me now. Cause I lied. I answered him by saying, 'Preacher, isn't it a sin to tell fortunes reading cards?'"

"He came right out and asked you if you read cards? Well, I never!" Aunt Mae exclaimed, and slapped her leg.

"Yeah, he sure did. Just came out and asked me. I didn't really lie and say the word *no.* I just answered him with a question. He sure did look funny."

"Reverend Buker Webster asked you a really nosy question, but he has a way of asking personal questions," Aunt Mae smiled. "He's been asking my family questions about Macie."

"About Macie?"

"Yes—personal questions, but since he preached her burial service, he probably has a curiosity about her."

"Mae, you're going to think it's queer, with me thinking this, but, I believe Reverend Buker Webster wanted his cards read."

Aunt Mae raised her eyebrows.

"Now, why do you suppose he needs his cards read, Grandmaw Taylor? Surely no preacher-man wants his cards read!"

"Don't go quoting me, now, Aunt Mae, but my gut-feeling tells me he's a scoundrel," Grandmaw Taylor sniffed, smiled and nodded her head knowingly.

"You see that in the cards?" Aunt Mae laughed.

"But, of course, I do!" Grandmaw Taylor cackled.

"A scoundrel! I guess we'll have to wait and see, Grandmaw Taylor. I'll keep it to myself, but do you care if I tell Hume?" she chuckled.

"Tell Hume. He'll keep it close. Speaking of the word *close*, you're a close-dreamer, Mae. Dreamed any more strange dreams, since you dreamed about that gigantic, black dove swooping down and getting that baby chick?"

"No, thank goodness!" She arose from her chair.

"Your dreams are interesting, and sometimes puzzling."

"Yes. Sometimes they are."

"Remember that little chick that got snatched away by the black dove—in your dream—I believe the chick was Macie," Grandmaw Taylor whispered.

"Oh, my God! Grandmaw Taylor, I can't believe you've thought of the chick as being Macie."

"Yes, I believe Macie is the little chick that the black dove came in for the kill, and the two chicks left are Caddie and Jake." Grandmaw Taylor stared at the clock.

"And the Giant Black Dove?"

"In your dream I believe the black dove that snatched the little chick up and away is Dan. But, I have no real reason to think that Dan's the black dove, except for interpretation. Dan was always peaceful like a white dove and such a good boy. I hate to think it!" Grandmaw Taylor sniffed loudly, and moved back in her rocking chair.

"I don't want to think it! I don't want to think it!" exclaimed Aunt Mae.

"I don't mean to hurt you. God bless you, Mae. God bless you." Grandmaw Taylor crossed her hands over her breast.

"You don't mean to hurt me—I know that, Grandmaw Taylor."

"Mae, everyone loves you. You know, if I could live my life over again, I'd do a better job of loving like you do. Be a little less stubborn too," she chuckled.

"Everyone loves you, Grandmaw Taylor. I don't want to rush, but I need to get back home."

Grandmaw Taylor stood up and balanced with her walking cane. "Thanks for everything, Mae. Lord knows Hannah is going to have a time with that baby without it having a paw and all." She lowered her voice. "Mae, don't hold back. Tell me if you know who is the paw of Hannah's little baby?"

The tick-tock of the clock invaded her thoughts. Aunt Mae's whispered, "I can't say I rightly know." She gave Grandmaw Taylor a sympathetic pat on the shoulder. "Do you?"

Grandmaw took one of Aunt Mae's hands and squeezed it. "I'm afraid to think what I think."

* * * *

"I appreciate your helping Hannah—my family. How can we ever pay you?" The sun reflected glints of coppery and auburn streaks in James Anderson's honey-blond, red hair. He furrowed his red eyebrows, and stared into Aunt Mae's blue eyes intently. "What can we do to ever repay you for all the things you and Uncle Hume do for us?"

"To name the child was enough." She smiled.

He seemed to have acquired a thousand more freckles since she had last seen him. He bent over the feed-sacks and busied himself tying them. When he looked up his eyes reflected a soft greenish-blue hue of kindness. "You'll find several things in the feed-sacks, Aunt Mae. Got some onions, sweet potatoes and a few apples. Didn't want to weight you down too much. So, I'll bring some more apples and potatoes to your house, later on. Missy put some of her good blackberry jam, tomato preserves, and pear preserves in one of the sacks. Believe it's in the one with the onions. I'll bring you a load of chopped wood next week. Hope this will do until you are better paid."

"Thank you, James. It's more than enough. Glad to help. I'll be back to check on Hannah in a couple of days, but come get me, if I'm needed before then." Aunt Mae mounted at an oak tree stump.

The sound of the honking geese and squawking guineas could still be heard faintly, as she approached the main road.

She breathed the fresh, clean air deeply, and rubbed her neck. Even though she felt exhausted, she was happy because the birth went so well. *Thank you, Father in Heaven, for helping me deliver such a fine baby-boy. Bless and guide Hannah, Benjamin, and their family in Your will. In Jesus' sweet name, I pray. Amen.*

* * * *

Aunt Mae rode her mule a very short distance, before she heard the sound of a wagon moving over the bumpy, rough red-clay road. She stopped, and waited for the wagon to appear.

She waved when she recognized George-West Meyers, with a hound-dog sitting beside him.

George-West leaned slightly forward in his board wagon, being pulled by a team of mules. When he saw Aunt Mae, he removed his black felt hat, smoothed his full head of dark black hair, and sat up straighter. He didn't look fifty years of age. His body was trim, youthful and muscular. When they got along-side each other, he pulled up. "Howdy, Mae. What you doing way out here? Kinda out of your way, isn't it?"

"Could say the same for you, George-West." She observed him closely, and noticed his handsome, tanned face reddened.

The dog growled in a low, guttural tone, and showed its teeth. George-West patted it on the head. "It's okay, Blue."

"Pretty hound-dog."

"Yeah, he's a right pretty Blue-Tick. Going down here to swap him for a good coon-dawg," he smiled.

"Heard John McIntosh wants to swap his dog."

"As a matter of fact, I'm going to John's place." He flashed a perfect smile.

"Been up all night delivering Hannah's baby!" Aunt Mae announced happily, and shifted her weight in the saddle.

"The baby's here, huh? Everything okay? Boy or a girl?" His penetrating blue eyes squinted when his eyes met hers, and his face flushed.

"All's fine. The baby and Hannah are doing just fine."

He held his head high, and his keen eyes met hers. "And you? Guess you're mighty tired?"

"I'm all right. They asked me to name that sweet baby boy, and I named him Benjamin."

"Nice name." He clucked to the mules. "Tell Hume hello for me, Mae. See you at church."

"Give my regards to Jessie!" She twisted around in her saddle and observed George-West Meyers, as he drove down the road a short distance and around the bend.

The sound of the Myers' wagon stopped.

She heard what she thought sounded like the clink of James Anderson's and Uncle Albert's metal mailbox being closed. Then, she heard the wagon move on again.

George-West Meyers must have left something in the mailbox for Hannah! Tears of dread swelled in her heart, as she remembered his blush. *If George-West Meyers is Hannah's lover, then Hannah's love is in vain! She's in love with a married man, a wealthy one, but a very married one, nevertheless! To think he's an elder of the church! And, he's married! Robbing-the-cradle, too! That hypocrite!* She began to laugh to herself. *Just because I heard a sound that I believe was a mailbox open and close, I let my imagination run rampant and now I'm accusing one of the pillars of the church to be involved with Hannah. What if I'm jumping the gun!*

On the way home, she thought of different scenarios, but none fit better than George-West Meyers being the father of Benjamin. She promised herself she would say nothing to anyone, except Hume, but would keep her eyes open.

* * * *

Aunt Mae sat on the front porch "looking" dried beans. She threw out a clump of dirt and a small pebble. Upon hearing the sound of a galloping horse, she glanced up. "Hume, come out here quickly. Jake's back." She stood up and placed the pan of beans on a small, wicker table, and waited anxiously for Jake's arrival.

"Looks like Jake's riding Reverend Buker Webster's horse, again." She rubbed her hands over the bib of her white apron, and smoothed her hair.

Jake's clothes were disheveled and wrinkled, and his blood-shot eyes were swollen, and sad.

"Come in here and eat something, Jake."

"You're looking well, Aunt Mae." Jake leaned over and kissed her on the cheek.

"You smell like a brewery, Jake!" she scolded. "You don't have any of that shine with ya, do ya? You know good and well how I feel about that!"

He raked his hand through his hair and rubbed the stubble of his whiskers. "I don't have shine, and yeah, I feel awful. Been home several days. Sorry I didn't come over right away."

"You're destroying yourself! You need to start taking care of yourself!"

"Let's have some coffee, Jake." Uncle Hume attempted to distract Aunt Mae. He grabbed the coffee pot and sloshed its contents.

"All right, Uncle Hume. Coffee sounds good. Got any pound cake?"

"We'll heat the coffee and have some cake," said Uncle Hume

"Hate to tell you that Dan's gone. Left his house and nobody had a clue where he went?" said Jake.

Aunt Mae opened the door to the pie safe.

"He disappeared?" asked Uncle Hume. "What happened?"

"Yes, he's gone only God knows where!" Jake exclaimed.

They gathered at the kitchen table, while Uncle Hume revived a fire in the wood-stove.

"Uncle Hume! Aunt Mae! Listen! Macie did have bruises on her body is what the undertaker's assistant said, but he wouldn't tell me anything because I got too upset when he answered a couple of questions. Said it was a family thing. Just the family got answers. I wasn't family. Said Dan's her family. No one else!" He slumped, and held his head.

"Well, I'm family. I'll ask some questions, myself," Aunt Mae exclaimed.

"We'll both ask that undertaker what we need to know!" declared Uncle Hume. "You too, Jake. You're family."

"Well, I got the Sheriff to say he'd question Betty Sue Mitchells about the suitcase she tripped over. Said he had heard nothing about a suitcase. I believe that packed suitcase is proof that Macie was ready to go—to leave—and Dan stopped her—killed her. The Sheriff said he'd look into the case further but not to get my hopes up that he'd find Dan. He still thinks Macie committed suicide."

"What suitcase?" asked Uncle Hume. He stood up, placed his hands on the kitchen table and leaned forward. His dark brown eyes flashed concern.

"Betty Sue Mitchells didn't tell us about a suitcase!" Aunt Mae said loudly, and stared at Jake long and hard. "She talked our ears off, but she didn't tell us something so important as finding a packed suitcase!" She sniffed.

"Yes, Betty Sue Mitchells tripped over a very heavy suitcase when she ran over to Dan's and Macie's house to check on Macie. The suitcase was in the middle of the floor at the front door. She picked it up and shoved it in a closet and kept on a' going until she reached the bathroom, and found Macie on the floor, bleeding—dead."

"Well, I never! Why didn't she tell us about a suitcase?" asked Aunt Mae.

"Told me it slipped her mind in all the excitement!" said Jake.

"Does the sheriff see this as proof Macie was leaving Dan and that Dan kept her from leaving?" Uncle Hume banged his fist on the table.

"Not exactly. Sheriff said he'd not been told about the suitcase until I told him. He was going to talk to Miz Betty Sue Mitchells and get her statement. Said it might look bad for Dan." Jake sighed.

Aunt Mae cut a slice of pound cake, placed it on a saucer for Jake and poured him a cup of coffee.

"Do you believe Dan might have killed her, Jake?" Aunt Mae held her breast and took a deep and quivering breath.

"I don't want to believe Dan had anything to do with her death, but Dan's nowhere to be found. Nobody has seen him since a couple of days after the funeral. He moved the furniture to Miz Mitchell's woodshed, and told the neighbors that he was on the way to Three-Mile Crossing. I paid Miz Mitchells for storage on Macie's furniture and paid to ship it to my cabin. It'll be located at my cabin, if Dan shows up. If not, I'll save the furniture for Henny-Penny and

Kackie. I wrote my address on a pocket note-book page and gave it to Miz Mitchells.

"Thanks, Jake."

"Dan probably killed Macie and now he's run off! That no good SOB!" Jake exclaimed.

"I can't believe the way he trembled, cried, and carried on so much, when we were in Tennessee, and then he didn't even come to Georgia for her burial!" said Aunt Mae. "We didn't ask him much about Macie's death because he seemed so upset. I can't believe the Sheriff wouldn't know the difference between suicide and murder," Aunt Mae sighed.

"We still don't know if it was murder. What makes us so sure?" asked Uncle Hume.

"Hume, I know you want to give Dan the benefit of the doubt, but, the bruises on Macie and the bruises and scars we found on the little girls tells us something. And also his running away! That incident shows guilt!" Jake grumbled. "How could we have let this happen to Macie? I loved her! I loved her," Jake wept.

"I know you love Macie—always knew you still loved her, Jake," said Aunt Mae.

"Macie needed help and we didn't help her!" Jake moaned. "This would have never happened, if she had been belonged to me!"

"Caddie sent Macie money for the train tickets for her and Henny-Penny and Kackie, even though she didn't realize the urgency of Macie's request. We can be thankful that she did that much for Macie."

"It was too late!"

"Yes, it was too late, but Caddie didn't know it at the time," said Aunt Mae.

"We didn't know she needed help, Jake. As far as our letting this happen to Macie, look here, we didn't let it happen. We don't have the answers. We don't even know the questions to ask. We all feel the guilt." Uncle Hume pulled the bib of his cap over his eyes.

"Oh! How I loved her!" Jake moaned.

Aunt Mae searched Jake's sweet countenance. She did not understand how Macie could have chosen Dan over Jake. Jake seemed more suited for her, but the decision had been Macie's. Macie apparently loved Dan, and he was her choice of the two.

Uncle Hume raised his voice, and flailed his right hand. "Jake, even if Dan beat Henny-Penny and Kackie and Macie, that doesn't make Dan a murderer.

Looks bad, though." Uncle Hume appeared to be shaken. "I don't want to believe Dan did this terrible thing!"

"Hush! You two lower your voices. Don't let the babies hear you talking!"

"You two remember Dan ever being violent? I can't remember him ever starting trouble or fighting, do you?" Jake questioned.

"No, I don't," said Aunt Mae.

"Dan was never a trouble-maker," Uncle Hume agreed. He arose from his chair and touched Jake's elbow. "Come on, Jake, your bath water is heating. Let's freshen up and rest, Son.

* * * *

Aunt Mae tidied the cabin and went outside to help Uncle Hume feed the guineas, turkeys, chickens and the livestock.

Later in the morning, she took Henny-Penny and Kackie on a hike to the mail-box. The dogs and cats tagged along behind them.

When they got to Three-Mile Crossing, she pointed in the direction of the brick schoolhouse across from the church. "See that nice red building? One day, soon, you'll go to that school. You'll learn your three 'R's in the first grade. Miz Locket Webster will be your teacher."

"Three R's?"

"Yes! You'll learn reading, writing and arithmetic. Just think, you'll read books that will take you to far away places in your imagination."

Henny-Penny and Kackie sat down on their knees to rest.

"I want to go to school now," said Henny-Penny. "I want to read about how to be a Princess."

"I don't ever want to go to school. I want to stay home with you for ever and ever," said Kackie.

Aunt Mae laughed, "Forever and ever?"

"Yes. And, ever."

Aunt Mae removed a white, cotton napkin from her apron pocket, unwrapped two buttered, blackberry jam biscuits and handed one to each little girl. She removed her bonnet, and wiped her brow on her apron. As they rested near a mossy and rocky creek, she read Caddie's letter:

"Dear Aunt Mae and Uncle Hume—I miss y'all, love y'all, and think of Macie all the time. I know how much you love Henny-Penny and Kackie, but I wonder how you are handling all the extra work it takes to raise them. I hate to add to your burdens, but I am homesick—so homesick!"

Aunt Mae decided to finish reading the letter later, and pushed the envelope into her apron pocket. Even though Caddie's letter disturbed her, she smiled. "Don't sit on that rotten log, baby girls. It's probably infested with chiggers. When we get home, I'll have to wipe you off with camphor. That'll kill the chiggers."

"What're chiggers?" asked Kackie. She crinkled her nose.

"They're the smallest little red bugs, you ever saw that live out here in the woods. They live in rotten tree trunks and on bushes and shrubs. They're little red mites, so small, they look like a little red-dot is crawling on you. When they burrow into the skin, they cause a terrible itch."

"Chiggers?"

"Yes, Chiggers. Isn't that a funny name?"

"Chiggers," they giggled. With cheeks full of buttered, blackberry jam biscuits, Henny-Penny and Kackie held hands, and began to circle and dance.

This little song was sung by the innocent children:

"Chiggers-Chiggers!

Don't you bite-bite-bite!"

Aunt Mae stood up and smoothed the back of her dress. "I believe I need to get in on this fun!" She made a funny face to make them laugh, grabbed their hands, contortioned her upper body, and they danced around and around in a circle.

"Chiggers! Chiggers! Don't you bite-bite-bite!" They laughed.

* * * *

Aunt Mae sat on the edge of her bed, and read Caddie's letter. She walked to the dresser slowly, and stood before the mirror. She turned her head from side-to-side, and stroked her face gently. She examined the deep wrinkles on her face, especially the crow's feet that fanned at the corners of her wise eyes, and pulled at the corners of the droopy eyelids until they became slits. She touched her once full lips that had begun to thin. *I am the same person I've always been, and my thinking and doing feels young, but the face Hume used to admire is hiding somewhere under all this sagging and tanned skin. Why don't I see smooth, and lily white skin after all of my many efforts to cure the aging?*

She removed the lid from her store bought jar of "Ponds" cream, and patted a stingy amount on her mask of aging. Then she smoothed a generous amount of her "special ointment" all over her face and neck. *Lord, please take exceptional good care of Caddie. Give me and Hume strength to take care of this family, and keep me "young" enough to do the job. In Jesus name, I pray.*

* * * *

Three-Mile Crossing nestled at the foot of the blue mountain range. Several small business establishments, sitting adjacent to each other on four short streets running in four different directions formed the crossing.

Judge Pewter moved back to Three Mile Crossing to practice law after he retired from his law practice and judgeship in Atlanta. He felt privileged to retire in the place he loved more than any other place on the green earth—his birthplace.

He renovated a two-story, red-brick service station into a quaint, but elegant office; installed window boxes to hold the flowers of the season, and hung his shingle on the front door for everyone to know an Attorney-at-Law/General Law Practice was in town.

Upon entering the front door of his office, it was obvious a wealthy lawyer worked in this interesting, and colorful place. Bookshelves filled with leather law books were dominant. Tapestries and original oil paintings hung on the walls over a spiral oak staircase, leading to the second floor. Oriental urns and vases sat upon antique tables at the ends of brown leather couches.

Even though Judge Pewter had gray hair, wore wire-rimmed glasses, was in his late sixties, and overweight, he appeared more youthful. He moved swiftly, usually walking with his head bent forward. He carried a brown weather-beaten briefcase in one hand and a black umbrella in the other. As he walked along the street, people stopped him to ask advice. They usually began their inquiry for a purported imaginary friend or asked hypothetical questions, but Judge Pewter knew the information they sought was for themselves. That was all right with him. They were all his potential clients. He answered their questions and invited them to his office. He worked long hours, and sometimes into the night. He reared his head back and laughed when he referred to the *law* as being his *mistress.*

* * * *

Jake parked his Ford under the front shelter of Judge Pewter's office, and went inside.

Judge Pewter said goodbye to a client, and held the door for Jake.

"Looking good, Jake. Come on in." Judge Pewter offered his hand. "How's the Sheriff's business coming along?"

"Usual arrests and stuff. You okay, Judge Pewter?"

"Doing fine, Jake. Come on back to my office. When have you heard from Ole Pem?"

"Not in quite awhile. What do you hear?" He sat down in a brown leather chair in front of Judge Pewter's antique, carved oak desk.

"You know Ole Pem still boards with my brother?"

Jake nodded his head.

"Brother Sam said Ole Pem's studying hard on his law books. You remember he's coming to work for me when he passes the Bar?"

"That's gonna be a great day!"

"You miss him a lot, don't you, Jake?"

"Sure do. Sure do," he sighed.

"You got the baseball team lined up to play at the school yard next Saturday?"

"Yes, sir. Sure do. Wanna come?

"I'll try to come and warm the bleachers a little while."

"What's on your mind, Jake? Macie?"

"How'd you know?" asked Jake.

"Guess I feel like I know you pretty good after all these years," he smiled. "What's bothering you, son?"

"You do know me well. I went to Tennessee to find Dan because he never has shown up here, like he said he would. He told Aunt Mae and Uncle Hume he'd be here at Three Mile Crossing within a couple of weeks after the funeral."

"Yes, Mae and Hume told me he said he'd be here in two weeks, but didn't show up. Joanie and Mr. Zanderneff are worried, too."

"Well, I went to Tennessee to Dan's house, the Sheriff's office and the undertaker's place in Tennessee, and came back without much news. I found out that Dan moved his furniture into a shed next door and left town—musta run off." Jake stopped talking and attempted to regain his composure.

"You don't say?" Judge Pewter looked alarmed.

"The undertaker's assistant told me that Macie had bruises on her body, when I asked him. But, he clammed up, when I started to ask questions. Said it's for the family to ask Not for me to ask."

"Bruises on Macie, you say?"

"Yes, Judge Pewter, I found out she had bruises on her body from the undertaker's assistant. Then I went to the Sheriff's office and he told me to 'let it be.'

He said Macie killed herself, short and simple! That's what the Sheriff said! But, I think Dan killed her."

"I'm so sorry, Jake. Dan's mother—Joanie—told me she's worried about him being late coming home. You remember Joanie works for me and Matilda. Been our housekeeper for years. I'm going to do all I can for all of you, but in the long run, I hope I don't end up with a conflict of interest. I want the Browns and the Zanderneffs to get along. You, too, Jake."

"I think Dan killed Macie."

"I feel so bad about Macie's death." Judge Pewter held his head and stared at his desk. He gained his composure and continued. "Now, let's take what you've just told me a little slower, okay? What makes you think that Dan killed her?"

"We want to know about bruises or scars on Macie. What we want you to do is help us find out from the undertaker a few more details about any bruises on Macie, and her condition at the time of death. We want a copy of her death certificate, and a copy of the coroner's report, if you can get it." Jake stopped talking and scrutinized the inside and outside of his hands. "What I'm trying to say is this. We need help."

"Jake, right now, I doubt that we can do anything from this distance, even if Dan did beat Macie. Maybe she did kill herself. Sometimes, we just have to brace ourselves—for the worst. Now, it looks really bad that Dan hasn't shown up. But, if something happened to him, he may be stopped-over someplace. We need to give the case a little more time, Jake. Also, remember proof, Jake. We need proof."

"Proof! Why Macie's next door neighbor, Betty Sue Mitchells, said that she tripped over a suitcase when she ran into Macie's and Dan's house and put the suitcase in the hallway closet. It felt heavy like it was packed. I told the Sheriff about it and he said he'd never been told anything about the suitcase, but would question Betty Sue Mitchells, and look into the evidence a little more—maybe re-open the case." Jake sighed, loudly.

"Easy, Jake. I'll write some letters for y'all immediately, and see what is required from this end. Now, listen, we're not the next of kin here, you know? Remember, Jake, you need proof that Dan did something. Don't go off the deep-end and do something drastic, you hear, Son?"

"Yes, Judge Pewter, I know that we need proof. Aunt Mae and Uncle Hume want you to write the undertaker and inquire because they are Macie's adoptive parents."

"Jake, may I ask why you wanted to question the undertaker. Why did you ask him if Macie had bruises on her body?"

"Oh, Judge Pewter, I thought someone told you. Aunt Mae found bruises and scars on Henn-Penn and Kackie."

"That's what I heard—it's sad."

"Yes. Now, we are wondering if Macie had bruises on her, also."

"You're wondering if Dan beat the little girls and Macie, too?"

"Yes."

"Jake, I haven't discussed anything with Aunt Mae or Uncle Hume about the bruises and scars on the children. Listen, we'd have to have proof before one thing could be done. Even if we learn bruises were on Macie's body, we'd need proof of who put the bruises on her, don't you see?"

"I know Judge Pewter. I know."

Jake's eyes fell on the bookshelves behind Judge Pewter's desk, laden with old leather-bound books, some in disrepair, some shiny and new. Newspapers and magazines, and legal documents were scattered and in much disarray. File folders stacked in neat piles were everywhere, all over his desk, tables and floor, on top of filing cabinets and windowsills.

Bessie knocked on the door, "Judge Pewter, forgive me for interrupting, but I need to get your signature on this letter before the mailman comes!"

"Sure, come on in, Bessie." He reached for his Schaefer pen set, marbled in greens and black. As his hand swirled and scrawled an illegible signature, light glinted on the gold point of the pen. He blotted the ink with a roller blotter, blew on his signature, and handed her the signed letter. "Here you are, Bessie."

"Excuse me again, Judge Pewter. You too, Jake."

A cool breeze blew through an open window.

"Judge, you're really busy." Jake noticed a pigeon perched on one of the window-sills. "I'm sorry to bother you." The Blue Ridge Mountains in the distance were hazy.

Judge Pewter pulled at his chin thoughtfully, and stared at Jake through steady inquisitive, wide-set, blue eyes. "Jake, I want to help you. Right now, all I can say is to try not to dwell on Macie's suicide so much that it eats you up alive. It's not that it's not important. It's important to me, too. Why, I loved that little Macie! So, this time of grief is hard for me, too. When you hear from Dan, come and see me immediately. In the meantime, I'll write some letters to Tennessee for Aunt Mae and Uncle Hume, starting with the undertaker." He arose from his squeaking chair.

"Thanks, Judge. I'll tell Aunt Mae and Uncle Hume."

Judge Pewter walked Jake to the door, and patted him on the back.

"What do you hear from Caddie?"

"She's fine but homesick."

"Caddie's a good catch for you, Jake—a delightful and intelligent girl."

"She's one of my very best friends," Jake smiled.

"The best kind of a catch, Son." They reached the front doorway. "Jake, I'll be in touch with you in a few days."

Thanks for your help, Judge," Jake said. He and Judge Pewter shook hands.

"Bye, Bessie." Jake smiled and raised his hand in a gesture of goodbye.

"Bye, bye, Jake. See you at church Sunday." She waved goodbye, and fluffed her short-bobbed, blond hair.

Judge Pewter held the doorknob, as he observed Jake walk dejectedly toward his car. His gut feeling told him that Jake would not "turn-it-loose." He became thoughtful and scratched his head, as he turned and went back into his office. His brown, leather chair sagged under his great weight, and he and the chair sighed aloud.

* * * *

The sun shone brightly through the colorful stained-glass windows and illuminated the pulpit. Some of the men wiped sweat from their brows with their handkerchiefs. Some of the ladies fanned with store bought folding fans, but, the majority fanned with "funeral-home," paper fans, which depicted a rendering of Jesus or another religious depiction on one side and a funeral home advertisement on the other.

Reverend Buker Webster read a dry, scientific sermon and compared hell to the planet Venus. He wiped his eyes and brow and replaced his glasses. "Brethren, hell is closer than one may think!"

Aunt Mae noticed Reverend Webster was rather handsome and boyish-looking without his glasses. Just as he mentioned the word *hell,* a ray of sunlight touched a drool of saliva trickling from both edges of his mouth, and as it trickled, it appeared to be as tusks, one on either side. The tusks became longer, as the drool moved slowly down each side of his chin. Reverend Webster wiped his eyes and mouth with his handkerchief, and replaced his glasses. Aunt Mae was so startled, she closed her eyes. *Lord,* p*lease let this pass; let this pass!* She opened her eyes, and looked at the Reverend's handsome face and everything seemed normal again. She blotted her face with her pink handkerchief, brushed lint from her lap and observed the people all around her. Nothing appeared to be out of the ordinary. No one else appeared to have seen the tusks and reacted as she had.

The men continued to wipe sweat with their handkerchiefs, and the ladies continued to fan.

Reverend Webster continued to read his message on the fires of hell and damnation, and Uncle Hume dozed, as did several others. When Aunt Mae punched him slightly in the ribs, he opened one eye and gave her a scowl.

As they stood on the front porch of the church, Aunt Mae looked into Reverend Webster's angelic, tan face, and searched for some kind of meaning in his penetrating eyes. She felt hypocritical when she said, "Impressive message," and shook his hand.

"Coming from you, that's a well-taken compliment," he smiled.

She was distracted by several young men that stood together under one of the large oak trees, laughing boisterously, talking loudly, gesturing and pointing to the meeting house. It was nice to hear them having so much fun, but little did anyone know that Reverend Buker Webster entertained the young men as an uninvited audience on many Saturday nights at the Meeting House.

* * * *

"Howdy, Deaver! Come on in. What's on your mind?"

"Howdy, Hume, how you been? Howdy, Mae."

"How's the family, Deaver?" asked Aunt Mae.

Family's fine, except Honey is going to kill me, if I don't get another well dug. She's getting red clay in the water—pitching a fit cause it's staining up all our clothes!"

"Sorry to hear about that, Deaver," said Uncle Hume.

"Hume, you're the best water-witcher in this country. Need you to come and witch for me?"

"When you need me?"

"Right now, if you're a willing to."

"Let me get my hat."

"Hope you don't mind, Mae," Deaver smiled.

"Sure, that's all right."

"Mae, here's you some of the best white-lightning in these parts. It'll make the best camphor you ever did see." He placed a pint jar holding a clear liquid on the kitchen table.

Thanks Deaver, but I don't have any camphor-gum."

"I knew you'd be needing camphor-gum." He removed a small packet from his pocket and handed it to her.

Aunt Mae removed the cellophane, and plopped the camphor gum into the jar of white-lightning.

"Henny-Penny and Kackie are really growing fast, and cute, too," said Deaver. "Let's go, Hume."

"Give my regards to your family," Aunt Mae smiled.

"Shore will. You haven't ridden in my new Ford, have you, Hume?" Deaver patted the front grill of his automobile, and gloated. "Ain't she a beaut?"

"Sure is, Deaver," Uncle Hume exclaimed, as he touched the car.

* * * *

Uncle Hume observed Deaver closely as he drove his new Ford down the county road. He was middle-aged, short, and a strong man of bull-like strength. At almost every social gathering, he removed his hat and shirt, and challenged anyone who dared to Indian-wrestle, or take-him-on, one at a time. He'd show them how he'd throw-em. Usually, a lot of the men stood on the meeting house porch, and watched Deaver mark boundaries in the red clay. After a match, Deaver wiped sweat off his face and chest onto his neatly pressed shirt. He laughed loudly, and gloated over his victory. Honey Clements always remarked in a disappointed tone, "Deaver, you know I just washed and ironed that shirt."

"County needs to scrape these roads. They're just like a scrub-board," said Deaver.

The men exchanged railroad and farm chit-chat.

Uncle Hume quietly examined the interior of the new car and surmised where Deaver got the money to buy his Ford. He didn't have any obvious way of making a living. The rumor was Deaver moon shined. Although Uncle Hume had never seen the still, he believed the rumor likely to be truthful. Deaver supplied Aunt Mae with moonshine to make camphor, but they never asked him where he got it. *What Deaver did or anyone else did was their business.* He didn't meddle in anyone else's *business,* and no one meddled in his. That was the way it had always been and that's the way it should be. It was the unspoken word in the mountains.

"Hume, I can't wait for us to get to my place. Wanna show you the best coon-dawg you ever did see. I just bought him and he's a good-un!"

"Cost much?"

"Cost me one hundred dollar bills. Worth it too." Deaver rolled down the window.

"Who from?"

"Bought it from George West Myers! I can get in there with the best of 'em."

"That's a lot of money, Deaver."

"Wal, you're gonna see he's worth the money, when we all go hunting."

When they arrived at Deaver's cabin, the dogs barked and goats bleated. Deaver cut himself a chaw of tobacco and offered a piece to Uncle Hume. "What do you need me to do? Want me to cut a limb or anything, Hume?"

"I'll pick my own rod. Just hope the saps not down. You need to be quiet and leave me be." Uncle Hume went into the dense woods, surrounding the house, and cut a springy forked stick from a young, wild cherry tree to use as his dowsing rod. He set out walking at random across the rocks and the cleared ground, all around the house. Deaver walked behind him. The pointed end of the stick stuck out in front of him and it looked like he carried a large sling-shot.

He walked fast as if drawn by a magnet. After a short time, he stopped, and yelled, "Here's a vein!" The dowsing rod pulled and quivered so hard, Hume could hear and feel the bark on the tree limb move, as it twisted against his palms.

"Deaver, mark the spot!"

Deaver ran in front of him and staked a place directly under the point of the stick.

"No, right where I am standing, Deaver! Stake the place under my feet! Not under the pointer!"

"You ole Sonavagun, how far down do you think is water, Hume?" Deaver asked as he staked an iron pipe in the ground.

"Oh, about 25 to 30 feet, I reckon." He wiped the palms of his hands on a red bandana handkerchief.

"Hume, let me see your hands," Deaver reached out to Uncle Hume.

"They're tingling some."

"Well, I've never seen anything like it, Hume. Look how red the insides of your hands are! Is that from the twig twisting?"

"Yes, it is."

"Let's go up to the house and pour cool water on them."

"That'd be nice, Deaver."

"Wish I knew how you do it, Hume. You told me one time that your Grandpappy and your Pappy both were water witchers, right?"

"Yeah. They called it divining, not water witching," he smiled, and sat down on a large rock.

"But, did your folks do the same thing that you do?" Deaver reached over and touched the palm of Uncle Hume's hand very gently.

Uncle Hume retold the story about how his Pappy and Grandpappy handed down this peculiar skill. Deaver listened intently, as if he had never heard him relate it before. "I remember seeing my daddy's hands after he marked the spot to dig a well. He'd sit down and rub his hands. They were cherry red—just like mine."

Little children peeped out the front door of the two-story cabin.

The hunting dogs continued to bark, "billy goats" and nannies bleated, and a rooster crowed.

"Honey, draw us a bucket of water and get us a brew!" Deaver called out, as he took off his shirt, wadded it up and threw it into a chair. Honey frowned at her husband, and stared at the shirt. "Hume has already witched us a spot for our well. You'll like it cause it's so close to the house."

"Thanks for witching us a new well!" said Honey Clements. She picked up the wadded shirt from a chair. "I'd just washed and ironed that shirt, Deaver," she moaned. "Saw you outside, but I been keeping these youngun's in the house. Deaver said witching requires quiet time."

"Glad to do it for you, Honey. Hope they dig you a well real soon."

"Uncle Hume, you see these youngun's. Everyone of them was midwifed by Aunt Mae. Oh, but you know that, of course," she giggled. "Where is Aunt Mae?"

"Mae's at home doing chores. Busy as a bee with Henny-Penny and Kackie. Lots to do."

"Wish Aunt Mae would come and visit sometime. Sure do like her." Honey said, as she knocked one of the little boys off a chair when he tried to climb on a table.

"Look here at my electric ice-box, Hume. Cost me like the dickens, but I said what the heck, and got me one. Got lights here in my house, and everything."

"Deaver, you've got lights! I'm saving my money to get power lines run to my house. Sure is nice to have ice, and an ice box to keep food cold."

"Yeah, electricity will change your life, Hume."

"Need to get home, Deaver."

"What's your charge, Hume?"

"Glad to do a favor."

"Wal, guess I'll have to bring a hawg over to your house in a day or two. How's that for pay?"

"That'll be fine, Deaver. Just fine!"

Goats and cattle grazed in a lush and green pasture.

Uncle Hume pulled his jacket closer to his neck and shoulders. Although he did not see anyone, he felt eyes gazing upon him.

* * * *

The next week Deaver came to the Brown's, just like he promised. He cut a chaw of tobacco, and offered it to Uncle Hume.

"Got my own, Deaver. Thank you. How's the family?"

"Honey and the young'uns are just fine. Listen to this, Mae. When Hume witched me that well, I asked him about how many feet down did he think it'd take to reach the water. Hume said about 25 to 30 feet," Deaver chuckled as he continued. "Well, guess what? We hit water 30 feet down! Now, tell me, Hume, how do you know about how many feet down it is that we need to bore for a water well?"

Uncle Hume smiled secretively. "I guess it's a gift."

"Wal, cuz you're so good to help me, Hume, I'm giving you a little something towards your lights fund—towards your dream—knowing how you want lights hooked up so bad." Deaver Clements extended a five-dollar bill.

"Uncle Hume beamed. "It's too much, Deaver. Too much!"

"Too much? Naw, take it, Hume. You're always helping me. That's for sure."

Uncle Hume fingered the money. "Thanks, Deaver. You're a good friend."

"Not only that, Hume. I've got that hawg tied in the back of my truck, just like I promised."

"A hawg, too?" Uncle Hume laughed.

"We best be getting that hawg off the truck!" Deaver placed his arm around Uncle Hume's shoulder, and they walked together to the truck.

* * * *

"Come in and make yourself at home, George-West. Just finished repairing your metal rake. I should say I made you a new one, it was in such awful shape."

George-West Meyers entered Uncle Hume's black-smith shed.

"Don't mind if I do rest a spell, Hume. Jessie and I had a nice, long ride, and thought we'd drop over to see you for a few minutes."

"Good. Good."

"So you got my rake done, huh? You remember I ran over it with the tractor."

"I fixed it almost good as new."

George-West examined Uncle Hume's repair. "This rake looks so good I guess I'll have to give you an extra quarter to go on your *Electric Light Fund.* He reached into his change purse and pulled out two quarters.

"Why, thank you, George-West. Mae's gonna be tickled pink when I get lights strung down here to the house."

"Yeah—I know Mae's gonna be thrilled to death."

"Won't she, though," Uncle Hume smiled and rubbed the two quarters together.

"Hang in, Hume. You'll get enough money for the lights real soon, I'm sure."

"I'm getting mighty close," said Uncle Hume. "Been saving my money for years."

"Listen—one of the main reasons I'm here is to give you a message from Jake. He telephoned, and said tell y'all he would be away for a few days. He's helping the Feds take some moon shiners down to Atlanta."

"Taking moon shiners to Atlanta!" Uncle Hume exclaimed. "Do we know any of the people?" He held his breath, when he thought of his friend, Deaver Clements.

"Don't know the people they arrested, as far as I know." George-West brushed the dust off his felt hat.

Uncle Hume sighed with relief.

* * * *

"Come on in the quilting house, Jessie, or we can go to the house," said Aunt Mae.

"I prefer the quilting house, please." Quilting frames hung from the ceiling, and colorful pieces of cloth of different kinds of material were neatly stacked on shelves attached to the walls. A small, round table and chairs sat before a fireplace.

"Why do you have the table prepared for tea. Are you expecting someone?"

"Hume and I planned to have tea. You and George-West are welcome to join us." Aunt Mae continued with her needle work.

"Aunt Mae, are you working on Cathedral Windows? I love that kind of quilting."

"Yes. I'm really enjoying myself."

"Aunt Mae, you know I am not good at any of those things. Can't sew good, can't cook good. Nothing. Wish I could do Cathedral Windows."

"Jessie, you have a lot of talents." She raised her right hand towards Jessie to quieten her, when she started to deny it. "I can show you what to do. It's fun to make and when you do each block, you not only have a unique design, but it has quilted itself on the back side." She turned the piece over for Jessie to examine.

"Show me what to do now, and I'll come back later." The evening sun caught gold highlights in Jessie's auburn hair.

"Jessie, I'll show you the basic steps now, but why don't you come next time the ladies are quilting."

"You know I'm in Matilda Pewter's Sewing Club."

"Matilda's nice."

"Matilda is very nice, but she examines my work. Makes me uncomfortable, especially when she turns my piece over and looks at the back."

"I'll give you a quick lesson, now, Jessie." After a few minutes of instruction, Aunt Mae had two of the blocks ready to show Jessie. See, it's sorta like an engineering job, putting it all together."

"I like it. It's a challenge." Jessie gazed out the window.

"What's wrong, Jessie," asked Aunt Mae.

"Nothing's wrong. Just bored. That's all." She flounced her hair with one hand and slouched at the window. She stood up, and pinched in her small waist with her fingers. "Think I'm losing weight?"

"You look wonderful!" Aunt Mae observed Jessie Meyers closely. "I'm glad nothing in particular is wrong, and you're just bored."

"I take care of myself, look good, and know George-West cares about me, but I'm trying to figure out what's wrong. If I didn't know better, I'd think George-West might be having an affair but he couldn't find anyone else as pretty as I am."

"You are pretty, Jessie." Aunt Mae quickly examined Jessie's slanted cinnamon-brown eyes and high cheek bones, and noticed that Jessie's right side was her best profile.

"Why do you think he's having an affair, Jessie? Anything special going on?"

"He's gotten where he dresses up more and puts on after-shave lotion every time he leaves the house to go anywhere—even when he goes to the barn. Makes me suspicious."

Aunt Mae looked up from her needlework. "Try not to worry, Jessie. Your husband is a businessman and has a reason to dress-up and go places. Maybe he's dressing-up for you. Thought about that?"

"I want things back the way they used to be, but I'm not sure how I can get things back the way they were. I am mighty worried." Her soulful eyes caught the light and she squinted thoughtfully.

"You mean get things back like when you were courtin'?" asked Aunt Mae.

"Yes, something like that."

"You have everything a woman could ever want. You have beauty, a good education, money and a good husband. Things always change. They are never like they used to be."

"Aunt Mae, please do me a great favor."

"If I can."

"I'd like for you to ask Uncle Hume if he knows anything about George-West running around on me, and then tell me what he says, okay?"

"Jessie, I can't do that. I don't *use* Hume, and I won't allow anyone else to use him, either. You understand, I'm sure."

"No, I don't understand but I am sorry if you are upset," she said haughtily. "Bet, if it was your Indian friend—that Laughing Eyes, you'd ask Uncle Hume," she snarled.

"No. You're wrong. Laughing Eyes would never ask me to manipulate my husband." Aunt Mae lifted her voice.

"How can you refuse me over her? She's just an Indian!"

"No, Jessie, not just an Indian. Laughing Eyes is my friend!"

"Okay! Okay! Let's just drop it!"

"Yes. Best we drop it. This subject is not about Laughing Eyes!" Aunt Mae snapped her quilting material into place, and it made a loud, popping sound.

Jessie raised her hand to silence her. "Listen! I hear something," said Jessie. "What's that horrible noise I hear?" Jessie stretched her neck to look out the window.

"Why, that's Henny-Penny and Kackie playing in their old, rickety wagon. Makes a terrible noise when they roll it over the river rocks and pebbles!"

"They are sweet children," Jessie sighed, and stared at them wistfully. "Never can have children, you know. My doctor in Atlanta said I'm infertile." She continued to stretch her neck and look out the window. "Such sweet little girls—I've always been partial to girls."

What a big bluffer Jessie is—acting uppity and mean. So, she does have a tender-spot—she would like to have children.

* * * *

Upon her return to the boarding house from an all day outing, Caddie met her landlady on the front porch. "Hi, Caddie. While you were out, a nice-looking gentlemen called for you."

"A gentleman?"

"He said his name was *Jake*, and he left you a note."

"A note! Where is it?"

"I slipped it under your door."

"Thank you Miz Meredith."

Caddie hurried up the stairway.

After all these years, Jake has finally come to see me and I missed him! But he left me a note!

She opened the door to her room quickly, bent down and picked up a most valuable treasure. She opened the envelope quickly and unfolded Jake's note. She read and re-read each word, looking for a clue that Jake might care for her, but she found no written evidence of his love. The real reason for the note stunned her, even though she knew he still cared for Macie.

She read the note in its entirety:

"*Dear Caddie—*

I am sorry I missed you today.

I had wanted to especially reminisce about Macie.

Love,

Jake"

She sat on the edge of her bed, held the note tightly to her nose, and close to her jaw. Just to know he had held the pen and placed the words, "Dear Caddie" and "Love, Jake" upon the paper had to be *enough f*or now. She held the tangible, treasured keepsake close to her breast.

For years, most of her idle thoughts had been of Jake. After Macie's marriage to Dan, Jake was always pleasant and sweet to her, but it was obvious he was still in love with Macie.

The distinction between love and obsession being difficult to make, her obsession nagged and nagged, not letting go, and throughout the years obsession tightened and chiseled away at her heart. She took a deep breath. She knew she must think and breathe more than obsession itself, but it was hard to shake the dream of having Jake one day for herself.

She closed her eyes.

Now that Macie is dead—is Macie able to know all? Know everything? Would it matter to Macie that I love Jake, especially since Macie never returned his love?

Caddie felt guilty because Macie probably knew at that very moment, while she sat on the edge of her bed, that she had always loved Jake. What did the Bible say? She searched her mind for scriptures trying to remember what was said about the dead. She believed it said that the dead are asleep.

If the dead sleep until Judgment Day, then Macie is asleep. Macie doesn't and couldn't know about how I feel concerning Jake.

She felt better.

She opened and closed her hand. *What triggers a thought to make me love the way I do? What triggers the thought that moves my hand? Where does it start? Where does it end?* She turned her hand from side to side, and stared at its movement.

* * * *

Caddie made herself a cup of mint tea in the share kitchen, went to the front porch of the old Victorian home, which had been her home away from home for several years, and sat in a creaking rocking-chair. She was homesick for the mountains, the rocks, the hills, the trees, and the water from the spring.

She gazed into the distance until she found green vegetation on a hill, trees and blue sky. She could almost hear Aunt Mae call to her. She could almost smell the aroma of hot-buttered yeast bread, fried chicken and banana pudding. She could almost taste the bitterness of the unripened pecan in the fall. She could almost taste the sweetness of peaches in the summer. She could hear bird calls. Faintly and then loudly, she could hear the call of the mountains, "Caddie, come home!" She awoke from her daydream and ran into the front hallway and up the narrow stairway.

She entered her pink and white flowered, papered sitting room/bedroom with its tall ceiling and sat in a chair before her dressing table. She turned the switch on a small, pink lamp, trimmed with wine and gold beaded fringe. In her restlessness, she moved brass candlesticks to the ends of the table one on each side, and back again to their original places. With her right index finger, she outlined the engraved flowers on a silver powder box which was a Christmas gift from her law firm. She looked into the mirror and examined her lovely reflection. She touched her high cheek bones, and traced her finger around the wide-open, blue-green eyes—eyes so wide they gave the appearance of naiveté. She traced her jaw bones on each side down to the pointed chin, thus making the outline of a heart-shaped face—the face of a beautiful girl. A girl who was intelligent except in one thing—loving the wrong man. But, she wanted to try to make him the right one.

She stood up erectly, and pinched in her slender waist. She turned back to the mirror, applied coral red lipstick, blotted her lips, and wiped her finger across her white teeth.

She walked to an antique wardrobe, unlocked it, removed a bank book, and flipped through its pages. The only money she had ever checked out of her savings account was for business college and money for Macie, Henny-Penny and

Kackie to buy railroad tickets. She placed the bank book inside her pocket. She knew what she had to do.

*   *   *   *

Uncle Hume hugged and kissed Caddie when she got off the bus. "Deaver brought me in his new car to pick you up, and Mae's at home cooking all your favorite foods! I'm so glad you're home!"

"Me, too! I've been so homesick, I could have died! I've missed you and I love you." She hugged him tightly around the neck.

Uncle Hume looked into Caddie's astonishingly blue-green eyes and noticed they slightly misted. He couldn't stand anyone's tears. "Look, here's Deaver!" He pushed Caddie towards him.

Deaver shook Caddie's hand. "Your folks are real excited about your being back home! They surely do need your help. If y'all need anything at all, let me know, you hear?"

"Thank you, Deaver. It was a long way for you to come to the bus station to get me. It's really good to be going home," Caddie replied. She pulled her coat tighter around her shoulders. "It's getting cold!"

"It was just a short piece down the road to come and get you," he smiled.

"It's a might cold," Uncle Hume agreed.

*   *   *   *

Aunt Mae awaited her with open arms. "I've missed you, precious child!"

"I missed you too, and I love you!"

The children jumped up and down when they saw her. The dogs barked and the geese honked. Caddie hugged Henny-Penny and Kackie tightly. "I missed everything! I missed your little smiles and pretty faces, the sounds in the woods, the smells, the rocks, the hills and the trees. I missed the mountains!" she exclaimed, as she looked at the mountain range on the other side of the creek.

"You missed Ole Jeb, too?" quizzed Henny-Penny.

"I missed Ole Jeb, chickens, and birds and bees and the most minute things. I've been so lonely, I haven't been myself!"

Aunt Mae removed a light blue, wool sweater from Caddie's shoulders, and smoothed her hair. "And, you missed Jake?" she whispered softly.

* * * *

Dan Zanderneff got on a train as inconspicuously as possible, hoping he didn't look like someone on the run. He sat beside a smutty window, and gazed at the countryside, which had become flat and less colorful.

It was a long trip, going to only God knew where. He settled down in his seat and covered his head with his worn, felt hat and rested his long legs on the seat in front of him. He dozed in a fitful slumber.

He awoke with a start, when his inherited seat companion gave him a nudge.

"I am sorry, sir. You were snoring."

He stretched his muscular arms and sat up erectly in the seat.

"Sorry, ma'am." He removed his hat, glanced briefly at the exquisitely dressed woman, and looked out at the sunset. Even though his brownish hair, with light blond streaks, was receding and thinning, he was physically attractive. His dark tan made his blue eyes outstanding and more appealing.

He slumped down in his seat and covered his head with his hat.

The lady observed the sleeping gentleman and noticed his being handsome beyond his unkempt person. She fanned her face nervously with a white lace handkerchief and wiped her neck and brow, the heat being extremely uncomfortable. A combination of "Old Spice," and sweat, mixed with the smell of coal from the train's smoke-stack, and the odors of all the other people on the train made her wish for a private compartment. She stopped the conductor. "You got a compartment now that those people got off?"

The train made so much noise, she could barely hear the conductor's response. "Don't believe we do ma'am. Let me see your ticket, please." She handed him her ticket. "Your ticket calls for a seat like the one you got ma'am. Can't change it now. Besides, you're almost at your destination." He left her at her seat, staggered, and balanced his way up the aisle.

"My husband's going to be upset because I couldn't get a private compartment. I've never seen so many people traveling. Wonder where in the world they are all going?" she exclaimed.

Dan Zanderneff spoke softly from under the brim of his hat, "Where you going, Ma'am?"

"Home, Mister, home! Mississippi's a good sight to see. I've been taking care of my sick mother. I'll be so glad to be back with my husband and little girl after being gone so long in Tennessee. Yes, sir, it's a gonna be good to be back!"

"I left Tennessee myself, sometime ago. Hope to find work in Mississippi. Need a job really bad."

"You got folks in Mississippi?"

"No, Ma'am. I'm all alone in this world. Sorta wandering, looking for a place to light." He yawned, and placed his hand over his mouth.

She looked into his sad, sky-blue eyes. "If I'm not mistaken, sir, your accent sounds more like Georgia than Tennessee. Tennessee accent is pretty distinctive."

"Oh, I lived in Georgia awhile back and my folks were from Georgia, too," he replied nervously. "Mind if I get up a moment and stretch my legs? They're getting a little cramped."

The lady made room for him to pass.

He held onto the luggage rack for a few minutes, stretched and stamped his feet and sat back down.

"You not going anywhere special, huh?"

"No, Ma'am, nothing special to do and nowhere special to go." An expression of sadness crossed his face.

"How'd you like me to introduce you to my husband? You could see if he needs somebody to work? We have sharecroppers who live on our land and work it."

"Why, Ma'am, that sure would be nice of you. I'd be much obliged." He smiled a shy smile.

The trained slowed, made a loud shriek, lunged, jolted and stopped.

Dan sat up.

"We're almost at the station," she said.

His smile projected a shyness, but an earnestness that she liked.

The lady nudged him, and pointed. "My husband and my daughter are standing together waiting for me. Look! There they are!" She stood up, as the train came to its final lurch. She staggered and almost fell.

He looked out at a large crowd on the platform trying to determine who belonged to her. He helped the lady with her suitcases. His cardboard suitcase was worn and cheap next to the lady's expensive leather luggage.

He adjusted his dark brown double-breasted jacket and stood more erect.

When they got off the train, a handsome gray-haired gentleman, and a beautiful teenage girl approached the lady.

"Mama! Mama!" The girl ran to her mother, and clung to her.

"Janelle! Janelle!" The lady laughed loudly, and kissed the lovely girl.

Then the tall, gray-haired gentleman held out his arms and smiled. "Mary, Mary, how I've missed you!" She fell into his arms and he swung her around. They laughed. "I missed you, Mary-Girl. I missed you!"

Dan stood aloof as he observed the lady's homecoming. He felt detached and alone. He wiped his sweaty brow with a smudged, white, handkerchief.

The lady turned towards Dan. "Please meet my husband, Mr. Davenport, and my daughter, Janelle. I am sorry, Sir. I failed to get your name."

"Dan. Dan Zanders." He shook her husband's hand. Then he turned and looked into the face of beautiful Janelle. She smiled. And said, "I'm happy to make your acquaintance."

The lady spoke to her husband. "Mr. Zanders says he needs a job."

"You'll find a boarding house down the street." He pointed towards a clump of houses. When you get settled in, come on down to the Davenport Farm and see me. I'll be glad to talk to you. Here's my card."

Dan took his card and read it. "Thank you, Mr. Davenport. I appreciate the opportunity."

Dan observed the beauty of the girl as she started to walk away. When she suddenly turned and looked back, her curious green eyes met Dan's blue ones. He smiled hesitantly—shyly. She flounced her long, dark brown hair, picked up one of her mother's cases and walked hurriedly towards a parked automobile.

A little boy "whipped-a-top" on the boards of the porch of the depot. Dan watched it spin until the top jumped the porch, and hit gravel.

* * * *

Caddie pulled the black, rounded trunk away from the end of her bed, and sat down on her knees in front of the trunk The lid was heavy and awkward to lift, the hasp being bent and uneven. She sneezed when her nostrils filled with a strong odor of moth balls, musty cloth and old papers. She grimaced and held her nose.

She picked up a brass-framed photograph, and wiped the dust from the glass onto her hip. Aunt Mae and Uncle Hume smiled at her from their aging and stained wedding day photograph. She replaced it among the treasures of the chest.

She caressed hers and Macie's adoption papers, and held them closely to her breasts, before she replaced the documents.

When she removed her natural mother's aging and yellowing, once white taffeta, wedding dress from the chest, and refolded it, she wondered what she was like: *Had she lived, would my mother have been as sweet and kind as Aunt Mae? Did she hold me just a little bit before she died? Or did she just die? Funny—I've never asked anyone that question.*

Uncle Hume said mother died birthing me, leaving me and Macie with Dad—Uncle Hume's drunken brother, Colonel. I guess he was overwhelmed with all his responsibilities when mother died, and he "dove into the bottle" a little deeper. Uncle Hume said he was a great person, when he wasn't drinking. How wonderful was my Daddy, really?

She removed the aged tissue paper which held one of her mother's unfinished pieced quilt tops, and spread "The Flower Basket" on the bed. After briefly admiring the beautiful hand-stitching, she folded it carefully, and replaced the musty smelling item.

She picked up a brown paper package, tied with a white, cotton, flour-sack string. It was marked *Manuscript by Macie Marianna Brown Zanderneff.* She untied the string, and removed a stack of papers, slowly and reverently.

The title page read:

M A N U S C R I P T
A FAIRY TALE
By
Macie Marianna Brown Zanderneff

The front page contained one paragraph written in English:

"Once upon a time there lived a handsome prince, whose name was Prince Imaginary, and a beautiful princess, whose name was Princess Reality. They were very much in love. One day they married. Their life was one of bliss."

(End, Page One)

Caddie smiled. *How sweet of Macie to write a fairy tale for Henny-Penny and Kackie!* She turned the page. Her heart jumped when she realized that the remainder of the fairy tale was written in code—a child's code—Pig Latin, which Aunt Mae had taught her, Macie, Jake, and Ole Pem, when they were little children.

She took a deep breath, scrutinized Macie's handwriting and discovered the Fairy Tale was really a Diary—Macie's thoughts—addressed to *"Di-Ar-Ree.* She began to read slowly but the more she read, the greater her translation speeded up, since she was familiar with the Pig Latin "language."

Macie's Diary Written in Pig Latin:

Earday Iday-Arway-Eeray,
Ouyay illstay erethay???
omewheresay???
Ovelay,
emay

—

Caddie's Translation of the Pig Latin:

Dear Di-Ar-Ree,
You still there—
somewhere???
Love,
Me

—

Earday Emay,
Esentpray!
Ovelay,
Iday-Arway-Eeray

—

Dear Me,
Present!
Love,
Di-Ar-Ree

—

Earday Iday-Arway-Eeray,
Iway amway adglay Iway amway away oth-ermay, utbay onday'tay antway otay 'owgray oldway' ornay alestay. Ybay ethay ayway, Iday-Arway-Eeray, ifway oneway owsgray "entallymay" oneway ancay evernay owgray "oldway"—ancay oneway? 'Oldway' isway enwhay oneway isway ustjay erethay ithway onay eelingsfay, oughtsthay orway ideasway; oneway ustjay "existsway' enwhay oneway isway oldway. Oneway eallyray oesday otnay "owgray" atway allway. Ightray? Iday-Arway-Eeray, Iway eednay omeonesay otay alktay otay esidesbay away ildchay orfay away angechay!
Ovelay,
Emay

—

Dear Di-Ar-Ree,
I am glad I am a mother, but don't want to 'grow old' nor stale. By the way, Di-Ar-Ree, if one grows "mentally," one can never grow "old"—can one? 'Old' is when one is just "there somewhere" with no feelings, thoughts or ideas; one just "exists' when one is old. One really does not "grow" at all. Right? Di-Ar-Ree, I need someone to talk to besides a child for a change!

Love,

Me

—

Earday Emay,
Alktay!
Ovelay,
Iday-Arway-Eeray Earday
Iday-Arway-Eeray,
Aturenay evernay akesmay ethay amesay istakemay icetway. Ouyay onway'tay indfay anotherway ersonpay ikelay emay alkingway aroundway, ight-ray, Ida-Arway-Eeray?
Ovelay,
Emay

Earday Emay,
!
Ovelay,
Iday-Arway-Eeray

Dear Me,
Talk!
Love,
Di-Ar-Ree
Dear Di-Ar-Ree,
Nature never makes the same mistake twice. You won't find another person like me walking around, right, Di-Ar-Ree?
Love, Me

Dear Me,
!
Love,
Di-Ar-Ree

*   *   *   *

Caddie laid Macie's diary aside, and wiped her eyes. *Macie you were clever to write your private thoughts in a child's language. Did this keep Dan from reading your thoughts? Did Dan think this was really a fairy tale? If he read any of this, he probably read page one? But, of course, I'm guessing.*

She continued to translate the diary from Pig Latin into regular English:

Dear Di-Ar-Ree,
I am cautious!
Love,
Me
Dear Me,
Get away! Leave!
Love,
Di-Ar-Ree

—

Dear Di-Ar-Ree,

He is drinking again. He started an argument in public. Said I mishandled the situation because I walked away. I will not be battered into ever saying I was wrong when I believe otherwise. I am stubborn and I hold steadfast to my beliefs! He raised his hand as to strike me.

Love,

Me

—

Dear Me,

When I tell someone I will do something, I try not to delay because I may not be here tomorrow to procrastinate. Don't procrastinate.

Love,

Di-Ar-Ree

—

Dear Di-Ar-Ree,

I feel sorry for myself today. Who has not had that feeling? The slime and coating of self-pity drips oozily with the sympathy I seek. I can sympathize more with myself than anyone else. How does another know HOW I wallow?

Love,

Me

—

Dear Me,

Snap out of it. Go back to the mountains.

Leave!! Go back! Do not be lethargic!

Love,

Di-Ar-Ree

Caddie stopped reading and sat up with a jolt! *Macie you were on the way back to the mountains—packed and on the way home! Oh! If only you had made it back!* She wiped her weeping eyes and runny nose on her sleeve. *My God! Macie! How'd you get by with writing a diary right under Dan's nose, and without him knowing about it?* She rubbed the knot in her stomach and became nauseated:

Dear Di-Ar-Ree,

The fight for survival makes me bitter and withdrawn. It is instilled in me to "fight" to the finish. Once I grab hold, I refuse to withdraw? Bitterness—what is this which eats at me? It could be said I have failed—if I want to see it that way, but I refuse.

I refuse failure.

Love,

Me

Dear Me,

Run!

Love,

Di-Ar-Ree

—

Dear Di-Ar-Ree,

Have you ever felt as if you should be doing something but don't know what? It is sort of like being hungry for something, but you don't know what you crave? I have this craving within me to be doing something, but what I am hungry to do is not clear to me—it is a restlessness, which grows into "hunger" pains. My brain never seems to still to a motionless state. My psyche appears "mad." It feels so sad!

Love,

Me

Dear Me,

Snap out of it!

Love,

Di-Ar-Ree

—

Dear Di-Ar-Ree,

When I was growing up, I was taught not to argue. And now, I know I did nothing wrong, yet he causes me to doubt myself. It overshadows my good thinking. I feel guilty because I can't cure the problem of self-doubt.

It's hard to believe I'm in a predicament where Dan not only doesn't love me—he doesn't like me. How did this happen?

Love,

Me

Dear Me,

Get out of this predicament! Get out!

Love,

Di-Ar-Ree

—

Dear Di-Ar-Ree,

I can't get through to Dan, anymore.

Love,

Me

Dear Me,

Anymore? Did you ever?

Love,

Di-Ar-Ree

—

Dear Di-Ar-Ree,

Dan becomes more remote/distant. He pulls an armor around himself. I can't get through.

Love,

Me

Dear Me!

Leave now!

Love,

Di-Ar-Ree!

* * * *

Henny-Penny and Kackie pushed open the door, peeped inside, and laughed. They made a dive for Caddie, and held her tightly around the neck. She placed the diary in the trunk, while she struggled with them. She pulled them down on the floor and tickled them under the arms and on the stomach, and made them laugh.

"Let's go outside, please Caddie?" Kackie begged.

"But, of course, we will. Let's go for a walk. Wanna go to the mailbox?"

"Will we get chiggers?"

"Hopefully not," Caddie laughed.

"Let's do the chigger dance!" Henny-Penny yelled.

Henny-Penny and Kackie jumped up from where they sat on the cold floor, held hands, and danced around while exaggerating their backsides.

"Chiggers! Wiggers! Chiggers! Chiggers!" they laughed.

* * * *

It was several hours before Caddie got back to the diary. She found the place where she left off reading when Henny-Penny and Kackie interrupted her so sweetly:

Dear Di-Ar-Ree,

I would not ask you to take a stand for me. It would be so hard for you to look around and see we would be on an island all alone. I would not ask that you do this act, and "put you on a spot." But, the greatest reason for not asking you to take a stand for me is because I wish to maintain an allusion, a myth of friendship and family harmony. I don't want to think the unthinkable; that if I said 'come stand beside me,' I would stand all alone, and you would not take that step to my island! I am exhausted.

Love,

Me

Dear Me,

Leave the bastard! Leave!

Love,

Di-Ar-Ree

—

Dear Di-Ar-Ree,

If I stay, I will be "blown away."

If I go, I will be blown away.

Love,

Me

Dear Me,

Leave!

Love,

Di-Ar-Ree

* * * *

Caddie stopped reading, and wiped her brow. *My God! Macie, why did you stay in that dangerous place with that horrible Dan? Some of your entries appear to be written by someone in complete denial, and oblivious to what's going on, yet your answers to "Me" seem so tuned into what is really going on. How could that be?*

It bothered her conscience to invade her dead sister's privacy, but she knew she had to read Macie's feelings and thoughts and try to unlock the secret of her reasons to commit suicide—or did she?

Dear Di-Ar-Ree,
I closed my eyes and opened them.
Thinking about being blown away is but a dream—a nightmare.
My lips moved, but they did not speak.
Love,
Me

Dear Me!
Leave!
Love,
Di-Ar-Ree

—

Dear Di-Ar-Ree,
You make it sound so easy.
I don't think I like you, sometimes ...
Don't you understand anything?
I am in a psychological depression! A dilemma!
Love,
Me

Dear Me,
Listen to me once in a while.
I like to talk, too.
I need to express myself, too.
Leave!
Love,
Di-Ar-Ree

—

Dear Di-Ar-Ree,
The fear!
Sinister shadows follow me.
Love,
Me

Dear Me,
Fear Not—you know the saying—
You must take a stand.
Love,
Di-Ar-Ree

—

Dear Di-Ar-Ree,

Do you remember when we moved here? I did not like it at all, did you? I have come to like some of the people. They are nice and very sweet. Dan does not want me to talk to them. He says they hate him—that they hate us.

Dear Di-Ar-Ree, are you listening? I know you are there, somewhere—someone has to be listening to me. I have to have someone to talk to. Right, Di-Ar-Ree?!

Love,
Me

Dear Me,
I'm listening.
Love,
Di-Ar-Ree

—

Dear Di-Ar-Ree,

Sometimes I feel as if I might drown in self-pity. The emptiness and aloneness is unbearable.

Love,
Me

Dear Me,
Dry off! Get back to reality!
Love,
Di-Ar-Ree

—

Dear Di-Ar-Ree,

I thought you liked me a little bit—what is this stuff about "drying off?"

Love,

Me

Dear Me,

Get out of the mire!

Go home! Go back to the mountains!

Love,

Di-Ar-Ree

—

Dear Di-Ar-Ree,

I want to get out of the mire—to go home. How can I leave my 1800's antique bedroom suit that Aunt Mae and Uncle Hume gave to me that I love so much—highly polished oak—with carved grape leaves from the top of the headboard and down the sides, its curly-cues, its beauty, its worth? How can I leave it? It's so dear!

Tell,

Me

Dear Me,

Leave! How can you not do otherwise? Is it worth it? You mean you are staying because of furniture?

Love,

Di-Ar-Ree

—

Dearest One,

One is loved by all.

Love,

U

Dear You,

Let us keep it just

as one.

Loved,

One

Dear One,
It is better to
be loved by all than one.
Love,
All

Dear All,
No person is ever loved
by all. Some are loved by some and some are loved
by none.
Loved,
One

Dear One,
All is the ego complete
Love,
Me

—

Dear Di-Ar-Ree,
He lost his job and he blames me!
How could I be to blame? Why can he not admit the blame to himself?
Is it failure when we admit that we are not happy? Surely, it would be more manly if
he admitted his faults! I am overwhelmed by rejection, bitterness and anger.
Love,
Me.

Dear Me,
Our soul hangs in the balance—
It knows all, sees all—Our
Soul is the balance—it must be.
Love,
Di-Ar-Ree

—

Dear Di-Ar-Ree,
I don't feel safe.
I feel so alone.
Love,
Me

Dear Me!
Go to safety! Home!
Go Home!
Love,
Di-Ar-Ree

—

Dear Di-Ar-Ree,

If I leave, I will be in even more danger. I want to leave, but I feel so inadequate and helpless. I hate failure.

Love,
Me

Dear Me,
Leaving is not failure!
Love,
Di-Ar-Ree

* * * *

Caddie heard a noise and looked up. Ole Jeb stood near the doorway and stared at her. "Come see me, Ole Jeb." Caddie snapped her fingers, and he walked over to her. "You reading my mind, Ole Jeb? Think I need a break? I believe I do, too." She patted him on the head. "Come on, I'll get you some bread and fresh water." She laid the diary upon her bed, and walked slowly to the kitchen. She wanted to continue reading, but the translation of her sister's thoughts had become more difficult. I agree *with you, Macie. Leaving is not failure—it's a continuation of life—but you knew that when you wrote that leaving would determine the continuation of your life. So why did you stay?*

She poured a dipper of water into the dog's bowl.

Ole Jeb lapped the water, looked up with solemn eyes, as if to say thank you, and drank thirstily.

Caddie patted him on the head. "Gotta get back and finish my reading, but first I'll get you some bread." She opened the pie safe, removed a jar of honey and a biscuit, bored a hole in the side of the biscuit with her finger, and filled the hole full of honey. "This is for being such a good doggie." She laid the honey-filled biscuit on his feeding bowl and licked the honey from her fingers.

* * * *

Dear Di-Ar-Ree,
I care, yet
I don't care anymore!
I feel, Yet, I don't feel anything, anymore.
I am in a tailspin!
Love,
Me

Dear Me,
Call home!
Love,
Di-Ar-Ree

—

Dear Di-Ar-Ree,
Dan's mentality is one of selfishness
Because he wants to share only his thoughts,
and he does not wish to hear the thoughts of others—my thoughts.
Dan tells me I am stupid! But, then, in the next breath, he says,
"I don't deserve you."
Love,
Me

Dear Me,
Leave!
You are wonderful!
You are intelligent!
You are not stupid!
Love,
Di-Ar-Ree

—

Dear Di-Ar-Ree,
He is jealous, but he has no reason to be.
Love,
Me

Dear Me,
You are amazing and intelligent!
Love,
Di-Ar-Ree

—

Caddie took the manuscript to the back porch, leaned against a wall and continued reading:

Dear Di-Ar-Ree,
We are all strangers here.
Staying only a little while,
As did our fathers.
Our days on the Earth
Are as a shadow.
None of us will be staying.
I Chronicles 29:5
Love,
Me

Dear Me
Snap out of it!
Love,
Di-Ar-Ree

* * * *

Rain pelted the tin roof. The wind began to blow and all the shutters throughout the cabin began to bang.

"Drat!" Caddie placed the diary on her bed and rushed around to close the shutters.

Aunt Mae and Uncle Hume hurried in from the porch, ran from room to room and closed the shutters.

"It's a bad storm," said Uncle Hume.

"Yes, really coming up a big one!" Aunt Mae said breathlessly.

"I'm afraid," said Henny-Penny.

"There, there! Don't be fearful," said Kackie. "You'll be all right. Ain't that right, Uncle Hume?"

"Yes, it will be all right. Come and sit with me. We'll light a coal-oil lamp and read a book."

"I'm reading some of Macie's papers and want to get back to it." Caddie said as calmly as she could.

Aunt Mae noticed Caddie's tear-stained face. "Macie wrote good stories, didn't she?" she asked as inconspicuously as possible. "Got any good fairy tales Hume can read to Henny-Penny and Kackie?"

"She's a good writer, but I don't have a fairy tale he can read to them, right now, Aunt Mae."

"Well, get back to your reading, Caddie."

Caddie went back to her room and picked up the diary.

Dear Di-Ar-Ree:

I finally put the humiliation and embarrassment aside and decided to ask for help. I went to the Sheriff's office, dragging the children. We were so hurt, so injured and so tired! I reported Dan, but it was several days after he beat us.

The Sheriff said, "What did you do to him to make him want to beat you?" I told him I didn't have to do anything to provoke him. The Sheriff said if he were beating me so bad, how could I get away to go to his office! He did not believe me. I tried to show him the girls' bruises, but he would not look. I said, "He wants to kill me and my children and kill himself!"

I kept trying to show him the girls' bruises, but the Sheriff said, "Teach them modesty for God's sake!" He would not look! He said, "Come back when you have hard evidence! Make a list of the dates and times he abuses you." What can I do? What is hard evidence? Death?

Dan followed me and the children to the Sheriff's office and he was waiting for us outside when we left the Sheriff's office.

I was so scared!

Dan beat us again, when we got home, but you know that as much as I, don't you, dear Di-Ar-Ree?

My trip to the Sheriff's office appeared to trigger Dan's anger more than ever, and now he is more violent.

I am embarrassed and humiliated.

Love,

Me

Dear Me,
Try to get enough money to go home!
Love,
Di-Ar-Ree

—

Caddie found the diary harder to read. The sordid details were too vivid to absorb without feeling Macie's pain. *Macie, surely you knew all along that I would send you the money. Did you see asking me for money as failure—embarrassment—humiliation—pain?* Caddie wiped the tears from her eyes, and blew her nose.

—

Dear Di-Ar-Ree,
I am glad we moved.
It will be a fresh start, but
I will miss my friends.
Dan said there are no friends.
I hope things will be better.
Dan promised he would be sweet.
Love,
Me

Dear Me,
Things have not changed.
The problems moved, too!
Love,
Di-Ar-Ree

—

Dear Di-Ar-Ree,
The moss so miry, lush and green, beneath my bare feet—
Oh! Butterfly ahead of me—in your fleet—
Come back and get me, Butterfly!
Carry me on your wings, to heights and depths
Only we will ever see!
Love,
Me

Dear Me,

Come out of it!

Get realistic!

Leave! Go back home! Go home!

Love,

Di-Ar-Ree

*　*　*　*

Kackie yelled, "Caddie! Caddie! Jake's here! Jake's here! He brought us some candy!"

"I love Jake. He says I'm his little girl," said Henny-Penny.

Caddie hurriedly placed the diary inside the trunk, and closed the lid. She glanced in the dresser mirror, dabbed her swollen eyes, brushed her hair quickly, and rushed to the front room.

*　*　*　*

Dear Di-Ar-Ree,

I don't know how to comprehend all this anger.

I've never had to deal with violence.

I feel so alone.

I feel so worthless.

Love,

Me

Dear Me,

I love you!

Love,

Di-Ar-Ree

—

Dear Di-Ar-Ree,

I feel like I am doing just great!

I listen, and don't speak.

It's better, after all.

He can never understand how I feel!

If I don't speak, he cannot say I am stupid, right?

Love,

Me

Dear Me,
Do not withdraw!
Do not withdraw!
Leave!
Love,
Di-Ar-Ree

—

Dear Di-Ar-Ree,
My mind became trapped by his rage. "What happened?"
What triggered his anger?
My fears have become a battlefield of rampant thoughts.
What happened?
Love,
Me

Dear Me,
Get out of the trap. Don't think of him!
Love,
Di-Ar-Ree

—

Dear Di-Ar-Ree,
I am in my private inner self—my private inner core—my private world—my eye of the storm. It is quieter here, but a cloud engulfs me.
Love,
Me

Dear Me,
Come out of the cloud quickly! Now!
Love,
Di-Ar-Ree

—

Dear Di-Ar-Ree,
He makes me feel like a nobody. I can not continue to stay in this acute depressive state much longer and survive. I need to think of myself, my children. I have allowed myself to be trampled for the last time, I hope. It is like being at the bottom of a deep pool. I either rush to the top and get air and survive! Or stay down here and die! I

jumped into this pool and allowed myself to be pushed under and have stayed under so long—my lungs burst now—desiring life. Where is my Surviving Spirit? Where is it? Is it still able to come forth with a big burst of energy forcing me to the top of the pool? A surviving splash at the top? Where is this beauty and inner strength I once held? Is it still available? Can it ever be brought forth again? Surviving Spirit, HELP!

Love,

Me

Dear Me!

Get out, fast! Swim fast!

Love,

Di-Ar-Ree

—

Dear Di-Ar-Ree,

The children and I left again. He brought us back.

I am unable to speak.

Love,

Me

Dear Me,

Tell someone!

Tell everyone!

Love,

Di-Ar-Ree

—

Dear Di-Ar-Ree,

Sometimes it's easier to stay than to leave!

Love,

Me

Dear Me,

Don't let it be easier to stay. You must get out now! Leave now!

Call Caddie!

Love,

Di-Ar-Ree

* * * *

Caddie stopped reading and rubbed her eyes. *Macie, you said, "It's easier to stay?" Were you physically hurt and couldn't move? Why was it easier to stay? Too much mental and physical effort to make that important, critical move? What?*

Reading the diary was depressing, but she wanted to finish reading all of Macie's words in their entirety. She realized how upset Aunt Mae and Uncle Hume would be when they read the Manuscript! It was no fairy tale!

She sighed aloud.

—

Dear Di-Ar-Ree,

I am now beyond humiliation! Help! Hear me! Hear me!

Love,

Me

Dear Me,

Caddie will help. Just get in touch.

Love,

Di-Ar-Ree

—

Dear Di-Ar-Ree,

I am humiliated! I am afraid!

Love,

Me

Dear Me,

Leave! Listen to your heart.

Love,

Di-Ar-Ree

—

Dear Di-Ar-Ree,

Why do I stay?

Love,

Me

Dear Me,
Do not find fault with yourself.
Love,
Di-Ar-Ree

—

Dear Di-Ar-Ree,

I have been in denial because I have said, "I'm staying for the children." I wrote some things down about the situation, Di-Ar-Ree, and when I did, I realized how much pain I have caused my own children by staying in this place of torment.

Why do I stay?
I stay for the children.
They need a father and a mother.
I stay for the children.
That's why I stay.
The children stay because they must
Each lick and pain becomes their own.
And I stay because
They need a father and a mother.
I stay because I want to live.
I'm not brave, you see?
I stay because
I'm afraid to leave.
Afraid he'll beat us
Until we can not walk;
And dismantle our jaws
Until we can not talk.
Sometimes, it's easier to stay
Than to leave—
I'm not brave,
You see?
I stayed because
The children need a mother and a father?
And, now I ask this question: Is one who abuses
His wife or his children
Really a father?
Love
Me

Dear Me,

Do not find fault with yourself!

Love,

Di-Ar-Ree

—

Dear Di-Ar-Ree,

Today is the fifth month, a year almost gone, and I have accomplished nothing. I am afraid. Why did I write the words, "I am afraid?" Am I really? If so, what am I afraid of—1. Failure; 2. Failure; and 3. Failure. I have failed in my marriage and I have failed myself because I have not fulfilled my expectations to the fullest.

Why have I gotten so passive? Sometimes I am so tired; I can hardly hold a pen upon paper to write. It takes so much effort.

Love,

Me

Dear Me,

Get out of this desolate grim terror. Get out! Accomplish that much for us!

Love,

Di-Ar-Ree

* * * *

Aunt Mae knocked lightly on the bedroom door. "Ready to eat, Caddie?"

Caddie laid the diary in her lap and looked up. "I'm not hungry, now. Maybe later. I need to finish something."

"Sure, darling. I'll leave the food in the warmer," said Aunt Mae.

Caddie leaned her head against the back of her chair. *Macie, you've written that word 'failure' again. I can relate to failure but this is to the extreme—and it pierces my heart!*

Caddie arose from her chair, rubbed her eyes, wrapped the original wrapping around the diary and placed it on the bed. She blew out the lamp, crawled into bed and held the diary to her breasts. *Macie—I hate Dan for what he did to you! I hate him!*

Caddie dozed fitfully.

—

Dear Di-Ar-Ree,

I am having a panic attack—anxiety pains me in the pit of my stomach. My frustration confuses me. Despondency! The pain is indescribable!

Love,

Me

Dear Me! Dear Me!

Snap out of it. Go back home! Leave!

Love,

Di-Ar-Ree

—

Hey, Di-Ar-Ree,

Are you listening to this dissertation? Dan listens to nothing that I say. He finishes every sentence that I start and most of the time it's nothing like what I meant to say at all. He is the poorest listener that I know, and the poorest conversationalist. He says, "I've already told you," if I ask him a question. He bothers to repeat nothing and says I have a hearing problem. My life is dull, when it comes to adult conversation. I only hear the conversations of my little children. I can't say I am not grateful, because that is what keeps me "sane." My children, at least, are very bright when they do speak, and they have a wonderful love for life itself. I am sane, Di-Ar-Ree, right? I am sane?

Love,

Me

Dear Me,

I am listening. I hear when no one else hears and I feel when no one else feels. I see you. I know you. I talk to you, but sometimes you do not listen. Listen! Listen, to what your common sense and your heart are saying! Listen! Get out, now! I am not underlining the word, NOW enough!

Love,

Di-Ar-Ree

—

Dear Di-Ar-Ree,

He and I had a lot of good times. We had a lot of bad times, too, but now we are really having a lot of bad times.

Love,

Me

Dear Me—Dear Me!

Fear and his terror control you. You must leave! Don't let terror hold you!

Love,

Di-Ar-Ree

* * * *

Caddie took a deep breath. *Oh! No! Macie you're giving in to Dan's charming ways—his winsome personality when he is not drinking—Why? Why? Why are you doing it, Macie? You know what Dan is like!*

She blew out the coal oil lamp, marked her place with a piece of newsprint, placed the diary in the top lid of the old trunk and went outside to complete her early morning chores.

It was hours before she got back to her room.

* * * *

Dear Di-Ar-Ree,

I pray. I read the Bible. I remember God and call upon Him. I remember He helps me when I help myself, but I am numb-like. I know I should, but don't understand why I can't seem to help myself? I am beginning to believe it is my fault that he has lost his job, and that I must not talk to anyone at my work. I am isolating myself. I am very quiet and introverted. I can not believe it! I try to be what I really want to become and what I am capable of becoming, but I am losing sight of what "that" is!

Love,

Me

Dear Me,

You are intelligent. Believe in yourself. Be your outgoing self! Talk to others. Don't fall in Dan's trap. He is the one who has a problem. Don't let his problem be your problem. You must not!

Love,

Di-Ar-Ree

PS: Leave!

—

Dear Di-Ar-Ree,

I have forgotten my goals. I don't remember what I wanted from life. All I want now is to be happy. I don't know how to be happy. I cannot concentrate.

Love,

Me

Dear Me,

Set one goal at a time. Try to reach one goal at a time. Your goal now: GET THE HELL OUT!

Love,

Di-Ar-Ree

—

Dear Di-Ar-Ree,

Sometimes he says he didn't really mean to hit me—that "I got in the way." He apologizes later—so charming—so charismatic. I want to forget his cruelty—I want to think it's only a nightmare—it didn't really happen. His apology gives me an excuse to stay.

Love,

Me

Dear Me,

Get out! The nightmare is real. You have no time to accept his apologies.

Love,

Di-Ar-Ree

—

Dear Di-Ar-Ree,

When it was just me getting hurt, somehow I handled it better than now. He is beginning to shove the little girls around. He's more determined to hurt them when I try to protect them. He pushed the child so hard, it hurt her back when she fell against a chair. Her pain is my pain! Oh, dear God, how can I protect my children? I am trapped. As an animal—Trapped! Help me, Di-Ar-Ree.

Love,

Me

Dear Me,

Take the children and get out, NOW!!! Leave NOW!!!

Think! Think!

Love,

Di-Ar-Ree

—

Dear Di-Ar-Ree,

I can not continue my allowing the girls to be in danger, and get hurt. I love them! I am leaving! I see how it really is. I have made up my mind. I will just leave when he is away. That's it! I will try it again.

Love,

Me

Dear Me,

You have finally come to your senses. Great thinking! Be careful.

Love,

Di-Ar-Ree

* * * *

Caddie stared at the diary. It was hard to conceive that Macie's mind was wandering one minute and thinking well the next. *Macie, you're coming to your senses! Great thinking!*

Caddie wrapped the original covering around the diary, slipped it into the trunk and headed for the kitchen. Even though her heart was sad, she called out to Henny-Penny and Kackie, as cheerfully as possible. "Let's make cookies!"

"Can I stir?" asked Kackie.

"Can I lick the bowl?" asked Henny-Penny.

* * * *

Dear Di-Ar-Ree,

I was packed and leaving and he came home drunk! Said, "Where you taking my babies?" I said, "I am going back to the mountains. I can't take it anymore." He pushed me back against the table, pulled a clump of hair out of my head, and almost broke my back. He got his pistol-gun and held it on the child's head. I rushed toward him, and he pulled the hammer back. I became numb; I could not speak. I knew it was "damned if I did, and damned if I didn't."

I wanted to go to the child. I could not move. I screamed at first. Then, I could not scream. It was as if I were not present in that place. I experienced my mind floating an immeasurable distance.

He pulled the child's hair and head back and held the gun to her temple. Said to me, "If you ever think of leaving, I will kill us all. I will kill each girl, then you, and then myself. Just end it all, you hear?"

Then, he let the gun drop to his side, and put it on the table. He hung his head between his hands and blubbered.

The girls ran to me, and I stood glued to the spot, resting my hands upon their little heads. I had been too afraid to move, to help them. I still can not make normal movements. My brain has closed down. I can't think properly. All my thoughts are gone—gone from my mind. I hear only the slosh of rushing blood—sloshing! Sloshing!

Help me, Di-Ar-Ree!

Love,

Me

Dear Me,

Control yourself! Think rationally. Think slowly. Think slowly.

Love,

Di-Ar-Ree

—

Dear Di-Ar-Ree,

My state of turmoil is not any better. It happened again. I could not move. I stood still, without moving—forever. Finally, he sorta shook his drunken head like he had sobered up, and said, "Y'all clean up this mess."

Di-Ar-Ree, I don't understand. I must be in a state of shock. The depression has left me lifeless and listless, and somehow it takes too much effort to move.

The next day I look at the child, but I make no effort to hold the child. I just stand motionless. My mind stops working. I want to move. I can not move!

Love,

Me

Dear Me,

You are a fool! You know that, don't you? A person who takes abuse is one who thinks he deserves the abuse! If you don't agree, why do you stay? Because you are in shock? Maybe. One day your body will be so injured, why have that mind of yours? What if you still have a body, but no mind, then what? What if he kills the girls, then what? What is it worth? It will take effort to get away and you must do it, while you have some physical and mental strength left, because, after all, you don't deserve this treatment! You must seek help.

Love,

Di-Ar-Ree

—

Dear Di-Ar-Ree,

I used to feel self-reliant, but, now, I lack the energy to think straight.

Love,

Me

Dear Me,

Think until it's "straight." Self-reliance is still within—here—somewhere. Think!

Love,

Di-Ar-Ree

—

Dear Di-Ar-Ree,

My head aches and pounds and pounds in confusion. I am not "fit for anything" in my great depression. He struck the child and I watched like a zombie—I wanted to reach out, yet I did not move. I could not. My mind "shut down." I seemed too listless, lethargic, and weak-kneed to attempt a rescue. Fear filled my ears and it whistled so loudly I could hardly hear the child cry out. My body quivered and my hands trembled. My heart numbed! I covered my ears. I did not want to be such a coward, but I am a coward! Please!

Love,

Me

Dear Me! Dear Me!

You know you must leave! Do it! You know you must!

Love,

Di-Ar-Ree

—

Caddie gasped for breath! *Oh! My God! This shows Dan's the one that hurt those innocent little babies!*

She placed the diary hurriedly in the top lid of the trunk and rushed outside to where Henny-Penny and Kackie sat on the doorsteps holding Spooky and Shadows. She snuggled between them, placed her arms around them tightly and squeezed them until they squirmed. "I love you two precious jewels—my little Henny-Penny and my little Kackie!" She kissed them on the top of their little heads. "Can I hold you a little while?"

"Sure, you can hold me all day long," said Kackie.

"You can hold me forever," said Henny-Penny.

"And ever," said Kackie.

—

Dear Di-Ar-Ree,

Said he'd kill me, if I told anyone. What to do? What to do? What can I do to calm Dan, when he's threatening and acting like such a stranger? It's all so mindless! Pointless!

Love,

Me

Dear Me,

Don't "work" on calming HIM. Calm yourself and Leave!

Love,

Di-Ar-Ree.

—

Dear Di-Ar-Ree,

He was in a drunken-stupor. He said he would kill me—kill us all. Said no one loved him; accused me of wanting to leave because I had never loved him. I said, "Yes, I want to leave!" He usually picks on only one of the girls, but today he beat both of them. Yes! That is too much to bear! Their bruises hurt me worse than my own bruises ever have or ever will hurt me! I know I must take action. I can't continue to wait. Help!

Love,

Me

Dear Me,

Get out of this pit of hell! Think! Act!

Love,

Di-Ar-Ree

—

Dear Di-Ar-Ree,

I can't believe I was so naive as to think my love could change him.

Love,

Me

Dear Me,

It is Dan's choice to change, after all. But, you're right, we can not change another.

Love,

Di-Ar-Ree

—

Dear Di-Ar-Ree,

Up until now, my injuries did not show. Dan placed them in perfect spots, so well planned: the top of my head, on my back, and on my buttocks.

Today, he hit me in the face so hard I am unable to work. People would see me and question me. I stayed home! I sat and stared out a window for hours—just numb, and dumb-founded. I grew up in a peaceful home. These actions are so foreign to me!

The girls play at my feet.

Love,

Me

Dear Me,

He's in more than a bad mood. He has never hit you so hard before, but now the bruises show! The licks used to be right between the shoulders and just below the neck. He was smart enough to place his strikes so the bruises would not show to the public-eye. But! What of your inner-eye? What has it done to your Spirit? And, today, he put a shiner on your beautiful face for the world to see. There is no fooling the public now. Who are you kidding? We won't speak of love. There is no such thing as a love-lick. You have been verbally and mentally abused. Your body won't stand much more. I, as yourself, will not tolerate it. He's becoming more dangerous and more volatile.

Take us back! Go! Think on it! Act on it!

Love,

Di-Ar-Ree

—

Dear Di-Ar-Ree,

It is the Dawn of my New Decision.

I am leaving, even if it kills me. I will work out a plan. I will keep my head. I will pray and ask God to guide me. Be with me, Di-Ar-Ree!

Love,

Me

Dear Me,

I'll help you leave today!

God, please help us!

Love,

Di-Ar-Ree

—

Dear Di-Ar-Ree,

I seek a sacred love like Aunt Mae and Uncle Hume have for each other. I want to sense a long-term connection like they have together.

Love,

Me

Dear Me,

You must leave to experience what you seek. You know you will not find it where you are. Listen! Act!

Love,

Di-Ar-Ree

—

Caddie held the diary tightly in her hands, and stared at the word *Experience. I want to experience life, too, Macie. I don't want to fall into a trap either—I left Atlanta and came back home to seek those things that I desire the most. I hope Dan never gets the nerve to ever come back here to this place! He doesn't deserve his daughters and none of us deserve his horrific treatment!* She sighed and attempted to feel the loneliness her dead sister must have felt.

—

Dear Di-Ar-Ree,

I told my preacher about what was occurring, and told him I needed to leave Dan. I asked to use the telephone but when he learned why I needed to use the phone, he said, "Try harder to make a good wife. What are you doing to make him so mad, so violent?" I was astounded at the preacher's response.

Di-Ar-Ree, I can't remember doing anything bad enough to be treated like this. I don't deserve punishment.

I said, "Preacher, I'm trying to be a good wife and always have. I've always tried to please Dan. I thought he'd change. I tried to change myself to get everything back like it was in the beginning, but nothing ever helped."

I told the preacher, "Dan is provoked about everything. I don't have to do anything to provoke him!

The preacher said, "It's against scripture for you not to regard your husband as the head of the household and you must be obedient to him."

I was dumbfounded!

The preacher said, "Lady, go home to your husband and try harder to please your husband, who is, after all, the head of the home!"

God continues to be my only stabilizing factor. I look to Him for help.

Love,

Me

Dear God!

Help Me! Help Us!

Love,

Di-Ar-Ree

—

A blank page separated the documentation to Macie's Diary and that of the last page of the Fairy Tale on page one.

Macie's Pig Latin continued:

The Fairy Godmother handed a Magic Wand to Princess Reality, with her blessing.

> *The handsome six-foot tall Prince Imaginary stepped forward and awaited his reward. Princess Reality waved the Magic Wand over her head three times, and sent brilliant golden and silver sparkles of light into the blue-black night sky. She touched the top of head of Prince Imaginary with the Magic Wand! He was magically changed into a small, twisted, bruised, yellow pumpkin with swollen, blackened eyes and a snaggle-toothed down-turned mouth. He flapped his long, purple, bruised and mottled yellowish green, spindly arms and legs against the ground.*
>
> *"Pick me up! Pick me up!" Prince Imaginary yelled loudly for mercy, out of his snaggle-toothed mouth. "Don't leave me!"*
>
> *Princess Reality placed the yellow Pumpkin Prince Imaginary upon a stone wall throne, and rode away from that place in her golden chariot to a quiet place in the woods.*
>
> *THE END*

* * * *

When Caddie realized she was holding her breath, she gasped deeply for air, and held her shaking hands to her heart. *Apparently Macie tried to leave and Dan stopped her! He killed her! He must have! I am so grateful that I sent Macie money when she asked, but she never got to leave! It was a horrible and evil encounter! She postponed and delayed, until it was too late. Oh! How hard Macie struggled!*

Macie's cries for help echoed in her mind: *Help me, Caddie! Hear me! Hear me!*

Caddie was guilt-ridden to have read the personal thoughts of her sister, and ashamed that she had not done more for Macie. *What more could I have done?*

She sat on the floor, unable to move and thought about how all of Macie's letters, written throughout the years, had been *happy* ones.

But, now that I think about it, the letters we received from you, Macie, were very much alike, except the letter where you asked me if you could borrow money and your last letter where you thanked me for sending you the money. I've always thought how lucky you were, Macie, to have such a smooth and complete life! Children! A handsome husband—one who made you happy!

How could I have been so wrong about your life? When you stayed with that abusive, horrible man—Dan—you ended up murdered! It couldn't have been suicide!

Macie! Why didn't you tell me or someone else in the family you needed help? Did Dan scrutinize your mail and everything that you did so closely you couldn't write? What about a telephone call? Were you so humiliated? So embarrassed?

Macie, in your Diary, you wrote that you '—could sympathize with yourself more than anyone else.' I would have sympathized and empathized, Macie. You know that I would have, if you had given me the opportunity. Macie! I would have listened! I would have helped you! Why didn't you give me that chance? Why?

Caddie wadded a corner of her grandmother's quilt small enough to cram an edge into her mouth, and continued her guilt-ridden misery.

Have I allowed my selfish and personal world and my love's obsession for Jake to be all that I ever thought about? Is that why I didn't realize your unhappiness? Why did you marry Dan? We all thought you and Jake would marry! What happened? I don't understand.

* * * *

Aunt Mae noticed a light under Caddie's door, knocked lightly, and opened the door when she heard no sound.

"Caddie, why are you not in bed? You'll be catching a death of cold sitting here half-dressed and barefooted on this cold floor!" she whispered. She assisted Caddie to her bed and pulled the covers over her. She could think of no time in Caddie's childhood that Caddie looked so distressed. "I love you, Caddie." She wiped the smudges from Caddie's tear-streaked face with a corner of the bed sheet. "I've noticed you staying in your room for a couple of days. I know you've been reading Macie's writings. Is that what's affecting you? What is it, Chile?"

Caddie reached down with a limp hand, picked up Macie's *Manuscript,* and handed it to Aunt Mae, without meeting her eyes.

"Wanna talk?" Aunt Mae asked sympathetically. She stood at the foot of the bed and ran her fingers around the edge of Macie's manuscript.

Caddie shook her head.

"The most important thing you need to do for the next several days is to get enough sleep. So, I'll leave you now. We'll talk in the morning, Caddie." She left the room as quietly as she had come.

After the door closed, Caddie held a pillow over her face, and her inner being screamed: *Dan killed Macie! Dan killed her!*

She leaned her back against her headboard and gazed at the ceiling, seeking the apparition of Macie. *Jake will want to murder Dan for what he did to you!*

Macie, I'd have taken a stand for you, if you had asked me. I would have come after you—done anything for you. If you had only let us know, all of us would have come after you! I sent you the money when you asked me so that you could buy train tickets for you, and Henny-Penny and Kackie. What happened?

Caddie dozed, nodded and her head slipped against the headboard. She slid under the quilt, and dreamed fitfully, and repetitiously:

"Come back, Princess! You're in for Reality. Your Prince was only Imaginary."

* * * *

Uncle Hume left home early to assist George-West Myers with some of his farming machinery and to doctor a sick cow.

Aunt Mae felt an urgency to read the manuscript when she remembered the horror in Caddie's eyes and a change in her whole countenance the last few days.

Even though it was late morning, she didn't disturb Caddie, Henny-Penny or Kackie, and let them sleep.

She scanned the Manuscript written in Pig Latin, hurriedly, with the intention of going back and reading very slowly every living and breathing word Macie wrote:

"—Dear Di-Ar-Ree,
Love, Me
Dear God,
Help us!"

When Aunt Mae finished scanning Macie's Diary/Manuscript, she laid the papers down slowly and carefully upon the kitchen table. She removed her spectacles and rubbed her eyes.

Macie! I see now that you couldn't have killed yourself. Some of your secrets about Dan are written here in your own handwriting! God love you! Talk to me, Macie! What other startling facts have you kept from us? Where did I fail you?

She leaned forward in her chair and rested her head in her hands, prayerfully.

Macie, you seemed to be so happy, when you and Dan were here. How could you end up unloved and murdered? You were defenseless in dealing with the unknown and inexperienced in dealing with an abusive husband—with Dan.

You wrote Di-Ar-Ree that you refused failure. When you knew you were in danger and might be killed, did you still see leaving as failure? I don't understand! I can't help but blame myself for what has happened.

Talk to me, Macie! Talk! Talk!

Aunt Mae held her fingertips to her temples and became very still. *I'm listening, Macie! Listening!*

All she could hear were Macie's unnerving cries for help.

Aunt Mae remembered her only child—Mandy.

I cradled little Mandy in my arms for only a few minutes before Laughing Eyes took her from me, and my yearning for Mandy has remained vivid, and indelibly imprinted in my soul.

When Mandy died, I lost interest in everything for quite sometime, but at no time can I remember thinking of taking my life—killing myself—it was so foreign to my beliefs. Macie, I know you loved your baby daughters. I never could believe you'd want to kill yourself and leave Henny-Penny and Kackie behind to fend for themselves.

Everything points to the fact that Dan killed you! Why didn't I feel Dan's involvement in your death at the time we were with him in Tennessee at your funeral? Dan Zanderneff not only fooled you, but he fooled us all! He beat you and bruised you, and Henny-Penny and Kackie! Your diary makes that very clear. What will we say to Dan if and when he ever comes back here?

Aunt Mae left her chair so abruptly, it tilted, wobbled and almost fell over. She ran outside, picked up newspapers, flowerpots, chairs and everything loose on the porch, and threw it into the yard. She had never been as angry in her life!

The dogs in their alarm turned their heads from side to side and stared at her with wide-open eyes, and ran under the house.

She slumped in her grandmother's rocking chair and caressed its wide, smooth, arms, worn slick with age, and use, and attempted to calm herself.

Much later, she returned to Caddie's room, and sat on the edge of the bed. Caddie kept her eyes closed.

"Caddie, Dan must have killed Macie! I read Macie's cries in her Diary, and I've never read anything like it! What are we going to do about telling Hume and Jake we've read Macie's Diary. They'll want to kill Dan!"

Caddie opened her swollen, blue-green eyes and stared at Aunt Mae. "Jake looks for Dan every weekend. Says he plans to kill him!"

"Caddie, Jake is still living in the past with Macie. I know you love him, but he might never love you back. Don't waste your life on Jake." Aunt Mae held Caddie's hands tightly. Go back to Atlanta, and find you some nice man—maybe a lawyer where you worked. You have your own life to live. We'll make do here. We'll miss you, but we'll make do. Please leave, and go back to Atlanta, before Jake breaks your heart!"

"Aunt Mae, I'm not wasting my life. I love being back here to live."

"You came back for what reason? You came back to Three-Mile Crossing to try to win Jake's heart?"

"Yes, Aunt Mae. Jake always loved Macie, and I knew I didn't have a chance with him, when we were growing up."

"That's what I'm trying to tell you, Caddie. He's still in love with Macie."

"I know that Jake still loves Macie, but I have to be here and see him, if I am ever going to get him to change his mind about me."

"I always thought Macie loved Jake, too. I figured they'd get married," said Aunt Mae.

"Well, I did too, but I was relieved when they didn't. I've wanted to move back for a long, long time so I could be near Jake," said Caddie. "Besides, y'all need help with the children."

"When Jake reads the Diary, he'll probably worry the rest of his life about not helping Macie, when she needed help. You might never have a chance to win him over, Caddie," Aunt Mae said softly.

"Why didn't she get word to one of us that she needed help?"

"It seems like Macie lost reality." Aunt Mae touched Caddie's face gently. "Why, you ask, and we all ask why? I don't know why, but I'm going to try and find out."

"Why? Oh, Why?" Caddie bawled. "Why didn't she let us help her get away from Dan?"

"I believe she did try to leave," said Aunt Mae.

"Yes, it's written pretty plain in her diary."

"Chile, Jake still loves the dead Macie, and you might never change his ways of thinking but if you think it's God's will, then go after him with my blessings. Just ask God if Jake is the one for you, but, listen to His answer. God's answer could be No."

"No?"

"Yes. His answer could be No. So, what then, Caddie? What if God's answer is No?"

"Surely, God wants me to have Jake. Surely, he wants Jake to love me, Aunt Mae!" She held Aunt Mae's hands tightly. "I feel awful! I've always been jealous of Macie having Jake in love with her, and now I feel guilty for my jealousy."

"Jealousy is human nature, Caddie. Don't feel terrible for loving Jake. Macie made a decision to marry Dan."

"After reading her diary, I wonder why she married Dan."

"Yes, it does seem strange in hindsight," said Aunt Mae. "Macie apparently loved Dan at the beginning. It was a choice only Macie could make. She chose to marry him, and then she chose to stay with him."

"But, why?"

"Caddie, I'm trying to figure out why she stayed. We know from reading Macie's diary that she did try to leave. Her diary gives us insight into many of her problems and one of those problems was dealing with how to leave Dan."

"I feel so guilty, Aunt Mae. Surely something could have been done differently."

"Caddie, I feel guilty, too, but I can think of nothing I could have done differently. Remember, Macie did not confide in us and let us know what was going on in her life. Somehow, Macie thought *it would be failure* to leave Dan. Yes, we would have helped her, if we had known."

"Aunt Mae, I was so homesick—so lonely before I came back!"

"We're very glad you're back here with us." She patted Caddie on the arm. "Remember, Caddie, this will always be your home."

* * * *

Aunt Mae's heart churned with a mixture of many feelings, overwhelming responsibilities and a lot of questions.

She wondered how Henny-Penny and Kackie slept through all the noise. She realized their wounds might be more mental than physical. *What can be done to heal their memories of a father who beat them? Can one erase the memories and scars of a wife-beater or a child-beater? Can they be erased or are they indelibly imprinted in the mind—in the soul?*

She went outside and sat on the porch. Ole Jeb turned his head with questioning eyes. She reached over and patted him on the head. "Ole Jeb, if you could talk, what would you say?"

He turned his head from side to side, made a little whimpering sound, as he wriggled on his stomach, and moved closer.

"Ole Jeb, I love you, too."

Ole Jeb wagged his tail.

* * * *

Aunt Mae prepared pork-chops, fried apples, green beans and cornbread and set the table.

Henny-Penny slammed the back door and ran to Aunt Mae and grabbed her around the waist. "Come quick. I saw a girl-frog on the back porch!"

"How do you know it's a girl, Henny-Penny?" Aunt Mae laughed. She wiped her hands on her apron and followed her to the porch.

"Because the girl-frog has a pink bow in her hair!" Henny-Penny whispered, excitedly.

"A pink bow?" Aunt Mae exclaimed, exaggeratedly, and followed Henny-Penny to the porch.

An ordinary toad frog minus the pink hair-bow, sat on the porch, quietly inhaling, exhaling, minding his own business. Aunt Mae laughed, reached down and picked Henny-Penny up and swung her around and around. Henny-Penny's eyes sparkled mischievously.

"Of course, that's a girl-frog. What else would it be with a pink hair-bow?" Aunt Mae laughed.

Kackie joined in the charade, and pointed to the frog. "See! See!" she giggled. "I can see its pink hair-bow!"

Aunt Mae gave both the children a hug.

"You know what? Henny-Penny and Kackie, sometime ago, your mother wrote a lot of words on a piece of paper and some of the wonderful words she wrote down were about both of you. She wrote: 'I am glad I am a mother'."

"Oh-o-o-o, that's sweet," Kackie smiled. "I miss her."

"Yeah, that's real sweet, Aunt Mae," Henny-Penny sighed. "She's coming back to see us again soon."

"She loved both of you adorable children very much."

Aunt Mae observed the little girls and wondered how long it would be before they realized their mother was not coming back.

"Look, the moon is shining in the sky!" Henny-Penny drawled.

"And, it's still daylight," Kackie squealed with delight.

"Yes, it's a full moon. You wanna sit up late tonight and see the moon? It'll be shining very brightly" Aunt Mae smiled.

"Yes! Yes!" Henny-Penny jumped up and down. "Will it shine bright?"

"Yes, it'll be so bright the moon will shine upon yours and Kackie's gorgeous faces," she smiled.

"And, your soft and wrinkled face, too, Aunt Mae?"

"Yes, mine and Uncle Hume's," she laughed.

"And, Caddie's?"

"Yes, of course, it'll smile on Caddie's lovely face, too."

"And, Ole Jeb?" asked Henny-Penny.

"Yes, and Ole Jeb," she laughed.

"And my girl-frog," asked Henny-Penny.

"The moon wouldn't miss a chance to shine on your girl-frog," she laughed.

* * * *

Jake fell into his chair completely exhausted. He scooted his chair a little closer to the fireplace.

Sheriff Olliff was told the Feds might need to use the lock-up that night—that a raid was taking place at Deaver Clement's place. He cringed to think of Deaver and his boys going to jail. He had known the Clement family all his life, and grew up with the boys. Depressing days, such as this one had been, made him wonder if being a Deputy Sheriff was really worth the effort. He felt sorry for his friends that had never made a living doing anything else except make moonshine whiskey.

Since Jake feigned sickness, and was not in on the arrest of his friend, Deaver, he wondered how long he could stay in a deputy's position and turn his head when his friends were in trouble. If a friend was in trouble, and probably going to jail for a long time, he wondered how he was supposed to feel?

He knew he had to adjust—to do the right thing or resign from his position. He had to help with arrests, regardless of who the law breaker might be. He worried enough until he was sick enough to go to bed. He wanted to do a good job, but how could he without becoming hardened and uncaring? He drank for medicinal purposes.

In the middle of the night, Jake awakened to someone calling his name, and banging loudly on his door. He stumbled to the door in his underwear, and opened the door slowly.

"Jake you still sick? We need you buddy! Deaver and two of his boys got away! The "Feds" are after them now and need us to help out."

Jake observed Sheriff Olliff and his deputy. He rubbed the stubble on his chin, and decided Deaver and his boys really had gotten away. "I feel some better. Let me get my clothes on!"

* * * *

That's the biggest goose I ever saw!" said Aunt Mae. She rubbed the side of the tow-sack that held the goose. The goose honked. "Look at that long neck!"

"It's a Chinese goose," said Uncle Hume. He rubbed the white feathers along its long neck. "Rueben said it'd make a good dinner."

"Why did Rueben give it away?" Aunt Mae asked, suspiciously.

"The goose has only one foot—got caught in one of Reuben's traps. He felt guilty about it and didn't want to keep it, so now we have it!" He handed the tow-sack to Aunt Mae.

"He's heavy!" Her arms sank under the heavy load.

Caddie and the children patted the goose on the back of its neck, but his loud honking scared them. It fluttered and made such a ruckus Henny-Penny and Kackie shied away. Their bright eyes widened in fear, yet curiosity.

Uncle Hume pulled the tow-sack tighter around the goose's neck. "Let me carry it, Mae. Just wanted you to see how heavy he is."

"I'll carry it to the pen," she said.

"Who is Reuben?" Kackie asked timidly.

"Reuben Caruthers and me worked on the railroad together for years and years," Uncle Hume smiled. "He's a good friend."

The plump gander, less one foot, distressed Aunt Mae. She stroked its long neck and took it to one of the empty rabbit pens. She whispered, "Settle down, I won't hurt you!" It attempted to reach around to bite her, but she held the tow-sack and the goose's neck, firmly. She placed it in a rabbit pen, gave it some water and chicken feed, and observed the stub of its leg.

That night after supper, they discussed the fate of the Chinese goose. Uncle Hume said he wanted a nice goose dinner with all the trimmings, and invite some company.

But, Aunt Mae said, "Hume, let's make him a peg-leg so he can walk, and we'll keep the goose. It's not fair he got his foot cut off in a trap!"

Uncle Hume laughed so hard at the thought of a goose with a peg-leg, he slapped his leg. "A goose with a peg-leg!" He laughed until tears ran down his cheeks.

"Yes, a Chinese gander with a peg-leg!" she smiled.

"But how?" He opened his hands wide and helplessly towards her.

"I don't know yet. I need to think of a way." She put her hand under her jaw and rested her elbow on the table. Her bright blue eyes became thoughtful.

The next few days, Aunt Mae tried different ways to make a peg-leg for the gander, but everything failed. She got angry thinking about Reuben setting a trap and forgetting about it. *A child could have stepped on the trap.* She shuddered just thinking it could have been worse.

Everyday she went to the pen where they kept the gander and stroked its feathers. She examined the stub of its leg and tried to determine how to make a peg-leg.

After several days of pondering, she finally decided she'd have to give in to Hume's wishes. She was disheartened to think the beautiful bird would have to be killed.

* * * *

"Come on, Baby Girls, let's go for a walk."

"Can Ole Jeb go with us?" asked Kackie.

"Yes, let's take Ole Jeb, too."

When Aunt Mae and the children walked through the woods, she related the names of many plants, trees, mosses and flowers, and made their world come alive.

Suddenly, she looked down and saw spent cardboard shot-gun shells lying in the pathway. She pounced on the empty shot-gun shells, and held them tightly in a fist close to her breast, as if they were a valuable treasure!

"Come on! Let's go back to the house as fast as we can go!" She started to trot and Henny-Penny and Kackie ran after her as fast as their short legs would carry them. Ole Jeb barked and followed closely.

Aunt Mae hurried to the rabbit pen that held the goose, and opened its door.

"Come on, you long-necked critter, let's try something." Aunt Mae whispered, as she wrapped her apron around the gander's head and long neck, leaving one short leg and a stub hanging out, and placed it on the ground. She knelt on the red, clay ground and held the apron tightly. The gander struggled, but she held the apron tightly and securely, and shoved one of the shot-gun shell casings over the stub of its leg.

The empty cardboard shot-gun shell casing fit tightly, perfectly, and formed a peg-leg.

She placed the gander on the ground, and removed her apron slowly.

The metal end of the casing braced the gander's leg enough to give support to its body.

At first the gander waddled slowly, awkwardly, and leaned slightly. Suddenly, the gander lifted its wings and floated gracefully around the chicken yard, occasionally touching the ground with its good foot and make shift peg-leg.

Kackie and Henny-Penny ran around the yard chasing the gander.

"Look! Look! He's floating! He's floating!" Henny-Penny yelled.

The chickens squawked, a rooster crowed, and Ole Jeb barked.

Aunt Mae smiled as she removed a handkerchief from her apron pocket, sat on a metal feed bucket and wiped perspiration from her face. "Hume's gonna be mighty surprised when he learns he's gotta find a substitute for that big dinner he's planning."

Henny-Penny ran to her and hugged her neck. "What're we gonna call him, Aunt Mae?"

"Let's call him Pegg. That'll be short for Peg-Leg."

"Come here, Pegg," Henny-Penny laughed as she chased the goose all over the chicken lot.

* * * *

When Uncle Hume walked into the kitchen late in the afternoon, he was surprised to find a extraordinary chicken supper prepared. Candles shone brightly upon a neatly set table. "What's the occasion? Why are the best dishes out? And, fresh wild flowers, too?" He picked up the vase of flowers and sniffed. "Smells good."

Aunt Mae smoothed her crisp, white, bib apron over a light blue dress and sat down. "You'll never guess the occasion, Hume."

Caddie and the children giggled.

"It's a surprise," said Caddie.

"What's the surprise?" he laughed. "Tell me, Mae! Tell me Caddie!"

"Uncle Hume, you'll never guess in a million years what Aunt Mae has done," Caddie slung her hair back and clipped it on each side with blue barrettes.

Uncle Hume glanced at Aunt Mae and began to guess everything he could imagine.

Aunt Mae just laughed.

After supper, the family walked Uncle Hume out to the chicken lot and stood before the gander's pen. "What are you up to?" he laughed.

Aunt Mae placed a spent shot-gun-shell over the stub of Pegg's leg, and placed Pegg on the ground.

Pegg began to waddle, leaning slightly to one side. He waddled faster and faster, and honked loudly. He spread his wings and "floated" around the barnyard.

"We named him 'Pegg,' short for Peg-Leg!" Henny-Penny squealed delightedly.

"Pegg?" Uncle Hume smiled. He was astonished at Aunt Mae's great ingenuity. She never ceased to amaze him. He threw his head back and laughed and slapped his hands together. "Well, I'll declare! I'll declare!"

Henny-Penny and Kackie chased the gander, and yelled, "See, we told you it'd be a surprise!"

"Caddie, can you believe what Mae has done? That's one lucky goose!" Uncle Hume exclaimed.

"Does this mean Aunt Mae can keep Pegg?" Caddie teased.

"You know the rules. We don't eat our pets," Uncle Hume smiled as he looked into Aunt Mae's dancing-blue eyes and knew how fortunate he was to have a wife who was happy with the simpler things in life. Little wisps of white curls framed her face. Her French-twist was coiled neatly on the back of her head except for the tiny ringlets that wriggled out at the bottom of the twist, and hung softly around her neck. He pulled on one of the wisps of her hair and watched the hair spring back into place.

* * * *

Uncle Hume bragged to their friends at church how Aunt Mae made the wonderful Chinese goose with a long neck and short legs a peg-leg with a spent (empty) shot-gun shell casing. The people exclaimed over her being such a cunning inventor.

Some of the elderly men socialized in a group close to the side door of the church.

Judge Pewter and Doc Stowe sat on a marble bench close to the Meeting House, and appeared to be in deep discussion.

The women exchanged recipes, and the events of the week in the front of the church, and the smaller children played close to their mothers.

The church folks hardly noticed the young boys standing under one of the big oak trees, whispering, laughing, and pointing towards the Meeting House from time to time.

"Jake, y'all gonna catch Deaver and his boys?" Joseph Daniels stood with his hands lodged in his suspenders, and rocked his muscular body back and forth.

And Jake stood with his hands in his corduroys, rattling change. "Still a 'looking," he said.

George-West Myers tamped tobacco in his pipe, lit it, and took a big draw. He held himself upright and sniffed. "You know Deaver is long gone. He's got folks up North. That would be the place you'd catch him, if anyone is crazy enough to tell you where that place is!" Everyone laughed. "Think I'll join Judge Pewter and Doc Stowe." He strolled towards the Meeting House and joined his friends at the marble bench.

"Jake, we know moon shining is wrong whar the law is concerned, but Deaver's been our friend a long time," one of the Elders said.

"I know. Believe me, I understand," said Jake.

Joseph Daniels cleared his throat. "You know, this is a gonna sound corny, but I'm mourning for Deaver. It's been a long while since he ran off in the woods. Hate to mention it, Jake, but your dad never came back after he went hunting that time when you was little and he went off. It's dangerous out deep in them woods."

"Yes, even though Deaver broke the law by moon shining, we still like him. Can't help that," said Jake.

As he listened to the men talk, Jake noticed Caddie sitting on the wooden bench at the Meeting Tree. She looks a lot like Macie today. He felt a twinge of jealousy when he noticed Tinker Daniels engaging her in conversation.

The Meeting Tree was an exciting and wonderful place for the children to meet when they were lonely and wanted to play. One of his favorite childhood memories was hearing the elders say: *Go to the Meeting Tree and sit on the bench, and stay for a very short time. Other children will join you at the tree, if they want to play.*

No one seemed to remember who built the first bench which surrounded the old oak tree, or sent the first child to the meeting tree to wait for other children to come and play, but it had been maintained as long as he or anyone else could remember.

"Hey, y'all, I'll see you later," Jake told the men.

As he started to walk towards the Meeting Tree, Jake heard someone say under his breath, "Everyone who is moon shining has got to be more careful."

"Hello, Jake. Glad to see you!" Reverend Buker Webster walked up to him and extended his hand. "Want to go horse-back riding tomorrow afternoon?"

"Sure would, Reverend. Call me at the office about noon, tomorrow. Gotta talk to Caddie, right now."

* * * *

Jake rushed up to Caddie. "Hi, Caddie! Can I walk you home?" he smiled.

She looked into his squinted, bright blue eyes and noticed his face was tanned a shade darker since she saw him last. "Yes, I'd love for you to," she blushed. "Aunt Mae, Henny-Penny and Kackie have already gone home."

"I was just about to ask her that same thing, myself," Tinker Daniels frowned. He straightened his jacket and stood taller. "I was gonna ask you to let me walk you home." His brown eyes met Caddie's blue ones.

Caddie smiled.

"Nope, I asked her first" Jake held his hand out to her.

She took Jake's hand and stood up. "See you later, Tinker. Enjoyed talking to you."

Tinker squeezed her elbow. "Me, too, Caddie." He slumped dejectedly as he watched Caddie walk away with Jake. "Maybe another time," he whispered to himself.

"Caddie, the main reason I wanted to walk you home is because I'm anxious to catch a glimpse of the new addition to the family. I hear its name is *Pegg.*"

She tried not to show her disappointment in his being interested in the goose and not herself. "Pegg's a fantastic curiosity," she responded without looking at him.

"A curiosity?" he laughed. "And a gander?"

"Yes, a curiosity and a gander." Her voice lifted slightly in her anger, but Jake didn't seem to notice.

"Can you believe how smart Aunt Mae is?" asked Jake. "Uncle Hume said that she's using shot-gun shell casings for a peg-leg. I'm gonna have to see this!"

"It's fun to watch Pegg try to balance himself."

"Why did y'all give a gander a girl's name—Pegg?"

"Pegg is short for Peg-leg. Can't call him *Peg-Leg.* It might hurt his feelings," she smiled, but her heart hurt from Jake's insensitivity.

"I'm sure Pegg would have hurt feelings," he laughed. He held Caddie's hand, as they walked towards the cabin, along the meandering of the creek which ran beside the rocky and narrow road. When his eyes met hers, he released her hand and placed his hands in his pockets.

Caddie's quick glance at Jake questioned his action, and he blushed.

Believing Jake was thinking of Macie, she couldn't help but feel a twinge of jealousy. "Pegg's gonna need a lot of spent shot-gun shells," she said, trying not to show her anger.

"Why is that, Caddie?"

"When Pegg gets his feet wet at the watering-trough at the barn or in the creek, the cardboard softens, comes apart, and won't hold him up.

"I didn't think of that."

"Pegg came to us at a good time."

"Sure did, Caddie." he agreed. "The words that Macie wrote in her diary are lying heavy on our hearts. We needed a distraction."

"I can't stand to think about her diary giving all those horrible details, and now our knowing how she needed me," said Jake.

"Needed all of us, Jake."

"Can you believe she wrote her diary in Pig Latin?"

"Yes. Macie would do something like that. She would write in code."

"I remember when we used to talk Pig Latin," he smiled.

"Me, too."

When they walked into the clearing at the cabin, Jake laughed when he observed Kathryn mocking Pegg's walk. "Pegg's really a sight to see—a curiosity, all right. He ran after the goose and caught it, held it in his arms to observe how the shot-gun shell worked on the stub of the leg. He shook his head in amazement. "Let's go inside and tell Aunt Mae she's a genius."

As Jake started to leave that evening, Caddie gave Jake a "Six-Egg Pound Cake."

"Thanks, Caddie, you're sweet," he hugged and kissed her on the cheek.

"Enjoy the cake, Jake. Don't be a stranger."

"Like I said, Caddie, you're sweet, but not as sweet at the cake," he laughed, and hugged her again.

* * * *

When Jake got home, he built a fire in the fireplace.

He sat at his kitchen table, cut himself a piece of Caddie's pound cake and sipped a cup of black coffee. He sniffed the aroma of vanilla in the pound cake, and savored each bite.

After he finished eating, he sat before the fireplace, lit his pipe, and whittled on a stick of soft pine, as he watched the dancing fire.

He chuckled to himself about Aunt Mae's inventive methods and how she worked so hard to get-her-way to keep the lame gander. He thought of Caddie and remembered the race of his heart and its leap, when he looked into her exquisitely blue eyes that afternoon. At that particular moment, Caddie had looked a lot like Macie.

Wonder what Tinker Daniels was talking to Caddie about? He's tall and pretty handsome, but not that handsome! He's not good enough for her! No, sir, Tinker Daniels better not get any ideas about Caddie.

Suddenly a twinge of guilt twisted his heart. *What would Macie think about me being jealous of Caddie?*

The thought of Macie's diary and her cries for help overpowered him, and he forgot Caddie, Tinker Daniels and whatever Tinker might have had on his mind that afternoon. He'd hardly been able to think of anything else since he read Macie's words of anguish. *Macie, I'm telling you right now that reading your diary was one of the hardest things I've ever done in my whole life. I hate Dan! That son-uv-a-bitch!*

He held his head in his hands, and slumped forward. The knife and the piece of whittled wood fell to the floor.

Why didn't you let me know you wanted to get away from Dan? I would have helped you! You know I love you! Nothing would have stopped me from helping you get away! Nothing!

He envisioned the troubled Macie, as she wrote her words of anguish. *Macie, oh, Macie! I would have gone to the ends of the earth for you! Why did you pick Dan? He was so wrong for you!* His soul ached with rejection.

He opened a kitchen cupboard and removed a pint of whisky.

Cats yowled and howled and scampered across the front porch.

* * * *

As Aunt Mae, Henny-Penny and Kackie walked to the spring, they heard the screech of a bird. She placed her water buckets on the ground quietly, placed her index finger to her lips and motioned for them to be quiet. She followed the sound of the bird's shriek.

"Look!" Henny-Penny whispered, and pointed to a sparrow caught in a saw-briar.

Aunt Mae removed a vine of thorns that wrapped around the body of the bird, and examined its grayish-brown breast. "Bet one of Deaver's boys or the Daniel's boys shot this little bird with his B-B gun! We mustn't shoot at anything unless it's for food." The girls listened intently with wide open eyes.

She held the sparrow in her hands firmly but gently, and began to hum an indecipherable tune as she brushed its breast feathers between her fingers, and rolled a BB shot into her hands. "Don't be afraid, little sparrow. Don't be afraid." She held the sparrow close enough for Kackie and Henny-Penny to observe. "Let's go back to the house and take care of this little critter. I have a bird-cage on the back porch."

They left their buckets on the path, and went back to the cabin to doctor the sparrow.

"I want me a pet bird," said Henny-Penny.

"Yeah, we want us a pet bird," said Kackie.

"Some things are best left untamed." She smiled at Henny-Penny and Kackie, and nodded knowingly.

Henny-Penny and Kackie were sad.

"He can be our pet until he gets well. Talk to the bird, and feed it and, hopefully, one day we'll open its cage and it'll fly away home to its family. To know God healed the bird will be something you'll always remember!"

She crooned to the sparrow, as she rubbed her special healing cream on its wound, and tied a bandage around its body. Then, she held the beak of the sparrow at its corners and forced the beak to open. She dipped her fingers into a bowl of water, held her fingers over its open beak and drizzled water into its throat. She hummed, "In the Sweet Bye'n Bye," as she placed the sparrow in a wooden cage.

* * * *

Aunt Mae worked her herb garden, while Henny-Penny and Kackie played in a rickety, wooden pull wagon just outside the garden gate.

Henny-Penny pointed her finger towards the woods, and giggled. "Look! I see Laughing Eyes."

"I see her, too! Look! Aunt Mae," Kackie yelled.

They ran awkwardly to Laughing Eyes as their bare feet crippled over the river rocks. She hugged them tightly. "I missed you two little mites."

"We're not mites—uh, what's a mite?" asked Henny-Penny.

"A mite is something very small," she laughed.

Aunt Mae looked up and smiled when she saw her friend. "You're a sight for sore eyes! I was just thinking about you.

"Thinking about something good, I hope." Her brown eyes sparkled, and the lines of her crow's feet surrounded her eyes in all the right places.

"Always good thoughts when you come to mind." Aunt Mae stepped outside her garden, closed the gate and they embraced.

A Blue-bird flew from one of the baby blue bird houses, which rested on top of the four fence posts, surrounding the herb garden.

"I brought you babies something good to eat?"

"What is it, Laughing Eyes?"

"Teacakes."

"Thank you," the little girls smiled.

"Brought Macie's Diary back." Laughing Eyes stared into the distance. "Macie had a sad soul and wrote sad words. My heart bleeds for her—for you."

"Yes, Macie's sad words—her cries keep me awake at night," Aunt Mae sighed.

Laughing Eyes touched Aunt Mae's shoulder gently. "Thank you for sharing this part of your life. It means a lot. Her writing the Diary in Pig Latin made it slow reading, but I finally managed to get the hang of it."

"I taught Jake, Macie, Caddie, and Ole Pem, too, how to speak Pig Latin when they were little children. They had a lot of fun with it."

"I remember Ole Pem speaking a strange language and when I'd ask what he was saying, he'd just laugh."

"Laughing Eyes, when you read her diary, did you notice that Macie writes to her inner-self, *Di-Ar-Ree,* and the answers *Di-Ar-Ree* gives to *Me* are good, sensible answers?"

"Yes, I did notice."

"Well, Macie knew what to do, but she didn't do what she knew had to be done," said Aunt Mae.

"Yes, Macie had choices to make. They were her *own* personal choices. I agree, it does appear that her inner-self, *Di-Ar-Ree*, told her clearly what to do to solve her problems," said Laughing Eyes.

"Yes, perfectly clear—good, clear and sensible answers. The *Me* who wrote seeking answers was not the *normal* Macie that I knew, but the inner-self who answered *Me* is the one I know as normal." Aunt Mae nodded her head.

"Mae, you recognized *Di-Ar-Ree* but not *Me?*" asked Laughing Eyes. "How can that be?"

"I recognized the astonishing, intelligent answers of the inner-self of Macie—*Di-Ar-Ree* but I did not recognize the Macie who signed herself as *Me.*" The one who had lost her confidence."

"How strange it all seems," Laughing Eyes sympathized.

"Yes, strange she would know what to do, but couldn't act on *just knowing.*"

"She tried to act. She had many obstacles. Mae, I'm very sorry for your great pain!"

"Laughing Eyes—in Macie's Diary, she mentions being mentally withdrawn and she *wallowed in the slime of self-pity.*"

"Yes, I remember reading that."

"I feel deeply guilty about not knowing she was having any kind of problems. I just can't figure it out. Why didn't she tell me she needed help and let me go and get her and bring her home, or why did she not just come home? Just take the girls and call us from somewhere—anywhere?" Aunt Mae wiped her eyes with the corner of her apron.

"Mae, I read Macie's Diary with a lot of concentration. It began as a fairy tale—but it turned out to be the story of a caring young mother bogged down in misery, loneliness, bitterness and confusion. It's a story about a young woman seeking a way out—a way to leave the husband who abused her and her children."

"Poor Macie's cries have sickened and depressed me." Aunt Mae stopped and stared at Laughing Eyes.

"Yes, her cries for help and understanding have touched us all," Laughing Eyes answered softly.

They walked up the back steps made of gray, flat rock.

Henny-Penny and Kackie followed.

"Mae, you do realize that Macie knew she was in danger," Laughing Eyes said, softly and apologetically.

"Yes, Dan beat her—hit her and the children and held a gun on them."

"Fear would be a reason to stay, Mae! F E A R is a horrible thing to experience, to endure!" Laughing Eyes whispered.

"Yes! Yes! F E A R!"

Laughing Eyes removed the neatly wrapped and tied diary from her split-oak basket and handed the document to her friend. "I took good care of Macie's sacred papers."

"Laughing Eyes, I want to thank you for your insightful thoughts. It helps me to discuss the words she wrote in her last days, even if it does make me sad."

"I am honored you allowed me to read such private papers. I loved Macie, too."

Aunt Mae rolled up the cuffs of her blue, cotton dress sleeves. "Let me freshen up a bit." She poured water into a wash-pan, washed and dried her hands.

"Mae, you know my brother was beaten by his wife. His abuse and pain were horrible, too. It's not just men who beat women. My brother is a quiet and gentle person."

"Is your brother okay, now?"

"Yes, remember, he divorced his wife? He's very happy, now that he left."

"Good for him," Aunt Mae responded. "Sit here at the table, while I put the kettle on."

Laughing Eyes observed the home of her friend. Dried onions, hot peppers, and "leather britches" hung at the fireplace. Rosemary, basil, parsley and other herbs hung from the rafters of the kitchen; Mason jars filled with colorful canned fruits and vegetables sat upon open shelves.

"Mae, might I have some dried herbs for soup?"

"Any kind in particular?"

"I'm making stew."

Aunt Mae opened a white pine, cabinet door and removed a jar of crushed herbs, which looked like pieces of sticks, dirty-looking brown leaves and a fine brown-gray dust. She removed a small paper sack from one of the cabinet drawers, filled it almost full of a variety of herbs, and tied it with a flour sack string.

"Mae, do you have any poke-berry dust? Need to dye a strip of cloth."

"Sure, I do. Come and see some more of my goodies on the back porch."

The porch was orderly. Its great depth gave room for tables, straight chairs and rocking chairs. A pie safe and several cupboards lined the walls. On one end of the porch was a water-well made of flat rock, the same as that of the porch steps, and the fireplaces in the front room and the kitchen.

Aunt Mae removed a jar of magenta and black-colored dust from one of the cupboards. "Here's some ground up poke-salat berries for your paints and dyes." She poured a generous amount of the dust into a little "penny sack," and tied it with flour sack string. She caressed the jar and admired its color, as she returned the jar to its shelf.

"Laughing Eyes, come and see what I've been working on," said Aunt Mae.

Laughing Eyes arose from her chair and followed her into a bedroom.

Aunt Mae unfolded her new crocheted pieces, her pieced quilts and spread them over her bed for Laughing Eyes to examine. They returned to the kitchen and held up fruit jars filled with canned vegetables and jellies, and enjoyed the green, yellow, orange, and red colors as they reflected in the light.

While they sat together on the back porch and drank a cup of calming chamomile tea, Pegg came out from under the porch.

"Aunt Mae, I'm fascinated by the way Pegg balances on his peg-leg. He doesn't walk. He waddles so fast, he floats!"

"Pegg was trapped and wounded but he was rescued from the trap. He's still wounded, yes." Aunt Mae hesitated and gazed towards the hazy-blue mountains. "Macie was trapped in her situation and she didn't get away. I would have helped her."

"Had you known about her trouble—you'd have helped her. It's not your fault. Your not knowing she needed help is not your fault!" Laughing Eyes spoke softly. "I wish I could find words to say that would bring comfort, but, I can find no words to soothe the pain of loss—the loss of a child."

"So true! So true," Aunt Mae sighed.

A Blue Jay fought with other Blue Jays in the trees, in the air, and made a nose dive to the ground where they continued their spat, close to the porch.

"What do the birds seem to be fighting over?" Laughing Eyes leaned forward to observe the birds more closely.

"I threw some corn out in the yard for Pegg this morning. I guess they've spotted some of the grains that Pegg missed. But, as you know, Blue Jays don't have to have a reason to fight."

A Red Bird joined the Blue Jays on the ground. All of the Blue Jays made a dive for the Red Bird.

"More tea?"

"No, thank you, Aunt Mae." Laughing Eyes laughed and clamped her hand over her mouth. "Look! Aren't those disagreeable birds typical of some of the people that we know?"

* * * *

Caddie walked up the stairs. "Been in the field. How're you, Laughing Eyes?"

"Fine. Just fine, and you, Caddie?"

"I'm feeling better since I moved back home. How's your family?"

"My people are fine. You remember Pem's in Mississippi. Works at the sheriff's office part time." Laughing Eyes smiled. "He never fails to mention you in his letters."

"I miss him, too. Is he still doing good in law school?"

"He is doing really well. He still lives with Judge Pewter's brother, Sam. The really good news is that Judge Pewter wants him to practice law with him here at Three-Mile Crossing when Pem passes the bar," she smiled proudly.

"It'll be a great day when Ole Pem gets back!" Caddie smiled. "Just think Ole Pem's studying to be a lawyer. Such Ambition!" Caddie laughed. "Laughing Eyes, excuse me, please. I need to eat a bite, before I go back to the field and finish the hoeing and weeding. It's been a rough day."

* * * *

From a distance, no one recognized the lady in the large, blue cloth work bonnet, the lady who hoed hills of squash and beans and stopped from time to time to wipe the sweat from her brow. The one that rubbed the calluses in her hands, examined new blisters, and wiped her stained hands on a blue apron. The lady who reached out carefully and removed a Lady Bug from a leaf, allowed it to crawl upon the back of her hand, and observed it intently. "Ladybug, I can crush you, and kill you, or allow you to crawl upon the jonquil-colored squash bloom. What'll it be?" No sooner said, she lifted her hand swiftly into the air, and a gentle breeze caught the Lady Bug in its breath and blew it to the other side of the field. *I must be out of my mind telling a little ole Lady Bug that I'll crush it, particularly since finding a Lady Bug is supposed to be good luck!*

She leaned her exhausted head upon the end of her hoe-handle. *Maybe I'm bitter because Jake is so unaware of me—so unaware of my feelings. I thought things would be different when I moved back here to be near him.* Caddie removed her cloth bonnet and wiped her forehead on the long sleeve of her cotton dress. She shook her head and combed her muddy fingers through her long hair.

* * * *

"Aunt Mae! Aunt Mae!" Rob-Hunter Daniels gasped for breath, and slumped on the front door steps. "You'll never guess what happened!"

Aunt Mae dried her hands upon her apron, and hurried to the porch.

"Maw was carrying a coal-oil lamp, and all of a sudden it just blowed up in her face, and she's burnt terrible bad! We can't find Doc Stowe nowheres! Paw said come quick!" He walked the length of the porch, and back again.

"How awful!" Aunt Mae hugged him and tried to console him. "Need to get my medicine basket from the Quilting House."

"Maw's in terrible shape! Face and chest are parched black, and her hair is burnt! Maw is praying and crying out, *My body's in hell!*" He motioned erratically, as he spoke.

Aunt Mae hurriedly filled her medicine basket with fresh herbs, her prayerfully blended ointments and cures, and a change of clothes. Rob-Hunter and Caddie saddled a mule.

"Caddie, please go back to the field and tell Hume where I've gone! Kackie, you and Henny-Penny, please help Caddie look after Uncle Hume, okay?"

Aunt Mae and Rob-Hunter rode hurriedly through the woods, riding "as the crow flies."

The Daniels' cabin nestled at the foot of a mountain, where a stream ran through the valley. Upon getting closer to the cabin, Aunt Mae observed a terrible eyesore. Old parts of farm equipment, parts of rusty cars, tin-cans, broken glass and furniture strewn to all creation junked up the yard. Her heart wrenched in disappointment knowing that some human beings lived in such an environment!

"Right there are the Donahoo boys, and brother, Wyllyam." Rob-Hunter pointed in their direction. Sandra Lou Donahoo's three little boys and Wyllyam Daniels ran along-side them, through weeds higher than their heads. "Mama said you can talk out fire! We want to see you talk out fire!" they yelled.

Sandra Lou Donahoo greeted them at the door. She wiped her sweaty face on the corner of her apron. "Don't let my little boys hinder you none, you hear."

"Want to see Aunt Mae talk out fire," they repeated.

Sandra Lou Donahoo shoved the boys back onto the porch. "Boys, go back outside. Go!"

"Maw! We want to see her! We want to see her bad!" they cried.

"Howdy, Sandra Lou."

"Aunt Mae," Sandra Lou Donahoo whispered, "Tinker came over to my house and got me. Mary's bad off. I said I can't doctor her, but I can cook."

Aunt Mae nodded and hugged her. "Thanks for helping out, Sandra Lou."

Sandra Donahoo resumed her cooking at the wood cook-stove.

Aunt Mae glanced at the walls of the dismal, darkened rooms, covered with black, tar-paper. When she walked to the back of the cabin, she noticed pieces of cloth hung in the doorways, as make-shift doors.

"I'm burning in hell!" Mary Daniels screamed.

Aunt Mae pushed a cloth door aside, and observed Joseph Daniels kneeling beside Mary's bed.

"Oh, thank you, God! Mae's here, Mary!" Joseph cried.

"Mary, I'm here!" she said, softly.

She heard the low whispers of the Daniel's children, and heard the words, *Healing-Woman.*

"She's going to lay hands on Mama!" Tinker Daniels whispered loudly.

The little Donahoo boys crawled under the bed, and Wyllyam Daniels followed. Aunt Mae lifted the bed-spread and got down on her knees. "Boys, come out from under the bed this very instant. Y'all need to go to the other room."

"Wanna see you talk out fire," said Wyllyam.

Aunt Mae smiled, "You boys are just *too* much!"

The little boys crawled out from under the bed, and began lamenting, "Just wanted to watch you."

"That you, Mae," Mary whimpered.

"Yes, I'm here beside you."

"Thank you, Jesus!" Mary cried.

Aunt Mae took Mary's hand, and almost gasped when she saw Mary's unrecognizable, swollen, parched face and lips.

"I hurt awful!" Mary moaned. "My body's in hell-fire."

"Mary, this is Mae. I'm right here with you."

"What have I done to deserve this awful pain?"

"You've done nothing to deserve pain." She knelt beside the bed, extended both her hands about three or four inches above the burned areas of Mary's body, and began to move her hands in circular motions. She closed her eyes, moved her lips, and began her prayer that talked out the fire.

She could hear the disappointed voices of the little Donahoo boys at the doorway, "I don't see no fire—don't see no sparks, neither. She's just talking to herself."

Mary moaned, "Mae, pray hard."

"Mary, try to calm yourself—you might scar worse if you don't settle your innards. Settle yourself. Calm yourself. Look at me, Mary!"

Mary fixed the swollen slits of her brown eyes upon Aunt Mae and made an effort to calm.

Aunt Mae prayed the same prayer she prayed when someone was bleeding or burned, a "secret cure" handed down in her family for generations.

She became aware of the sickening odors of boiling cabbage, mixed with the odor of Mary's burnt and parched skin.

Aunt Mae removed *The Log Cabin* quilt from the bed, folded it and placed it on a chair. She stripped the feed-sack sheets from Mary's bed. "Boys, let's get the wash-pot boiling in the back yard. We need all of these bed linens washed." They stood amazed that a woman's work was expected of them.

"Washing clothes is women's work. It's Ratchel's place to do it," said Rob Hunter, and the other boys nodded.

"We're gonna need a lot of hot water to get this job done. Best be quick about it."

They were hesitant at first, and then everyone scurried.

While other preparations were underway, Aunt Mae mixed several ingredients to apply to Mary's burns. She measured her herbs and powdered roots precisely, and ground them with a pestle, until they were as fine as dust. She prayed as she mixed the ingredients she used for an important reason—or bad sickness. Prayer was the power. That most crucial ingredient.

Ratchel-Robin Daniels—the Daniels only daughter, brought home-made feed sack sheets and pieces of red flannel cloth, and handed them to Aunt Mae.

Aunt Mae opened the wood stove's oven door and placed the home-made sheets on the oven racks to sterilize them.

She and Ratchel-Robin cut away Mary's clothes as gently as possible, and made-up the bed with the sterilized feed-sack sheets. She removed some of the parched skin with small scissors, and cleansed the burns with her special mixture. After cleansing, she applied more ointment, smoothly and gently, to all affected areas. "We don't want Mary to sweat." She covered Mary loosely with a sterilized homemade sheet, and wrapped her feet in a red flannel blanket. "Ratchel, let's keep her lightly covered and fan her to keep her cool and keep the flies away.

She spoon-fed Mary a unique broth made of meal, flour and several herbs hard to decipher by taste. "It's bitter as gall, Mae," Mary moaned and frowned.

* * * *

Aunt Mae prayed as she walked through the woods and cut fresh tree bark and foraged for leaves and roots to prepare a sedative for Mary. When she returned to the cabin, she measured and mixed the tree bark, roots, and herbs exactly and precisely—knowing too much of some of them might be toxic. She gave Mary the sedative, and sat beside her until she began to drift-off to sleep.

Aunt Mae observed Ratchel-Robin. *I wonder if my little Mandy would have been as pretty as Ratchel, had she lived.* She reached over and stroked Ratchel's long sun-streaked, blond hair and the girl smiled timidly. "I love you, Ratchel. You're a gorgeous young lady."

"I love you, too. Thanks for healing Mama."

"Ratchel, God is the healer. Not me. Sometimes God says, 'No,' when we ask for healing. I don't know why. God might say *No* at this time. You understand?"

Ratchel smiled at her, and shook her head. She did not understand why God might say *No*.

"Aunt Mae, mama told me one time that your little girl would be a big grown up lady, if she didn't die," Ratchel said hesitantly.

"That's right. My daughter's name was *Mandy*. Every time I see you, I think about her."

"You think of your little girl, when you see me?" Ratchel was obviously pleased. She twisted her collar and ducked her head.

"Yes, I sure do. I always think of her when I see you. Did anyone ever tell you that you look just like an angel."

"Naw, they never did tell me that. I don't know what to say, Aunt Mae."

"*Thank you* is all you ever need to say."

"Thank you," Ratchel giggled.

"You spoil her, Aunt Mae," Sandra Lou Donahoo said, approvingly.

"Not near enough," Aunt Mae sighed.

She tiptoed through the house, opened the back door, and found Joseph lying on a cot on the back porch. He sat up when he saw her. "I'd take the pain from Mary, if I could," he whispered.

"I know you would, if you could. I know how much you love her."

* * * *

Aunt Mae organized everything from cutting down weeds, raking yards, making a nursing chart, and a list of household duties. She detailed the junk in the back yard being hauled down to a far away ditch—out of sight. Since the boys wanted to do men's work, she gave them men's work, and they didn't question her.

She smiled when she remembered the day each of the four handsome, young, scowling men were born. She midwifed them all, including Ratchel-Robin.

* * * *

Doc Stowe arrived at the Daniel's home a couple of days later. "Mae, you've done an amazing job with Mary. You know you missed your calling. You should have been a doctor." His blue eyes twinkled.

He didn't know how Aunt Mae instinctively knew how to treat the sick. He didn't try to change her medicines and superstitions. He just blended his medicine with hers. She was the greatest midwife and practical nurse he had ever known. He complimented her and spent time catching up on the news. Since his wife passed away, he seldom talked to anyone about his personal feelings, but from time to time he confided in Aunt Mae.

After Doc Stowe and Aunt Mae discussed Mary's condition, he said, "Let's go outside, walk a bit, and talk about you. We haven't talked since Macie died." He smoothed his white hair on each side of his balding head, held the edges of his vest and snapped it into place.

"All right."

"How's Hume?"

"Lovely! Lovely! He's just perfect."

"Glad to hear it. Rest of the family—Caddie? And, your granddaughters?"

Delightful! Just delightful!" Henny-Penny and Kackie are adjusting well.

"Naturally, you're sad about Macie. What's on your heart, Mae?"

"Doc Stowe, I'm very upset, even more so since I read Macie's diary. We learned that she had severe problems with Dan. He mistreated her, and beat her and the children. I hear her cries of anguish, when I lie down to sleep." She wiped her face on the corner of her apron.

"I never had children, but know it must be a terrible thing to lose a child," said Doc Stowe.

"Macie, never in her lifetime, let us know she ever had a problem. But when I read her diary, I was amazed to learn what a hard time she and the girls had with Dan. If you read her diary, Doc, you'd know more about what I'm thinking and feeling."

"Yes, Mae, let me read it."

"After we read her diary, we don't know how he did it, but we believe Dan killed her." She wrung her hands.

Doc Stowe stopped walking and turned to her. He took her hands in both of his, shook her hands slightly and let them drop. "I know it has to hurt a lot to think about the things she wrote."

He touched her elbow, and they began to walk again. "Do the Zanderneffs stay in touch? They supportive in all this?"

"No! And that's a funny thing, too. They've distanced themselves."

Doc Stowe raised his eyebrows. "You know this is serious business. Grand-maw Taylor and Laughing Eyes showed me Henny-Penny's and Kackie's bruises, but that was after they had already treated both the little girls."

"Yes, it really grieved me when I saw their bruises. I couldn't believe that no one showed their bruises to me."

"Yes, your friends were very concerned. I'm the one who told the ladies to wait about showing you their bruises. You had enough on your mind. Besides that, Henny-Penny and Kackie were being looked after. They okay, now?"

"Physically, yes."

"And, mentally, can you tell how they are? Are they coping okay?"

"They're skittish and hold on to each other a lot, but seem to be doing well," said Aunt Mae.

"It's funny how things turn out sometimes. I always thought Dan was a very nice, and gentle young man."

"Doc Stowe, when you read Macie's diary, you won't believe you ever knew Dan. He turned into a stranger."

"It's very hard to handle deception. Let's go back and get some coffee, Mae."

* * * *

Several days passed, and Mary improved remarkably.

Aunt Mae walked into the kitchen, and found Sandra Lou Donahoo standing at the kitchen stove, stirring a large pot of oatmeal. "Sandra, the Daniels and I are lucky to have you here to help out. I have to leave today. It's not much, but I picked you some wild-flowers early this morning, and put them in fresh water in that cooking pot setting on that table. Can we find a fruit-jar to put them in?"

"The flowers are lovely, and smell wonderful. It's so like you to remember me here in the kitchen. I was glad to be of help. We're sure gonna miss you!" she whispered.

* * * *

When she told the Daniels she had to go home, Joseph Daniels offered payment, but she refused. "Joseph, maybe you can do me and Hume a favor sometime."

"My boys will come over and bring a wagon load of cut-up hard wood and while they're working, tell them what you need fixing," said Joseph. The young boys stood nearby and smiled.

Aunt Mae reached out to Wyllyam Daniels and pulled him to her. She smoothed his red hair, and patted him on the back. He smiled a big eight year old smile, and snuggled to her. "I just can't get over how big you're getting and how much more handsome you become every time I see you."

Wyllyam's green eyes held her gaze, and he smiled. "Mama says I'm gonna be the biggest and tallest when I grow up, cause I'm just like her daddy. He was tall and big."

"Well, that's the truth because you're so handsome now."

Wyllyam held her tightly around the waist. "Mama says you're the sweetest woman in the whole world!"

Aunt Mae smiled. "Thank you Wyllyam. You sure do know how to treat a woman." She looked toward Wyllyam's brothers, mischievously. "Need a chicken house repaired and need a new rabbit pen, and I have a lot of clothes that need to be boiled and hung on the line."

"To wash?" they screamed. When the young men realized they were being teased, they laughed out loud.

"The cut wood will be a mighty good gesture. Thank you!"

"Then it's the wood you'll get."

Being a good "horse-trader," Aunt Mae liked the "swap."

* * * *

The mule jogged along smoothly and easily. Aunt Mae took a long sweeping glance over the freshly raked yard and smiled as she remembered how badly strewn with junk cars it was the day she arrived, and how neat and trimmed it turned out to be after the big clean up. The Daniels' yard looked as if it had gone back to nature—except for the little cabin and barns. She looked back and waved as she faintly heard the Daniels and the Donahoo boys yell, "Bye, Healing Woman."

* * * *

"Fine dinner, Mae. I love your fried chicken and banana pudding," Doc Stowe complimented. He took a long drink of tea from his glass, and handed it to her.

"Oh, yes! It was outstanding!" Reverend Webster agreed. "You're a great cook."

"Thank you. Glad y'all enjoyed the dinner."

"Mae's a very good cook," said John McIntosh. "I love everything she makes."

"Mae, I went by the Daniel's place and checked on Mary yesterday. She's doing so well just applying your special ointment and treatment that I didn't change anything. What's really amazing is how comfortable she is. She is not in pain," said Doc Stowe.

"Glad she's improving so well."

"So am I," said Doc Stowe.

"Reverend Webster, we missed Locket being here with us. Will you tell her, please?"

"Locket will be sorry she missed this outing, but she has to go and visit her family in Atlanta from time to time."

"If you'll excuse me, I need to help Laughing Eyes and Caddie clear the table," said Aunt Mae.

"Doc Stowe, what you're saying about Mary not being in pain is amazing!" said Reverend Buker Webster. "You mean to tell me Aunt Mae makes herbal and root medicine that will knock people out and make them sleep? Medicine that takes away pain? She needs to try to get it patented, or whatever you do to make money."

Doc Stowe narrowed his dark brown eyes, and stared at him, "She doesn't charge."

"She doesn't make money on her healing," said Uncle Hume. "It's a gift from God."

"But she could make money if she charged! Doc Stowe, is it true that Aunt Mae's a faith-healer and can talk-out-fire. It's so interesting! Do you think it's mind over the physical that heals?" Reverend Webster questioned, being oblivious to his irritating manner. "Does she do incantations?"

"Preacher, laying-on-of-the hands and faith healing is old stuff here in these parts. We just accept it, and don't try to change it. Some people do it. Some don't. It's that simple."

"It's archaic and superstitious, isn't it? As a doctor, how do you handle it? Doesn't it bother you?"

"Doesn't bother me, at all. Apparently, it's bothering you?" he sniffed loudly, and crossed his legs deliberately.

"Doc Stowe, you use scientific medicine. How do you cope when other people like her, are doctoring, too? With herbs and grease and stuff?"

"I work around it and with it. Whatever works for the people is what's the best for them."

"Even though it's superstition?" Reverend Webster laughed sarcastically.

"Even though it might seem to be superstitious to you, it could be religious to someone else. Don't judge what you don't understand, sir. Best you stay with your preaching."

"I'm sorry. Guess I am getting too personal."

John McIntosh looked startled. He stood up and walked into the cabin. "Think I'll see what the women-folk are doing."

"Preacher, the people around here mind their own business. To be happy living here, you live by their code. Not yours." Doc Stowe left his rocking chair and walked into the yard with his hands in his pockets.

Jake arose from the door-steps where he sat, and walked hurriedly into the yard to join Doc Stowe.

"Uncle Hume, I believe I went too far with Doc Stowe," the Reverend apologized.

"Reverend Webster, Doc Stowe's one of our own. He understands how things are," said Uncle Hume. "It'd be best not to talk about Mae's gift. You best not talk about Mae to me at all."

"But, the occult is so interesting!" Reverend Webster continued.

"You'll find absolutely nothing occult about what Mae does. She's superstitious, all right, but her prayers go straight through to the throne. She's got her faults, but not enough it should bother you." Uncle Hume answered, gruffly.

"Sorry I offended you. I'm just curious—that's all. I think Aunt Mae's an awe-inspiring person. I didn't mean to alienate anyone, really." Reverend Webster stood up and stretched. "Guess I better be going."

*   *   *   *

That evening Reverend Webster sat at his desk in his study, bowed his head, and prayed:

Dear Mother—I went too far today. I must control my curiosity!

*   *   *   *

Aunt Mae dreamed a black crow flew over a freshly plowed field. It flapped its wings hard and furiously, made a nose-dive, hit the ground hard with its sharp beak, and bored its beak into the ground. It's black wings flapped and flapped. Its beak bored a hole, bigger and bigger. When she awoke, she remembered that someone in her dream exclaimed, *You've dreamed about another black bird! Oh! No! This is troublesome!*

The next morning, Uncle Hume noticed she hardly said a word. "Anything wrong, Mae?"

"I'll tell you after breakfast." She removed fried fat-back from an iron skillet, browned flour in the grease, added sweet milk, salt and pepper, and stirred it into a thickened, white gravy.

He observed her closely as she poured the steaming gravy from the iron skillet into a brown ceramic gravy bowl, and made no further comment.

After they ate breakfast in silence, Aunt Mae told him about her dream.

"What you make of it, Mae?"

"It's not good! It's not good! Why do I have such nightmares!"

"Mae, I'm not concerned about why you have the nightmares but the affect they seem to have on you. That's what bothers me—the affect."

Uncle Hume hated dreams.

*   *   *   *

Reverend Buker Webster sat in his office editing one of his publication papers entitled, "The Disciples of Death." He scratched through the word *Death* and changed it to ***Life.*** The marbled green fountain pen, trimmed in gold, became scratchy and ran out of ink. He re-filled the fountain pen with black India ink and laid it down upon his desk.

He walked to one of his many bookshelves filled with encyclopedias, theology books; sermons written by the most well-known scholars, books referencing occult practices, and best sellers. Novels and non-fiction. He chose a book, "Do the Spirits Communicate?" He sat down at his desk and began to read. When his eyes tired, he leaned his head on his hands and rubbed his temples. His thoughts and emotions became convoluted with the memories of his mother. *I wish you were here with me, Mother!*

Rain splattered the window panes and the wind rattled the shutters.

Mother, you spoiled me, pampered me, spoon fed me when I was sick, read the classics to me and entertained me all day long by teaching me constantly … mainly teaching me the things that interested you, but that was okay.

Mother, I remember when you combed my long, black hair around your fingers and made curly locks. I had no problem with wearing my hair in those long, girlish curly locks when I was at home, but the mean remarks of the boys and girls at school and their malicious and vicious attempts at humor really stung me, and hurt my feelings. I can't believe you allowed that to happen to me—your only child.

Buker Webster shook his head to remove those early childhood thoughts. He remembered how the children in the first grade called him, a *Sissy* and a *Mama's baby. I cried and ran away from the bullies' cat-calls. They threw rocks at me.*

He covered his ears, attempting to hush the children's cruelties—their chants.

The reality of his childhood encompassed his mind. *I was lonely then—lonely now. When I told daddy what the children did or said to me, he always said, 'I'm not here at home very much, so do what your mother says, Son.'*

Buker Webster smiled as he remembered with great affection the teacher who wrote a note to his mother:

"*Your son's hair must be clipped very neatly above the ears and neck. This is a school policy. Please cooperate in this matter. Our administrators don't want to file a complaint against you.*"

That note didn't make you conform, Mother, until I took drastic measures in my own hands. It was a horrible day when I chopped my own curls off with those dull scissors. You were furious with me, and just cried your eyes out! Said you'd never forgive me, but you took me to the barber shop and had him smooth the nicks out of my black curls. When I told you how the children called me ugly names and made my life miserable, you consented to my boy's haircut.

Mother, what was the teacher's name that wrote you the letter telling you to have my hair clipped? He pressed his head firmly and tried to squeeze out the name of his caring teacher. *I can visualize her face. She had thick, blond hair. She looked just like Locket. Yeah—she looked like Locket. O-o-oh! It makes me mad when I can't remember!*

I remember the time right after I had shorter hair, I began to have fewer problems with cat-calls, but I still had no friends. I studied hard under your supervision, Mother, and I retained many of the things you taught, and could repeat them well, but I don't remember things as well now, as I did then, and sometimes the names of people escape me.

"Where did my little precious baby-girl go?" You'd say. And you'd ruffle my hair, and hold me so tightly, I'd squirm.

He smiled as he reminisced.

You kissed me every day when I left home to go to school.

He touched his cheek and frowned.

When I got home at the end of the day I'd find those frilly pink lace dresses laid out on my bed along with a blond wig that had long, dainty curls. I love you, Mother, and wear the girls' clothes because obeying you makes you so happy.

I still remember our farm and that old Victorian-style home, south of Atlanta. It was white, lacy, and airy on the outside, but the inside was dark and rambling. It was spooky! I wonder who those night visitors were that set appointments for visitations, for séances, for palm and tarot card readings, and seeking a link between life and death. They came in and out of our house all hours of the day and night! I didn't want to leave our lifetime home when we went to Europe, but Mother, you never missed a beat! You advertised in the newspapers as "The Beautiful Madame Madras, with uncanny, and unbelievable powers," and took up where you left off in Georgia.

Oh! Mother, you're so charming and dear! People came from everywhere in the world to meet you as a medium, and a giver of hope to those seeking hope.

He laughed and rubbed his eyes. *Of course, you gave more hope to those who held the most money. I wish daddy had stayed home with us more and didn't have to go out of town for such long periods of time. I know he was a noted speaker, and went away to make money, but I was less afraid when he was home.*

That dank and dreary cellar that I sat in, or I should say that I waited in, was filled with flies and sometimes mosquitoes. It smelled musty and old. Is old a good word? Yes—old and boring. I was bored sitting all alone on a stool awaiting a signal—waiting for a light tap on the floor overhead that you made, Mother. I'd hear the knock you made with a walking cane, and I'd know you'd started the séance proceedings. While I waited for your signal, I caught flies and pulled off their wings and watched them as they writhed and struggled in their last living moments of life, and I'd pretend I could hear them scream. Now don't you scream, Mother, when you hear me reminisce about this. I know how you hate creepy things.

He smiled when he remembered how he burned their bodies with matches or squished them between his fingers.

The compartment in the cellar where I sat was directly under the dining room table. Mother, you remember daddy prepared an iron rod to go through the floor and into the middle supporting leg of the dining-room table? When I pushed the rod ever so slightly, the table moved. I'd raise the table 'til you were satisfied with the height, remember, Mother? Then, you'd tap-tap-tap on the floor with a walking cane. I loved doing the next stage of the game! I put on those girl things—those flowing gowns of white gauze, and walked gracefully and slowly throughout the rooms that adjoined the dining room, and give just enough time to allow those visitors a glimpse of the other world. I could hear the titter of their excited voices as they sat at the séance table, and glimpsed the other side! That nether world!

As I danced through the rooms, Daddy dimmed and dimmed the lighting. Daddy was so good at everything! Remember those illusions he formed with electricity and candle light, too. I could never understand where the reflections on the walls of those strange, creepy images of shadowy, eerie demon-like people and animals came from.

After the séance was over, I'd change into my boy's clothes and stand at the door with you and daddy, and I'd say good night to the guests. The people seemed to look through me as if under a spell. You'd introduce me as your only child and no one suspected the "girl-ghost" who skipped daintily throughout the rooms was me—Buker Webster—and not the visitor's own beloved, dead relative.

* * * *

The wind blew the rain hard against the window, and lightning flashed.

Buker Webster walked to the parsonage window and looked out. Lightning struck a tree close to the lake, and he thought of the beautiful lady walking at the lake that morning. *Was her name "Miranda? Miriam? No! No!* He closed the curtains, went back to his desk and sat down. He couldn't remember the beautiful lady's name, but he fantasized his most vivid and meaningful memory. He touched his smooth, moist lips with his index finger.

His face became hot and sweaty:

One day Mother (Madame Madras) sat on the veranda, which faced south and caught the rays of the sun. A vision of loveliness, a gorgeous woman, a regular visitor, sat across from Mother at a square, metal table. A crystal ball sat in the middle of the table, along with tarot cards spread in a traditional formation.

The beautiful lady's greenish-blue eyes were unforgettable. I loved the way her dark, wavy black hair hung down to her waist. She was always so kind and sweet and always spoke very gently.

It was summertime. I hid in the room next to the veranda, as close to the open window as I could get and I could hear Mother and the beautiful lady talking very distinctly.

"Now, first of all," Madame Madras said, "if the law comes tell them you're here to purchase some turnip greens, you hear? My husband's picking the greens, as we speak, and that's just in case the law should come. The law does not hold lightly to fortune-telling or tarot cards, you see?"

"I understand," the beautiful lady said.

"Did you remember to bring what I told you to bring with you?" Madame Madras asked.

"Yes. Here is a paper sack and an egg is inside, just like you said to do."

"Now, my dear, did you remember to place your husband's handkerchief around the egg, before you placed it in the sack?"

"Why, yes I did! You know, Madame Madras, I felt so funny doing this. It felt sort of like I was cheating on my husband, when I did what you asked me to do. Getting his handkerchief, you know!" She giggled nervously.

Madame Madras shuffled the tarot cards and laid them on the table. "What do you want to ask? What do you want to know?"

"I want to know—I want to know the name of the woman, he's cheating on me with!" The beautiful lady stammered.

"Cut the cards."

The beautiful lady touched the cards.

Madame Madras got up and held the paper sack to her forehead, and walked back and forth on the porch, as she talked. "Is black your natural hair-color, my dear? It's so lovely!" She walked behind the beautiful lady, and snipped a small piece of her long, black hair with a concealed pair of scissors. It was so fast no one would have believed it! She placed the lock of hair inside the paper sack, just as fast, while she paced.

I sat very still and real close to the window. I held my breath, fearing the beautiful lady could hear me breathe. I pushed my back tightly to the wall and listened intently. Madame Madras sat back down in a rocking chair next to the table. "My dear, you're such a lovely lady. So lovely! Are you sure your husband is unfaithful?"

"Yes, yes," she said. She lowered her humiliated voice and I envisioned that she closed her saddened eyes.

Madame Madras placed the paper sack on the table in front of the beautiful lady and said, "Make your wish."

I peeped around and saw the lady open her eyes and she appeared to hold her breath.

"Now, my dear, you must crush the egg in the paper sack. Hit it very hard! Hit it with your fist, very hard!" Madame Madras insisted dramatically.

The beautiful lady struck the sack very hard, and the small table wobbled under the impact.

"Hand the sack to me, my dear." Madame Madras reached her hand out for the sack, placed it in front of her, pulled the sack apart exaggeratedly, and revealed the broken egg soaking through the handkerchief and paper sack. She unfolded the inside of the white handkerchief to reveal the broken shell, smeared yellow yolk and translucent white, surrounding the snippet of black hair that she had secretly clipped from the beautiful lady's hair and inserted into the handkerchief.

The lady began to scream, "What is it? What is it? What is that ugly, black thing in the egg?"

I peeped out again and saw the lady immediately begin to rub her shoulder and arm. She stared at the lock of black hair, mixed in a yellowish slime oozing from the paper sack.

"Why, it's a sign of the demon you carry in you, my child. See the black hair. It's a part of a demon. We have some of the demon's hair here, my dear, but we did not get the entire demon," and Madame Madras settled back in her chair and rocked slightly. "We'll have to do this again."

"A demon! A demon! How? How could this be? I'm a good person!" The beautiful lady stared in horror at the paper bag and its contents and continued to rub her left arm and hand.

"My dear, you need to be treated for the demon within you first of all, and, then, and only then, upon its disbursement and leaving your body totally will we know the secret you need to know. The name of your husband's lover will be shown to us at the time the demon is removed from your body. The knowledge you seek will be revealed to us immediately upon your cure of the demon."

"A demon lives in me? Something so horrible lives in my body! What can I do?" Oh! No!" She held her hand over her mouth, bit her knuckles, and held her stomach.

"My dear, you must come to me every week at this same time for a while. Do you have any money?"

"Only a little. A little," she murmured. "My husband would kill me if he knew I was spending his money like this."

"But, my dear, you can not tell him, can you?"

"No! No! Madame Madras! My husband must not know!" She gasped. "He mustn't know!"

"I will give you a good price for my services, my dear, because you have been such a faithful customer. I want you to be rid of this demon that is destroying you." Madame Madras sympathized. "Do you want to bury this part of the demon in the graveyard? Or do you want me to bury it for you? If you choose to bury this part of the demon in the cemetery, you must do it tonight at midnight." She held the brown paper sack towards the lady.

The beautiful lady held her breast and cried out. She rubbed her left arm and hand and screamed, "I am in terrible pain! The demon must be overtaking me! My arm is numb!"

"My dear, you mustn't cry out so loudly. I'll get you some refreshment." Madame Madras stared at her customer intently, and arose from her chair.

Suddenly, the beautiful lady toppled over towards the table. Madame Madras screamed, "Buker! Help me, Buker. This lady's having a spell! Help me!"

I rushed outside to Mother and helped the beautiful woman lie down upon a white wicker lounge. Her head rested upon a large pink rose and her long, black hair flowed upon the design of green leaves.

Mother ran to the telephone, called a doctor, and rushed back to the side of the beautiful lady. "My dear, the doctor will be here soon." She gazed keenly at her customer, and quickly removed the paper sack that held a part of the demon. "Buker, stay with her and I'll find your father. He's probably in the garden or the cellar!" Mother ran back into the house.

The beautiful lady gasped.

I looked around and upon seeing no one in sight, I touched the beautiful lady's long, dark hair that I had secretly desired to touch for so long. I stroked her hair, and assured her, "It'll be okay. It'll all be okay." The beautiful lady stopped breathing. I kissed her upon her cheek and then the lips. "Breathe! Breathe!" I begged. She became very still.

When the doctor came, he pushed Mother and me and my father aside, and began to examine her. "Let me get to this lady!"

"Why, the lady just fell over, while we were chatting, that's all. She came to get turnip greens. Here is the sack!" Mother brought the large paper sack of greens for the doctor to see.

As the doctor worked with the beautiful lady, I noticed the crystal ball upon the table reflecting one of the tarot cards. It magnified the Hanged Man, wearing a red tuxedo jacket and black tights. Just as I became somewhat hypnotized by the reflection,

Mother quickly removed the crystal ball and the tarot cards, and took them into the house.

When the Sheriff arrived, he demanded to know the reason for the beautiful lady being at their home. "What has happened here?"

Mother insisted the beautiful lady came to our house to purchase turnip greens. "By the way, the sack is still sitting here." She reached down on the veranda, and picked up a sack filled with turnip greens and attempted to hand the sack to the Sheriff. "You may have the turnip greens free, now that the lady won't be buying them."

The Sheriff refused the sack.

I was afraid everyone would know I kissed her, and I left the porch and went to my room.

The beautiful lady died shortly after entering the hospital.

The next night about midnight, I sneaked over to the funeral parlor, and entered an unlocked basement window. I found the lady lying on a marble slab next to a coffin. When I heard people talking and walking upstairs, I became very quiet. I smoothed her hair. I touched my lips to her cold face, her cold lips. I was fourteen years old when I had my first encounter with the dead.

The paper reported that an autopsy was held on the beautiful lady, and it was determined that she had a history of heart problems. My parents were relieved to hear that this was not her first attack.

And, then, immediately after the occurrence of the beautiful lady's death, Mother and Father decided to go on an extended vacation. We toured all over Europe, beginning with Paris. I can't remember much about Europe.

* * * *

It was Saturday, and a work day at the church. Some of the young men met under an old oak tree behind the meeting house. They leaned on their rakes, whispered to each other, and laughed boisterously in their camaraderie.

In the meantime, a few of the Elders met at the old rock well at the side of the church, shared a common gourd dipper, and drank cool water together. They talked about feed, livestock, draught and their need to fill the pulpit with a more dynamic preacher. "We need to discuss a plan of action to be rid of Buker Webster," said Elder One.

"Yeah," Elder Two replied.

"He's too scientific—reading encyclopedias and stuff in the pulpit, you know. Not talking about the bible at all, you know," answered Elder One.

"Yeah—where's the gospel?" asked Elder Three.

"Not a good preacher at all. He's a queer man—strange I'd say!" insisted Elder One.

"Not a bit consoling to people at a time of death or in their other troubles," Elder Four chimed in.

"Naw, not at all," said Elder Two.

"Can't carry on a decent conversation," Elder one added. "He asks too many questions to suit me."

"Acts bored," said Elder Four.

"Yeah, he tries to be uppity and all," stated Elder Three.

"Don't need anyone like this Reverend Webster" said Elder Two.

"George-West Myers would not want to hear that the church folks want to get rid of him," said Elder One.

"He wouldn't want to have to pay more money to get someone else," said Elder Four.

"Where is the preacher right now?" asked Elder Three.

"Hiding I guess. Or he might be polishing one of his fancy cars in his garage. Wonder where he got so much money?" Elder One responded.

"Somebody said he's got inherited money. Got it when his folks died," said Elder Two.

"He's sure not working here with us cleaning up the church and the church yard."

"Look!" Elder Two pointed his finger towards the lake.

The Elders looked where the pointed finger guided them and observed Reverend Buker Webster standing alone, and from time to time skipping a stone on the water.

"What's he doing over at the lake by himself?" asked Elder Two. "He's wading in the water and stuff. Suppose he's practicing for a baptism?"

"God only knows," laughed Elder Three.

"We're standing here talking about the preacher and just look at us! We've reneged on our own work long enough. Let's get back to fixing the meeting house," said Elder Four.

The cherry wood walls and pews of the chapel gleamed after a hard polishing by the ladies of the church. Pewter vases holding wildflowers sat on mahogany tables at the front and the back of the church.

Dogwood tree limb brooms made a "swishing" sound as some of the ladies joined the young men and raked the church yard. The squeals of happy children running and playing echoed in the valley and blended well with the progressive sounds of sawing and hammering. While some of the ladies swept and dusted the meeting house, others prepared lunch under the large oak trees in the churchyard. They sang as they worked, "When We All Get to Heaven—"

Aunt Mae and Laughing Eyes dusted the wooden picnic tables with damp cloths.

Aunt Mae turned around and almost bumped into Judge Pewter. "Sorry Judge Pewter. I'm clumsy."

"I would never call you *clumsy.* Say, Mae, how's the family?"

"Still wondering where Dan is, but we're getting along as well as can be expected. No letter—no word of any kind from Dan," she responded.

"How's Caddie taking everything since she returned home?" he quizzed.

"Caddie's a miracle worker. Don't know what we'd do without her. Helps us in the field and with Henny-Penny and Kackie. She stays busy all the time. She's down at the "Pewter-Mapps Little Store" right now buying nails for the men to repair the meeting house."

"I need to see her right away."

"All right. I'll tell Caddie." She tried to determine what he would need with Caddie. "How are you and Matilda getting along, Judge Pewter?"

"Matilda and I are fine. She's gone to Atlanta to her social club this evening. Be back late tomorrow."

"Give Matilda my regards," said Aunt Mae.

"Mae, listen, I'd like to talk to Caddie about working in my office."

"Glory be!"

"Bess is expecting, you know, and she's not planning on coming back to work after the baby is born. Her husband wants her to stay at home."

Aunt Mae smiled so broadly, the crinkles almost closed her bright blue eyes.

"Bess said she'll be glad to show Caddie around the office and get her acquainted with my work. Wonder if Caddie wants to get back into a law office?"

"I can't believe you're telling me this! I'd hope she would want to get back to work in an office! Caddie had business school, and worked for those lawyers in Atlanta."

"Yes, and they speak well of Caddie. Anytime will be fine, but just tell her to see me soon." His eyes twinkled. "Be nice for Caddie to have a job so close to home, wouldn't it, Mae?"

"Oh! Yes! A Godsend."

"It'd be a Godsend for me, too, Mae."

He tipped his gray felt hat, and walked away.

Aunt Mae watched him walk towards the lake. "Thank you, Jesus!" she laughed.

Laughing Eyes hugged her friend, "The Lord has His hand in this!" she exclaimed.

Uncle Hume walked up behind them, and grinned. "What was on the Judge's mind?"

"A miracle, Hume! A miracle!

* * * *

Aunt Mae stood on the church house porch, holding Benjamin, while she talked to Hannah.

George-West Myers passed them and lifted his felt hat, "Howdy, Mae. Howdy little boy."

Aunt Mae noticed that he kept his head lowered and avoided looking at Hannah, and passed them hurriedly.

Jessie Myers came immediately behind her husband. She sniffed at Hannah, and flounced her head as she glanced at Benjamin. "Aunt Mae, what piece of trash is this you hold?" She pointed at Benjamin and snickered. "A piece of trash—" She held her fist under her jaw and preened. Her large diamonds flashed gold, blue and sparkling wealth.

"I'm holding a treasure—can't you see. I was just telling Benjamin how lucky he is that God created him to be so handsome!" Aunt Mae patted his strawberry blond hair. Benjamin stared at Jessie Myers through innocent sky-blue eyes, framed by perfectly arched, white eyebrows.

"A piece of trash, and you know it, Mae," she hissed. "To think I came to you and asked for a favor! You refused me, but you cater to this—this trash!" She raised her head haughtily and passed.

Benjamin instinctively grabbed Aunt Mae around the neck and held her tightly.

Tears came into Hannah's eyes. "Why is she so mean to him? Benjamin is just a little baby."

"Ignore that remark, Hannah," said Aunt Mae. "Jessie is mad at me about something I wouldn't do."

They walked towards Caddie and Jake. "Caddie, Hannah needs company while I take Benjamin for a walk."

They stood together and observed Aunt Mae as she walked into the woods with Benjamin, down a winding path which led to a spring. She stopped and pointed at a wild-flower.

"Aunt Mae's showing Benjamin all kinds of things and talking to him, just like she would if he was a big boy." Hannah fluffed her carrot-red hair, highlighted by the gold of the shimmering sunset, and uncovered large ears that fit close to her head.

Jake touched Hannah on the shoulder. She turned and looked towards him and smiled.

"Hannah, don't you remember your walks with Aunt Mae?" Jake picked a honeysuckle from its vine, bit the end of the blossom, and sucked the sweet juice.

Hannah blinked solemn gray-green eyes. "Yes, I do remember but things are different now that I have Benjamin. Sometimes I forget this world still has kind people." She looked wistfully towards a group of men standing behind the church. Her lower lip pouted.

Caddie followed her eyes, wondering which *gentleman* her eyes sought. Hannah's wistful look and sigh told her she apparently loved someone standing in that group that did not love her back.

"I'm really worried about how ugly Jessie Myers treated Aunt Mae because of me. I'm sure it hurt her feelings," Hannah lamented.

"Aunt Mae can handle herself." Jake reached for another honeysuckle blossom.

"I can't believe she spoke so cruelly in front of Benjamin. He's a precious little boy," said Hannah.

When Aunt Mae brought Benjamin back to Hannah, he clung to Aunt Mae.

"Tae! Tae!" Benjamin called. When Hannah took Benjamin into her arms, he jumped and lunged, and leaned towards Aunt Mae.

Aunt Mae smiled, and patted him on the back.. "Benjamin, I'll be back and play with you later." She kissed him on the cheek and walked hurriedly towards The Meeting Tree.

Immediately upon being seated on the bench at The Meeting Tree, most of the little children ran to her, and yelled, "Aunt Mae's waiting for us to play! Aunt Mae's at The Meeting Tree!"

Aunt Mae laughed and stood up. She held her finger to her lips. When the children became very quiet, she led them into the woods.

*   *   *   *

After the activities were over at the church, Reverend Buker Webster held Locket's elbow, and guided her towards the parsonage. "Buker, you're such a put-on! You have no compassion, no empathy and no desire whatsoever to change. How can you keep on fooling all these people?"

"Hush! Someone might hear you," he said under his breath. He clinched his heavy jaw and narrowed his yellow-gray eyes into slits.

"We need to decide what to do about our marriage—or our so-called marriage!"

"Locket, I'm content the way everything is. Why should I change? I have what I want. You should have no complaints. Especially since I don't bother you." His face twisted in disgust.

"But, you do bother me—" Locket tried to pull her arm away from his vice-like grip on her elbow, but he held her tighter.

He spoke very sternly under his breath, and looked straight ahead. "I'm your husband and you'll do as I say. Someone could be looking at us right now this minute, and see you snatch your arm away. Don't do that again. I intend to hold your arm until we get to the front porch. Then, I'll turn it lose," he uttered between gritted teeth.

"Buker, you're so different from the days before we married. You were gentle, and entertaining. Now, I realize that I've never really known you at all. And, I have no idea what you're thinking."

"I'm thinking I am very content with the way things are. By the way, so are you," he growled.

"No, Buker. I'm not content. I don't like to hurt your feelings, but you have a double personality—you're a preacher one hour in the church—in the pulpit—and someone else the next. You are nothing like the man I married!"

"No, I'm not a double personality! I'm who I am!" he whispered.

"Well, if you are not a double personality, Buker, then who are you?"

* * * *

The cicadas sang a song of summer's ending.

Aunt Mae joined the children on the wide back porch, where they were playing paper-dolls from cut-out Sears Roebuck Catalog pictures. "You've been so good, we're gonna have a tea-party."

Uncle Hume came in smiling. "Looks festive, like some kind of a celebration or a party. What's the occasion?" The table was set with her handsome, most prized tea set.

"It's a surprise."

"A surprise," he asked.

"Yes, it's a celebration."

"Now, Hume, you know it's not our anniversary or anything." Aunt Mae smiled sweetly.

He sighed with relief, learning he had not forgotten an important date. "What's the surprise? What? What?" His eyes twinkled mischievously. "You can't fool me," he drawled.

"You're the bestest teacake maker in the whole wide world, Aunt Mae!" exclaimed Henny-Penny. She and Kackie jumped in their chairs with excitement.

"Let's be ladies. Please place your napkin in your lap. Hold your cups still, very quietly and properly." They obeyed Aunt Mae's instructions.

After they ate their teacakes and drank their tea, Aunt Mae said, "Let's all go and sit on the back porch." She poured tea in a cup, diluted it with water, and placed the cup and a teacake on a saucer. "Come with me!"

"Do we get to see the surprise now?" Henny-Penny and Kackie asked.

"You will see it now." Aunt Mae removed the hanging bird cage from its hook, set it on a table, removed the bird from its cage, and placed it on the table beside the cup and saucer. "Come, Sparkle Sparrow. Have some tea and teacakes!"

Sparkle Sparrow dunked his beak into the cup and drank. Then, he pecked at the teacake which she held in her hand. The bird turned its head from side to side and blinked.

"Look! His eyes are blinking," said Henny-Penny. She caressed the bird on the tail.

"Blink! Blink!" Kackie blinked her eyes and laughed.

The sparrow perched on Aunt Mae's finger, turned its head from side to side, observed, listened, and listened, as she crooned. "Don't be afraid, Sparkle Sparrow." The bird stretched and fluttered its wings.

"Look! He's winking at us!"

"Henny-Penny, you and Kackie need to say goodbye to Sparkle Sparrow."

"We want to keep him! He's our pet!"

"No! We have to turn him loose." Aunt Mae caught herself before she added the words, "He needs to go to his mother!" She balanced the bird steadily on her finger, and walked carefully down the rock stairwell. When the family gathered around her at the foot of the steps, she lifted her hand swiftly toward the sky and the sparrow flew high into the air.

Henny-Penny and Kackie waved at the sparrow, "Bye, Sparkle Sparrow. Bye-Bye-Bye!" They jumped up and down, giggling and yelling, "He's well! He's well! He can fly!"

Sparkle Sparrow flew high, high into the sky. But, suddenly, the bird made a dip towards the cabin.

"He's coming back down to tell us goodbye," Kackie yelled. She jumped up and down and pointed towards Sparkle Sparrow.

Just as quickly, the bird ascended and soared. Then, it was gone.

"Oh, No!" Henny-Penny screamed. "He's gone! Gone! Gone forever and ever!"

"Don't cry, Henny-Penny." Tears streamed down Kackie's face, but she placed her consoling arms around her sister. "Don't cry."

Uncle Hume rested his hands on Henny-Penny's and Kackie's shoulders. "There, there! It's gonna be all right," he whispered.

"You did it, Aunt Mae! You did it! Sparkle Sparrow can fly! You made him well!" Caddie yelled.

Aunt Mae placed her hand on her forehead and peered into the sky. "Yes! Can he ever fly!"

A feeling of homesickness overcame Uncle Hume. "Well, I'll declare!" He removed a handkerchief from his hip pocket, and wiped his face. "I'll declare!" he whispered. He gazed into the sky and observed the bird fly higher and higher, and Macie's words came to mind*: Carry me on wings to heights and depths, only you will ever see.*

* * * *

As Rob-Hunter Daniels rode up the path, he screamed, "Aunt Mae! Doc Stowe couldn't do nothing for Ratchel. Her neck's broke," he cried. "You can heal her. Please help her!"

"Ratchel, dead? How? How?" Aunt Mae's knees buckled under her and she held onto the gate. Anxiety pains hit her in the stomach.

"Ratchel fell in that old well at the clothesline! Come, quick, please! You can heal her!" He held both his hands out to her pleadingly. "Doc Stowe said her neck is broke and she's dead, but mama and daddy said for you to come quick and heal her!"

"If Ratchel's dead, there's nothing I can do—nothing, Rob-Hunter, except go to your mother." Her body trembled but she held on to him, and attempted to console him.

"But, you're *The Healing Woman*," he howled.

"Caddie, help me get ready to go to the Daniels' house, please. Then, go to the parsonage and tell Reverend Webster and Locket that the Daniels' need them.

"I'll saddle the mule, Mae," said Uncle Hume. "I'll look after things here." He wiped the tears from Aunt Mae's eyes and held her tightly.

"Hume—it's gonna be awful over there. You heard what Rob-Hunter said. They think I have healing powers—enough to bring Ratchel back from the dead!"

"Gonna be rough on you. Mae, but Doc Stowe's over there at the cabin. You're gonna be all right."

* * * *

When Aunt Mae arrived, Mary ran out of the cabin, wringing her hands and crying out, "I knowed you'd come and heal her!" She looked into the faces of Mary, Joseph Daniels, and the young men—faces seeking hope—hope and faith that Ratchel would be okay, right now—now that *The Healing Woman* had arrived.

Doc Stowe held her elbow firmly and guided her into the cabin. "Mae, Ratchel's neck is broken. She's dead." His sadness weakened her.

"I told Rob-Hunter I couldn't heal her. That I'd come over here to be with his mother—the family," she said. They walked to Ratchel's bedside. "Rob-Hunter doesn't believe me."

"Mae, they didn't want me to cover her face with a sheet. The Daniels are looking for a miracle," said Doc Stowe.

"Doc, this is so horrific!" She held on to the iron bed-stead.

"Heal her! You can make her well, Healing Woman!" Mary Daniels pleaded.

"Doc Stowe's done all he can," she whispered. She gazed upon the unbreathing, lovely girl lying on the bed. She appeared to be asleep but no sleeping girl would have clumps of red mud streaked in her long, blond hair. Aunt Mae reached down for the sheet.

"No! No! Don't cover her face! Please heal her, Healing Woman!" Mary begged. "Don't cover her face."

Aunt Mae could hear Joseph and the young men mumbling under their breath. "If only she'd lay hands on her! She could heal her! Lay hands on her! Bring her back!"

"Only God can give life," Aunt Mae whispered.

"No!" Mary screamed.

"I'll help you bathe Ratchel, and get her ready for the undertaker, Mary."

A white, blue-eyed cat, with three black paws and one yellow one, jumped from the loft onto the bed. Mary and Aunt Mae screamed.

Doc Stowe took the cat outside, and returned to stand between them.

As the young men left the room, Aunt Mae heard the mumbled words, *Healing Woman.*

Rob Hunter lamented, "It's my fault. I should have clumb down in that ole well faster, and got to Ratchel Robin quicker. Daddy says I'm the fastest climber in the whole bunch!"

"No!" said Tinker. "It's not anybody's fault! The old well caved in! Being quicker to get to her wouldn't have helped. She was already dead."

Doc Stowe patted her on the arm. "Mae, how about me making us some coffee?"

"That cat jumping on the bed unnerved me. Coffee sounds fine, Doc, fine," she sighed.

Joseph Daniels stood in the middle of the floor, never moving the whole time they spoke, "I told Mary it was in God's hands!" He walked across the room and opened a cupboard. "Doc, let's have something stronger than coffee!" He set a crock-jug upon the table.

"Joseph, I don't like to tell anyone what to do, but let me tell you this. Seeking consolation in that jug just makes everything worse. You know it, and I know it." Doc got a cup from one of the apple crate shelves, uncorked the jug, poured Joseph a drink, re-corked the jug, as he talked, and placed it back into the cupboard. "Now, let that be it! Listen, Joseph, you and the boys have a lot of work to do."

The odor of moonshine permeated the room.

"Whatcha mean, Doc? Me and the boys have some work to do?"

"That abandoned well Ratchel fell into has to be filled up, and marked." Doc patted Joseph on the back. "Now, where's that coffee?" He poured Aunt Mae and Mary a cup of coffee, and carried a cup and the coffee pot with him to the back porch.

As Aunt Mae watched Doc Stowe leave the cabin, she wondered how he could continuously cope with birthing and dying. *Why is my wonderful Ratchel gone—so young—just starting in life—never a misdeed—so good! Why? Why did she have to die?"*

"Mary, will the body remain at the funeral parlor? asked Aunt Mae.

"Joseph and I will ask the undertaker to bring her back home."

Aunt Mae looked into the bedroom wardrobes until she found a "Sunday" dress she had seen Ratchel wear many times. "Mary, do you want me to press this dress for Ratchel?"

Mary nodded.

"Mary, you losing Ratchel makes me remember my Mandy," said Aunt Mae.

"Lordy, I remember that sad day, Mae. I just realized you understand how I feel and know how I'm suffering. God gave Ratchel to us a lot of enjoyable days here on this earth. You never had one day with Mandy. Not one live minute—not one day."

"Yes, it's hard to lose a child," Aunt Mae sighed, and wiped her eyes on her apron.

"Two of your daughters are dead—Mandy and Macie. I know you must understand how I feel."

"Yes, Mandy, Macie and now Ratchel," Aunt Mae whispered.

"But, Mae, you seem to take all the children, everywhere, into your heart. I guess it helps to fill that empty spot. I guess what I'm trying to say is this, Mae. I believe a lot of substitute Mandy's have been in your life. Since Mandy died, I believe a lot of lucky Mandy's have had the privilege of knowing you."

Aunt Mae stared into Mary's eyes, and realized her wisdom. She had never admitted to herself that she searched for Mandy in the company of all the little children.

* * * *

Aunt Mae nudged Uncle Hume, and pointed towards Reverend Webster, standing in the Daniel's front room taking photographs of Ratchel in the coffin. "I can't figure out why anyone would ever want a picture of somebody dead. It's hard enough to forget the death scene, as it is."

Uncle Hume glanced around the crowded room filled with the Daniel's relatives and neighbors, and lowered his voice. "Lots of people want those pictures and hold tight to them, but I'm glad we don't want any pictures of dead people." He rubbed his chin and observed Reverend Buker Webster as he became the center of attention while taking photographs of Ratchel. He was handsome dressed in a dark blue suit and tie and white shirt. He noticed that the preacher's dress shoes were shined, which was so unlike him, and he wondered for how long.

Uncle Hume walked over to Locket Webster, who stood alone in the middle of the floor. "Locket, you're looking well."

"Thank you, Uncle Hume. You're always so kind and such a gentlemen."

He offered her his arm. "Locket, how's about some coffee and cake? Mae makes the best pound cake in the world, and I'm about to look for her box. How's about it?"

She smiled and took his arm. She nodded towards her husband. "Uncle Hume, don't her parents mind that Buker is taking pictures of Ratchel?"

"Locket, some people seem to be very pleased to have a picture of their loved one when he's laid out in a coffin. Everything suddenly becomes more important about that person who just died. You'd be surprised how many here in this cabin that don't have a picture of their relatives, except the ones taken at a wake. Some of them are grateful and want those pictures." He looked down into her innocent-looking blue eyes. Little wisps of golden curls swirled about her face. "Locket, let's you and me get our coffee!"

* * * *

Reverend Buker Webster read his repetitive funeral sermon at Ratchel Robin Daniels' graveside service. The significant words of *Amazing Grace* and the loud thuds of thick, red clay hitting the coffin echoed throughout the graveyard.

After the service, Reverend Webster shook hands with the Daniels family. He squeezed Mary Daniels' hand. "I must come by and talk to you about your lovely daughter. I know words don't make up for the loss of Ratchel, but talking might help."

* * * *

The Daniels' boys stood together beside their parents, and from time to time they glanced sullenly at Aunt Mae.

Aunt Mae observed them and wished there were something she could do to help them. *To think that some people believe I have powers to heal people and bring them back from the dead is scary. Don't they know that I'm grieving, too? Ratchel had a way of getting close to our hearts. More than likely, she has never harmed a soul in the world, but God saw fit to take her—young. God took Mandy before she had a chance to live at all. Some of the meanest folks I've ever known lived to be old. I wonder why? How does God make that distinction?*

Uncle Hume stood beside Aunt Mae while she laid a bouquet of varied wild flowers upon Ratchel's and Macie's graves.

She walked to Mandy's grave, and stood quietly fingering the locket which held a lock of Mandy's auburn hair. She laid a small bouquet of wild purple and white flowers in front of her tombstone, which was inscribed: "Mandy, We Will Walk with You in Heaven Some Sweet Day."

Uncle Hume placed his arm around her waist, and as he turned her away from Mandy's gravesite, Aunt Mae pointed towards the invisible world at the Taylor plot, where the ghost of three-year old Billy Taylor played on his wild flower laden swing.

* * * *

Aunt Mae held Henny-Penny and Kackie by the hand, and walked along the path. Suddenly, she freed their hands and pointed to a toad-frog sticking its head out of a hole near a rotten tree trunk. She motioned for Tommy and Bobby to join them.

"Sh-h-h," she hushed. She placed a finger to her lips.

She walked cautiously up to where the toad looked out from its hiding place, and squatted down. "Little toad in the hole, camouflaged from the world, why do you hide?"

The toad blinked its eyes nervously.

"We're all toads camouflaged against the world. We won't hurt you," she crooned.

The toad blinked.

"See he understood me. He winked at us!"

The children laughed.

"What does camouflage mean?" asked Kackie.

"It means 'disguise.' The toad is disguised, so he'll blend into his surroundings."

"I want to pet him." Bobby reached his hand towards the frog.

"Will it bite me?" Henny-Penny asked. She squatted down beside Aunt Mae, and stuck out her finger.

"No, actually, it looks a little shy. We've intimidated the little toad."

"I want to hold him," said Bobby.

"No! Let it be," Aunt Mae whispered.

"Let it be," Henny-Penny mocked, and laughed.

The toad hopped into a bed of leaves. Aunt Mae shoved the leaves away from the toad-frog, picked it up between finger and thumb, and held it under the arm-pits. It dangled in an undignified way.

The frog belched.

The children laughed.

"I want me a toad-frog for a pet," said Henny-Penny.

"We need to leave him here at his own home." When Aunt Mae smiled, the wrinkles and the crinkles almost hid her blue eyes.

She placed her index finger to her puckered lips, and the children became very quiet. "Listen! Listen to the gentle humming of the pine trees swaying in the wind. The woods are alive with lots of critters and flowers and energy."

"I hear something humming in the wind, and feel the breeze, and I can hear that little frog," said Tommy.

"When you really listen, you can hear the whisper of God," Aunt Mae smiled.

Henny-Penny lowered her voice, and attempted to whisper. "How will I know that it's God whispering,"

"You will hear His voice in the gentle breezes, and you'll feel a tug in your heart." She clutched the bib of her starched, sky blue apron and wadded it in her right hand.

A black widow ran under a rotten tree trunk to join termites, sour-bugs and other creepy, clammy things. Spiders in their webs, hanging overhead, watched closely. The sound of a woman's chuckles and the giggles and laughter of the children was foreign to the "critters," but their sounds blended well with the other noises of the woods. The song of the wind filtered the treble of the rays of the sun, through the trees, leaving a whispering, soft, gentle lingering sound. It was a haunting in the mind—as haunting as an unfinished waltz. Its tune? It's tune?

* * * *

Henny-Henny-Penny and Kackie sat on the doorsteps holding Shadows and Spooky. Locket handed them two small, straw baskets full of cookies. "I baked some teacakes, just for y'all." They threw the cats down and reached for the baskets.

"Wash your hands before you touch the teacakes, Babies." Aunt Mae beamed.

"Come in, Locket. You're a sight for sore eyes. Let me make some tea."

"May I join you in the kitchen, while you prepare the tea, please? I like to see how you do things."

"Of course, you can, if you'll ignore my untidy kitchen."

"Your house is immaculate, Aunt Mae. I don't see how you do all that you do."

"I have a lot of help!" Aunt Mae went to a cupboard and removed her china teapot and cups to match. "This tea set has been in my family for a couple of generations."

Locket touched the pink, and white flowers with green leaves, and scrolled her fingers around the gnarled, green vines of one of the teacups. "How exquisite and charming." She was enchanted by the kitchen, which had only shutters, no windowpanes, and no electricity. "I love this stone fireplace. It's almost tall enough for me to walk inside!"

While Aunt Mae prepared a delightful mint tea from her herb collection, Locket read aloud the labels on the little jars that set on a kitchen shelf: "Mint, Sassafras, Sage, Sunflower Seeds, Basil, Holly-Hock, Bay, Parsley, Thyme, Mixtures, Dried Jimson Weed, Maypop, Mistletoe, Comfrey, Morning Glory, Dandelion Root, and Dandelion Seeds."

"I like the way you do things, and if I might ask, Aunt Mae, what are the long, stringy-looking things hanging on the fireplace?" She touched them and they rattled.

"Why that's Leather-Britches! You know, dried green beans. Next time I cook some, I'll bring you a dish."

"Amazing! What a quaint name—*Leather Britches*?"

Locket walked into the front room, stood before an easel and observed one of Aunt Mae's oil paintings. Two little girls sat at a child's table and chairs, under the drooping limbs of a Weeping Willow tree. Upon that table sat a miniature teapot and cups, exactly like the one in Aunt Mae's kitchen, and exactly like the one she had just caressed. A beautiful woman with long, dark brown hair, apparently playing hide-and-seek stood behind the tree and peeped out at the children. Her very transparent, delicate wings gave the illusion of an angel. "Aunt Mae, this is such a lovely painting! Please tell me what you were thinking as you painted."

"Well, I thought I'll paint a Weeping Willow tree with its head a-bowing, and then I said, O, Willow Tree, lift your head. You're just a *drawing*!" She chuckled.

Locket realized she was being teased and brightened. "Do you talk to everyone and everything, including inanimate objects?"

"Everything is as important as we make it. That painting is as alive as I choose to make it. Yes, I talked to that tree, to that angel, and everything in that picture, and it came to life!"

"I knew it. I just knew it," Locket smiled. "The lady in the painting is Macie, isn't it?"

"Yes. It's my Macie looking out for her babies."

Aunt Mae caught a glimpse of despondency in Locket eyes. She noticed that the expression of sadness in Locket's eyes went away as suddenly as it appeared.

When Locket started to depart and they embraced, she held onto Aunt Mae a little longer than usual. Aunt Mae looked into Locket's eyes again, and saw so clearly the unhappiness in the young woman's soul that her heart gave a saddened pang of empathy. "Locket, you know I love you. We all love you."

Aunt Mae walked in step with Locket a short distance. Pegg came floating by them, as if he knew they needed a distraction.

"Pegg's so comical," Locket smiled.

"Yes! Pegg is a joy."

"I loved every minute. Tell Uncle Hume and Caddie hello for me!"

* * * *

When Locket got to the first bend in the path, she stopped, looked back and waved.

Aunt Mae held Pegg under one arm and waved with the other.

* * * *

It was "Old-Fashioned Day" at the church house.

Uncle Hume hitched a team of mules to a wagon, while the family completed the finishing touches on their Ole-timey dresses and bonnets that mimicked days gone by. He came into the kitchen and picked up a large basket filled with food. "Boy, howdy, this food smells so good, I think I'll eat before we leave!" He set the basket down, and rubbed his skinny and bony hands together.

"Hume, if you keep eating, you're going to be as big as this cabin!"

He placed the basket in the back of the wagon. "Hope it doesn't rain." He nudged Aunt Mae, and pointed towards Caddie.

The wind blew Caddie's hair and she pulled her light, blue bonnet tighter upon her head. Her white dress billowed and quivered in the wind. "Jake hasn't been around in a while."

"Yeah—sure do miss Jake." Aunt Mae sighed and studied Caddie as she stood looking forlornly at the mountains. "Hume, Caddie's wearing her mother's wedding dress today. Wish Jake would wake up and see what a sweet and smart person she is."

"Listen to me, Mae. Jake says he's *very* busy handling matters of the law, but, don't be surprised if he's not home drinking again," said Uncle Hume.

Aunt Mae cringed at the thought.

Uncle Hume lifted Henny-Penny and Kackie into the back of the wagon, and covered their legs with one of Aunt Mae's pieced quilts.

Caddie walked towards the wagon and smiled. Uncle Hume tipped his hat in an exaggerated manner and offered his arm. "You look very beautiful today, young lady. May I assist you?"

"Thank you, Uncle Hume. She lifted the hem of her long, white skirt and climbed into the wagon.

* * * *

When they arrived at the church house, Jake rushed up to Caddie and took her hand.

Aunt Mae sighed with relief.

During the program, Aunt Mae looked across the aisle and observed Hannah holding Benjamin. When she caught Benjamin's eye, she held her hands out to him. He pushed away from his mother, got down from her lap, and toddled over to Aunt Mae. She picked him up, held him closely, and patted him on the back. When, she looked into his bright blue eyes, Benjamin smiled back at her, and laid his head on her shoulder. She remembered the important night he was born and she named him. He fell asleep in her arms. Beads of sweat appeared on the bridge of his little nose, and she wiped it away with her white, lace handkerchief. She observed Hannah, just as George-West Myers glanced at Benjamin and then his eyes met those of Hannah. When George-West Myers met Aunt Mae's glance, he turned away, quickly. *Yes, George-West Myers just might be the father of Benjamin. That would explain the expensive baby blanket and baby clothes, his glances towards Hannah, his actions, but Hannah's family also has money and could afford the expensive baby stuff. George West has money enough to buy that expensive watch too. Hannah knows that I know her lover bought the Bulova. Benjamin's father has to be George-West Myers. She waited for any glance made towards Hannah, again. Aha! his eyes met Hannah's! I wonder if they are still seeing each other.*

Henny-Penny and Kackie sat on each side of Aunt Mae, leaned their heads against her, and snuggled a little closer.

* * * *

The church pews were filled with people! Funeral fans scarcely stirred the air. During the services, Aunt Mae noticed the young men passing notebook paper notes, as they exchanged mischievous glances, and sniggered aloud. Their parents frowned, shook their heads and made faces at their sons, in a scolding manner. Usually Tinker Daniels sat with the group and kept them quiet. She looked around and spotted Tinker sitting on the back pew beside Jake and Caddie.

Reverend Buker Webster stood behind the podium and looked out into the audience. His eyes fell on the eight or ten young boys, who always sat together and who never seemed to take their eyes off of him. They wrote notes and passed them back and forth, and laughed. He stared at the young men, and tried to read their faces. He held his temples and looked closer at his hand written notes of grandeur and wiped his mouth with his handkerchief. "Please bow your heads and let us pray. Oh, Father, hear our pleas for holiness and wholeness." He squeezed his aching head. "Bless us as we have a good time at our Old-Timey, Old-Fashioned Day. May we all have a good time singing, dancing and playing. Keep us safe, we pray, O, Lord."

* * * *

After the program was over, George-West Meyers stood up and announced: "As Head of the Grievance Committee, I am calling a short meeting for all of the men-folk."

The women filed into the front church yard and put "dinner on the ground" while they waited for the men to conduct their meeting,

Aunt Mae carried Benjamin into the church yard, and Henny-Penny and Kackie ran ahead of her.

Caddie said, "Let me help you place the food on the table!"

"Be my guest!"

"I'll go and get the other boxes," said Caddie.

Aunt Mae looked towards the back of the church and saw Joanie Zanderneff staring after Henny-Penny and Kackie as they ran away. Hannah walked up to Aunt Mae, holding out her arms, "I'll take Benjamin, now. Believe he'd just go live with you for a little!"

Aunt Mae handed Benjamin to Hannah. "Thanks for letting me hold him. You're doing a fine job with Benjamin. He's so handsome. By the way, Hannah, I love your dress."

"Why, thank you, Aunt Mae!" She smoothed her long, white muslin dress, gathered at the waist with a green satin sash and touched her green bonnet. "You know, I made it myself."

Aunt Mae retrieved Henny-Penny and Kackie from the front steps of the church. "Y'all can play with Tommy and Bobby, but stay close enough for me to see y'all."

Laughing Eyes placed a pound cake on the table, next to Aunt Mae's box. "I made your favorite, and hope you'll like it," she smiled.

"I'm going to be so big and fat from eating all this food! You look nice, Laughing Eyes."

Laughing Eyes smoothed a long sky-blue taffeta dress with a white lace collar and white apron. Her black hair was pulled back into a bun at the nape of her neck. "Thank you, Mae, so do you!

Caddie and Aunt Mae added their food to the tables that groaned under the weight of the tremendous amounts of delicious dishes that were prepared by all of the church ladies. Wondrous odors of food permeated the air: green beans, lima beans, peas, potato salad, cakes, pies, other salads, banana pudding, fried and baked chicken, ham, pork chops, pork roast, beef roast, canned peaches, bread and butter cucumber pickles, chow-chow, breads, rolls, biscuits, corn-pone, sweet tea, sweet-milk, and butter-milk to name only a few good things.

Grandmaw Taylor walked up behind Aunt Mae and touched her on the shoulder. "Mae, turn around here! You're dress is perfect for this occasion. Got a new bonnet, too?"

"Thank you—"

"I just wore my usual stuff. All my stuff's ole-timey," Grandmaw Taylor cackled.

"Grandmaw Taylor, you always look great! I love your bonnet, too."

"Can't climb up in the attic no more, but Missy can. She has on one of her great Grandmother Perkins' hats today. She's real cute in her red taffeta dress and hat to match—really cute. Look! I had to add some new flowers and some new feathers to my hat. Why, would you believe this is a Blue Jay's feathers? Suits my personality, don't you know." Her eyes sparkled mischievously, and she tapped the brim of her hat.

Aunt Mae laughed. "You a Jay-Bird? Never! Your hat's gorgeous, Grandmaw Taylor. I can't wait to see Missy's outfit. Did you bring your delicious hickory-nut cake?"

"Why, this whole bunch of people would run me out of the church yard if I didn't bring my hickory-nut cake?" she laughed.

"It's Hume's favorite. He'll be looking for your basket."

Grandmaw Taylor began removing bowls of food from wooden apple crates, and cardboard boxes. "Know what I did the other day? I walked up to that preacher and I said, 'Reverend Buker Webster, did you ever get anyone to read your cards?'"

"You didn't, Grandmaw Taylor! When was this?"

"I did this after church services last week. Know what he said? He said he was waiting for me to read his cards. And then he just walked off," She cackled.

"You going to give him a reading?" Aunt Mae laughed. "Gonna read his cards?"

"Of course not! God would just zap me good and strike me dead, if I read cards for a preacher-man. I'm not that big of a fool." She cackled again.

Bobby and Tommy ran up to Grandmaw Taylor and yanked on her dress. "Grandmaw, you want to know what them men folks are talking about?"

She bent towards them and peered over her glasses, "How would you young men know? Tell me what are they saying?"

"We looked through that keyhole in the door. Grandmaw Taylor, what does *actions* mean?" asked Tommy.

"Actions? I guess it would mean taking action to do something about a situation, or perhaps it could pertain to someone's behavior. What did you hear?" She whispered.

"Mr. George-West Meyers says, I'm surprised at the actions of the young gentlemen. They all looked sad," said Bobby.

She frowned, and said, "First of all, you little boys have no business listening at keyholes. Someday, you just might have to forget something you wish you hadn't heard! It's very bad manners. What you have heard today, you must not repeat to anyone else. You've already told me." She smiled and patted them on the heads. "You didn't know better this time, but now you do."

"But, what does *actions* mean?" asked Bobby.

"It means *get a move on*!"

Bobby and Tommy chased each other to the Meeting Tree.

Aunt Mae smiled. "Bobby and Tommy are so cute. I believe what they just told us is that those young men, who misbehaved in church this morning, are in for a hard time, when they get home."

"Yes, Mae, it beats all I ever saw. I can't imagine what's gotten into those boys, talking and laughing in church, but I can tell you this. I just know it's mischief." She rested her chin on her hand, and looked very hard at the church house. "It's mischief, all right."

Judge Pewter walked up to Aunt Mae and Grandmaw Taylor, and tipped his hat. "Good morning, ladies! Is this a good place for me to place my black-berry cobbler?"

"Sure is. Put it right here in front of me," Grandmaw Taylor cackled. "This is the best place you'll find anywhere on this long table." Grandmaw Taylor smiled a toothless smile. "Just to know you're a lawyer and cook, too, just amazes me! The men folk at my house never cook a thing."

"I like to cook desserts, Grandmaw Taylor." Judge Pewter smiled and placed a long aluminum pan on the table. "Mae, could you have Hume bring you by my office this afternoon after four?"

"Sure, Judge Pewter. Why're you working on Saturday?"

"Finishing up a brief, Mae, and doing some personal business. See you this afternoon! By the way, Caddie's doing a superb job for me!"

"Thanks, Judge Pewter. We'll see you this afternoon."

"See you ladies later." He tipped his black, high-top-hat.

"Mae, you know its times like this that I take note of who's here and who's gone on to meet the Lord," said Grandmaw Taylor.

"Doesn't seem like Macie should be gone," said Aunt Mae.

"Yes, and Ratchel, too."

* * * *

After they ate "dinner on the ground," most of the people square-danced and sang. Young couples walked along the path next to the creek, or gathered wild-flowers from the nearby fields. Some of the young men met behind the meeting house and laughed and talked in lower tones. The children played "Tag," "Red-Rover," "May-I", "Simon-Says," "Hide-and-Seek," "Hop-Scotch," "Marbles," "Checkers" or "Chess."

The older folks reminisced, and laughed at the same stories they heard at every gathering.

A contest was held for the best Ole-Timey costume. Locket Webster played the piano, while everyone paraded in a circle and the judges decided the winner. Reverend Buker Webster announced, "The winner of the Ole-Timey contest is—The Winner is—" He hesitated and smiled, as he held up a piece of paper, and waved it in the air. "The winners for the best lady's costume, and the best man's costume are Missy and James Anderson!" The audience clapped and cheered loudly, as the Anderson's held hands, walked around the room of the meeting house, and modeled their old-fashioned costumes.

Jake called, "Shake a leg, Missy and James! Give us your best winner's dance!" Everyone clapped as the fiddler played.

Uncle Hume grabbed Aunt Mae's hand.

Jake adjusted his three-piece, black suit, reached for Caddie's hand, and called, "Everybody join in!"

* * * *

Aunt Mae and Uncle Hume walked to Judge Pewter's office just before four in the afternoon. "Looks like Joanie's changed her ole timey clothes and cleaning windows over at Judge Pewter's today," said Aunt Mae.

"Yeah, looks that way. That ladder's a might high for her," said Uncle Hume.

"Howdy, Joanie. How are you?" Aunt Mae called out.

Joanie climbed down from the top of the ladder. "Hey, y'all. I'm doing fine. Except a little tired."

"Joanie, we're wondering about Dan. Ever hear from him?" asked Uncle Hume.

"Nary a word have we heard from Dan. Mr. Zanderneff and I are mighty worried. We've called the sheriff's office in Tennessee and asked the sheriff to check things out, but he has heard nothing from Dan."

"We're worried too."

Purple and yellow bruises were evident on Joanie's left eye and both of her arms.

"Say, Joanie, what's wrong with your eye, and your arms?" asked Uncle Hume.

"Ran into a door. Just about killed my eye. Bruised my arms a little, too." Joanie turned her arms around for them to observe.

"So sorry you hurt yourself," said Uncle Hume.

"I'll give you some camphor to doctor with, Joanie," said Aunt Mae.

"That'd be mighty nice of you." She reached over one of the window-boxes and began to wash the windowpanes on the ground floor.

"Is Judge Pewter in his office, Joanie?"

"I believe so."

Uncle Hume lifted the door knocker attached to the elaborately carved door of his office.

Judge Pewter opened the door and chuckled, "Come on back here to my office, people! Back here to the messiest office you ever saw!"

Aunt Mae and Uncle Hume followed him.

"We'll have some hot tea, and that'll give me an excuse to eat some of my black-berry cobbler. Mind you, my herb tea won't be as good as yours, Mae."

"Thank you, Judge."

Upon entering his private office, they observed neatly stacked papers in one area of the office, along with strewn file folders. Yellow legal pads and wadded papers were scattered everywhere in another section of the office. The floors next to the walls, and his desk were piled high with legal-sized typed papers and hand-written note book sheets. Three open law books were stacked on the left hand side of his desk.

"I'm working on a very complicated brief for the Court of Appeals, and this place is a mess!" He shook their hands and motioned to chairs sitting before his desk. His facial expression became serious. "What do you hear from Dan? Anything?"

"Not a thing. Not a thing. We're all wondering where in the world Dan can be," said Uncle Hume.

"We're very concerned," said Aunt Mae.

Judge Pewter poked the fire in the gray, flat-stone fireplace and sparks flew. He sat down at his carved, oak desk, and cleared his throat, "Joanie Zanderneff says she hasn't heard a word, either." He gazed into the fire, shook his head and frowned.

"Just like he disappeared off the face of the earth," said Uncle Hume.

"Yeah, we just asked Joanie about Dan, when we saw her outside washing windows. Said that she and Mr. Zanderneff haven't heard from him and they're worried to death!"

"Yes, I'm sure all of you are worried," said Judge Pewter. "Me, too."

"We don't want to believe that the incidents that Macie wrote about Dan are true, but after reading her diary, we think Dan killed her," said Aunt Mae.

"Then, he ran off," said Uncle Hume.

"Doc Stowe told me Macie's diary was one of the saddest things he ever read. It's worded sorrowfully and meaningfully, but Doc Stowe said it's heart-wrenching and awful hard to read," Judge Pewter sighed. "Said it was written in Pig Latin. That seems unusual."

"Macie probably wrote it in Pig Latin so Dan wouldn't pay any attention to what she was writing. Judge Pewter, you wanna read her diary?"

"Yes, I'd like to see what the diary says about Dan. A lot of time has passed and I've come up against a stone wall and haven't been able to locate him," said Judge Pewter.

"Judge Pewter, see if you can decide why Macie didn't just leave and come on back home," said Uncle Hume.

"We thought Dan was a good boy until we read Macie's diary," Aunt Mae sighed.

"Thanks again for your inquiries to the Sheriff and the undertaker in Tennessee," said Uncle Hume.

"We appreciate all you do for us, Judge."

"Wish I could help more."

"Joanie and Mr. Zanderneff never inquire about Henny-Penny and Kackie. They never try to see them or anything," said Aunt Mae. "Does that seem normal?"

"Told Mae we'd see the Zanderneff's in court, if they do try to get those children away from us," Uncle Hum huffed.

"Since we adopted Macie, surely Henny-Penny and Kackie belong to us as much as they belong to the Zanderneff's, isn't that right, Judge Pewter?" Aunt Mae inquired.

"Believe you could back that up with some law," Judge Pewter said softly, "but I have a conflict of interest, being close to you and to Joanie. I'd hope the Zanderneffs and both of you would share the love of Macie's and Dan's babies, if push comes to shove."

"But, so far the Zanderneffs don't try to visit with the girls at all," said Aunt Mae. "So we might be worrying for nothing."

"It does seem unusual—the Zanderneffs not claiming their own flesh and blood, and, especially since Joanie seems to care so much for Dan," said Judge Pewter. "Maybe the Zanderneffs are embarrassed about Dan not showing up?"

"Could be," said Uncle Hume.

"What else can I do for you? I've waited for you to come back to see me so you could tell me what you want me to help you with. As your friend, I want you to know I'm here to help. I also wonder where Dan can be." Judge Pewter held his chin in his left hand and tapped a Blue Horse tablet with his closed Schaefer fountain pen with his right.

"We have no idea where Dan could be, Judge."

I'm trying to help you, but, I need to keep some loyalty to Joanie, too. She's been an outstanding housekeeper and a dear employee for me and Matilda for a long, long time. Why, Joanie's a friend, too. Just like y'all are."

"We understand."

"Joanie has a black eye and some awful bruises on her arms. Said she walked into a door," said Aunt Mae.

"Yes, that's what she told me, too," said Judge Pewter, without meeting their eyes. He slid his carved, teakwood pencil holder from the right side of his desk to the middle of his desk.

"Looks like Joanie is in bad shape to me," said Aunt Mae.

Judge Pewter moved the pencil holder back to the left side. "Yes, bad shape," he sighed.

* * * *

Aunt Mae and Uncle Hume walked hurriedly along the narrow and winding road towards their cabin. "What do you suppose those boys were writing about? What's in those notes the boys passed in church?"

"Don't know, Mae. It looks like it might rain."

"Rain—yes—you're changing the subject," she said. "Now, Hume, all of a sudden these boys are laughing and snickering in church and doing the same thing in the church yard. Y'all call a crucial—a critical meeting about it and now you say you don't know what's going on? I already know what you talked about."

"Mae, it's hard for you to believe, I guess, but I have no idea what they're writing. I've never written or passed a note in school or in church in my life! Today, all I saw was dirt-daubers darting in and about their nests, atop the door to the Sunday School room. That's all." He searched her face. "How did you know what we talked about in that meeting?"

"Dirt-daubers? Hume, I didn't see any dirt-daubers. So, you say you were looking at dirt-daubers and not those mischievous boys?"

"Yes, dirt-daubers. How'd you know what we talked about in the meeting this morning."

'I didn't think we had dirt-daubers except in hot summer time." Aunt Mae exclaimed. "I can't figure out why those boys changed their ways. They've always been quiet in church. I'm worried about them. That's all."

He grabbed her hand, and began to run. "Hurry! It's beginning to rain!"

The rain came down in heavy sheets and the earth turned dark red, miry and slippery.

* * * *

Jake and Caddie walked to the graveyard, and placed wild straw flowers on the graves of Mandy, Macie, Jake's mother and Ratchel-Robin.

Jake placed his arms around the base of the marble angel as far as his arms could reach. "This beautiful angel has been standing guard and watching over my mother for a long, long time. And, now, it's nice to know the Storey Angel is looking over my mother and Macie, too."

"The angel is more than beautiful, Jake." She rubbed her finger over the sir name, "S-T-O-R-E-Y," carved in the base of Jake's angel.

"I come here real often, since Macie died," he said. "It's like I'm drawn here like a magnet. Stay a few minutes and leave. I come to mama's grave, and then to Macie's grave."

"Are you saying that this piece of marble—this rock angel gives you comfort, Jake?" She scrutinized the exquisitely carved, marble statue, and stared at Jake. "It symbolizes a heavenly being, but I've never thought of anything in a graveyard giving a person comfort."

"Of course, it gives comfort, Caddie." He scratched his head.

Caddie noticed that he needed a hair-cut. His blond, curly hair coiled around his ears and it gave him a boyish demeanor.

"Listen, Caddie, I haven't told you yet, but I finished reading Macie's diary again. Reading her words made me feel close to her but it's also one of the worst, hardest, and saddest things I've ever done." He looked far into the distance. "Caddie, do you still think Dan killed Macie?" he asked gently.

"Yes, I am sure he killed her!" Especially after I read Macie's diary about Dan's horrible physical and mental abuse and all the hurt he caused Macie and the little girls. I just wonder where that evil Dan is?"

He reached down and picked up a withered grave blanket from his mother's grave made of chicken wire and cedar limbs. "I need to get some cedar and freshen this up." He looked into the distance. "God only knows where that killer—that S.O.B. is! You already know that I go looking for him every weekend, and it just won't do for me to find him." He pulled a leaf off a sweet shrub that grew on Macie's plot, and stripped it down to its stem. He crushed and smelled its sweet aroma.

"I didn't know you went out looking for him every weekend."

"Yeah—Dan couldn't have loved her. He hit her. He beat her and he treated her awful. I just wish Macie had asked me to help her."

Caddie pulled weeds from Mandy's grave. "I can't get Macie's cries out of my mind," she sighed.

"It bothers me day and night, Caddie. Let's go now," he said abruptly. He pulled her to her feet and dropped her hand quickly. "Caddie, do you think my mother and Macie see us and hear us?" He walked to a rusty, lacy-wrought iron fence, which enclosed the grave site, and gave the rusty gate a shake. He looked back and waited for her reply.

She joined him at the gate. "No, Jake. They're asleep," she whispered. "I've questioned that issue, myself."

"You don't think they hear me when I talk to them?" He removed a white handkerchief from his pocket and wiped the rust from his hands. "I tell them I miss them."

"No, Jake. They don't hear us." She felt the force of his rejection. *He lives and breathes Macie. Why must I be so jealous of my own sister? My very lovely sister! Why can't Jake look at me adoringly, just once, like he used to look at Macie?*

"We had a great childhood didn't we, Caddie?"

"Yes, it was wonderful."

"I wouldn't have missed growing up with you, and—"

"—And Macie," Caddie supplied the words for him.

"Yes, you and Macie," Jake sighed.

* * * *

________________, Mississippi

Ole Pem smoothed his black hair, straightened his brown tie, knocked on the well-kept farm house door, and waited nervously. He twisted and untwisted the neck of a brown paper sack. He smiled as he anticipated a glimpse of the attractive young lady that lived at this address, and he was still smiling when she opened the door.

"Good afternoon, Pem. What brings you by?" She smiled a half-hearted smile. He caught a slight glimpse of her slanted green eyes before she looked away.

"Since the Sheriff knew I passed your home on my way home, he asked me to stop by and see if you've heard anything from your husband."

"Not a word. It's not like him to just go off and not let me know where he is. But, I've already written that in my Missing Person's Report."

"Yes, that's why I'm checking—because he's missing, and we're concerned."

"Would you like to sit a little while on the front porch?" she asked.

"I brought some lemons. Do you like lemonade?" He handed her the brown, paper sack.

"Would you like for me to make some lemonade?" she asked, shyly.

"That would be nice," he smiled. He hoped he could get a better look at her clear, glassy green eyes, but she failed to make eye-contact.

"I'll be right back. Make yourself at home," she said softly.

He relaxed in a rocking chair, and observed the many acres of a ready to pick, white cotton field that flowed in front of the house and in every direction as far as he could see. *I wonder why her husband just left without a word. No notice from him of any kind, and he hasn't come back in days and days, and she says she hasn't heard a word from him. She's very attractive—Oh! I shouldn't even be looking at her—*

The screen door opened, and she was back.

When he stood up, his tall, muscular body towered over her. He waited for her to be seated before he sat down.

"I hope the lemonade is sweetened to your liking. My husband always says I make the best in the world." She sighed in dismay, and glanced briefly into his inquisitive greenish gray eyes.

They sipped their refreshment, and rocked in high back oak rocking chairs that set on the long, front porch.

"I was just noticing your cotton field. It's about ready to pick, isn't it?"

"Yes, it is. Wish my husband was back to oversee it, but I guess Papa will handle things by himself now that Daniel's gone."

"You own the land?"

"No, Papa does. He has sharecroppers. My husband is an overseer."

When he wasn't looking at the pretty girl with long, black hair, green eyes and exquisite body, Ole Pem mostly scanned the expansive sea of the white cotton, and kept on rocking. Something about the cotton field began to gnaw at him. *It's strange to see just one spot in the middle of the field that the bo-weavils got into. They just killed that one small rectangular spot right in the middle of the field.*

"You know, Janelle, I was just noticing something. He pulled on his square jaw. The field is perfect except one small, brown spot in the middle of the field. Why do you suppose that brown spot happened? It seems very strange that bo-weavils have affected only that one spot." He pointed to the brown colored rectangle, which marred the otherwise perfect white field.

"I can't imagine why," she said nervously.

Ole Pem's stomach knotted. He arose quickly from his chair, leaned over the porch railing, and spit out a mouthful of bile, mixed with sweet lemonade.

* * * *

Sheriff Olliff answered the telephone, "Howdy, Ole Pem! How's it going? Glad to hear your voice—" He tapped the end of a pencil on his desk.

"Was just logging some cases. Miss seeing you around here, Buddy. When you coming home?"

"You're kidding, Ole Pem! Sure. Let me get Jake before he leaves. He's going out the door. Sure, I'll get back on the phone after y'all talk." Sheriff Olliff placed the telephone on his desk and called, "Jake! Ole Pem wants to talk to you on the telephone."

"Thanks, Sheriff." Jake picked up the telephone. "Ole Pem! You son-ova-gun, where you calling from?"

"Glad to hear your voice, too," said Jake. "Yeah, we're all okay."

"Oh, you're at home—in Mississippi. Thought maybe you were home. Tell Mr. Sam I said *Hello.*"

"Yeah, we've had all bulletins out for Dan. Nobody's heard a word from him. It's getting very exasperating—"

"Yeah, Ole Pem I'm listening."

"Yeah, I can hear good. Go ahead—"

* * * *

"Caddie! Hume! Come quick!" Aunt Mae yelled as she rushed out of the kitchen, "Jake and the Sheriff are here!"

When Jake and Sheriff Olliff got out of the Sheriff's vehicle, Ole Jeb and Baby Jeb barked, but stayed close to the porch.

"Something's wrong! Jake doesn't look right—he's slumped and holding his head down," said Caddie.

"Howdy Jake. Howdy, Sheriff." Uncle Hume shook hands with Sheriff Olliff. He touched Jake on the shoulder, and tried to make eye contact, but Jake turned his head away.

Aunt Mae wiped her wet hands on the bottom of her apron, smoothed the moisture into its blue-checks, and adjusted her glasses. "Something's wrong?" She searched their faces.

"What's wrong, Jake?" asked Uncle Hume.

Jake slumped on the doorsteps, and shook his head, "I've never been this tired."

Caddie sat down beside Jake. "What's the matter, Jake?

"What's wrong Sheriff?" Aunt Mae pushed a rocking chair towards him.

"I'll let Jake tell you." Sheriff Olliff sat down in the rocking chair, took his hat off, and turned the brim of his hat around and around in his hands.

Uncle Hume patted Jake on the back. "What's the matter, Son? Been 'a wondering about you. Haven't seen you in a few days." Uncle Hume furrowed his brow with concern.

"I'm trying to clear my mind." Jake held both sides of his head, tightly, and frowned. "My head is killing me," he moaned.

"I'll get you a gourd of water." Caddie arose from the door-steps, and went into the house.

"Where are Henny-Penny and Kackie?" Jake asked.

"In the bed asleep."

"Good! They don't need to hear what I'm about to tell y'all." He drank deeply from the gourd dipper and handed it back to Caddie.

He clenched his jaws so hard, the hinges worked.

Sheriff Olliff cleared his throat. "I'm gonna let Jake tell you what's happened—let him tell you the news, since he got it first hand."

Everyone glanced at each other, puzzled.

"Ole Pem called me on the telephone and said he needed to talk about a young girl he met."

"In Mississippi?"

"Yes, in Mississippi." Jake became very quiet, held his hand out to the little puppy, Baby Jeb, and it began to lick his hand. He rubbed the puppy's head and ears. "Ole Pem called me at the Sheriff's office and said he wanted to tell me something about a beautiful girl who came to the Sheriff's office one day, and told them her husband was missing."

"When did Ole Pem call?" Aunt Mae asked.

"Couple of days ago was when he called. Ole Pem said she's about the most attractive little thing with dark hair and green eyes he's ever seen."

"Hope Ole Pem's not in trouble," said Uncle Hume.

Jake continued. "After the girl made her Missing Person's Report, the Sheriff out there in Mississippi—Ole Pem's supervisor—went out to the girl's house from time to time, or he sent one of his deputies to see if she had heard anything from her husband."

"Oh! No! A husband!" Aunt Mae exclaimed. "Her husband came home and found him there with his wife! Oh, No!"

Jake handed the empty gourd dipper back to Caddie. "Thanks for the water."

"I know what you're gonna say now," said Caddie. "Her husband came back—I can't believe Ole Pem's in trouble—"

"No, Caddie, not that," said Jake. "I wish things were that simple. Sometimes Ole Pem said he went to the girl's house mostly to look at her because she's the most beautiful girl he's ever seen."

"So, Ole Pem's in love," Aunt Mae whispered, and shook her head.

"Time went on, and one day Ole Pem decided to check up on the girl and he took a sack of lemons. She invited him to sit on the front porch while she made lemonade." Jake sighed loudly. "Ole Pem said they sat rocking in some rocking chairs on the front porch, justa talking and drinking lemonade."

"Well, I've never heard about anybody taking lemons to a girl's house and ask the girl to make lemonade when they were courting. I'd never think to take lemons to a girl's house," said Uncle Hume. He sat down on the steps beside Jake. "Sorry to interrupt. Go ahead, Son."

"Ole Pem said that he sat in that rocking chair, and rocked and looked across the road that ran in front of the house, and gazed beyond that road into a white cotton field, ready to pick. When he wasn't looking at that pretty girl, he mostly scanned that beautiful, white cotton field, and kept on rocking in that old rocking chair." Jake became quiet and stared into the distance at the hazy blue mountain range.

Everyone followed his gaze and tried to figure out what news he heard that made him so hesitant to share.

Aunt Mae wiped the bib of her apron with her open hands. "Jake, you need to get on with the story. You're making me mighty nervous."

"Me, too! Jake, please don't tell us that her husband showed up, and beat-up Ole Pem! Don't tell us Ole Pem's hurt!" begged Caddie. She held her hand to her stomach, and bent over.

"No, Caddie, Ole Pem's not hurt," said Jake.

"Want me to finish telling them, Jake?" asked Sheriff Olliff. "I can tell it for you, but I don't want to interfere. This is sorta private news."

"No," Jake sighed, "I'll tell them. I know they're anxious for me to finish telling them what I came to say."

"We're sure anxious."

"Well, Ole Pem told me he enjoyed looking at that sea of whiteness—those perfectly formed cotton fields which stretched for miles and miles in front of that girl's house. He said he mostly scanned that white cotton field, when he sat on the front porch, but something about that field began to gnaw at him."

"What was gnawing at him, Jake?"

"Right out in the middle of that cotton field directly in front of the porch where he sat, he saw a brown spot—a brown patch in the middle of the field in the shape of a small rectangle. He thought how strange it was that the boweavils had eaten and killed just that one small spot, and nowhere else in the field." Jake hesitated, turned around and looked at Aunt Mae.

"I think I know what you're gonna say, and I don't think I need to hear the rest," said Uncle Hume.

"Did he decide what was bothering him about the field?" asked Aunt Mae.

"Ole Pem said that he'd just taken a big swallow of lemonade, when the idea came to him of why that spot in the middle of the field might be brown. Ole Pem said that he stood up and leaned over the porch and blew that lemonade out of his mouth. It spewed everywhere!"

"Oh! No! What happened? What did he see?" asked Caddie.

"Ole Pem told the girl he had to leave—that he was sick." Jake stopped speaking, and lit a cigarette.

"He got sick? I don't understand," said Caddie.

"Yes! Sick—very sick!" Jake knocked the ashes from his cigarette onto the ivy that grew beside the steps. "He rushed to the Sheriff's office pronto, and told the Sheriff about that little spot where the cotton was all brown and the leaves and stalks were all affected in the middle of the field! He told the Sheriff that he thought the girl's husband might be buried there in that brown spot."

"Oh! No!" gasped Aunt Mae.

"I'm not believing such an awful thing happened to Ole Pem!" Caddie got up and stood in the yard.

"Well, the Sheriff didn't want to believe it could happen, either, but he decided he better go and investigate the situation, anyway. So, the Sheriff went out to the farm, and without telling the girl what he was going to do, he picked up a long stick, and just started walking out into the cotton field. It didn't take much effort for him to poke around the dead cotton stalks and determine that something bad was wrong."

"Glad it was him and not me that had to do that," said Sheriff Olliff. He shifted his weight in his chair.

"What was wrong? Was her husband buried in that field?" Uncle Hume asked solemnly. He stood up, brushed the seat of his pants and stood in the front yard beside Caddie.

"Ole Pem said that the Sheriff walked back to the girl's house from the field, and asked to use the telephone to call his Office. A crew came out and dug in that brownish-colored area. They pulled back the dirt and found a rag rug covering a mutilated body that was buried under the cotton stalks. Just a body. The body had no arms, no legs, and no head." Jake's sad eyes met Uncle Hume's.

Uncle Hume drew his arm tighter around Caddie.

"Poor Ole Pem! This is too, too sad!" said Caddie. "Poor Ole Pem."

"Found a gun, too," Jake whispered.

"A gun?" asked Uncle Hume. "Had the husband been shot, too?"

"Don't know, but a gun was lying on top of the body. Ole Pem said you have never smelled such a horrible odor that permeated the air when they pulled the rag rug off the body and exposed it to the elements!" Jake exclaimed.

"Jake are you sitting here and telling us that pretty girl that Ole Pem likes killed her husband? The girl that Ole Pem likes so much?" asked Aunt Mae. "How horrible! I know Ole Pem's devastated!"

"Yes, that's what he's a' saying," said Sheriff Olliff, and he shook his head in horror. "She killed her husband all right."

"What happened to his head, arms and legs?" asked Uncle Hume.

"Ole Pem said that the girl broke down right away and told the Sheriff that she killed her husband! Said after she killed him, she went out in the middle of the field, dug up and pulled up cotton plants, dug a hole and then she buried her husband. She placed the plants back over his body. Since she didn't bury him very deep, the decay of the body killed the cotton stalks and made that dead, brown-colored patch out in the middle of the cotton field," said Jake. "That brown spot was where her husband was buried—"

"Well, I'll declare! Ole Pem saw the husband's grave when he was sitting on the front porch!" said Uncle Hume.

"Yes, that's what caused the brown patch in the cotton field," said Sheriff Olliff.

"No wonder Ole Pem got sick!"

"Did the sheriff find the rest of the body?"

"No, they sure didn't."

"I'm so sorry Ole Pem had to go through such an ordeal," Caddie said sympathetically.

Jake interrupted, "Listen, y'all, the rest of what I'm about to tell you is even worse. That girl killed her husband with an ax, chopped his head, arms and legs off and his head, too, and then she burned all those body parts."

"This bad news is more than awful!" Aunt Mae gagged.

"Yes, it's awful—terrible," said Jake. "The Sheriff said that girl burning her husband explained the unusual, acrid and putrid burning odor some of the people in the neighborhood had complained about, but the sheriff's department could never pin down exactly where the odor was coming from."

"Ole Pem must have been horrified!" said Aunt Mae.

"Well, when the beautiful girl realized Dan's body was too heavy to carry; she chopped his head, arms and legs off, and dragged the rest of his body out in the middle of the field and buried it under the cotton plants."

"She just burned parts of her husband? Not the body?" asked Uncle Hume.

"Yes. That's right."

"Did I hear you say his name was *Dan*? Did you say, 'burned parts of Dan'?" Caddie held her hand over her mouth.

"Yes, that's what I said. I've tried to make it easy on you when I called the man *her husband.* They identified the body as Dan Zanderneff," Jake whispered, sorrowfully. "Dan changed his name to *Daniel Zanders.*"

Aunt Mae gasped, "Oh, dear God! That couldn't be *our* Dan!"

"You mean to tell me that Dan was married to some girl out in Mississippi! And, you're saying that some girl in Mississippi killed Dan!"

"How do they know for sure that it's him?" asked Uncle Hume. He held his hand over his heart. "I have to sit back down."

Jake moved over to make room on the door steps for Uncle Hume to sit down.

"The Sheriff found a photograph of Dan in his personal papers inside the house, and it depicted Dan standing beside Macie, Henny-Penny and Kackie," said Sheriff Olliff. "Ole Pem recognized all of them, of course."

"Where did they find the photograph?" whispered Uncle Hume.

"In Dan's and his wife's house—in a dresser drawer."

"Oh! No!" Aunt Mae sobbed. Uncle Hume guided Caddie up the porch steps to Aunt Mae's side, stood between them and cradled them in his arms.

Jake's concern was evident. "They found a photograph of Dan and Macie—and uh—And, the girl told them that was her husband standing with his sister and his nieces."

"Dan lied to her! Lied and said that Macie was his sister?" screamed Caddie.

"—and the Sheriff poked around in the fireplace in the kitchen, and the ash-heap in the back yard and found enough human bone fragments to determine the girl burned parts of Dan!"

"I just can't believe that girl killed Dan!" Tears ran down Caddie's face.

"Ole Pem said he was horrified that such a gorgeous girl could have committed such a gruesome murder, and was strong enough to drag Dan out in the field. She appeared to be too small to lift someone so heavy!"

"Oh! No!" screamed Caddie. "How awful! I can't believe it! He killed Macie and ran away and got married again!"

"So, Dan did run away," murmured Uncle Hume. "I always believed something happened to him, but nothing like this. I always took up for him!"

"Ole Pem said the girl told them that when she and Dan first married, he was good to her, and then, one day, he got drunk and just started beating her for no reason. This treatment went on for about a year. The last beating was so bad, Dan nearly killed her."

"I know I have to hear, but I don't want to hear!" Aunt Mae wiped her eyes and nose on the corner of her apron.

"The girl told them that Dan held a gun to her head, and he tried to make her slit her wrists with a straight razor. While he was trying to make her kill herself, Dan just all of a sudden fell to his knees, leaned against the kitchen counter, stayed in that position for a few minutes, vomited, and then he just toppled forward in a drunken stupor. He passed out and laid in his own vomit."

"Dan tried to kill this girl? Oh! My!"

"The girl ran out to the back porch where she saw an ax, took it back inside and found him still lying in his own vomit. She killed Dan with the ax."

They sat dumbfounded. "This is really an ordeal!"

Aunt Mae held her temples between her fingers and closed her eyes. When she opened them, she stared at the mountain range as if she'd never viewed it before. "Dan's dead," she whispered in disbelief.

Jake's jaw quivered with emotion. "I asked Ole Pem how could this girl hate Dan enough to ax him and burn him? Then, Ole Pem said the girl claimed that for several months before she ended up killing him, Dan beat her and one day he stomped her when she told him that she thought she was pregnant. It turned out she was not pregnant, but the damage was done to her body and psyche. She decided to leave him."

"Oh, that poor girl! Sounds like he drove her to kill! How sad!"

"I'll declare! I'll declare! Just think we have been wondering where Dan got off to. He killed Macie and ran away!" Uncle Hume held his head and closed his eyes.

"Dan must have killed Macie exactly the same way. He probably held a gun on her. He made it look like suicide! He must have!" said Jake.

"And he left Henny-Penny and Kackie here with us? His own flesh and blood!"

"Dan never has contacted Joanie and Mr. Zanderneff, as far as we know," said Sheriff Olliff. "They are very hurt, and mystified."

Jake beat his fists on the rough boards of the door steps. "It's hard knowing Dan killed Macie! But, I never could believe Macie committed suicide. I just knew he killed her!"

"So, it looks like Dan probably tried to kill two girls—Macie and now his second wife," whispered Uncle Hume. "But, this wife beat him to it. She axed him to death!"

"Dan deserved to die!" Jake clamped his square jaw tightly.

"What's that girl's name?" asked Aunt Mae

"Don't remember the girl's name, for sure, but I believe it's *Janelle Davenport,*" said Sheriff Olliff.

"Janelle? Don't believe I've ever heard the name *Janelle.*"

"The Mississippi Sheriff wanted someone else other than Dan's wife, and Ole Pem to identify Dan's photograph. We received the photographs here in my office yesterday, and we know for sure that man in the photograph is Dan, all right. He was standing beside Macie, Henny-Penny and Kackie in one photograph and in another one, Dan was standing beside a real pretty girl who is supposed to be the wife who killed Dan." Sheriff Olliff cleared his throat.

"Well, I never—"

"Just think, his wife—Janelle—didn't know Dan was ever married and had a family, so she claims. Said Dan told her that it was a photograph of his sister and her little girls, and she believed him!"

"So, Dan abandoned Henny-Penny and Kackie, but kept their photographs! How could he stand to look at their pictures every day?" Jake opened and closed his fist, drew his jaws shut, and worked them in anguish.

"You have to tell Dan's folks about all this," Uncle Hume said feebly.

"We told Dan's people before we came over here. We had to wait for the photographs to arrive here first, and had to get them verified. We had to do this before we could tell you and the Zanderneff's."

"I feel sorry for Dan's maw and paw. I prayed to God for vengeance, but Dan's brutal death seems more awful than anyone could ever imagine. He got more than his *just dues.* It's so awful!" Aunt Mae whispered under her breath.

Caddie started to laugh, hysterically.

"I need to tell you something else. Dan's people want his remains brought back to Three-Mile Crossing. They want him buried next to Macie."

"I just don't know what to say," Aunt Mae whispered. She clutched the front of her dress and rolled it in her hand. "This has to be discussed with the Zanderneffs."

Caddie's hysterical laughter turned into screaming. She began to run towards the path that led to the spring, and Ole Jeb and Baby Jeb ran after her.

Jake started to follow Caddie, but she was out of sight before he could get off the front steps.

"Let her be, Jake. She'll be all right," said Aunt Mae.

*   *   *   *

Uncle Hume got up from his chair, and staggered to the door. "Mae, hope you don't mind, but I need to lie down." He rubbed his chest.

"Hume, you okay?" Aunt Mae frowned.

He nodded, but he continued to hold his chest.

She held his arm, and walked with him to the bedroom. "I'll get you some warm milk."

"I'll help you," said Jake.

Sheriff Olliff followed them into the bedroom. "Let me help you, Uncle Hume." Sheriff Olliff pulled the bedcovers down, and sat down in an oak rocking chair beside the bed. "I'll sit with you a little while. I want to be sure you're all right."

"Thank you, for your kindness," Aunt Mae said. She patted Uncle Hume on his shoulder. "I'll be right back. I have to go to the kitchen."

"Uncle Hume, what can I do for you? You okay?" asked Jake.

"I'll be okay, Jake. Don't worry."

"That's right, Jake, try not to worry. I'll sit with Uncle Hume for a bit. See if Aunt Mae needs any help," Sheriff Olliff insisted.

Jake followed Aunt Mae to the kitchen.

"Aunt Mae, I have to find Caddie," Jake said, humbly. "Will it be okay to leave Uncle Hume? He's holding his heart. I knew he'd take it hard about Dan, but I didn't know how to tell y'all any easier."

"You knew no easy way to tell us, Jake. No easy way." Her hands shook as she poured milk into a small pan.

"I need to find Caddie, Aunt Mae."

"Leave her be, Jake. She'll be okay."

*   *   *   *

Early the next morning when Caddie returned, the dogs followed behind her.

When Jake ran to meet Caddie, Ole Jeb and Baby Jeb wagged their tails the moment they saw him. "Caddie, forgive me for not considering your feelings when I told y'all about Dan being murdered. I just blurted everything out. I knew you'd take the news hard, but I should have been more gentle—more understanding. I should have been more sensitive."

Caddie remained quiet.

"Sweet, sweet, Caddie," he whispered softly. He wiped tears from her puffy eyes and face, with his handkerchief.

"I don't blame you for the way you told us about what happened." Caddie sobbed, and wiped her runny nose and blood-shot eyes on her blouse sleeve. "How could you have found an easy way to tell us about Dan getting killed?"

"Caddie, I am sorry for so many bad things happening to you—to us." He tried to rub the smudges off her face with his fingers. "Caddie, where did you go? I've been *so* worried."

"The tree house."

"The tree house? Why the tree house?"

"I wanted to go back to a place where I've been happy and back to a less complicated time, when we were all little children."

"Going back is impossible," Jake sympathized. "If I could go back, I'd try to change a lot of things."

"About Macie?"

"About Macie. About me," he whispered.

"About yourself? What do you mean?"

"Yes, I'd change a few things about myself. Caddie, you've always been right beside me—you're one of the sweetest friends I could have ever asked for. I should have appreciated you more."

Tears came into her eyes because she knew he was wondering what he could have done to win Macie's heart. How he could have gone to her rescue and brought her and the little girls back safely to Three-Mile Crossing, and away from Dan.

"Yes, Jake, if we could go back, we'd all try to change things."

"There. There," Jake soothed. He placed his arms around her, and scratched his stubble of whiskers against her face.

* * * *

Aunt Mae placed a kettle of water on the wood stove, and wiped her hands on her apron. *Did I do wrong to ask Jake not to follow Caddie? I pray my probing into her affairs did no harm. Jake's so wrapped up in poor, dead Macie! Poor Caddie!*

Oh, Macie! I hated Dan for what he did to you and Henny-Penny and Kackie. I wondered what I'd do when Dan showed up here one day, and gave us some lame excuse for being late in his arrival. But, Macie! Dan got married to a girl out in Mississippi. He was so mean to her, just like he was to you that it caused her to retaliate.

He tried to make her slit her wrists, just like he did you Macie, but she killed him, before he could kill her! And she burned him!

Oh! It's terrible what that girl did to Dan.

Many times I've asked God to please "handle" Dan. Now, I am humbled by how drastic Dan's outcome turned out to be! Oh! Macie, I have to pray for forgiveness. I have to ask Him to remove hatred from my heart. I should have prayed, 'Vengeance is in Your hands, Lord.' I didn't mean for God to kill Dan.

God, please be with Ole Pem! And, please, please remove my hate for Dan. I can't believe you dealt with him so harshly.

A black kitten ran between her legs and almost tripped her. "Spooky, you scared me to death! I almost walked on you!" She picked up the kitten, held him evenly with her face, and looked into his yellow-green eyes. "Hug me close," she whispered and curled him in her arms.

Thank you, dear Lord, for showing us Macie didn't kill herself. We felt so much failure! We felt so much guilt about not being able to hear her cries for help! And, Lord, that poor girl out in Mississippi needs Your help. They said her name is Janelle.

Thank you, dear, dear Lord, for all Your blessings!

Your will be done!

* * * *

Aunt Mae awoke knowing she had seen a portion of Macie's heaven. For the first time since Macie's death, she felt not an absence, but a presence.

When she went into the kitchen that morning, she patted Uncle Hume on the back. "Hume, thank God, you seem to be feeling better."

"Yeah! I just got a little over-excited last night, when I heard about Dan. I'm having problems believing he's dead, specifically being murdered."

"Me, too, Hume."

"Don't worry about me, Mae. "Everything's gonna be all right."

"If you say so, dear. You know, Hume, I had an unusual dream last night!"

"Well, can you tell me before breakfast?" he inquired, as he slipped his arm into a navy blue sweater, and examined her sweet face, closely. Her face was radiant. It glowed.

"Of course, I can. It was a spectacular dream!" She removed crisp, fried fat-back from a black skillet and cracked an egg into the hot grease.

"Well, thank God!" he exclaimed. "It's about time we had a nice dream to talk about before breakfast!" He set the table and she told him her wonderful and exciting dream.

"Hume, I dreamed I walked hand-in-hand with Macie along a luscious, thick carpeted, green, winding, wooded path, along a clear, blue-green, babbling brook.

"Get your breath! Get your breath! He laughed.

"Oh! How adorable Macie was! She was very young—maybe twenty—very vivacious and laughing. The colors of the woods and flowers were more vivid in color and more gorgeous than anything I've ever seen in *real life***.** The air was filled with all of nature's music, perfume, and energy.

"We were walking along that exquisitely formed path of flowers and greenery, and suddenly, Macie stopped and released my hand. 'This is as far as you can go!' she said.

Aunt Mae smiled. "I stood at that luscious green place on that breath-taking path where Macie left me, and I watched her walk until she got to the top of a hill. A blue, blue sky framed her misty gold aura. Behind Macie, way off in the distance was a dome of a bright blue-white light that covered tremendous space.

"Macie turned around, waved and smiled. I waved back, and then, Macie continued to walk upon that mystical bright green, colorful, floral path, far into the distance, towards that stream of light, that stream of life. Oh! It was such a restful and soothing dream!"

Uncle Hume patted her on the hand, and smiled. "It is a welcome dream. For a while, I thought all our dreams would be nightmares. But, this is different. You walked on the pathway to heaven, I suppose." He arose from his chair and reached for a milk-pail. "Macie let you know she's okay. Thank God for your enlightening dream."

Aunt Mae stood in the doorway and observed Uncle Hume walking towards the barnyard and behind that barn scene was the brightest, most colorful sunrise she had seen in many a day.

* * * *

Tinker Daniels met Ole Pem in Gainesville, Georgia at the Southern Railroad Station. "Good to see you, Ole Pem."

"Good to see you too, Tinker."

They shook hands.

"It was nice of Mr. Zanderneff to send you to pick me up."

"Yeah, he's a nice man. He and Miz Joanie are taking Dan's death real hard."

"Yeah. I talked to Mr. Zanderneff on the telephone."

"So, they say ye spotted Dan when you were sitting on that lady's front porch? Did you think it was Dan buried out there when ye saw a brown, dead patch in the middle of the cotton field?"

"I didn't know there was a body buried in the field. I didn't even know the girl was married to somebody that I knew."

"Wal, you knew that it wasn't boweavils that made that brown patch?"

Since Tinker Daniels was usually a young man of few words, Ole Pem was surprised at his inquisitiveness.

Ole Pem laughed, and patted Tinker on the shoulder. "Listen, I don't want to cut you short, but I don't like talking 'bout it, okay?"

"Okay, Ole Pem. Didn't mean to get into your business. Just have a curiosity, don't you see? All of us wonder why Dan settled down so close to where you live."

"I have a lot of curiosity about it, too."

As they traveled the winding mountain roads towards home, Ole Pem's mind kept wandering back to Dan's wife. *How could she kill him? Why didn't she go for help when Dan was down on the floor? I can't believe she committed such an awful, gruesome murder! Why doesn't she hate me for calling the Sheriff's attention to that brown spot in the cotton field?*

"Ole Pem, let's stop when we get around the next curve and put some water in the radiator at that little creek."

"Did you know Mr. Zanderneff's truck had radiator problems before you left home?"

"Sure I knew. It's nothing new. Always having problems of some sort or another." He pulled the truck off the road. The access road to the mountain stream was narrow and muddy. "I'll get the water can so we can fill the radiator."

"That radiator's hissing pretty bad, Tinker."

"Yeah, but it'll be all right. It's just a mite of a leak."

"Tinker, we're lucky we're not on top of the mountain and can't get to water easily. How'd you expect to get back over the mountain with this radiator needing work?"

"Figured we'd camp, while the radiator cooled off."

"Cool off and camp! Camp and cool off!" Ole Pem couldn't believe Tinker could be so nonchalant.

"Yep. Told everybody not to expect us until late tomorrow. You make us a fire, while I try to get us a couple of trout." He threw Ole Pem a box of matches. "If we need water, I'll pee in the radiator if I have to—"

"Pee in the radiator?" Ole Pem laughed.

"Just kidding." Tinker pushed his unruly black hair off his forehead. His brown eyes twinkled.

"Got us a can of pork 'n beans, and a loaf of bread, but betcha I get us a trout."

Ole Pem made a fire, pulled his jacket closer to his chest, fed small twigs to the smoldering, hard to start fire, and rested cross-legged before the campfire.

Tinker returned with two small trout. "See, it's a good thing you didn't bet. Ye would have lost!" He removed a pocket knife and began scaling the fish. "I'll open a can of beans, so we'll have enough to eat." He grinned.

"Thanks, Tinker. Say, it's getting a little late to be starting over the mountain with the radiator leaking. I can't believe Mr. Zanderneff sent you to get me with a truck that's in such bad shape!"

"I heard him tell daddy that he believes if he lets me drive the truck long enough, I'll fix everything that's wrong with it."

"Always tinkering around on things since you were a little boy," Ole Pem smiled.

"Mr. Zanderneff knows I'll put water in the radiator. He let's me use the truck all the time. Mr. Zanderneff's a real good guy."

Tinker wove a green stick through the bodies of the fish and hung them over the fire until they became a crispy brown. They became quiet while they ate.

"It's getting late. Let's try to get some rest." Ole Pem sat down next to a dogwood tree and leaned back. "It was a long train ride," he muttered, and rubbed his right knee.

"Here's you a blanket. See, it's not so bad. Just like an outdoors, top-notch hotel," Tinker laughed.

"You're a good guy, Tinker. I know you think I'm too quiet but I can't get Dan's murder out of my head."

"I understand," said Tinker. "We'll get on up the road after the radiator cools."

* * * *

Dan crowded Ole Pem's dreams, and his sleep became fitful and sporadic:

Dan held a football and ran through a green, green cotton field, which turned into a sea of white, and then the sea of white became marred by one small brown spot in the middle of the field.

Dan called, 'Ole Pem, ya wanna play? Wanna play?' And, suddenly, Dan jumped into a brown, dead section of the cotton-patch, and the ground swallowed him.

A gorgeous girl handed Ole Pem a glass of lemonade.

He awoke gasping, and couldn't go back to sleep. He didn't want to think about the horror of Dan's murder. He forced himself to think about his handsome father and his lovely mother who were at home awaiting his arrival.

Suddenly, he shivered with an unnatural cold. *A rabbit just ran over my grave!* He pulled the blanket closer to his neck.

"Ole Pem, you awake?" Tinker whispered.

"Yes, been awake most of the night." Ole Pem squinted his tired, sleepy eyes, and noticed Tinker sitting before the fire wrapped in a blanket.

"Me, too. Let's get out of here, Ole Pem! For some reason, I'm getting the Heebie-Jeebies." Tinker smiled sheepishly.

* * * *

"Hume, I tell you that preacher's crazy as a Betsy-Bug. He reads the same sermon every time we have a funeral, and I'll bet he reads it again today at Dan's funeral," said Aunt Mae. "If he does, it won't be suitable."

"I know. I know. The Elders need to say something, but they don't want to make George-West Myers mad, because he's the main one who brought Reverend Buker Webster here in the first place, don't you know."

"Yes, I know, he's the man with the money."

"That's right, and it's a very good reason," he smiled sadly.

"Think we're doing the right thing allowing Dan to be buried beside Macie?"

"Well, we're allowing it because of Henny-Penny and Kackie. Hopefully, having their parents buried side by side will make it easier for them, mainly when they get a little older," said Uncle Hume. "Besides, we really don't know positively that Dan killed Macie."

Henny-Penny and Kackie stood beside the Zanderneffs at the gravesite, along with her and Uncle Hume. Laughing Eyes, John McIntosh and Ole Pem stood behind Aunt Mae and Uncle Hume.

After the burial service, Ole Pem walked over to Caddie and Jake, where they stood beside the marble angel. He shook hands with Jake. When he placed his long, muscular arms around Caddie, she looked into his sympathetic eyes and leaned her head on his shoulder. "I surely have missed you, Caddie. Sorry I couldn't be with y'all for Macie's funeral," he whispered. He pulled her close to him, and kept his arms around her.

"Missed you too, Ole Pem. Can you believe Macie and Dan—both are dead? We believe that Dan killed Macie?" Caddie blinked her sad, green eyes.

Ole Pem cringed, and looked into her ashen-colored face. "Heard that's the news in the grapevine. How do you know that Dan killed Macie, for sure?" He pulled Caddie a little closer and smoothed her long hair.

"You need to read Macie's diary, and then you can decide for yourself."

He felt her body shiver, and held her a little tighter. "I'd be curious to read her diary—heard it's written in Pig Latin, and that makes it very hard to read. You think so, Caddie?"

"At first it's hard to read. After you get the hang of it, you can read it okay?"

"Listen, Caddie, as you know, I'll be clerking for Judge Pewter while I'm here. So, I'll be seeing you at the office. Let's get together and discuss old times, whatcha say?"

"Sure, I'd like that," said Caddie.

"I've missed you so much, Caddie. I can't wait to get back here to Three-Mile Crossing for good," he whispered.

"I guess your Mama told you that I ask about you all the time?"

"Yes, Mama always tells me when you ask about me, and it means a lot. Just think! We're gonna be working in the same office. Won't that be something?"

"Yes, Judge Pewter is very nice," she smiled. "I'm looking forward to working with you—for you, Ole Pem."

"Me, too, Caddie." He dropped his arms, and squeezed her hand as he searched her concerned eyes.

"Please come over to the house and see us when you can. Aunt Mae and Uncle Hume are anxious to have you spend time with us."

"Looking forward to visiting with your folks." He smiled and his brown eyes twinkled. "And what about you? You anxious to have me spend time, too?"

"But, of course, I am." She blushed when his eyes met hers.

"I look forward to visiting," he said.

"Wanna play some pool later, Jake?" Ole Pem raised his voice loud enough for Jake to hear.

"Sounds good." Jake placed his hands in his brown gabardine pants and rocked his feet back and forth on the river-rock pebbles.

"Meet me at Sojo's Hall about five, okay, Jake?"

"Okay."

"You come, too, Caddie." Ole Pem squeezed her elbow, tightly.

"I'd love to!"

When Ole Pem's twinkling eyes held Caddie's, Jake stared at Caddie and then at Ole Pem.

* * * *

After the burial, Aunt Mae approached Joanie Zanderneff. "Do you feel like walking up the road a piece, Joanie?"

"Of course." Joanie fingered the buttons on a brand new, store bought, navy blue faille dress. She glanced nervously towards Mr. Zanderneff. "Where in the world did all these strangers come from, Mae?"

"Sight-seekers—I know it's nerve-wracking!"

As they walked along the dirt road, towards the parsonage, Aunt Mae put her arm around Joanie's shoulder, and pointed towards the parsonage. "Let's walk over to that bench setting beside the preacher's flower garden. I want to say something that's been bearing on my mind quite a while now, and I can't wait any longer."

"All right, Mae." Joanie stopped, rubbed her narrow back, stood rigidly, and glanced at Aunt Mae nervously.

Aunt Mae guided Joanie to a bench. "Joanie, I'm so sorry about Dan! His death is such a horrible, horrible thing!"

"Thank you, Mae. Dan was my sweet, baby boy. So sweet!" She held her head in her hands and closed her eyes.

"Joanie, I also remember Dan as being a sweet boy when he and Macie married."

"Poor Macie. That wonderful child—poor, poor Macie. I loved her," Joanie Zanderneff whispered. "I know I haven't shown my love to you, since Macie's death."

"I know you loved Macie, and Macie knew you loved her. Joanie, I need to talk to you about something, but I didn't want to talk in front of the men. Now, what I have to ask is why have you never asked to take your granddaughters to your house to visit or even to live with you? Bad as it hurts me to ask, I have to hear it. I have to know. Lord, I know you have to love them. They are so precious. It doesn't make sense, somehow, that you don't visit with Henny-Penny and Kackie. Can you tell me, Joanie?" she asked very gently.

Joanie began to cry, "Mae, I'm ashamed. So ashamed!"

Aunt Mae stood up. "Let's go back where the others are, sweetie. I'm sorry I upset you. Shouldn't have asked you about the little girls here at the cemetery. I'm a terrible person to approach you right now, and I'll be the first to tell you. You say you're *ashamed*? Why, I am the one that should be ashamed! Let's go back to the graveyard."

Joanie nodded, and stopped walking.

"Forgive me, Joanie. I love those little children 'til I'm obsessed with them. I was afraid that one day you'd walk up to me and tell me you or Dan wanted to take those baby girls and that I'd never see them again. We've never talked about their welfare. Now that Dan's passed on, I decided we needed to talk, that's all."

They walked back silently toward the graveyard.

"Mae, uh, Mae," Joanie stammered.

"Yes, Joanie."

"I love them very much. They are so precious to me! They're Dan's flesh and blood, and also my flesh and blood. But, listen good, Mae, cause I can't tell you again, you hear?"

"Surely."

"Wal, Mae, I want Henny-Penny and Kackie, mind you! I really do want to be with those precious granddaughters! But since Mr. Zanderneff beat Dan unmercifully all his life, I just couldn't stand the thought of him mistreating Henny-Penny and Kackie, too. Just like he beat Dan!" She shivered. "I know Mr. Zanderneff would beat 'em, if we had them! Just be glad my husband doesn't want those little girls, Mae. He can be really mean!" She held her hand over her mouth, closed her tearing eyes and shook her head. "He's very cruel and mean-spirited."

"Joanie, I never knew! I never knew! Mr. Zanderneff always seems calm enough to me. I never suspected Dan had a welt on him, when he was a little boy! Let's start to walk." She hugged Joanie's shoulder tightly.

"You mustn't tell anyone, not anyone at all, you hear, Mae. Not ever, you promise?"

"I promise."

"Sometimes Mr. Zanderneff is sweet to me, especially after he's beaten me. He tries to make up for mistreating me, but I don't want to make up with him. All I've ever wanted is a life full of peace. You mustn't tell anyone what I just told you. Not ever, Mae!"

"Of course, I'll never say anything to anyone, but do you care if I tell Hume?"

"Just Hume, and that's all, because he's got to know why I don't come around to visit those precious children. I'd be so attached to them, and all. I don't want Hume to think I'm a terrible person, or to dislike me. I see him look at me kinda funny-like!'"

"Hume has wondered why you don't pay attention to Henny-Penny and Kackie, but he doesn't dislike you."

"I can't take a chance on having Henny-Penny and Kackie get beat by Mr. Zanderneff. It's best they never visit us because I'm afraid he'd find some reason to hurt them."

"Oh! Joanie! I never realized your great worry and pain!"

"All my hopes and dreams are buried back there in that cemetery. Dan was my sweet, little boy, my whole life! I loved him!"

"You must think of yourself, now, Joanie." Aunt Mae spoke, gently.

Joanie shook her head and her chin trembled. "No, Mae. All is gone!"

"Not unless you decide your life has to be that way. You have a lot to live for."

"I wish I knew what to do!" Joanie cried.

"I wish we'd talked much earlier. Listen, Joanie, I'll tell you what we'll do. We'll make a plan for you to play with Henny-Penny and Kackie—places like church. I'll see to it! Joanie, don't be afraid to get attached. They need all the love and kindness they can get! You're their grandmother! You need their love, too!

"I'm so humiliated!" Joanie cried.

"Let's plan for Henny-Penny and Kackie to sit beside you at church and we'll do lots of things—just girl stuff. Come see them at my house, as often as you want to. Do it, Joanie," Aunt Mae encouraged.

Joanie stared at her without responding

They walked back to the grave site in silence.

Mr. Zanderneff lifted his hat towards Aunt Mae, and took Joanie's arm firmly, "Joanie! About near took you long enough!" he said under his breath.

"Sorry—it was my fault," said Aunt Mae.

"See you later, Mae. Thanks for coming. We appreciate it." Mr. Zanderneff guided Joanie to their beat-up Chevie.

Joanie glanced back at Aunt Mae, and her frightened eyes explained many things.

I wonder why I never knew Mr. Zanderneff is a wife-beater and a child-beater! I saw Dan throughout his childhood, and never suspected any mistreatment. I remember seeing bruises on Joanie from time to time, but never inquired as to what caused them, except that day outside Judge Pewter's office when Hume and I saw her.

"Thank you for taking that walk with me, Joanie. That crick in my back is almost gone since we walked that little piece down the road!" She put her hands on her hips and reared back.

"Did you need to yell quite that loud, Mae?" Uncle Hume slipped his arm around her waist, guided her down the hill, away from the cemetery and to the church. Caddie, Henny-Penny and Kackie followed behind them.

"Did I yell too loud?" she whispered.

"What you up to, Mae?"

"Not up to anything."

"Did you and Joanie come to an understanding about the children?" He stopped and observed her sad, blue eyes.

"Yes, we did. I understand many things more clearly," she sighed. She walked up the front steps of the church and opened the door.

Uncle Hume removed his felt hat, and scratched his head in bewilderment.

* * * *

Jake opened his kitchen cabinet door, and removed a fruit jar of moonshine. He placed the jar to his lips, and took a big swallow. Drinking the acrid liquid, directly from the jar, burned his throat and caused him to grimace and shiver.

He sat down in a rocking chair before his fireplace, and reflected upon the day. He peeled an apple with his pocketknife and fed himself the thin slivers of apple. Macie, I w*onder who all those strangers were that came to Dan's funeral today*? He stretched his arms over his head, and held onto the knobs on the back of the rocking chair.

I couldn't make myself go over and shake hands with those strange people. They'd want to talk about Dan, and I don't want to even think about him. It's a good thing that gal killed him, cause I was going to do it myself if I ever caught up with him.

He pulled off his mud-spattered hunting boots, brushed them, and placed beeswax to water-proof where the leather met the soles. His thoughts turned to the time he spent with Caddie and Ole Pem at Sojo's pool room. *I couldn't believe how Caddie's eyes lit up when Ole Pem hugged her at the graveyard. Then, later, she played pool like she always does—aggressively and just like a tomboy. Ole Pem must think she's attractive the way he kept looking at her and smiling. Why should it bother me if Ole Pem likes to play pool with Caddie, or if she leans her head on Ole Pem's shoulder? If he wants to hug her that's normal. We all grew up together. When she leaned over to shoot, her beautiful hair shimmered in the light and it's so long, it fell on the pool-table from time to time.*

Jake gave an extra hard brush to the sole of his boot, and let it fall on the floor. He picked up the other boot and applied beeswax.

When Caddie shook her head and flounced her hair over her shoulder, it was sorta like when Reverend Webster's horse shakes its head, and its mane shimmers in the light. Ole Pem reached out and brushed her hair off her shoulder, and smoothed it from her face from time to time. He never took his eyes off her all evening, and I heard him say, "I missed you, Caddie Brown."

After that one real good shot, Ole Pem sure was standing close to her, and when she stood up and turned away from the table, she almost ran into him. They laughed, and he hugged her.

A jealousy and a desire for Caddie overcame his being, and the newness of the feeling alarmed him.

He emptied the remainder of the moonshine from the fruit-jar, and stumbled to bed. He tossed and turned, and dreamed that he held Caddie in his arms! *Macie pushed herself between him and Caddie. She shoved Caddie away from Jake, and whispered seductively in his ear, 'Jake, you love me! I didn't choose you before, but I choose you now!'*

* * * *

Joseph Daniels and his boys came up on the porch laughing. "Howdy, everybody! Let's go coon-hunting! Hume, you and Jake come on! Let's go run the dawgs!"

"Howdy, boys! Coon-hunting's not in season, but it's gonna be a mighty cool night."

The boys became quiet when they saw Aunt Mae.

"Howdy, boys!" Aunt Mae greeted with a smile.

"Evening, Aunt Mae. Maw said to give you a hello message," said Wyllyam.

"Tell Mary *hello* for me, too," Aunt Mae smiled.

"We're just gonna run the dawgs. Not after no game, nor nothing," said Joseph.

"Believe I'll go. Come on, Jake. Let's go with 'em," said Uncle Hume.

"Let me see what clothes I have stored up in the attic." said Jake.

"Y'all come on in, while Jake and I get dressed." Uncle Hume pulled the kitchen chairs away from the table and close to the fireplace.

"It was awful about Dan getting killed. We're all mighty sad."

"Surely is sad, Joseph. We're dealing with it the best we can. Come on in."

The Daniels came inside and gathered around the kitchen fireplace.

"Henny-Penny, you and Kackie don't be fooling around with the dogs," Caddie called. "Come back inside."

Joseph Daniels spit in the fireplace and wiped tobacco spittle from his chin.

"John and Ole Pem will meet us at the creek, where my land meets John's at the old home place. John can't wait to try out his new hunting dawg. Supposed to be the best coon dawg you ever saw."

"Have to be a good-un to beat Ole Jeb!" said Uncle Hume.

"You know what, Aunt Mae? We're probably in for a bad winter," said Joseph.

"Why do you think that Joseph?"

"Well several of us men-folks sat outside Pewter-Mapp's Store, and I was whittling and chewing my tobacco, and I learned quite a bit," he smiled.

"What did you learn, Joseph?" Aunt Mae asked.

"Somebody said that fall's early this year. The sumac leaves have already turned red, and some of the trees are already dropping their leaves."

"I suppose you can tell when you see that happen, Joseph," she smiled.

"I know it's gonna be a cold winter because the corn husks are thick and all of my dogs' and cats' hair have thickened up."

"I've always heard that's a sign," she laughed.

"Yep! It's gonna be a cold winter, all right."

"Did you ever hear it's a sign of a bad winter if spiders are in the house!" asked Tinker.

"No, I don't believe I've heard about that sign."

"Well, we've got cobwebs everywhere!"

Aunt Mae laughed, "I guess you have all the right signs."

Jake walked overhead in the bedrooms and the ceiling floor creaked.

The attic floor squeaked overhead. "Those footsteps sure don't walk around in the attic soft enough for it to be a ghost," Joseph Daniels chuckled.

His boys clapped their hands together and laughed.

"I'm ready! Let's go!" yelled Jake, as he ran down the stairway.

"Uncle Hume probably has an extra shirt that'll fit you," said Caddie.

"If I put on just one more piece of clothing, I'd topple over!" he smiled. "I'll see you later, Caddie." He squeezed her hand. When Caddie's eyes met his, he turned away, and left the porch quickly. "Let's go, boys," he yelled.

"I'm still gonna beat ye playing pool, Caddie," Tinker teased.

"We'll have to see about that," Caddie teased back. "See you, Tinker," she smiled.

Uncle Hume took a lantern off the kitchen wall and handed it to Jake. "I'll get us another lantern out at the barn."

* * * *

"Into bed, little girls," Aunt Mae said to Henny-Penny and Kackie.

"We want to sit up with you!"

"Not tonight. We've already said our bedtime prayers. Off to sleep with you, now." She hugged them tightly, and pulled the covers over them. "Oh! Nobody knows how much I love you little babies."

"We're not babies. We're precious little Henny-Penny and Kackie is what Uncle Hume says," Henny-Penny corrected.

Kackie giggled.

Aunt Mae was amused. "Yes, and Henny-Penny and Kackie are growing up too fast! Good night." She whispered and closed the door to their bedroom.

"I'm turning in, too, Aunt Mae," Caddie took a deep breath, and yawned.

"I know you're tired. Hope you rest well."

"Aunt Mae, I believe Jake likes me more than he used to. What do you think?"

"What do I think? I'm sure he likes you Caddie, but maybe not as much as you might want him too."

"I suppose you're right, because if he really likes me, why did he go hunting tonight, and not stay here with me?"

"Oh, guys all like to get together. You'll have to get used to that with any man. But, Caddie, I imagine Jake's still struggling with his feelings about Macie."

"Jake always brings up Macie's name." Caddie muttered.

"Even though you hear me speak of Macie, it doesn't mean I think less of you because I love you very much, Caddie. So does Jake," Aunt Mae gave her a reassuring pat on the arm.

"Sometimes when Jake looks at me and says something sweet, I think he really likes me, and then in the next breath, he'll make a remark about what he and Macie did together or tell me something she said. It changes everything."

"It's frustrating I know. Goodnight, Caddie." Aunt Mae leaned over and kissed her, and smoothed a blanket over her shoulders. "By the way, did you enjoy playing pool with Jake and Ole Pem the other day?"

"Jake got upset when I won, but Ole Pem thought it was funny. He said it was like old times. He's lots of fun! Tinker was hanging around, and Jake kept telling him to go away. He kept coming back and teasing me. A lot of other young people were with us and it was nice. Jake and Ole Pem played a game of chess and when Ole Pem won, Jake showed a lot of temper. Ole Pem told Jake it was just a game!'"

"I'm glad you had a good time." She closed Caddie's door, gently.

Aunt Mae added a log to the fire, moved close to the lamp-light, and settled down to crochet, knowing that the hunt would probably last a long time.

Her eyes rested a moment on a child's stool that sat beside the hearthstone—an important place! She missed the family when they were in bed, but she appreciated a few moments to herself. She pulled a gray wool shawl tighter across her shoulders. She poked at the fire, re-arranged the logs, and dug deeply into the red coals.

The dogs barked for quite sometime. It was exciting but sad to hear a wild chase—the hound dogs chasing after a coon, a opossum, or a red fox—a frightened animal running for its life!

Firelight flickered on the wall.

Macie, I've been worrying for nothing. The Zanderneffs don't want to take Henny-Penny and Kackie away from me and Hume after all. But, you already know that, you being in heaven and supposed to know everything. Or, are you sleeping and I'm talking to myself and God? What was it like to see Dan's spirit?

Did Dan tell you that his father beat him when he was a little boy? Did he tell you that Mr. Zanderneff beats Joanie? Joanie is afraid he'd beat Henny-Penny and Kackie, too, if they visited with the Zanderneffs, because Mr. Zanderneff still beats Joanie. Just like Dan beat you, and Dan beat his wife in Mississippi. Oh! It's too hard to comprehend.

I wonder what will happen to that poor girl out in Mississippi that killed Dan—what fate? What verdict will a jury decide?

She set her crochet aside, rubbed her eyes, cleaned and adjusted her spectacles, and picked up her bible.

* * * *

Uncle Hume nudged Joseph Daniels, and gave him a signal to be quiet. He turned to the young men, and tried to keep his voice serious. "Boys, we'll stop here at Ghost Hollow, and listen to the dogs run."

"We're not in Ghost Hollow, are we!"

Since the boys had heard so many ghost tales about *Ghost Hollow* being haunted, they huddled together. Uncle Hume and Joseph laughed and slapped their legs at the boys' reactions. The other men smiled.

"I'm cold," Wyllyam Daniels shivered.

"Yeah—we're cold. Let's go home. Our feet are wet from wading in the creek," Rob-Hunter agreed.

"Don't scare the boys like that, Hume," said John McIntosh. "You've got them wanting to go home. We're not even close to Ghost Hollow."

"Wanna bet," Ole Pem laughed. "We've been in Ghost Hollow for quite a spell, and now we're almost back to Uncle Hume's land."

"Naw. We're not in Ghost Hollow. I was just joshing the boys," said Uncle Hume. "Just wanted to see what Wyllyam would say." He patted the little boy on the back, affectionately.

"Toughen up, boys. Toughen up," Joseph Daniels said.

"If you boys only knew, neither Joseph nor Uncle Hume wants to be in Ghost Hollow. Probably more scared than you boys are." Jake slapped Uncle Hume on his shoulder. Everyone laughed.

"Heard a lot of mysterious tales about Ghost-Hollow. Let's get out of here." said John McIntosh. "People have wandered around for days trying to find their way out."

"You're right about that!" Uncle Hume and Joseph Daniels agreed.

They heard the dogs strike.

"Listen, Jake. You hear Ole Jeb? He's got the lead. Now, isn't that just like music to your ears?" Uncle Hume laughed and slapped Jake on the arm.

Everyone became quiet.

"He's in the lead, all right. Ole Jeb's got more lung power than any dawg I ever heard."

"Ole Jeb's getting old, but he still likes to hunt. John, you hear your dawg yet?"

"I hear him, but he's way behind the pack, dad-nab-it. Paid too much for him!"

"He'll be okay, Dad," encouraged Ole Pem. "You've just got to run him a little."

"John, you know Ole Jeb will train him right.

"I hope so, Hume. Sure hope so."

They slowed down to listen to the barking dogs, and determined the direction the dogs were running. The hunters hurried over hill and dell, through briar patches, and crossed over creeks. Limbs slapped their faces as they ran through the under-brush. Water soaked their feet and coldness invaded their bodies.

Wyllyam Daniels ran as fast as he could, but no matter how hard he tried, he lagged behind.

Ole Pem backtracked, picked Wyllyam up and placed him on his back. "Come on, little guy. I'll help you catch up."

Wyllyam held on tightly, leaned his head closely to Ole Pem's back, and was thankful for the piggy-back ride.

"Listen! The dogs *treed!* I hear Ole Jeb! Doesn't he sound sweet?" Uncle Hume laughed. "Listen! It's music to my ears!"

When they arrived at a large persimmon tree, Uncle Hume yelled, "Ole Jeb was the first to tree!"

Ole Pem placed Wyllyam down on the ground.

Wyllyam shivered with cold, and his teeth popped. "I'm powerful grateful to you, Ole Pem. I'm obliged to you for helping me out when I was dragging behind."

Ole Pem patted Wyllyam on the back. "You're welcome. Let's get in on the fun and see what the dogs treed—maybe it's a big ole coon."

The hound dogs reared and jumped up all around the tree. The Daniels boys held up their lanterns, and Uncle Hume shone a flash-light into the top of the tree. Looking back was a hissing, shiny-eyed opossum, his sharp teeth showing.

Clouds covered and uncovered the full moon.

"Looks like a big-un," called Jake, as he ran to the other side of the tree to get a better look. "Look, here, Ole Pem!" He shone his flashlight on the scared animal.

"Yeah, he's a big un, Jake," said Ole Pem.

"Rob-Hunter's the best climber. Come on, son, climb up and get him!" yelled Joseph Daniels.

"Leave it in the tree!" Ole Pem called.

"Leave it!" Uncle Hume called. "We're just giving the dawgs a run—and we don't want the Game Warden after us!"

"This is Ghost-Hollow!" Ole Pem yelled. "Leave the opossum!"

Rob-Hunter climbed the tree, carefully caught the opossum by the tail, and placed it in a tow sack. He tied the sack with a string, and dropped it down to his father.

Jake called out, "Joseph, y'all don't need that opossum. Let it go. You know we're hunting out of season."

"We're in Ghost Hollow, boys," Ole Pem shouted. "Let it go!"

"Naw, we're not. Keeping it anyhow, Ole Pem. I'll fatten it up in my pen and it'll make some good eating, later on. He's a big'un," said Joseph. "Mary can bake us a good opossum and sweet tater dinner. We'll pour vinegar over it and go to town. I can smell it now! Man won't that be good!!"

The dogs barked and pulled at the tow-sack.

"I'd leave that critter be. We've made a complete circle and we're in Ghost Hollow!" Uncle Hume said, nervously.

"We've crossed and re-crossed the creek," said John McIntosh "Let's get out of here!"

"Won't hurt nothin' to keep that ole opossum. You'll see!" Joseph insisted.

They rested at the persimmon tree and waited for the dogs to strike again.

"Joseph, y'all need to let that critter loose right here," Uncle Hume pleaded. "It's not even hunting season."

"Let the opossum go, Joseph!" Jake insisted, but Joseph held the tow-sack tightly.

"Naw! He's the biggest opossum I ever saw," exclaimed Joseph. "I'm gonna keep him." He stood up, pulled the opossum out of the tow-sack and held it up for everyone to see. Even in the dim light cast by the lanterns, the opossum appeared to be extra large, and have extra white hair. "I'll put him in a pen and fatten him up, and keep him until Hunting Season gets here. Then, we'll eat him." He carefully placed the opossum back into the tow sack.

John McIntosh's dog pulled at the tow-sack that held the opossum, and growled. John McIntosh yelled, "Git! Git! Git away!"

"Bet he's old," said little Wyllyam Daniels. "His hair is white and shaggy just like Uncle Albert's." His teeth chattered and he pulled his sleeves over his hands. "I'm wet and cold."

"My bones feel chilled to the core and my teeth are chattering, just like Wyllyam, here," said Uncle Hume. "Let's get on home!"

"Listen! Do any of you smell smoke?" asked Ole Pem. He sniffed loudly.

"Naw! I don't smell nothing."

"Believe I do smell smoke."

"Well, if I smelled it before, the scent has left me. Hope the woods aren't on fire. Let's put some distance between us and Ghost Hollow, boys!" Joseph Daniels set out in a trot and they all followed.

"Pem and I are gonna cut through the woods right here and head on to the house. See y'all Sunday at the church house." John McIntosh grabbed his hound dog, and placed it on a leash. "Come on, Pem. Let's get this dawg on home."

"Glad you could go with us, Ole Pem. It's like old times!" Jake slapped Ole Pem on the shoulder.

"Yeah, old times," said Ole Pem. "I've missed all of you guys."

"Hey Ole Pem, I know it's been rough thinking about Dan and his wife killing him."

"Yeah, I've been having horrible dreams about Dan's murder," said Ole Pem.

"I'm having terrible nightmares about Macie," said Jake. "The main thing I dream is that Dan is killing Macie in the bathroom, and blood is everywhere.

Some nights, when I dream about it, I see Dan hit her, blow by blow and I see him cut her wrists and blood spurts everywhere when they struggle. I wake up in a cold sweat."

"Who'd ever think we would become so burdened and heavy-laden at our young age?" Ole Pem said softly.

"Wanna play pool tomorrow?" Jake asked.

"Yeah. See ya tomorrow at Sojo's. Say about five?"

"Okay. See you then."

"Let's ask Caddie to come, too, okay?" asked Ole Pem.

"Not tomorrow. Maybe another day"

"I'll see you tomorrow, Jake," said Ole Pem.

* * * *

"Nice to come into a warm place, Aunt Mae." Joseph Daniels stamped his feet on the hearth and rubbed his arms.

"We all have wet feet and just a freezin' to death." Tinker held his hands out to the fire. "Where's Caddie? Gone to bed, already?"

"Yes, she's already asleep, Tinker," said Aunt Mae.

Wyllyam stood close to the fire, and held his hands out to warm them.

Aunt Mae noticed his trouser legs and feet were wet. She reached into her sewing basket and pulled out a pair of socks.

"Take your shoes off and put these dry socks on, Wyllyam. They're a little big for you, but they're dry. We don't want you to catch a death of cold."

His green eyes shone brightly and his expression was all the thanks she needed. He hurriedly took his shoes off and pulled the dry socks on.

"Thank you, Aunt Mae. You and Ole Pem are really kind people. Know what Ole Pem did? He carried me a piece on his back, all up and down the hills. He's the strongest man I know."

"That was kind, Wyllyam, but we're all supposed to do kind things for each other."

"Lookie—here, in this sack. Wanna see the biggest opossum anybody has ever seen?" Rob-Hunter opened the tow-sack slightly and peeped in. Then, he held the sack towards Aunt Mae.

"He's mighty big," she agreed. She stood at a distance and stared in the sack at the very large opossum with an abundance of white hair on its shaggy head.

When the opossum hissed, all the younger boys jumped back.

"Y'all look cold. Come closer to the fireplace." Aunt Mae noticed the hand-me down clothes of the Daniels family were ill-fit. The sleeves of Rob-Hunter's jacket were too short, and Tinker's jacket was too big. Little Wyllyam's coat fit snugly, but he had a hole in the knee of his thin pants. "Y'all strike a coon, too?"

"No. We just got a opossum."

"Not going to keep it, are you?"

"Yep."

"It's out of season," she said.

"Keeping it 'til it gets in season," Joseph Daniels laughed.

She shook her head in disagreement, and turned to Jake. "Did you have enough hot tea?"

"Yes'm. Sure did. Cake was great, as always. Listen, I'm going on upstairs to bed. Will you tell Caddie I'll see her at the church house Sunday. I'll probably be up and gone when y'all get up in the morning."

"Sure, Jake."

"See y'all later, boys. Hope you enjoy eating that opossum," Jake laughed and he went upstairs.

"You're invited to eat opossum and taters, Jake!" Joseph Daniels called out to him.

"How did John McIntosh's new dog make out?" asked Aunt Mae.

"John's a little disappointed. But, it's just a young dawg and not trained yet," said Tinker. "John paid a good bit for him, too."

"Oh, Ole Jeb'll train him. Not to worry," said Uncle Hume.

"It's getting late. See y'all at the church house Sunday." Joseph stood up from his chair, and pulled the legs of his pants over his boots.

As they left the front porch, Rob-Hunter said, "Aunt Mae, we got skeered at Ghost Hollow. We got real spooked!"

"You were in Ghost Hollow?"

"Yes! But we didn't mean to be."

After they left, Aunt Mae approached Uncle Hume with a frown on her face. "I can't believe y'all went to Ghost Hollow!"

"Got paid back for teasing them boys," he laughed.

"Hume, what mischief did you get into?"

"Just having fun with the boys. That's all. Thought I'd scare them a little and ended up spooked, myself."

"You spooked? Naw, not you," she teased. "You brag about not being superstitious."

"Yeah, all of a sudden I thought about Dan and Macie, when we were in Ghost Hollow. I got this feeling they were with us, and I got really spooked.

"Hume, I hoped the hunt would do you good," she said.

"Me, too."

Uncle Hume limped across the room, went to the bedroom and fell into bed exhausted. Aunt Mae warmed blankets at the fireplace, wrapped them closely around his body, and pulled a goose down coverlet over him.

She heard Jake walking around in the attic rooms, and then the loud sound of one of his boots dropping on the floor. She looked up and waited for the second boot to drop. It fell to the floor loudly, as if on cue.

The cabin was quiet except for Uncle Hume's snoring. She listened intently. She heard a scampering noise. Something ran across the attic floor just above her head.

Is that a squirrel? Or could that be a ghost?

The thought of a ghost being in the house became unnerving. She banked the fireplace, blew out the kerosene lamps and hurried to bed.

She snuggled close to Uncle Hume, striving to make herself comfortable.

He jumped when she placed her feet on his. "Mae, you've got the damnedest, coldest feet!"

* * * *

"Like I said last night, Mae, I got paid back for teasing them boys. I got chilled to the bone," he chuckled.

"But, why didn't y'all leave that opossum at Ghost Hollow?"

"Joseph insisted on taking it home so he can fatten it up. Get the wild taste out of it. Mae, I reminded them to leave it!"

"You know the superstitions. If you take any critter out of Ghost Hollow, the ghost of Ghost Hollow will come and haunt you!" she said.

"You believe that, Mae? It's just a superstition. You really do believe that, don't you?"

"I sure do. You remember that's where Jake's father probably went hunting. He never made it back."

"Mae, the superstitions are just made up tales. You know good and well that a long time ago the Indians were smart enough to start a tale about Ghosts and Spirits in that area, so no one would go in their territory after the animals. It preserved the wildlife. It scared everyone off."

"Well, Hume, I don't think the Indians concocted that old tale anymore than you did. Now, don't be surprised if anything strange happens." She pressed her temples and hesitated. "Maybe moon shiners started the rumor. That would keep people away from their stills."

"Naw, I don't believe so," he said. "Everybody around here is too scared to moonshine in Ghost Hollow." He shook his head emphatically.

"Regardless of how it got started. I don't like to think about you hunting in that God-forsaken place! Something could happen!"

"Don't be teasing me about strange things might start going on Mae."

"I'd never tease anyone about a superstition."

Hume examined her face, and saw the fear in her eyes when she became occupied with superstitions—the unknown.

"Rob-Hunter's the one who took the critter out of the tree. I set no store in superstitions, but, then, sometimes I get spooked like the rest of them," he excused.

"Um-m-m—"

By the way, while we were out there in Ghost Hollow we thought we smelled smoke. Hope the woods are not on fire."

"You see fire?"

"No, didn't see fire. Just got a whiff of smoke."

"We're really in for it, if the woods are on fire."

"You can say that again. We got out of Ghost Hollow fast, when we got to feeling uneasy-like. The smoke smelled like it was a long ways off."

"Well, I guess we'll see."

* * * *

Reverend Buker Webster stood at the dining room window gazing at the lake. He raised a white, stoneware coffee cup to his lips, and sipped.

"Buker, we need to talk."

He placed the cup on its saucer.

"You broke my train of thought, Locket!" He rasped. His handsome face became gnarled, and ugly.

"Let's decide what to do, Buker."

"About what?" he snapped.

"The farce we live. That's what!"

"You wanted to be a preacher's wife. You got your wish. It's no farce."

"Our life as husband and wife is a farce, Buker. You pretend to be so sweet when you're in public but at home you act differently. You act weird. And, we've never slept together. That's not normal. I wanted children."

"I'm happy enough. You have this delightful place to live, Locket. You should be happy too."

"I'm not happy. Buker, you're so detached. I don't believe you care about anything but yourself."

"Detached? You're saying that I don't care?" He raised his eyebrows. "I don't care?" He laughed haughtily, shook his head, and tapped his chest, as he emphasized the word *I*.

"Yes."

"I'm happy! And, you're happy!" he yelled. He usually lowered his voice and whispered accusations with rudeness in a very precisely, enunciated monotone, but that morning his voice became loud and cruel. "You're trying to mess up a good thing!"

She batted her wide-open eyes. His yelling startled her so much she thought he might hit her.

"No, listen to me, Buker."

"Listen, you say?" Reverend Buker Webster drank the remainder of his coffee, and placed the cup and saucer on the dining room table. He placed his hands in his pockets, rocked his feet, back and forth, and scowled.

She recoiled, clinched her fists and closed her eyes, hoping he'd leave the room.

"Locket, if you had wings, I'd clip them, but you don't have wings, do you?" He hissed.

Her eyes opened wide. "That's a weird kind thing to say, Buker. What are you inferring? If you're saying you'd like to clip my soaring wings, you've already clipped them."

"No, stupid. Like an insect. Like a bug," he sneered.

"Yes, you've clipped my wings, and you've taken the wind right out of my wings, my sails. Humiliated me!"

"Right," he drawled and rolled his eyes.

"Buker, do you have any wants or unfulfilled needs?"

"Of course not! Let's just drop the subject. It's going nowhere."

"Buker, do you have a mistress?"

"A mistress? Well, let me think." He placed his hand on his chin. "Yes! Death is my mistress."

"You mean you want to die. You're just waiting for death?"

"No, I'm flirting with death," he laughed, and shrugged his shoulders indifferently, as he turned back to the window.

A horrific cloud of the unknown covered her being. She gasped, "Buker, we need a divorce. I can't stay here with you any longer. Like I just said, we're not really husband and wife, since we've never even slept together." Tears came into her eyes. "I intend to start packing today."

"You are so pathetic," he drawled. "So pathetic." He shook his head, and stood at the window looking out.

"Buker, I need to say something," she held her clenched fists to her stomach, and bent over.

"Say it."

She smoothed her blouse, and looked timidly into his scowling face. "I met with Judge Pewter at his office, yesterday," she said hurriedly.

Reverend Buker Webster turned around and faced her with clenched fists.

"I talked to Judge Pewter about a divorce," she said hesitantly.

"You did what?"

"You heard me." She lowered her eyes.

"Are you out of your mind? What will Judge Pewter think of me now? He and his secretary know you want a divorce, and now the whole community will know. Is that what you want? We'll have to leave Three-Mile Crossing Church—this perfect place! Is that what you want?"

"No. Just a divorce. His office will keep a confidence about the reasons."

"A divorce. Just like that. A divorce? The stigma of a divorce! Are you out of your mind? When the petition is filed, everyone will know."

"It's not just 'like that' really, Buker. It's an annulment. Since we never slept together—the marriage has not been consummated. Therefore, Judge Pewter said the process would really be an annulment."

"We're husband and wife, Locket. Like I said just now, you told me when I first met you that all you wanted in life was to marry a preacher. Well, you got your wish."

"No. I didn't get what I wished for. I wanted a husband who loves me and cares about me. I want children."

"You'll never find a more peaceful place to live, Locket. As for me, I plan to stay here for the rest of my life. If you carry out your plans and get a divorce, my career will be over. And, think about it—your career will be over, too. You won't be able to stay here and teach."

"I'm sorry, Buker." Her blue eyes opened widely. "It's not peaceful."

He walked over to her and placed his long, strong fingers on each side of her face, and pulled her face towards him, until her face was even—face to face with his.

She stood on tip-toe, but he towered over her.

Since she didn't know he drank, she was startled when the odor of stale alcohol filled her nostrils. He crushed her face so tightly, her teeth cut the inside of her jaws. Blood oozed from her mouth, and tears came into her eyes.

"You're sorry? You won't be doing anything like filing for a divorce, you hear? Or you will be sorry!" He pushed her away.

She fell against the china cabinet. Dishes rattled.

He crossed the room to the doorway, turned around angrily, and screamed, "You hear me Locket? You won't be doing this stupid thing!" He gritted his white teeth and squeezed his eyes into thin dark slits. "If you attempt to leave, you'll never leave in one piece! I think *I will* clip your wings! Now, just think about it—" He came back to where she hovered against the cabinet. "Don't open your mouth to Judge Pewter or anyone else again, if you know what's good for you!"

Tears streamed down her face, and she shrank away from him.

He grabbed her red face tightly and squeezed. "If you think shedding a few tears will help you, tears won't help," he snarled. He held tightly to the jaw-line and slung her bruised face away from himself, backed away from her until he reached the door, and shook a threatening finger at her. He slammed the back door and the screen door so hard, both doors rattled.

Locket realized that all the time she had known Buker, he had shown only a good side of himself that he had wanted her and the world to see. She feared the demon that hid behind his disguise of Reverend.

She felt her face, caressed her swollen left eye, her bruised jaw and worked it back and forth. She looked out one of the kitchen windows. Buker Webster walked hurriedly towards the barn. She hoped he would saddle a horse and leave. Instead, he got into his new sports car, lit a cigar, and sped out of the driveway, throwing rocks in every direction.

She ran to Buker Webster's office, hoping it would be unlocked. The doorknob turned. She stepped inside the stale, dusty smelling study and walked slowly into the immaculate and orderly room. She crossed over to the office desk and tried to open the drawer. It was locked. Two highly polished oriental-designed, carved wooden boxes that sat on his desk were also locked.

She rushed to the clothes closet that Buker Webster had turned into a dark room when they moved to the parsonage. She opened the door. Stagnant, and whitish-colored developing chemicals stood in the sink Pungent and acrid fumes escaping from those stale fluids filled her nostrils. She held her nose, as she pulled a chord to the overhead light. It swung back and forth, throwing dark, and mysterious shadows on the peeling, scaly gray wall. She hesitantly glanced around the small room. A large piece of cardboard, covered with hundreds of photographs, was tacked to the right hand side of the wall. When the swinging overhead light became still, she examined hundreds of photographs that depicted a collage of men and women in their coffins.

She became chilled, and her teeth began to chatter. All of the photographs were unknown to her, except the photograph of Ratchel Robin Daniels. She remembered when Buker Webster took the photograph of Ratchel Robin in the front room of the Daniels' home. A chill of dread ran up her spine, through her stomach, and weakened her knees.

She hurriedly closed the dark-room door, and leaned against it. She held her face, worked her jaw back and forth, and held back the nausea. She grabbed a bath cloth from the bathroom, ran outside to the well and pumped a bucket of water. As she bathed her face, and held the cold wet cloth to her eyes and bruised jaws she prayed: *Dear God, get me out of this nightmare. Please intervene!*

She ran to the telephone and picked up the receiver. She recognized Matilda Pewter's voice on the party line. She hung up the telephone quietly, and anxiously waited her turn to get the line. Finally, she dialed the operator, "Good morning, Jan, I need to talk to my sister in Atlanta. Please ring the number: _________. Thank you, Jan." She could hear the telephone buzz on the other end.

"Mrs. Webster, I'm sorry but the number is still ringing—no answer. Do you want me to keep trying the number and call you back??"

"Yes, Jan, please do. And, Jan—thank you for your help. This is a very important call." Locket went into her bedroom, locked the door and began to pack.

* * * *

Reverend Buker Webster returned to the parsonage late in the afternoon, and went directly to his study. He felt an irresistible urge, an urgent desire to be alone, to reflect, and sort out his personal feelings. He opened a desk drawer, removed a bottle and a shot glass and poured.

The alcohol burned his throat and nose.

He set the glass down on the desk, and listened intently. *Locket said she was leaving. She's still here. She's a scared little mouse. Women are so weak!* He laid his arms and head on one of the boxes, and remained in an immobile position for a few moments.

Upon his brief reflection, he forgot his wife as quickly as she had come to mind.

He removed an antique, carved treasure-box from the bottom drawer of his desk, and placed it on the top of his desk and leaned forward. He opened the box, removed a letter and a black and white photograph of his mother from his treasure-box and smoothed it with his long fingers, slowly and lovingly. He examined her stunning floor-length black dress. Wide white lace surrounded the collar and engulfed the cuffs, and his mother held a bouquet of white roses. She smiled at him with a knowing smile.

He placed his mother's photograph on his desk, walked to a dresser, looked at the handsome stranger in the mirror, who turned his head from side to side, and smoothed fine-lined wrinkles on his throat, and jaw line.

Be still mind. Be still!

He pressed his fingertips into his aching temples, tightly.

I don't want to think. Mother! Help me!

He sat back down at his desk, lit a *Lucky Strike* cigarette, removed a fountain pen with the widest nib, and set his hand to write:

Mother, dearest, I saw the beautiful lady again today. She arose out of the lake, reached out and beckoned to me. A deafening, cold wind blew so hard, her beautiful dark hair twisted and whipped in the breezes and grew longer and longer, until it almost touched the water. I left the bank of the lake and waded out to her! Just as our fingers touched, I heard someone call my name!

I turned around and saw that it was Jake Storey calling me. He wanted to know what I was doing, and he pointed at my wet and muddy boots.

* * * *

"What in the world, Hume! Not another lame goose!"

"No, Mae, she's in perfect condition. It's Pegg's bride. Happy birthday, Mae!"

"I'll declare, Hume, whoever heard of a husband giving his wife a goose for her birthday! I believe this is Pegg's birthday present—not mine." She laughed.

Pegg stood nearby and turned his head from side to side, and stared with curiosity.

"Look! I think Pegg likes her!" Kackie exclaimed.

"What's her name, Uncle Hume?" asked Henny-Penny.

"Why don't we call her *Bride*?"

"Bride?" Kackie grinned.

"Why do you want to call her Bride?" asked Henny-Penny.

"Because she's going to marry Pegg!" said Uncle Hume. He removed the goose from the tow-sack, cut the string from her legs and placed her on the ground.

Pegg spread his wings, balanced well, and he and Bride scurried to a dammed-up place in the creek.

Uncle Hume removed a small package from his coat pocket. "Here's your real birthday present, Mae."

"Why, Hume! What a lovely barrette! The sky blue stones are gorgeous! Thank you!"

"It'll look perfect in your beautiful hair." He tugged a white curl that hung behind her ear. His brown eyes twinkled as they met her sky blue ones.

* * * *

Jake peered over the rocky ledge of a cliff, before he sat down on a log, and gazed at the Blue Ridge Mountains and far into the deep valley. He was overcome by the majestic beauty of the moment, and a surge of God's presence filled his soul as he relaxed, and emptied worldly thoughts from his mind. If Heaven is more awesome than this place, it's going to be mind-boggling!

From time to time, he glanced towards the thicket of the sweet-gum trees where Caddie sat on stacked flat rocks, and told the story of the Legend of the Indian Mound to Henny-Penny and Kackie.

The whispering voices of the spirits sighed through the pine trees, and lingered in his mind.

Macie, I find myself listening for your voice—your whisper in the wind! I listen for reasons and answers.

He walked over to the rock where Caddie sat, leaned over and kissed her on the cheek.

"A little kiss for old times' sake," he said. "Let's have our picnic!" He pointed to a gray cloud forming in the distant sky. "Believe a cloud is coming up."

Henny-Penny and Kackie chased each other.

"Jake kissed Caddie!" Henny-Penny laughed. "Jake kissed Caddie!" she yelled.

"Let's eat! Let's eat!" the little girls yelled, and jumped around happily.

Caddie stood up, and pulled her red cotton sweater over blue cotton slacks. She searched Jake's eyes, his face, and it made her happy to see that his whole countenance appeared to be less uptight.

"Okay, Henn-Penn and Kackie. Let's spread our picnic," said Jake.

He removed a blue and white tablecloth from the picnic basket, and spread it over a stack of rocks. "You're wonderful, Caddie."

"You are too, Jake," she whispered. She waited to hear what she longed to hear, but he remained quiet and smoothed the tablecloth, never looking up.

"You're so sweet to take such wonderful care of Henn-Penn and Kackie."

"It's one of my greatest pleasures."

They ate a picnic lunch of deviled eggs, and fried ham between slices of home-made loaf-bread. "Ready for pound-cake, Jake?"

"You bet I am!"

"We are too," said Henny-Penny.

"Jake, we saw you kissing Caddie," Kackie teased.

Caddie handed Jake a glass of lemonade.

"I kissed her because she's so sweet," he smiled, and took a big swallow of his drink.

"Wish we had ice for the lemonade, Jake," said Caddie.

Jake spit a mouthful of lemonade upon the ground, and held his stomach.

"Remember the trouble Ole Pem got into when he drank lemonade!"

"Oh, No! Jake, I wasn't thinking!"

* * * *

Caddie strummed the banjo, and Aunt Mae played a pump-organ which was so old and rickety, its pedals creaked, knocked, and made such a racket it almost drowned out the music. They sang while Uncle Hume and Jake taught Henny-Penny and Kackie how to Two-Step and Square Dance. Ole Jeb and Baby Jeb howled so loudly, everyone screamed with laughter.

Uncle Hume called a square dance:

"Docie, do. Step to the right, step to the left."

* * * *

After everyone went to bed that evening, Aunt Mae went out into the yard, looked up at the constellations, and continued her practice of meditation and feeling the presence of God.

She wrapped her apron around her chilly arms, and thanked God for the lovely day, and the wonderful evening.

On her way to bed, she saw a light under Caddie's door and knocked.

"Come in, please."

Aunt Mae opened the door and peeped in. "Everything okay?"

"Yes, Aunt Mae, today has been a great day!"

"I was just passing the door, and I saw your light," she said.

"You'll like to hear that Jake and I are communicating much better. We talked about his being obsessed with Macie's ghost and my being obsessed with him," she smiled.

"Y'all can surely work everything out, darling."

"Aunt Mae, I'm afraid Macie might always come between us. I just wonder if Jake will ever propose."

"How do you feel about that, Caddie? What if Jake did propose to you, but he didn't love you? You realize that if you did accept such a proposal, you might not ever be happy with Jake."

"Aunt Mae, he kissed me on the cheek, today." She touched her face with her well-groomed, long fingers. "And I was surprised because it was for no apparent reason, except to be a sweet guy."

"And, that has given you new hope, hasn't it, Caddie?"

"Yes, new hope," she nodded and smiled brightly.

"Perhaps you shouldn't read too much into his kissing you on the cheek. Why was it so special?"

"I think it was the way he looked at me just before he kissed me. I'm not sure."

"Caddie, remember to ask God for His will in your life. Sometimes we get what we ask for and it might not always be the right thing for us. I am praying for you, Caddie, and my number one prayer is for your happiness."

* * * *

Jake spent most of his Saturday evenings with Caddie, and the rest of the family. They sat around the fire, sang and played musical instruments, popped popcorn in a wire corn popper over the fire in the fireplace, and talked about old times. Sometimes they played checkers or dominoes or someone read aloud to the family. Sometimes they sang or listened to the Grand Ole Opry on the squawking radio. Uncle Hume and Jake spent a good part of their time adjusting tubes, batteries and the radio knobs, for a better connection, and hoping for less static. When there was too much static, and they couldn't hear the radio, Aunt

Mae pulled out her records. Uncle Hume sat close to the Victrolla, and made sure the handle stayed cranked.

* * * *

Locket took the telephone off the hallway table, placed it on the floor of her bedroom and locked the door. She dialed the operator. It buzzed and buzzed.

To think I've tolerated Buker Webster all this time, just because of what people might think. I should have left a long time ago, when I realized things were not working out. I've lived a lie, pretending to be happy. It's so embarrassing! Of course, the people here in this place can look at me, and know things are not right with Buker and me. Living with him has been such a waste of time. Such a waste of my life! I've told him he's a fake and I feel like a fake, too! I've waited for a miracle that never happened!

"Operator? That you Jan? Good! Jan, let's try my sister, again. Thank you, very much," she whispered. "Sorry to constantly bother you, but it's very important."

"Sorry, Ms. Webster. No answer. Want me to keep trying."

"Thanks, Jan, I'll call you back. My sister must be out of town."

* * * *

Reverend Buker Webster felt an electrical tingling in his being—a restlessness. Reading many journals dating back to his childhood, sorting stacks of correspondence, examining the possessions he had accumulated in his travels and just being in the privacy of his office did not curb the anxiety that he felt in the pit of his stomach. He gathered up his letters, tapped them neatly on their edges, placed them in one of the carved boxes on his desk, tucked them under his arm, and left his study.

A Hooting Owl called to its mate.

The bright moonlight elongated and exaggerated the shadow of Reverend Buker Webster's tall and muscular body as he walked from the parsonage up the steep, and rocky hill to the cemetery. He kept his eyes on the long, outstretched arms of the Storey angel, and felt its pull and beckoning. He took a deep breath when he reached the wrought iron gate which surrounded the Brown's gravesite. He held the small boxes in his arms and under his chin, opened the wrought iron gate to the small outdoor room, and walked slowly and reverently to Macie Zanderneff's grave. He placed his boxes gently upon the mounded earth, and knelt. He took it as a good omen when he noticed a shadow of the Storey angel and the lacy shadow of the wrought iron fence fashioned by the moonlight, reflecting directly on her gravesite.

He wriggled his knees, and made himself more comfortable on the hard clay of the grave site.

"Oh, Mother of Darkness—" he prayed.

An owl swooped down into the confines of the wrought iron fence, snatched a field mouse by the back of its neck with its sharp talons and lit on the left shoulder of the Storey angel. The shadow of the owl holding a dangling mouse struggling for its life, its tail twitching, twitching until it could twitch no more, fell across Macie's grave.

The spirit of Billy Taylor moved his swing. The silvery blue ribbons intertwined in its ropes shone brightly in the moonlight, and its frayed ends fluttered in the moaning wind.

* * * *

Reverend Buker Webster left the cemetery hurriedly and headed for the meeting house. He entered the front door and laid his prized carved boxes on a church bench.

He located two coal-oil lanterns, lit them, and hung them on nails on the wall. Then, he placed a wooden, four-foot plank between the rails of two split rail chairs.

He unlocked a small closet in the back of the room, found a bottle of bourbon hidden inside the door frame, removed its cap and took a swallow. He removed a white tablecloth and placed it upon the wooden plank.

He admired his work and lit two more coal-oil lamps. He placed the small lamps, one on each side of the make-shift altar and moved one of the coal-oil lanterns to the opposite wall.

The moonlight shone brightly through a window at the back of the room, and created a perfect setting for his weekly ritual.

He placed a round object on the altar, covered in a black, velvet cloth and slowly removed the cloth to reveal a crystal ball. He placed the crystal ball in the middle of the altar, carefully and precisely. He leaned a tarot card of The Hanged Man against a side of the crystal ball. "The Hanged Man with a painted white face and black eyes wearing a red tuxedo jacket and black tights was the same tarot card that had belonged to his mother, and the last image "the beautiful lady" probably saw the day she died on his parent's verandah.

He removed a red velvet tuxedo jacket from the closet, brushed and smoothed it with both of his hands, pulled it through his long arms, buttoned it, and patted his muscular chest.

He removed a grass rope from the closet, tied a noose and threw the rope around a rafter. He pulled both ends between his hands, making the rope see-saw back and forth over the rafter. Back and forth. He tied an end of the rope to a chair nearby, all the while inaudibly muttering to himself.

He removed a mirror and a small metal box from the closet and set them on the altar. He knelt down, opened the small metal box, removed several small, metallic paint tubes and placed them on the altar. He gazed into the mirror and smiled at the reflected handsome image of himself. He opened a tube of white paint and smeared it upon his eyelids. He opened a tube of black paint and outlined the white paint with black circles around his eyes, and mouth. He wiped his hands on a white cloth blotched with black paint, and removed his muddy pants, exposing a ballerina-type black tights. He smoothed his tightly bound legs and admired them.

Excitement rushed through his veins, as he admired his camouflaged face in a small mirror, feeling a flicker of vulnerability, without accountability. He shook off vulnerability, taking on a new persona, with a new and superior power. Every muscle in his body appeared exaggerated in the dim light.

He placed one of the carved, wooden boxes upon the altar, removed envelope after envelope, doted over the contents, and placed the envelopes back into their specified places in the box.

He walked back to the rope, untied it and see-sawed it back and forth over the rafter and re-tied it to the back of the chair.

He knelt down and placed his hands upon the altar and posed as a channeler, doing those things he'd seen his parents do many times in the past. He called upon the dead in a loud voice, "Come forth! Make your presence known. Macie! Ratchel!"

His body wretched, and slumped forward, and caused the altar to shake and tremble. The lights of the coal-oil lanterns flickered. His lips mumbled a message from an unknown world and gave reality to the shadows in the moonlit room.

When he reached consciousness, he picked up the bottle of bourbon that sat on the floor beside him, and drank deeply from the bottle.

"Take me to your unknown world! Show me its dancing lights and its contrasting blue-black darkness! Be with me and help me see the truth of your mysterious world!" He cried out, and moaned.

He stood up, twirled around the room until he staggered. He held onto one of the chairs that held the make-shift altar.

After he got his bearings, he knelt down, and returned to his ritual. He opened the flap of one of the envelopes, and removed a photograph of a naked Ratchel Robin Daniels lying on a colorless marble slab. He kissed the photograph and placed it upon the altar.

He read one of the letters aloud.

"Dearest Ratchel—

I knew that I loved you, on that day I came to know you!"

He replaced the letter on the altar along with the photograph of the naked Ratchel Robin Daniels. He shouted his torment to the demons of the darkness, and bared his searching soul.

Ratchel-Robin, come forth! Come forth!

Ratchel Robin's photograph slipped slightly ajar. He adjusted and readjusted it.

Moths flew around the globes of the coal-oil lamps, bumping-bumping against the glass.

Buker Webster knelt before the altar.

A "Luna Moon-Moth"—its species prevalent around light on a warm night—danced in the wings of the altar's stage. When the moth bounced against one of the lanterns, Buker Webster grabbed it between his long fingers, held it up and examined its furry white body with pale, pea-green wings and streaming tails that appeared fairy-like.

He stood up and walked to a shelf where he found a box of craft supplies that were used for church activities. He removed embroidery scissors, and glue.

He held the moth carefully and securely, and clipped the wings from the moth, very precisely, with the scissors.

While he glued the moth's fairy-like wings to the shoulders of Ratchel in the photograph, the remains of the moth writhed and gyrated.

His ritual intensified with his preoccupation, and the movement of the dying moth added to his arousal and excitement.

He laughed when he heard the moth crying out in a moth's mother language only its mother could interpret.

He removed another letter from the carved box, and read it loudly, as he held a photograph to his heart.

"Dear Mother of Darkness!

I love you. my angel! You are my angel—my one and only angel. Each person has one to call his own. You are my angel who hears and cares—my angel who listens when I call and my angel who lifts me up when I fall! Oh, guardian, why invisibility, when I scream for visibility! My Angel*!*"

He replaced the letter in the carved box.

He viewed his face in the small mirror, squeezed white paint from a metal tube upon the tips of his fingers, and smoothed the white paint upon his eyes and face.

A ghostly face with blackened round eyes sat upon the shoulders of a demon-like-man in a red tuxedo that pranced around the room, holding one photograph after another.

"Come forth, Mother of Darkness!"

"Come forth beautiful lady who walks upon the waters and torments me everyday!"

"Come forth, Macie!"

"Come forth, Ratchel! Find me alluring and enduring!"

He closed his eyes and awaited their presence.

Suddenly, a brisk wind rattled the door.

He stopped prancing, opened his eyes and held his arms out towards the door and the invisible visitors.

"Welcome! Welcome!" he called. "Join me here at this altar."

"Observe the test of my love!"

He knelt down, and held his hands tightly around the globe of one of the coal-oil lanterns. His hands smoked. He groaned when he felt pain, and smelled the stench of scorching flesh. With that pain he felt power and "masculinity" rush into his being, entering through his burning fingers.

He stood up, walked to the chair, and pulled the chair, which held the rope, nearer to the altar to enable him to see the photographs he had placed close to the lamps. He untied the rope, put the noose around his neck and pulled it tightly with his red, and blistered hands. He stepped upon the chair, gripped the loose-end of the rope tightly, and swung away from the chair.

The chair toppled over! He held the rope, and hung silently a few moments. The rope cut the flow of oxygen. A sensuous exhilaration rushed to his brain. He released his fingers from the end of the rope, but it remained attached to the rafter, and the noose continued to tighten around his neck. He didn't fall down to the floor like he always did. He tried to jiggle the rope, but it was entangled, and caught on a nail on the rafter. He panicked, as he struggled, and his burnt and blistered palms hindered his working and loosening the rope.

The juices of his body began to excrete, and he gasped, gurgled, and struggled, as death came slowly.

* * * *

It was a cool evening, the night Jake left the Brown's house. He walked the path towards Three-Mile Crossing.

The stars shone brighter than usual.

An owl hooted—hooted.

All the smells in the atmosphere and the night noises seemed more distinct. The world felt more alive than usual, and a full moon reflected his shadow as he walked along the pathway.

As he got near the church at Three-Mile Crossing, he heard a low, whinnying sound. He stopped and listened. It sounded again. He knew it was definitely the sound of a horse snorting. He became more alert. In the moonlight, he saw several saddled horses tied to scrub bushes near the path. He moved slowly away from the path towards the horses. It was a strange sight to find horses tied in the woods, away from nowhere, and particularly after midnight. He continued to walk slowly. Dry twigs snapped under his feet. He stopped, and listened, and looked around.

He noticed a dim light reflecting in a window at the meeting house. He began to creep slowly and quietly towards the light. A feeling of dread filled his stomach and apprehension overwhelmed his being.

Is it bootleggers? Who else would be out here in the woods this late? Oh, my God! I don't have my gun!

He held his stomach tightly, sucked in a deep breath, while listening, listening intently. He started to go to the front door, but decided to go around the back, instead. Something did not jibe—his gut-feeling told him to be cautious.

He slipped to the back of the meeting house. He was astonished but relieved when he saw the reflection of a dim light shining through some of the small cracks of the logs, and onto the faces of eight young men that leaned forward with their hands placed on the meeting house wall, peering through them like peep holes. The dim light reflecting from the inside of the meeting house made their faces glow. They acknowledged Jake with a nod, and turned their wide-open eyes back to their observations.

Jake said nothing, but adjusted his boots in the soil, leaned forward and rested his hands on the meeting house wall and peeped through a chink-hole.

* * * *

When Jake looked through the chink hole, he saw a skeleton-faced man with a white face and dark circles painted around his eyes dancing around the back room of the meeting house. At first, he didn't recognize the painted face.

Bile rushed into his throat and nausea filled the pit of his stomach, when he realized it was Reverend Buker Webster who danced.

Reverend Webster called upon the dark spirits of the unknown to make their presence known. "Come forth!"

The wind began to blow and the door to the meeting house rattled.

Jake pulled his hat tighter upon his head, and heard the murmur of the boys. "Did you see that?"

And, Tinker whispered, "Quiet—he'll hear ya."

Jake stood mesmerized watching the bizarre performance. He was glued to the spot. He held his breath, and the wind whistling in his ears became temporarily deafening. The sickening, pain-induced actions, and performance of Buker Webster made Jake's legs rubbery.

When Jake saw Buker Webster place a rope around his neck and swing out from the chair, Jake gasped out loud. He was stunned! He couldn't move!

Buker Webster's struggled with the rope, making an attempt to loosen it. His eyes became wide open, his tongue bulged out of his mouth, and he gurgled.

Jake shook himself back to reality and ran to the back door of the meeting house, as fast as he could run.

The young men followed closely behind him.

Tinker Daniels, Rob-Hunter Daniels, Wyllyam Daniels, the Donahoo boys and the Myers boys ran in the meeting house directly behind Jake. Tinker grabbed Buker Webster's legs and pushed his heavy body upwards.

Jake picked up the over-turned chair and stood up in it. He hacked the rope with his pen-knife until it cut through. Jake removed the noose of the rope from Buker Webster's neck, placed him on the ground and worked to revive him. He yelled at the young men, "Hey! You, boys, go and get Doc Stowe! Believe he's across the road visiting with Judge Pewter. Run fast for me, Rob Hunter! Rob-Hunter, run fast!"

But Rob-Hunter didn't hear Jake. He stood at the make-shift altar with the coal-oil lamps on each side, and knelt down. His body became rigid, and his eyes became riveted to a photograph of his sister, Ratchel Robin, which depicted her naked body lying on a funeral-home marble slab. Fairy-like, pea-green moth wings were glued to her shoulders. Rob-Hunter screamed, "Oh! No! No!"

All the young men were inside the meeting house at that time, and Jake yelled, "I said for somebody to go and get Doc Stowe! Turn on the lights, quick!"

"Some of you other boys go and get Uncle Hume and Aunt Mae, and tell Aunt Mae to bring her medicine basket!

"Ain't the preacher dead, Jake," Tinker Daniels whispered, as they knelt on the floor next to Buker Webster.

"Believe he's dead or 'most dead." Jake whispered. He continued first-aid.

"Ain't that about the ugliest red coat you ever saw," Tinker Daniels whispered. He pulled the lapels back and looked inside the lining. And, look at those sexy tights. Now, ain't that some kind of a preacher?"

"Yeah! Silly coat and wicked preacher," Jake agreed. "Tinker, you need to go for help."

"Me go for help? Let God help him," he sneered. He held his wide open hands out towards Jake and backed away. "Think I'll just spit on him!"

* * * *

Reverend Buker Webster's body floated to the top of the ceiling and he looked down. He saw Jake hovering over someone lying on a wooden floor. *Why are those people crying over a clown in a red jacket?* He looked closer and gasped. *Those people aren't crying. They seem to be mad about something.*

Reverend Buker Webster floated back down to the floor and observed the clown, again. *It's I! It's I! But how could it be? I see young boys, and a gentlemen and a lady. Why it's Aunt Mae! Oh, no! Now she knows. Now they all know!*

After the body gurgled and struggled to breathe, it lay quietly. His spiritual body came nose to nose with his own physical face! He hovered above the physical body and slowly floated to the ceiling again.

He heard someone say, "Let's get him out of here, and fast like!" It sounded like Doc Stowe. "Gotta get him to the hospital!"

Now I remember. I burned my hands with the lamp, and couldn't work the rope!

He floated through the ceiling into a mint-green mist, and found himself lying prostrate at the silvery, metallic feet of a man. No word was spoken, but he knew it was the unknown—Death! He became aware of a deafening noise—the sound of shrill, loud and humming machinery. He held his ears and cried out in pain, as he lifted his eyes, and gazed upon the embodiment of "Death."

Death had the body of a man, four scaly arms and hands and the face of a giant cicada. Upon the head of the giant cicada were wriggling antennae and two horns. Across the forehead bore the name, "Necromancer." He wore a suit of armor, and across his breastplate were the words, *IT IS TIME*! A hang-man's noose hung from his left shoulder-plate. His four hands carried different instruments: a cycle, a small, carved wooden box in the shape of a coffin; a bronze vial from which spilled vile, putrid, smoking vapors. He placed the bronze vial upon a table of thick, green mist, removed a smoldering coal of fire, and held it in his hands towards Buker Webster.

The black cape of Death hung to his feet, its hood covering only the back of his insect-like head. His colorful mint-green wings were shaped as a Luna Moon Moth and moved slightly, as if they breathed.

Buker Webster was too horrified to scream! He looked into myriad eyes and realized that the thunderous machine-like noise was that of possibly millions of moths, flies, bugs and giant cicadas singing a song of death, rubbing their legs and antenna together in unison. They surrounded him, moved slowly towards him, and glowered with their shiny and revengeful eyes.

The spiritual body of Buker Webster took flight from the physical one. He felt the outline of his aura with his helpless hands. The aura was but a shadow, and a mere personification of his worst faults and weaknesses.

He wept, but no tears came.

He laid his face forward into a sea-green misty cloud and cried, "Have mercy!"

His body began to spin, and the green cloud tightened around his body and swirled him into darkness. The thunderous noise hurt his eardrums. He was pulled swiftly, as if he were drawn by a magnet through a dark, narrow, funnel. When he saw light at the end of the narrow funnel, he breathed with relief, but at that same moment, he caught a glimpse of the silhouette of a giant of a man, with outstretched arms, blocking the exit. The man opened his gold and brown "Monarch Butterfly" wings, and his enormous wing-span touched and covered both sides of the tunnel.

The recesses of his mind emptied and the recall of every good and every bad deed he'd ever done in his life reeled before his eyes.

* * * *

When Aunt Mae looked down upon Reverend Buker Webster 's body lying on the meeting house floor, she saw the old and new bruises and the rope burns upon his neck. And, suddenly, she realized the raw burn Reverend Buker Webster referred to as a razor-burn was not that of a razor but the burn of the noose of a rope. "Doc, Buker Webster is an impostor!" she whispered between her teeth.

"He is indeed that and maybe more, Mae. See about Rob-Hunter and the other boys, right away, please, Mae!" Doc Stowe pleaded.

"Doc, I'm glad you're here. I don't believe I could have worked with The Reverend."

"You'd do it if you had to, Mae. See about Rob-Hunter, please," Doc Stowe raised his voice.

Aunt Mae moved slowly through the nightmare.

She found Rob-Hunter sitting before the make-shift altar holding a photograph of Ratchel Robin. She removed the photograph from his hand, laid it upon the altar, walked him to a bench and spread her shawl around him.

Rob-Hunter stared straight ahead with unblinking eyes, without moving. His body shook and his teeth chattered.

"Let's get you warm and make you comfortable," said Aunt Mae. She removed a red flannel blanket from her medicine basket and spread it over him.

Uncle Hume removed his coat, spread it over Rob Hunter's shoulders, and sat down beside him. "Lean on me, Rob Hunter." He put his long arm around the boy and drew him close to his body. "It's gonna be all right. You're gonna be all right," he whispered.

Aunt went back to the make-shift altar and observed a contortioning and suffering wing-less moth, only then realizing that the moth's fairy-like green wings were glued upon the shoulders of Ratchel Robin's photograph. She yelled for Jake to come quickly! She pointed to the suffering, furry-white body of the Luna Moon Moth and Ratchel's photograph. "Please put that poor creature out of its sweet misery!

"Aunt Mae, we have to leave all this for Sheriff Olliff to examine. Don't let anybody touch anything," he whispered. He placed his handkerchief over the writhing body of the moth and left it on the altar. "Somebody, please go and get your maw and paw. Bring Mary and Joseph here," Aunt Mae said urgently. "Get some quilts from the parsonage!"

"So—this is what that preacher had in one of the boxes—nude pictures!"

Tinker handed Aunt Mae a cellophane packet, which held a photograph of Macie. Monarch Butterfly wings were glued to her shoulders. "That preacher is a sicko."

Jake placed his arm around Aunt Mae's shoulders and held her tightly. "I can't believe he touched our Macie!" he whispered in disgust. "Our Macie! Our Macie! I should have let Tinker spit on that son-uv-a-bitch! That so-called preacher!"

"What is it?" asked Uncle Hume. "What're you looking at?"

She handed him the photograph. He was dumbfounded when he gazed at the nude body of their beloved Macie. Uncle Hume placed his handkerchief over the section of her nude body and allowed only the top of her head to show.

"Jake, we need to call the Sheriff! This picture was taken of Macie after her body was brought back here to Georgia."

Uncle Hume removed the photograph from Aunt Mae's hand very gently.

"Sheriff Olliff's on the way." Jake took the photograph from Uncle Hume and laid it face down upon the bench. "Let's get away from all this, Aunt Mae. It'd probably be best if you sit down," he said gently. "We shouldn't be handling all this stuff—it's evidence against Buker Webster. Let's wait for Sheriff Olliff to get here and don't touch anything else."

The young men began talking all at once, "That preacher man dressed up and danced around here every Saturday night. He talked to invisible people and stuff. He called for the Mother of Darkness to come forth. It was amazing! No wind ever came up before, but tonight a strong wind came up all of a sudden and it blew really hard. The door to the meeting house swung open!"

"And he yelled for angels to come and help him and he'd say he was declaring his love for the dead people and stuff!"

"He talked to his mama, and stuff."

"Yeah, and he'd get on that chair and hang from that rope and stuff!" They agreed excitedly and loudly.

"You boys have been through a lot. Let's sit on the bench beside Rob-Hunter." Uncle Hume rolled his jacket and placed it under Rob-Hunter's head and spread Aunt Mae's shawl across his body. Rob-Hunter stared wide-eyed. "You've been through a lot, Son, but everything's gonna be all right," he assured, as he patted him on the shoulder.

"Place some song books under his feet. Elevate his feet," said Tinker.

"He don't look good."

"He's in a bad way," said Aunt Mae. "Doc needs to help with him."

"Hume, that Luna Moon Moth is a summer moth. It's late in the year for one to be here in this place tonight, and alive."

"But, this Summer Moth is right here before our eyes, and its being here at this time is a crazy occurrence, just like everything else happening around here."

"Yes, crazy. It's a bad omen."

"You know that preacher's crazy! He took a picture of Macie and Ratchel and God only knows who else. I want to kill him!" Uncle Hume's voice shook with anger.

"He's evilness, itself!"

"Hume! I just thought of something!"

"What, Mae? What?"

"Remember—" She held her heart and closed her eyes. "I told you something bad was going to happen when y'all took that critter out of Ghost Hollow!" she whispered.

"You're just too superstitious!" said Uncle Hume. He shook his head. "We don't know that us catching that opossum caused anything," he emphasized.

Doc Stowe yelled, "Call Jenkins' Ambulance. Let's get Buker and Rob Hunter out of here, boys!"

"You mean that evil preacher is still alive?"

"It's awful, ain't it? Just awful—the things he's been doing," the young boys lamented.

"Look at Rob-Hunter! He won't do nothing. He won't say nothing! He just stares at me! Speak to me! Say something, Bubba!" Wyllyam cried out to him.

Jake and Uncle Hume helped Doc Stowe place Rob Hunter in Doc Stowe's Buick, and Aunt Mae covered him with a quilt.

"Be careful on the highway, Doc."

"Jenkins' ambulance will get Buker Webster to the Downey Hospital quite a bit ahead of me. I'll take Rob Hunter with me. We'll be all right.

Tinker got into the automobile with Doc Stowe, and placed his arm around Rob Hunter. "Gonna take care of brother."

* * * *

Aunt Mae walked to the make-shift altar and looked at the photographs again, and especially the one of the nude Ratchel Robin Daniels lying on the marble slab next to her coffin.

Laying the photograph aside with a trembling hand, she opened the lid of one of the small carved boxes, and peered inside. "Ever see anything like it, Aunt Mae?"

She jumped, and screamed. "Jake, you scared the dickens out of me!"

"Did I startle you, or did the contents of the box startle you," he asked, as he squatted down beside her. He took the other box into his hands and opened it. "Look! Inside this box are thousands of insect wings. Every possible insect and bug wing you can imagine is in this box: flies, cicadas, butterflies, moths, and God only knows what other critters' wings are here in this box." Jake drew a deep and exasperated breath. "Now, let's put all of this stuff back where it was, and let Sheriff Olliff take over."

Aunt Mae handed him the photographs of Ratchel Robin and Macie. "The man is sick. Buker Webster had to have been at the funeral-home laboratory, here at Three-Mile Crossing, in order for him to take these photographs."

"Aunt Mae, it was all I could do not to go over to him and finish killing Buker Webster, after I saw the photographs of Macie and Ratchel," said Jake. "I wanted to go over to that evil preacher and choke him!"

"He was barely hanging on, when Doc Stowe took him to the hospital a few minutes ago. He might not make it," said Uncle Hume.

"Buker Webster is evil and sick. It's obvious he tortured critters and cut their wings off while they were alive and watched them die because we've got a dying moth lying under your handkerchief, and a box of dried insect wings, right here before us to prove it!" Aunt Mae pointed to the carved box which held the insect wings.

Jake shook his head in bewilderment. "I remember the day Buker Webster became entangled in a spider's web and wanted to kill the spider, but I thought it was just because he messed up his glasses."

"Look at this little box! It's in the shape of a coffin. It's chunked full of addressed envelopes. They apparently were never mailed."

The board resting between the chair slats shook, and the lamps flickered.

"Who is this evil man?" Jake whispered.

"He's the same strange person that wrote these letters and glued wings on the rest of these photographs?" Aunt Mae held the box tightly in her hands.

Uncle Hume reached into the wooden box, while Aunt Mae held it between her hands. "Look at these photographs, Mae. Here's one of an attractive woman with butterfly wings attached to her shoulders." He turned to the back of the photograph. *Mother* is written on the back of this picture." The woman wore a dark beret close to her left eye, held her head upright, and with dignity. Her dress reflected a shiny substance, perhaps taffeta, and it was obviously a design of good class.

Uncle Hume's hands shook.

"Let's leave everything where we found it," said Jake.

Aunt Mae kept her gaze on the lady's face and took the photograph into her hands hesitantly. "Yes, she's a very pretty lady."

"Here's a picture of that same woman." The lady stood beside a lovely little girl, with long black curls, also dressed immaculately. "On the back of this photograph I see some hand-written words that say, M*e and Buker.*

"Me and Buker!" He exclaimed. "That's a little girl in the photograph. That couldn't be Buker Webster and his mother." Uncle Hume held the photograph closer to his eyes.

They examined some of the other photographs of the little girl, about five or six years of age, and most of them were labeled *Buker Webster.*

"Look, here, Hume. Try to keep the cellophane wrapped around the photograph." she whispered.

Uncle Hume took the photograph in his shaky hands. "Well, I'll declare. I've never seen anything like it." He shook his head in amazement.

"Every photograph has insect wings or butterfly wings glued on the shoulders of the people," said Jake. "No wings are on any of Buker Webster's own personal photographs!"

"Guess he glued wings only on the dead people." Aunt Mae closed her eyes, and held her hand over her mouth.

Sheriff Olliff, Judge Pewter and Ole Pem rushed into the Meeting House.

"What in the world is going on?" yelled Sheriff Olliff.

Aunt Mae shouted, "We've been hoodwinked by Buker Webster!" She wiped tears from her eyes, and blew her nose.

Ole Pem walked up to the make-shift altar, and whispered, "Well, I'll be—"

"Leave everything like it is!" said Judge Pewter.

"Let's not touch anything else," Sheriff Olliff said gently, as he surveyed the room. "Okay? Let's everybody move to the back of the room." He placed his hand on Aunt Mae's and Uncle Hume's shoulders. "Y'all have to come, too."

"Where's Locket?" asked Judge Pewter.

"She's still at home, as far as we know," said Uncle Hume.

The young boys slumped on a bench.

"We've been deceived by a crazy man," Uncle Hume whispered.

Ole Pem placed his muscular arms around Aunt Mae, and pulled her to his chest. "This is quite an ordeal, Aunt Mae. Want us to take you home?" he asked, soothingly. She nodded against his chest.

"Jake, go over and keep Locket at her house. We don't need her over here." Sheriff Olliff whispered.

* * * *

Locket Webster was on the front porch, ready to come down the steps, when Jake came into the yard.

"What's going on, Jake? What's all that commotion? It's Buker, isn't it?" She held one hand to her breast and grasped her robe with the other. "What's wrong?"

"Locket, let's make a pot of coffee." He touched her elbow and guided her back into the house.

"Tell me, Jake. What has happened?"

"Locket, I don't know how to tell you."

* * * *

At daybreak, everyone sat around the kitchen fireplace, drinking tea or coffee, and speculating on what had taken place the night before. Caddie and Aunt Mae prepared breakfast.

When the dogs barked, Aunt Mae threw her shawl across her shoulders and rushed to the front porch. Ole Pem and Judge Pewter assisted Locket Webster as she got out of his Cadillac.

Locket fell into Aunt Mae's arms and sobbed, "Buker is still alive! They took him to the hospital but say he'll have to go to the Milledgeville Hospital, Aunt Mae. He's gonna be locked up! They said Buker is crazy! I need to know what to do."

"You're welcome to stay here with us, Locket. We have plenty of room. We're just about to put biscuits in the oven." She touched a bruise under Locket's eye with her index finger.

Joseph and Mary Daniels stood at the door and stared at Locket Webster and Judge Pewter.

"Morning, Mary. Morning, Joseph," Judge Pewter reached for their hands. "Doc called me on the telephone and told me that Rob-Hunter is progressing well. He'll bring him and Tinker back here with him this afternoon. I'm sorry for everything that's happened to you folks."

"Yes, thank you, Judge. Rob Hunter must be taking everything worse than the other boys. Wyllyam is asleep in one of the attic rooms upstairs, and the Daniels and Myers boys are at home. Pore ole Rob-Hunter," Mary muttered and frowned. "Pore ole Wyllyam. Pore ole Tinker. Pore boys! How will all this horrible stuff touch our young boys?"

"Well, time will help, I'm sure. We'll get them some professional help." Judge Pewter encouraged.

Ole Pem stood beside Caddie, "You holding up all right?"

"As well as can be expected—horrified is the best way I can describe how I feel. Will you eat breakfast with us? The biscuits are almost ready to come out of the oven."

"Don't go to any special bother, Caddie," Ole Pem smiled.

"It's no bother, really. We're glad to have you."

"I need to take Joseph and Mary out on the back porch for a short conversation," Judge Pewter said.

"You want ham with your biscuits?" asked Aunt Mae, as she moved the iron skillet onto the eye of the wood stove.

"Just whatever you were going to fix. No special bother for me," said Judge Pewter.

The Daniels followed Judge Pewter and Ole Pem to the back porch.

"First of all, I want to tell you I represent Locket Webster, and I am speaking for her, as her lawyer. The most important thing I need to say is that I talked with Doc Stowe on the telephone, and Doc said Buker Webster will end up at Milledgeville."

"Well, he needs to be cuz he's crazy," said Joseph Daniels.

"Doc Stowe said Buker Webster's spine is dislocated and his larynx is crushed but somehow, he has miraculously lived! Rob-Hunter and Tinker are on the way back home with Doc Stowe and we'll see them just as soon as they get back to Three-Mile Crossing."

"All right."

"In the meantime, Doc Stowe wants you to keep a sharp eye on all of the other boys."

"Sure, we will."

"Locket Webster didn't know the first thing about her husband's weird Saturday night activities."

"Locket's his wife! She'd have to know!" Joseph Webster snarled.

"Locket Webster did not have the slightest idea that Buker Webster collected anything unusual. She knew he took photographs of dead people and gave the photographs to relatives, but that's all she knew. She didn't know anything about his sexual perversions, such as his hanging from the rafters at the church, and doing all these rituals and stuff."

"We're mad about the whole thing!" Mary Daniels cried. "We thought Reverend Buker Webster was a true minister and a man of God, when he took the time to console us, and told us our beautiful daughter was greatly missed at church. He'd hold our hands, and look into our eyes like he was so concerned! But, in reality, he was not a true man of God. He was mocking me and Joseph." Mary frowned and squeezed her eyes shut.

"If you have any grudge whatsoever, direct your anger towards Buker Webster. You understand what I'm saying? You hear? Locket is innocent."

"Reverend Buker Webster stripped Ratchel Robin's clothes off and took a picture of her naked body when she wuz at the funeral parlor! He cut off the wings of a summer moth—a Luna Moon Moth, and pasted the wings on Ratchel Robin's picture! Locket Webster knew he was doing these things and she didn't care!" Mary Daniels sobbed. "That crazy preacher took pictures of dead women! He was sick! Locket knew it! She knew he took pictures of poor little Ratchel Robin and Macie, too!"

"No, Mary! Locket Webster didn't know her husband was doing anything unusual. She didn't know he pulled wings off living insects or dead ones, either, for that matter."

"Locket Webster had to know Buker Webster loved dead people—that he did unnatural things to them at the funeral parlor!"

"No, she didn't. That's what I'm here to tell you today. She does not condone his actions!"

"It's hard to believe he did all these crazy things and Locket didn't know about it. Don't you think so?" Joseph Daniels frowned, and wrinkles ran from the corners of his eyes into his cheeks, making deep indentations all the way down to his mouth.

"Not necessarily. We don't always know all the things that our spouse does. Anyway, Locket's going to have a hard time getting a new start. I hope you will help her."

"We won't cause Locket no trouble, if you say she didn't know what wuz going on." Joseph held his chin with his tanned, bony hand and methodically scrutinized the conversation. "But, that evil preacher needs to pay. Some way he needs to pay for what he's done to all these boys. He needs to go to jail."

"I personally want Locket to stay here at Three-Mile Crossing and not move away. She's an asset to the community. She's a good influence—a teacher—a lady!"

Mary Daniels slumped into one of the chairs on the porch and wove a baby-blue handkerchief in and out of her fingers. "No—she'll be the laughing stock if she stays here in this place."

"I thought that crazy preacher hanged himself to death, and I was proud of it! Now, I hear he's still alive and I want to kill him with my bare hands for messing with Ratchel Robin, and confusing our young boys with all his wild shenanigans," said Joseph Daniels.

"Did the boys tell you anything about what they saw?"

"Every Saturday night, our boys and the neighbors' boys—you know the Donahoos and the Myers—George Myers' nephews—have visited or spent the night at each other's houses. They always packed biscuits, cheese and ham for a picnic."

"The boys said they'd get together and ride their horses 'til it started to get dark, and then they'd wait out in the woods for Buker Webster to begin his rituals." Joseph Daniels sat down and held his head in his hands.

"Yeah, and after that crazy preacher went home, the boys went inside and spent the night in the meeting house," said Mary Daniels. "The boys said they ate their biscuits the next morning, and dressed for church."

"We saw the boys at church services the next morning, and didn't suspect anything!" said Joseph Daniels.

"You're not planning on whipping your boys, are you?" asked Judge Pewter. "I don't believe whipping them is an answer to their observing Buker Webster's autoerotic actions, and rituals."

"No. We don't plan to whip them, but we don't understand what's happened enough to talk to them about it! We don't nothing about autoerotic—whatever it is you said."

"Nobody understands it. Don't worry. Nobody knew. Let's get back to what the boys observed at the meeting-house every Saturday night. That has to be the reason those young men have been laughing in church, all this time, and probably the subject of what their notes contained, as they passed them back and forth in church?"

"What notes, Judge Pewter?"

"You remember the notes they were writing in church and passing back and forth and some of them were laughing? Then, they'd pass it on to another boy. They created such a commotion, a meeting was called about their actions, remember?

"Lordy, I remember now. My mind is so cluttered from what's happened last night, I forgot for a moment, Judge Pewter."

"If I can be of any help whatsoever, please come to me. The boys need counseling, you know?"

"Yes, we know!" Mr. and Mrs. Daniels said, sadly. "Can you counsel them?"

"I'll talk to Doc Stowe just as soon as I can. We'll decide what we all need to do. Probably have to call a specialist to come up here and help us."

"Let's get Preacher McClure to counsel the boys," said Mary.

"Mary and Joseph, you need to know that Buker Webster is a very wealthy man. We'll ask the court to have him pay for the boys' counseling bills, ask for damages, and whatever else comes up, okay?"

"You talking about a lawsuit against that preacher?"

"Yes, that's what I'm saying. We'll come up with something. Might take some imagination, but we'll think of something."

"Thank you, Judge Pewter. You're a good man."

* * * *

Many cups of coffee washed down buttered-biscuits, fig preserves, muscadine jelly, grits, sausage patties, fried eggs and ham.

Judge Pewter split open one of the biscuits and inserted a pork sausage patty which was heavily seasoned with sage, and topped it off with fig preserves. "Good breakfast, Mae."

"Caddie cooked the biscuits."

"Caddie, you make superb biscuits!"

"Thanks, Judge."

"Yes. They're delicious, Caddie," said Ole Pem.

"Delicious—Scrumptious biscuits," Jake replied, thoughtfully.

"I hate to eat and run, but you know better than anyone else here, Caddie, that I have to rush," said Judge Pewter.

"Yes, we all understand."

Silence overcame the group.

"Caddie, do you want to go with me and Judge Pewter to the special called meeting at the church?" asked Ole Pem.

"Thanks, Ole Pem," she said, softly. "I—"

"Caddie is going with me to the meeting," Jake interrupted, and frowned.

"Okay, then I'll see you and Caddie at the meeting," Ole Pem smiled as he searched Caddie's sky-blue eyes. Her expression gave no indication that she was disappointed in not accepting his invitation.

"Hume, you need to go. We're out of a preacher now," Aunt Mae said solemnly.

"Okay, if you say so, Mae. I'll help you with things around here, when I get back after church."

"Judge Pewter, I just happened to think about Matilda. Where was she when everything was taking place?" asked Aunt Mae.

"Matilda's in Atlanta with her garden club friends. She'd really be in a dither about now. She can't handle any kind of pressure."

After Judge Pewter, Ole Pem and the Daniels left, everyone settled down.

Jake said, "I've heard of strange things happening, such as somebody hanging from a rope, just for the hell of it, but I still don't understand it."

Caddie glanced at Locket.

"Locket, are you sure you want to hear?" asked Aunt Mae, as she raked imaginary crumbs from the table cloth into her hand.

"I need to learn what my husband—what Buker Webster was really like!" Locket glanced quickly at Jake. "Tell everybody what you found last night, Jake," she whispered.

"After I talked to Locket last night, Sheriff Olliff and I took her over to the meeting house and let her see the cut rope hanging from the rafter and the make-shift altar and everything on it. We went through all of it carefully. From what we could gather, Buker Webster had a box full of love letters to dead people that he had personally written and kept in a box. It's in the shape of a coffin."

"Did Sheriff Ollie go over to the parsonage, too?"

"He's investigating Reverend Buker Webster's past. Mainly, he investigating him disturbing the dead," said Jake. "Buker Webster wrote letters to people he once knew, men and women, who are now dead. Each envelope had a "love letter" with a photograph. His letters sounded as if he'd had relations with some of the dead people, but, of course, he could have been fantasizing.

"I've heard if a person loves the dead or has a relationship with them the dictionary has a word for it called *necromancy* or that person is called *a necromancer.*" Aunt Mae rubbed her forehead. "But, I thought it was all made up stuff—make-believe stuff that just happened in horror tales."

"Yes, Aunt Mae, it is horror," said Jake. "Some of the photographs had the wings of moths or butterflies glued carefully and meticulously to the photographs, along the shoulders of the people."

Caddie scooted her chair closer to Jake.

"It's hard to conceive the pain he inflicted upon butterflies, moths and insects!" Jake stopped talking as he remembered the moth's suffering and tortured body contorting on the make-shift altar.

"Do insects and bugs endure pain?" asked Uncle Hume.

"Talk lower. Henny-Penny and Kackie are still asleep," Aunt Mae whispered. She poked the logs in the fireplace. Sparks flew. "And, Wyllyam is asleep in the attic." She pointed her finger at the ceiling.

"Last night when I saw those boys staring through those cracks, you know those chink-holes at the meeting-house, and I leaned forward to see through one of the peepholes, I didn't know what to expect. I never imagined how it would change all our lives," said Jake. "I didn't want to believe what I saw. All of a sudden, I was like one of the boys—just caught up into a peep-show, caught up in a play. I was floored!"

"Locket, we are so sorry!" Uncle Hume sympathized, and patted her on the hand.

Locket nodded.

Aunt Mae refilled Jake's coffee cup.

"Rob-Hunter's mind might be affected, Jake. Seeing Ratchel Robin's photograph on that altar was devastating to him! All those boys will be affected, somehow," said Aunt Mae.

"Buker Webster has been an appalling example for those boys. I'll never forget seeing the picture of Macie's nude body lying on that—that—altar, whatever it was! Never!" Locket's hands trembled, when she rubbed her swollen blue eyes and blew her swollen red nose.

Jake followed Uncle Hume to the back porch.

"Jake, I've been thinking. When Buker Webster painted that mask on his face, he became someone else. That way he didn't have to accept any guilt, because he'd become another person," said Uncle Hume.

"Uncle Hume, I don't believe he was capable of feeling guilt. I don't believe he has a conscience. He's not only crazy but an impostor. No real preacher would ever touch Macie! Nor Ratchel!"

"None of us deserved such treatment!"

"I've heard that when someone ties a rope around his neck and just hangs there, but not really meaning to kill himself like Buker Webster was doing, it has something to do with sexual matters. It purportedly causes intensity in ejaculation. A quick rush of blood supposedly goes to the brain or something like that."

"How in the world would anyone know about doing such a strange act as he was doing?"

"I don't know. It's weird anyway we look at it."

"Remember we found a tarot card called *The Hanged Man* on the altar, propped up against a crystal ball. Buker had on a red tuxedo jacket and black tights just like the picture on the card. When Sheriff Olliff and I went through his things last night at the parsonage, we learned that his parents were fortune tellers."

"Well, in that case, that crystal ball might have belonged to his parents—to his mother."

"Will Buker Webster ever be able to tell anyone, himself?"

"I doubt that even if he gets better, he'll ever want to tell anyone about his sordid life."

"As old as I am, Jake, I've never heard anything to top this." Uncle Hume always prided himself in being a real-man, a tough one who could really 'take it.' As tears flowed from his eyes, he didn't realize his gentleness was one of his greatest, masculine assets.

* * * *

Jake removed a pack of papers and a bag of tobacco from his pocket. "Smoke, Uncle Hume?"

"No, thank you, Jake."

"Uncle Hume, you got any brew or corn to drink?"

"No, Jake. Let's keep our heads clear, okay? Everyone's depending on you son."

"Sure. Everyone's depending on me." Jake stood up and stretched. He clenched his fists as he thought of Macie.

Dan beat you, killed you, and if that wasn't enough, that make-believe preacher violated your body! Macie what could I have done to prevent your death! This violation! This horror!

"Sit with us, Jake."

"Best be going on home, Uncle Hume," Jake said in a tired voice.

"Please stay here with us—Jake!" Uncle Hume insisted, and raised the tone of his voice.

But, the call of the bottle was louder.

* * * *

Aunt Mae led Locket to one of the attic bedrooms. "Thanks Aunt Mae."

"You're welcome, Chile. When you get into bed, I want you to drink this cup of tea that I brewed especially for you."

Locket sniffed the steam rising from her cup. "I can't determine its aroma."

"It'll make you sleep." She looked into Locket's eyes and knew that her life was shattered—probably forever.

"Aunt Mae, I don't know what I'm going to do. I'll have to move out of the parsonage!"

"Stay with us as long as you like. You need to rest, now."

"Thank you, Aunt Mae," she whispered. "You know I've been so worried because Buker didn't want to sleep with me. Now, I'm so happy that we never did. I just couldn't go on living, if we'd ever slept together."

"You don't say!" Aunt Mae studied her face.

Locket laughed sarcastically. "To think he loves dead people."

"You mean to tell me you and Reverend Buker Webster never slept together as husband and wife?" Aunt Mae raised her eyebrows and widened her eyes.

"No, he never touched me." She turned her face toward the wall. "Aunt Mae, I'm so ashamed. When Jake came to the house and told me Buker hanged himself, I told him that Buker and I had quarreled—that I had told Buker I wanted a divorce. I told Jake I didn't know Buker cared enough for me to try and hang himself."

"Don't feel ashamed."

"Jake had to tell me that the reason Buker was hanging himself was due to sexual perversion, and it had nothing to do with our marriage—with my trying to leave. I am so embarrassed—so humiliated."

"Best be glad it's the way it is, Locket. You need to thank God he never touched you."

"Aunt Mae, Buker threatened me and said he'd clip my wings. Now I know he wasn't just trying to scare me!" She touched the bruise under her eye and rubbed her jaw.

"You're in a safe place now. We'll talk again." Aunt Mae closed the door.

* * * *

Locket sipped her tea.

Nothing makes sense!

Her anxiety mingled with horror and resentment.

God, let this be a dream. It can not be real. She placed the red pottery cup on a an oak table next to the bed, and snuggled down into the bed.

I've wasted so much time with Buker.

She slept fitfully, and dreamed:

A strange man offered her a rope. "Will you please tie a knot?" he asked.

"What kind of knot? A wedding knot or a hangman's knot?" Locket asked.

And the man said, "Is there a difference?" As his face floated away from his body, it laughed and mocked her!

She fell, with a lurch, away from the man and the floating face, swiftly. Then, she floated slowly and peacefully through soft shimmers of pink light. She grabbed a soft, pastel, pieced-quilt cloud of rainbow colors, tucked it under her chin, and slept, deeply.

* * * *

"Our meeting was terrible, Mae."

Yes, Hume, I know it must have been horrible!"

"Mae, those boys said they heard him talking out in the graveyard every Saturday night. Even, if it rained, he walked around in the rain and mud. His clothes and boots would be filthy."

"Hume, I saw his boots muddy a lot of times. Didn't you?" She helped him take his coat off and hung it on a nail on the wall beside the fireplace in the kitchen. "Can you poke up the fire, a little, please?"

Uncle Hume placed a log on the fire, and rearranged the coals with the fire poker.

"Listen, Mae! Sheriff Olliff, Jake, and the Elders found several posters on the dark-room closet wall located in the study. They found a lot of photographs of dead people in their coffins glued to the posters. Jake said they didn't recognize anyone in the pictures except Ratchel Robin and Macie. Sheriff Olliff took the posters to his office—the ones that had dead people all over it."

"George-West Myers is fit to be tied! He helped the sheriff go through some journals that Buker has been writing since he was about fourteen years old, along with letters, newspaper clippings, and old documents they found at the parsonage. That's the way they learned a little about his Maw and Paw."

"Were they wealthy?" asked Aunt Mae. "His mother's photograph looked like a lady of wealth."

"Apparently, his parents were fortune tellers—mediums or whatever you call them," said Uncle Hume. "His mother was known as *Madame Madras.*"

"Fortune tellers?"

"Yeah, Buker Webster still owns his old home place down in south Georgia. The pictures looked like a big Victorian house, Jake said."

"So, Grandmaw Taylor was right about Buker Webster wanting his cards read," Aunt Mae nodded for emphasis.

"She was probably right. Maybe Grandmaw Taylor reminded Buker Webster of his mother."

"So, he took pictures of other dead people before he moved here. I wonder if he tortured human beings like he did insects?"

"Don't know. Sheriff Ollie said they found no indication that he ever harmed anyone, but they're looking into that possibility."

"Locket is afraid of him."

I can't believe those young boys didn't tell their parents about Buker Webster."

"The boys said they knew Buker Webster was deceiving everyone—wanted to report him, but it got out of hand when they waited so long. They grew afraid to tell anyone about the Saturday night rituals."

"Buker Webster was a stranger when he got here and he's even more of a stranger now."

"I'll always hate him for what he's done, for touching Macie and Ratchel Robin."

"Buker Webster is gonna be in a lot of trouble with the law I'd say, when he leaves Milledgeville," said Aunt Mae.

"You mean *if* he ever leaves that booby-hatch!"

* * * *

That night Uncle Hume dreamed*: He walked along a barren, lonely road where he'd never walked before, and a strange man he'd never seen walked up to him and handed him a rope.*

"Here, ring this church bell," the stranger said.

When he started to pull the rope to the church-bell, he discovered the rope was around his own neck, tightening and choking him.

The stranger laughed hysterically.

Uncle Hume pulled and tugged at the rope around his neck!

The same stranger handed him a photograph. "Look upon this photograph—for there is a lesson here—a lesson—a lesson here—a lesson!" The laughter echoed.

The photograph of the stranger began to swirl in slow motion and the face, appearing to be a wrinkled mask, slid off his skull and rested upon his neck and chest, leaving the bareness of the bone of the skull, and blood. The face—the mask was held to the skull by its eyeball strings coming through the eye holes, and extended from the brain.

"Stranger, why do you show me this vile and horrible thing! No! No! I don't want to see!" Uncle Hume screamed

The strange man's laughter caused a vibration of the face, and the face slid completely off the photograph and into mid-air.

The floating, stretching elongated white face with blackened eyes floated closer. Blood flowed from the mouth of the face, and formed the words: "It's just a mask. You wear a mask. I wear a mask. Your own face is just a mask!"

Uncle Hume screamed and awakened the household.

* * * *

The children were not allowed to make noise on the Sabbath. Therefore, they played quiet games such as old-maid cards, checkers, chess, hop-scotch or marbles. Some of the children read or sat on their front porch steps, and yearned for a week day, so they could run and play.

Several cliques formed in the yard. Some of the men chewed tobacco, dipped snuff, tamped their pipes and refilled them with Prince Albert, or rolled their smokes in leaf papers. Some of the men just talked or whispered, but mostly they bickered about the deception of Buker and Locket Webster.

What will happen now? Who will preach? We wouldn't trust a new preacher if we had one?

Is Locket Webster standing by her husband or is she really getting a divorce as the grapevine and party lines have "throbbed."

Where did Buker Webster come from, anyhow? How could he have slipped one over on us?

"Sheriff Olliff said he wants to talk to Buker Webster's relatives."

"Locket thinks they're all dead. She's sure his mother and father are deceased."

"When's Locket moving?"

"Renting a room at Aunt Mae's and Uncle Hume's, so she can finish out the school year. Doesn't know what she'll do after that."

"Hume, that's mighty kind of y'all to take Locket Webster in."

"Glad to help her if we can," said Uncle Hume. "Locket had no idea Buker Webster performed rituals and tortured insects and collected their wings, and she didn't know about him loving dead people."

"Anybody sitting around torturing insects or torturing any kind of animal is sick—a very sick man! Just think the boys said he yelled to the dead people out in the graveyard and told them that he loved all of them."

"Y'all are saying that Buker Webster bothered them young ladies when they wuz at the funeral parlor? I just can't believe that he could do that."

"Yeah, he's sick."

"What does Locket plan, Jake? Is she divorcing that deceitful, son-uv-a-gun?"

"Yes, she doesn't mind anyone knowing she plans to divorce Buker Webster."

"Whar's Locket now?"

"With Caddie, Aunt Mae and Laughing Eyes."

"Heard Jessie Myers say we should kick Locket Webster out of the school house. She doesn't want us petting her," said John McIntosh.

"Don't get me started on Jessie Meyers!" yelled Joseph Daniels. "She's just a meddling fool!" Anger flashed in his cinnamon-brown eyes. "If anyone should be mad, it should be Mary and me and our boys!"

"Yeah! That's right!"

"I want to kill Buker Webster for touching Ratchel Robin and Macie Zanderneff. It's a good thing he's off in that hospital for crazy folks," Joseph Daniels muttered.

"Guess we are all mad and feel that way, Joseph."

"George-West Meyers said he can't believe Reverend Buker Webster fooled him the way he did. He's mighty sorry."

"He's not a *Reverend*, Joseph. *Devil* would be more like it. He's not a real preacher, even if he did go to a seminary. He's an impostor."

"Yes, he's a deceiving devil."

* * * *

Locket Webster walked downstairs timidly. She buttoned the fitted jacket that matched her black chiffon dress, and smoothed her hair. "Do I look okay?" She pulled on white lace gloves and donned a black, broad-brimmed hat, which enhanced her short, curly blond hair.

"You're perfect. Just perfect." Aunt Mae patted her on the shoulder.

"Thank you. Everyone's going to be gawking at church. You don't know how much I dread going," said Locket.

"Just remember, Locket, if they gawk, it's because you're so pretty," Uncle Hume encouraged.

"Thanks for everything you do for me. Every one of you are so sweet—so wonderful!"

"Everything's gonna be all right, Locket. We need to go. Henny-Penny and Kackie are waiting outside," said Uncle Hume.

Caddie walked out of her bedroom into the sitting room. "So—do I pass inspection?" She pulled a short brim black hat, decorated with one black rose, a black leaf and stem, over her left eye. "Think Jake will like it?" She twirled around as they admired her black voile, olive green and black striped skirt. She tugged long black gloves onto her hands, and shuffled her feet in her black patent-leather shoes, and turned around for inspection.

"You look so good, Caddie! Jake will be crazy in the head if he doesn't agree," Locket smiled, and smoothed wisps of Caddie's long blond hair. "Jake would be crazy not to think you're the greatest."

"I'll declare, if Jake doesn't think you're something, some other man will," Uncle Hume laughed.

Aunt Mae placed her arms around the attractive girls and pulled them close to her. "You young ladies just out-did yourselves today! Both of you are gorgeous!"

* * * *

After the church services were over, Locket walked into the church yard, heads turned, and some of the people whispered behind their hands. And, some talked aloud, "Can't tell me Locket didn't know what her husband was doing. Maybe she's sick, too!"

When Aunt Mae noticed Locket standing alone, she nudged Ole Pem. "Please go over and speak to Locket. She could use a strong arm to lean on. I'll ask Caddie to go over to Locket, too."

"Sure. Be glad to, Aunt Mae. Come on, Jake. Let's walk Caddie and Locket home."

Ole Pem had the good looks of both his parents. His mother's traits showed in his black hair and olive skin, and he was tall like his father. He walked casually over to Locket and offered his arm. His green gray eyes twinkled mischievously. "May I walk you home, Locket?"

Jessie Meyers snickered, and pointed towards Locket. "Just look at that hussy! If she thinks she's going to get Pemrick McIntosh, she has another guess coming."

"Don't stir up anything else, Jessie," said George-West Meyers.

"Well, Buker Webster is gone, and she needs to be gone, too!"

"Leave Locket alone, Jessie. Everything will be different when Reverend Jason McClure takes his place. He'll be a good interim preacher," said George-West Meyers.

*   *   *   *

Caddie opened the door to the wooden springhouse, where they kept churns of buttermilk, and crocks of cream and butter.

"Look, Henny-Penny and Kackie! Spring salamanders, minnows and crayfish live in here."

"Can we catch them in a jar and hold them up to the light?" asked Kackie.

"We'll look at them, but then we'll let them go free," said Caddie.

"Caddie, you sounded exactly like Aunt Mae," Jake laughed.

"I want to be just like Aunt Mae when I grow up," said Henny-Penny.

"I believe you're like her already," Caddie laughed.

"I want a pet salamander, Caddie," said Kackie.

"We'll just play with them here. They live here in the spring, Kackie," said Caddie. "I know you want a pet. I'll get you a gold fish next time we go to a big town."

"I'll catch some minnows and put them in a jar, so you can look at them up close," said Jake.

After they played with Henny-Penny and Kackie, Jake and Caddie removed a crock of buttermilk and a cake of butter from the spring-house. "This butter is going to be good with hot biscuits and sorghum syrup." Jake threw the cake of butter high into the air and caught it.

"Careful, Jake, that wax paper could slip. If it does, it'll knock the bird and flower design off the top of the butter. Aunt Mae will be upset."

"I won't drop it."

"I want hot, buttered cornbread and butter-milk."

Jake re-wrapped the wax paper more tightly.

"That sounds really good."

He put one of his arms around her, pitched the butter high into the sky and caught it with one hand.

"Watch it, Jake! Don't drop it," she laughed.

"I'm a good catcher," he laughed.

"Jake, you wanna go to Sojo's when we get home?"

"Any reason in particular?"

"Just to see who's at the place. Get some coffee. You know," she begged.

"Wal, I suppose, if you wanna go."

"I do wanna go."

"That's a good idea, Caddie. We need a break. I still can't get over Buker Webster touching Macie. I'd like to kill him!"

"We're all angry, Jake. We're all devastated."

"Not like me! Not like me!" He beat the cake of butter against his chest, emphatically.

She appraised him calmly. "Yes, Jake, just like you."

No," he whispered, adamantly. "Never! Never, like me!"

* * * *

"We're gonna need a passel of plain salt to sprinkle around the meeting house. Iodized salt won't work."

"Why's that, Mae? Why do you need salt?"

"Hume, quit reading the newspaper and listen. We have to sprinkle a line of salt around the meeting-house and the parsonage—so evil won't cross it again. Salt is purifying. You know? We'll start at one side of the church and sprinkle salt all around the church house—make a line of salt and form a circle."

"Why are you wanting to do that, Mae?" Uncle Hume raised his voice slightly.

"To purify it, Hume. To purify it. Sometimes you just don't listen."

"Mae, you can't purify the church by just pouring a line of salt around a building."

"I'm gonna make a stab at purifying it. I'll hold the sack and pour the salt out in a thin line all around the church."

"No, Mae. The church is the people—the spiritual body." He shook his head.

"Well, regardless of what you think about it, I need that salt!"

"If it makes you feel better, Mae, I'll get the salt." He turned back to his newspaper."

Mae is such a religious woman to be so darned superstitious. But, regardless, I believe I'll keep her. Suddenly, Uncle Hume started laughing, "Mae, I just thought of the funniest thing!"

"What? What? Now it's not fair to laugh so hard without telling me. Tell me!"

"I can just imagine you and Grandmaw Taylor both thinking you're gonna solve this problem all by yourselves, and on a really dark night both of you decide to sneak over there to the church house at the same time, unbeknownst to the other. One will start on one side of the church and one on the other side, and you both bend down and begin to draw a line of salt around the church house, and all of a sudden you run into each other, and just scare hell out of each other!" He screamed with laughter, and slapped his leg.

"That is not funny, Hume," she giggled.

"Just run into each other, butt to butt," he yowled, and slapped his knee.

"Hume, I said, that's not funny." She pushed his shoulder, and laughed with him.

* * * *

"Joseph, you still got that ole opossum you and the boys got over at Ghost Hollow?"

"Sure do, Aunt Mae. He's just a butterball. Been giving him food scraps and chicken feed to eat." He grinned a snaggle-toothed smile and placed his tongue in the hole of his missing front tooth.

"Joseph, I'm surprised you still have that ole opossum."

"Yeah, he's still got it," said Mary.

"Been feeding him real good—trying to get the wild taste out of him, Mae," said Joseph.

"Yeah! That wild taste," Mary chimed in.

Aunt Mae went out to her mule and began to untie a tow-sack. "Listen, here's a young, tame, white rabbit in this tow-sack. I want to swap it for the opossum y'all caught at Ghost Hollow."

Joseph Daniels would never refuse her anything, but he frowned when he heard her request. "Why, shore, Aunt Mae, you can have him. Anything you want, you can have it."

"You sure can have him, Mae. Sure can have that ole 'possum," said Mary.

"Thanks."

"Been wondering why them dawgs was jumping up on the side of your mule," said Joseph. "And, now, I know they're after a rabbit."

"Yeah, I was wondering, too," said Mary.

Joseph Daniels took the rabbit to his pen to make the swap.

For Aunt Mae to be such a smart woman, she sure has some strange notions. She doesn't even eat opossum. She doesn't realize how attached I am to Big-Un. Bet if she knew, she'd let me keep him, but I don't have anything to swap her. She has never asked for anything that I can ever remember, so what can I do but give her Big'un?

He retrieved the opossum from its pen, held it up, examined the fattened animal, and admired its weight. It snapped, and showed a mouth of sharp teeth. A whitish, sticky drool dribbled from its angry mouth. Joseph walked back slowly.

Aunt Mae's so superstitious and all, bet she's taking Big'un back to Ghost Hollow and turning him loose. Joseph pretended to be happy, and slapped his hands together after he tied the tow-sack, which held the opossum onto the saddle. "Mae, here's that ole Ghost-Hollow opossum. He's a big'un. You might need some help getting home with him."

"I'll be okay."

"Mae, that hunt was one to remember! That ole persimmon tree was loaded with ripe persimmons! Big-Un was right on the tip-top of the tree, and Rob-Hunter clumb that tree like nobody's business, and got him. He could always climb the best of any of my boys." He exclaimed loudly.

"Yeah, Rob Hunter always clumb the best of the youngun's," Mary agreed.

Wyllyam interrupted. "Mama says I have the best mind for memorizing and Tinker has the best mind for numbers." He smiled a snaggle-tooth smile and his green eyes twinkled.

Aunt Mae placed her hand on his head. "Keep up the good memory work, Wyllyam. You're gonna go places."

"Yeah! Rob-Hunter clumb up that tree and got a hold of Big-Un, and you know the rest," Joseph smiled.

"Bet that was awful exciting, Joseph," Aunt Mae tried to appear jovial even though she was still concerned about the hunters taking the animal out of Ghost Hollow.

"Mae, will Rob-Hunter ever climb again?"

"Joseph, I believe he'll do a lot more than climb. Give him a little time. He'll be all right."

Mary Daniels beamed lovingly at Aunt Mae. "We hope so," she sighed and her chin quivered.

"Tinker, get me a poke and a pencil," said Joseph Daniels.

Tinker went into the cabin and returned with a brown paper sack and a stub of a pencil.

Joseph Daniels wet the end of the pencil in his pursed lips, and drew lines and marks on the brown paper sack. "Where I have this big 'X' marked on here is where we got Big-Un." He pointed the stubby pencil. "Right here, at Yeller Medder in Ghost Hollow." He stabbed a big **X** on the paper sack.

Aunt Mae took the paper sack and examined it. "Yeah, I know where this is—it's close to mine and Hume's property line."

"Ye wouldn't be taking it back to Ghost Hollow today, would ye?" He squinted his eyes and grinned knowingly.

"Yes—that's what I aim to do."

"I thought so, you being so superstitious, and all. Want company? Want one of us to go with ye?"

"I'll be all right. I'll get Hume to go with me." She crossed her fingers, knowing that she wouldn't ask Hume to go with her to Ghost Hollow.

"Wal, be careful."

The Daniels' dogs yelped and jumped enthusiastically around the tow-sack that held the opossum.

"Hold that tow-sack tight, Aunt Mae. The dogs are getting a whiff of Big-Un," he grinned. "Since you're turning him loose, the good Lord willing, maybe I'll catch 'Big-Un' again, but on my property or your property." He sighed.

"Let me say good-bye to Rob-Hunter, before I go." Aunt Mae went back into the cabin.

"I'll go with you, Mae," said Mary.

She found Rob Hunter sitting in a chair on the back porch. She leaned down and whispered in his ear. "I'm taking that big ole opossum back to Ghost Hollow. Do you understand?"

He nodded, slowly.

"The Ghost Hollow spell will be broken. You understand?"

Rob-Hunter stared at her.

She held his face gently with both her hands and gazed into his eyes. "We all love you very much Rob-Hunter. You're gonna be well because you *will it to be so.*" She removed her hands from his face, and backed away from him.

His eyes never left her face.

"You do understand, don't you, Rob Hunter?" He nodded.

* * * *

When she arrived at the persimmon tree on the other side of Yellow-Meadow at Ghost Hollow, she dismounted and tied her mule to a scrub bush. She removed the tow sack carefully from the saddle and peeped inside.

The opossum hissed, and she jumped. *I'm as nervous as a cat.*

When she got a whiff of wood-smoke, she raised her head and sniffed. The smell left as quickly as it had come. The combination of thinking about the ghosts, spirits, and a forest fire made her shiver.

She grabbed the opossum by its tail, stretched and lifted the opossum onto a small, lower limb of the persimmon tree.

Suddenly, an arm came up from behind her. "Best you let me help you with that, Mae."

She whirled around and knocked her elbow into the muzzle of a shotgun. "Deaver!" she screamed. "You scared the living daylights out of me!" She gasped for breath, and rubbed her elbow.

"Hope I didn't hurt you none," Deaver laughed. "You screamed so loud, Mae, you scared me and every living creature out here in these woods. Hope the revenuers didn't hear ya."

"What you doing here? I thought you left for parts unknown!"

"Mae, this is *parts unknown.* What you doing here alone—all by yourself? Ghost Hollow is no place for a woman."

"I'm returning that ole opossum that Rob-Hunter Daniels took out of this persimmon tree."

"Superstitious, ain't cha, Mae?"

"I suppose you could call me that," she grimaced, and continued to rub her elbow.

"Figured you would be. Figured that one day soon, you'd be bringing that critter back, because that's the way you are. Guess our forefathers made us superstitious that'a way, huh?"

"And, our mothers—"

"Yes, I guess that's so." He nodded his head in agreement.

"Yes, I am superstitious, but I'm trying to right a wrong. You know about what happens when you take an animal out of Ghost Hollow."

"Of course," he said. "Bad things happen if anybody takes a critter out of Ghost Hollow."

"Everybody knows," she exclaimed.

"Mae, things go wrong whether we're superstitious or not. You placing that big ole fat opossum back in this here persimmon tree won't change anything that's already happened."

"I'm not trying to change things, Deaver. I just don't want anything else bad to happen."

"Yes, I know everyone has had a whole lot of changes—Honey keeps me informed."

"Honey! How can she? Your house is so far away!"

"Of course it's far away, but we manage. I know about Dan Zanderneff's new wife being in jail for killing him. And, I know about that crazy, no good preacher. That son-uv-bitch!

"Deaver!"

"I told everybody he was as crazy as a 'Betsy-Bug,' all the time, and we needed a new preacher. Now didn't I? It was awful bad when Ratchel Robin broke her neck. I hope Locket finds a man who'll appreciate her. Hear tell Rob-Hunter's tetched."

"You're keeping up with the news, all right, but Rob-Hunter's getting better."

"So, Jake's finally wised up and started courting Caddie, huh? And Macie's little girls, are they okay?"

"Henny-Penny and Kackie are growing up fast. Caddie and Jake do a few things together, and they are a handsome couple."

"Caddie's a good woman, and Jake better wise up. Thought I lived here just like a hermit, didn't you? I keep up with everyone."

"Yes, I believe you do keep up with all of us," she said and shook her head in amazement. "It's so hard to believe you are still here, so close—"

"Yes, I'm close and hope to stay that way."

"Will you ever come home again, Deaver?"

"I am home."

"Hume sure has missed you, Deaver."

"Me, too. This here is a dangerous place. You need to get on home, Mae, and don't tell nobody you saw me here. We'd have a peck of trouble. Tell Hume don't come back into Ghost Hollow! Will you do that for me?"

"Sure, I will, Deaver."

"I'm trusting you, Mae. Don't come back, you hear? It's not safe." He put his shotgun on his shoulder. "Mae, Honey's expecting a baby. Will you see about her? I'll pay you."

"A baby?"

"Yes, a baby," he acknowledged, sadly.

"Of course, I'll see about Honey."

"You know a lot of speculation will be going on about who the father is. Me being gone and all. I just want you to know, I am the father of that baby." His chest puffed out like a stuffed turkey.

"I will do my best to help Honey, when her time comes."

"Thanks, Mae. Another thing. You know that sweet-gum tree that Hume rests under almost every weekend? There's a rock right under that tree. He rests his arm on that rock sometimes."

"Yes, I know where that sweet-gum tree is, Deaver."

"And the rock?"

"Yes, Deaver."

"Would you put a pink thread or a blue thread under that rock, after the baby is born, so I'll know whether the baby is a boy or a girl? Don't leave a note or nothing."

"Okay, Deaver," she whispered.

"When Honey's laid up, I won't see her for a pretty long time."

"I'll place a thread under the rock—a pink one for a girl—or a blue one for a boy."

"You won't tell anyone but Hume, of course."

"Of course."

"God sent you here today, so's I could ask you to see about Honey. I really believe that."

"Deaver, I smell smoke. Could the smoke be coming from your campfire?"

"It is sort of a campfire. Now, get on your mule and high-tail it out of here, Mae. Don't even look back. I don't want any of the other guys to see you." He stood at the tree and waited for her to ride away.

Of course, she didn't look back, and she didn't see Deaver climb the persimmon tree and retrieve Big-Un.

* * * *

She rode home as fast as the mule could trot, not daring to look back. She dreaded telling Uncle Hume she had gone beyond the boundaries of Yellow Meadow and crossed into Ghost Hollow, deliberately and alone!

Hume, will never understand. He will be so upset!

That evening Uncle Hume kept glancing at Aunt Mae, and wondered why she was so quiet. He wondered if she were grieving for Macie, Ratchel, Dan or all of them. "Something's bothering you, Mae. What is it?"

"Hume, I can't bear to have you mad at me. You're going to just die."

"Mae, tell me. If I do get mad, I'll just try to get over it. Now what is it?"

"I went into Ghost Hollow, today." She closed her eyes, and lowered her head.

His eyes widened with fear. "Yes," he drawled slowly. "And—" He motioned his hands for her to continue talking.

"When I was at the Daniels' today, I exchanged that young rabbit we had in the pen for the Ghost Hollow opossum."

"Yes? And—" He leaned forward in his chair.

"Uh—and I took that ole opossum back and put it in the persimmon tree." She bowed her head, leaned forward, and placed her hands on the top of her head.

"You didn't!"

"Yes!"

"All by yourself?"

"Yes—" she hesitated.

"But, why did you go alone?"

"Since that ole persimmon tree was so close to our property line, I thought I'd ride to Ghost Hollow real fast, let the opossum loose, get back quick and nobody'd ever be the wiser."

"That's why you went alone?"

"I didn't think you'd see the importance of taking the opossum back."

"You didn't think I'd see the importance of your superstitions? Is that it?" He raised his voice.

"Because you don't think Ghost Hollow is haunted. But, that's not the worse part!"

"Did something happen? Did someone—" He stood up, placed his hands in his pockets, and waited, expectantly. "Did—"

She interrupted. "While I was putting that critter back in the persimmon tree, a hand reaches up to help me!"

"A hand!" Uncle Hume grabbed his heart.

"Yes, it was Deaver's hand." Her chin trembled.

"Deaver's hand reached up to help you! He's living in Ghost Hollow? Of all the darned places!" News of his friend brought a temporary smile to his face, but it quickly turned into a frown. He scratched his head behind the left ear. "I'm puzzled."

"Hume, listen," she said meekly. "Deaver lives there."

"Where?"

"Said not to tell anyone else but you that he's living in Ghost Hollow. I need to tell you something else, Hume—"

"Don't tell me that it's gonna get worse! He didn't lay a hand on you, did he?"

"No. I felt sorry for Deaver. Said that Ghost Hollow is his home now."

"He knows the revenuers will never give up on him. You know that?" he replied, with fear in his eyes.

"Hume, Deaver sees his family all the time. Honey's gonna have a baby, and he wants me to mid-wife her."

"And—"

"I told him I'd be with her."

"And—of all things—there's gonna be a baby! What was Deaver thinking!"

"That's what Deaver told me and that's what Deaver asked me to do, Hume," she replied meekly. "Are you very mad at me? I know it was irresponsible of me to go to Ghost Hollow alone, but I just had to do it. I want everything to be like it used to be before y'all took that critter out of that haunted place!"

"I'm too upset to be mad. I am too frightened to be mad with you. I am too thankful you're back safely to be angry. You were in a lot of danger today. Not necessarily from Deaver, but the men who are there with him. Did you know that?" He shook his head as he spoke.

"I know that, now."

"Promise me you'll always ask me to buy salt or anything else you want to carry out any of your superstitions. I'll even climb on top of the parsonage, the meeting house and the church house and toss salt to the four winds, if you ask me. If you want a opossum put back in a tree, ask me. I'll never turn you down." He shook her shoulders firmly, but affectionately, pulled her to him, and wrapped his long, lanky arms around her tightly.

* * * *

Reverend Jason McClure was a good man. On that particular day, he felt small and humble as he stood behind the pulpit of "The Church at Three-Mile Crossing." He smoothed his balding, white hair, smoothed his vest, and buttoned the coat to his three-piece black suit. He prayed for the right words—no more and no less. He saw his good friends, Judge Pewter and Matilda Mapp Pewter, and her father, Jason Mapp, sitting in their regular places on the left side, the second row from the front. Their somber expressions troubled him.

Jessie and George Myers sat in the middle, the third row from the front. Jessie Myers kept turning around and staring in the back.

Doc Stowe sat on his regular pew, the second row from the front, on the right-hand side. His poker face was unreadable.

Hume and Mae Brown sat on the right towards the back, and he noticed that they were surrounded by children. Locket Webster sat beside them. He also noticed that the young nephews of George-West Myers, the young boys of the Daniels, and the young boys of the Donahoos were not in attendance, but their parents were.

The church pews were packed with regular church members, but mostly curiosity seekers.

He stood and addressed the congregation. "Ladies and Gentlemen: "We are gathered here today, to pray, to meditate and to come together in some kind of understanding. An impostor came here to this place, lived among us and deceived us. Buker Webster pretended to be a man of the cloth. His pretending piousness crushed us, mentally and physically. It has crushed our faith in man, our faith in preachers and our faith in God. Some of us are crying out to God and asking him why he allowed this awful thing to happen?"

"If we ever see him again, we'll kill him!" A stranger yelled from the right side at the back of the church.

"Unforgivable!" Someone else in the audience shouted.

Aunt Mae turned around and stared at the stranger. He sat with a large group of people that she'd never seen before.

Reverend McClure continued. "Let's settle down, and get through this thing. God will help us get through it."

"God let us put up with that imposter and He didn't do anything about it!" The same man yelled.

"Amen!" A man on the left hand side yelled.

Reverend McClure held up both his arms as if to calm them. "—the difference was Mr. Buker Webster was a professional impostor. Anyone of us can be an impostor but he was a professional impostor."

Reverend McClure stopped, wiped his mouth with a white silk handkerchief, and viewed the congregation.

The depression of the church was evident in its body language.

Jessie Meyers shook her head, huffed in disgust, and wiped her eyes with a white lace handkerchief. George-West Meyers placed his arm around her and attempted to comfort her.

"—Buker Webster attempted to hang himself, and he was taken to Milledgeville. For those of you who don't know about Milledgeville, it's a hospital for the mentally ill." Reverend McClure took a deep breath.

"—Sheriff Olliff and some of the Elders examined the parsonage, the church office and Buker Webster's personal possessions, and found many different kinds of fake credentials, but this might come as a surprise to you when I tell you that Mr. Buker Webster does hold a legitimate degree in theology. He is a bonafide preacher. He has held a lot of different kinds of employment, in many capacities and in many towns. He has been a college professor, an undertaker, and a preacher."

A murmur stirred throughout the audience.

Joseph Daniels yelled in a booming voice, "That crazy preacher ruined all our lives. He needs to be sued! He was a demon and a fake!"

Judge Pewter turned around and stared at Joseph Daniels until he made eye contact. He shook his head at Joseph Daniels, and placed his index finger over his lips.

Joseph nodded his head and whispered to Mary, "Don't wanna mess up that law-suit our boys are gonna have against that crazy preacher. So, I'll stay quiet-like."

"I say, let's find him in Milledgeville, and give him what's coming!" The same stranger yelled again.

Many of the people in the congregation murmured and nodded their heads in agreement. "That's not Christian for him to do this to us!"

Reverend Jason McClure held his arms up and raised his voice. "I suppose you could say Buker Webster was good at being an impostor because no one knew the truth about his being a fake, until this last major mistake—the one which brought finality to his error."

Jessie Meyers stopped crying and tossed her head haughtily, snorted indignantly, and loudly. George-West Myers crossed his arms, and shook his head in bewilderment.

"One of the people who is hurt the most is Locket Webster. She didn't realize her husband was an impostor."

A loud moan echoed in the church house.

The people stared at Locket Webster, and, then, at each other.

Locket bowed her head and closed her eyes.

Aunt Mae glanced at Honey Clements. Her stomach bulged slightly. While she wondered if anyone else knew that Honey was pregnant, Honey met her eyes and gave a nod.

Aunt Mae stood up, motioned for Henny-Penny and Kackie to follow her, and on the way outside, she motioned for Tommy and Bobby, and Benjamin to come with her. She led them outside. "How about a game of tag? Aunt Mae will sit here on the doorsteps, and watch you have a big ole time running and playing."

The children ran excitedly to the meeting tree. They climbed upon the oak bench and walked around and around the tree.

She listened intently, and heard Reverend McClure say:

"We've discussed a little bit about what's happened. Now let's discuss what we can do now?' It's human nature to retaliate, and strike out when we have been mistreated, but when it comes to our faith, we know there is no healing process in retaliation. Healing takes a lot of patience and endurance.

"We practice patience in our daily lives. We prepare our fields, we plant, and then we wait patiently. We wait for rain, and good weather. Our crops grow, but we still must have patience and wait until it's time to harvest our crops. We go on working and doing other things like getting our other fields ready to plant. We are busy. We trust God. We give Him and nature time to run the course.

"See, you already know patience."

"We've already shown too much patience. We should have kicked that preacher out of here a long time ago!" The stranger shouted, again.

"Yeah! That's right!" one of the church members agreed.

Reverend McClure raised both his hands and held them toward the congregation. "Let's settle down and get through this meeting. I admire all of you. I've known most of you a long, long time. In the past, when trouble came along, you never sat down and whimpered and gave up. You have moved on in life. Because you have *hope***.** I've looked into your faces throughout the years, and they have held various expressions. I've observed your smiles, love and hope. I know you're angry because of the great deceiver!"

A murmur sounded. Heads nodded.

"Let's ask ourselves who the real deceiver is? Satan, the fallen-angel, is the deceiver.

"Luke 8:17 says: For nothing is secret, that shall not be made manifest, neither anything hidden that shall not be known."

He searched the faces of the congregation. They were staunch in their pain and his message had not moved them. He wiped sweat from his brow and looked heavenward.

"Buker Webster pretended to be a man of God, but he was a deceptive Angel of Light. He became as Satan, himself!

"We must not focus on a person to blame for the way we feel, but we must focus on our hope. We must focus on mending our suffering, and broken spirit. How do we mend? We must pray for strength and endurance and patience."

Reverend McClure wiped his brow and continued. "In our prayers we must ask God to send His Holy Spirit to guide us, to help us, to teach us, and to heal us. We must ask God to release anger from our souls, and remember that heaven, hell and judgment all belong to God.

"Don't be embarrassed that we were taken in by a deceiver, that we believed in him and perhaps some of us even loved him before we learned about his deceit.

"Let's forgive ourselves, and let's forgive all of those who have deceived us.

"We pride ourselves in our high integrity. Let us go on-with-life and live our lives to the fullest!"

George-West and Jessie Myers shook their heads, as if in dismay.

"To get all we can out of life, we must be happy and cheerful!"

Reverend Jason McClure raised his hymnal. "Turn to page 32."

The audience stood and sang, "Praise God from Whom all Blessings Flow."

Reverend McClure looked into the troubled faces of the people. He stretched his long arms and hands above his head, and whispered, "Go about Your Father's business, in peace and love!"

A holy benediction fell upon that moment.

* * * *

Locket held onto Ole Pem's arm. The soft scruff of their Sunday shoes sounded in the leaves, along the pathway.

"I'm glad you're staying with Aunt Mae and Uncle Hume." When he glanced down at her, Locket looked up, met his eyes, and glanced away, quickly.

"Aren't Aunt Mae and Uncle Hume the most fantastic people, Ole Pem?"

"Can't be beat!" he said.

They stopped at a bridge which ran over a little creek. The water lapped against smooth stones.

"I smell rain," said Ole Pem.

"You can't really smell rain, now can you?"

"To answer your question, it's the smell of moisture upon the dry trees, upon the leaves. Yes. I can smell it. It's the most woodsy and heavenly odor. I love to smell it!"

"Will you teach me to smell rain?"

Smile wrinkles appeared at the corner of his gray-green eyes. "Why, Locket, I'd try to teach you 'most everything I know." His searching look was one of gentleness, and one who appreciated what he saw. He squeezed her hand and she looked away.

"When you going back to Mississippi, Ole Pem?" she managed to ask.

"To tell you the truth, Locket, my finances are up in the air. I need to work at the saw-mill with Dad long enough to make some money, but I also need to get back in school as soon as possible. Judge Pewter's making a place for me in his office, when I pass the bar."

Their footsteps sounded hollow and echoed on the wooden bridge, when they crossed the creek.

"I wish only the best for you, Ole Pem."

"Locket, may I see you, while I'm here? That is, will you go to a movie with me sometime? Or maybe we could go to a play in Atlanta or go to dinner. It's a long way into town to a theater, but we'd get there. Bet we'd have fun too?" He hesitated.

"Of course. Thanks for asking, Pem." She blushed when she met his eyes. He squeezed her hand in reply.

A gust of wind caught her wide-brimmed hat and blew her skirt. She laughed as she turned his arm loose and grabbed her hat and skirt. The red silk scarf wrapped around her neck began to flutter in the wind.

Ole Pem reached out and caught her scarf, and chuckled.

"It's sprinkling rain. You did smell the rain!" She laughed again.

"Does your laugh always harmonize with the wind?" he asked.

She looked into his twinkling eyes, and smiled. "Always."

*   *   *   *

After dinner, everyone sat on the front porch, sharing the newspaper, and the Sunday "funnies," and chatted amicably.

Aunt Mae gave Henny-Penny and Kackie some bread to feed the ducks. "Drop the bread on the ground and don't hold it. The geese and ducks might snap your little fingers."

Aunt Mae noticed Uncle Hume slip off the edge of the porch quietly. He put his finger over his lips for Aunt Mae to be still, and say nothing.

Aunt Mae motioned for everyone to be quiet. They watched Uncle Hume tip-toe behind Henny-Penny and Kackie.

When Henny-Penny and Kackie reached their hands out to feed the geese, Uncle Hume sneaked behind them. At the same time he reached his hand out to pinch Henny-Penny and make a loud noise, Pegg came up behind Uncle Hume with his long neck stretched and bit him on the back side, just inside the inner thigh.

Uncle Hume jumped and screamed, and scared Henny-Penny and Kackie so much they yelled and grabbed each other around the neck.

Uncle Hume fumed, as he hurried back to the porch rubbing his inner thigh. He unbuckled his pants and hurried inside the cabin.

Everyone yelled and screamed with laughter. Uncle Hume rushed into the cabin.

Ole Pem slapped his leg hard and rocked back and forth, as he laughed. He stood up and glanced inside the house. "Wonder if he's hurt badly?" He sat back down beside Locket.

"Pegg got the joke on you, Uncle Hume! I've never seen anything like it in my life—it's so funny." Jake held his stomach and laughed until tears ran down his cheeks.

"It's one of those things you don't believe, even when you see it." Locket held her hand over her mouth and tried not to laugh.

"I can't help laughing," Caddie sputtered. "But, I do hope he's not hurt too bad." She sat down and wiped the tears of laughter.

"I know, Caddie, he might be hurt really bad, but I can't stop laughing," said Ole Pem. When his eyes met Caddie's blue-green eyes, his heart felt warm, and he welcomed the feeling.

Henny-Penny and Kackie danced and shrieked with excitement.

Caddie was still laughing when she left the front porch and hurried towards the outhouse.

"Uncle Hume!" Ole Pem called. "Will it be all right for me to tell Dad?"

"You better not tell John!" Uncle Hume called through the screen door.

"He could be hurt bad." Jake careened his neck towards the door with both curiosity, humor, and concern.

Tears of laughter ran down her cheeks as Aunt Mae followed Uncle Hume to the bedroom. She continued to laugh so hard, it was difficult to examine him. "Mae, don't you dare tell any of your friends about what's happened today!"

* * * *

AT THE QUILTING HOUSE

Aunt Mae looked forward to her quilting-bee session that week. She loved piecing memories of days gone by, over teacups of nostalgia and welding and bonding the hearts of those who stitched together, but she couldn't wait to tell them the story of Uncle Hume and Pegg. "Ladies, you should have been with us Sunday. Funniest thing you ever saw to see Henny-Penny and Kackie reaching their hands out toward the geese and ducks to feed them—and Hume reaching his pinching fingers out directly behind them, and Pegg stretching and reaching his long, long neck out—all in a row. Hume and Pegg pinched at the very same time."

"The timing was perfect!" Missy Williams screamed with laughter.

"But, not for Hume," Grandmaw Taylor cackled.

* * * *

Ole Pem leaned over and kissed Aunt Mae on the cheek. "Let's go for a walk." His broad grin showed even, white teeth.

"All right, where do you want to walk?"

"Just down to the spring."

They strolled to the spring, down a familiar path they'd walked together many times. Somehow the path had taken on more meaning Ole Pem thought as he enjoyed the scenery, and the sounds of the woods. He looked down at the top of Aunt Mae's white, curly hair and realized how much she meant to him and how much she had encouraged him to be a lawyer.

"Remember the day that old rattle-snake made its sound? He was ready to strike, right about here." She pointed towards a rotten log. "You were a little boy but you just plopped a forked stick about its neck and we killed it. You were never afraid of anything."

"Yeah, it was really close to my foot!"

"If that rattlesnake had bitten you, I don't know what I would have done. You could have died."

"But, you killed the rattler, and I'm still here," he grinned.

"Thank God, for that!" She spoke loudly as she recalled that dangerous moment.

He squeezed her arm, gently, in response.

She beamed at him. "What do you remember most when you're away from home, Ole Pem?"

"Wal, I think of home all the time when I am in Mississippi. Get homesick especially for mama. But, the main thing I think of when I was a little boy, is all the times you took all us young'uns into the woods, and you'd say, 'I'm going to show you something no living soul has ever seen before.' Then you'd say, 'Sit down a while and be still.' On all our quiet adventures with you, I learned to respect every living creature. That's what I like to remember."

"Yes, and also to listen and to hear," she nodded, as if to prompt him.

"Yes, to really hear. That's what I like to remember."

"Ole Pem, you've learned something very important!

"I'll always remember the day I finally heard the music—and I felt it here." He touched his heart with his right hand.

"Yes, I remember seeing your face—when it came into your heart."

"I learned there is music here in these woods, and I felt the presence of God."

"You never told me!" She stopped and touched his arm and looked into his twinkling eyes.

"It was a perfect feeling—a perfect day," he said.

"How nice!"

"My favorite thing to do these days is to search for another perfect day." He looked into the distance and searched the Blue Ridge Mountains.

They commenced to walk along the path again.

Henny-Penny and Kackie ran ahead, stopping now and then, to pick up a stick or throw a rock.

"I have cherished memories of my childhood and my good friends, and without exception Caddie and Macie and Jake and Dan—" he hesitated. A cool breeze touched his jaw, and he felt an unseen force in the woods, and acknowledged a kindred ship to what he knew was there. He took Aunt Mae's hand, as he had done many times as a child, and swung her arm back and forth.

A weather-beaten bench awaited them at the spring. "Let's sit here for a moment," Ole Pem said gently, and he placed the water buckets on the ground.

They sat quietly for a little while, not saying a word.

Aunt Mae glanced at him and searched his face. She knew he held something in his heart that he wanted to say.

The spring—a small trickle of water oozed from a crack in the rock and spilled into a very small, round, rocky pool which then spilled over more rocks, stacked by nature's hand. Lush, yellowish-green, velvety mosses cushioned their feet. Snake-doctors (dragonflies) darted upon the water seeking their next prey.

Ole Pem remained quiet and looked into the distance. The caw of a crow, and the rustle of leaves blended well. "Gonna be getting cold, soon, Aunt Mae." A murder of crows flew over their heads.

"Yes. The sights and the sounds will be different here soon."

"Aunt Mae, it was bad about Macie. Really a tragedy."

"Sure was, Ole Pem. Such a waste! Such a waste!" She agreed, and wiped her face on her apron.

Ole Pem's voice faltered, realizing he was touching an open wound. "Aunt Mae, it was real bad about Dan, too. Huh?"

"Yes, Ole Pem."

"I think about all that's happened, a lot. Can't get it out of my mind. Discovering Dan's body has really unnerved me."

"Care if I ask you some questions about Dan's wife? Janelle's her name, isn't it?

"I don't mind."

"Well, what did Dan's wife say concerning her marriage to Dan? About Macie? Can you tell me why Dan killed Macie?"

"I used to go over to Janelle's house and talk to her a lot. I used the excuse that I was checking up on her husband for the Sheriff—to see if she'd heard anything from him. She really gave no information about Dan before she was locked up. She only talked to me about Dan when I saw her at the jail."

Aunt Mae raised her eyebrows. "You went to see her at the jail?"

"I've tried to figure out things too, Aunt Mae," he frowned. "I've thought back on the times when we were little boys playing together. Dan never seemed to be ill-tempered or the type to kill anyone or anything. I was sure surprised he tried to kill Janelle—you know he tried to make her slit her own wrists, but she ended up killing Dan, instead."

"Isn't that ironic?" Aunt Mae held her head in her hands. "Can you believe it? He tried to make Janelle slit her wrists, too. Just like Macie—her wrists were slit. Macie didn't live to tell it."

"Of course, Janelle believes Dan musta killed Macie. Janelle was surprised to hear Dan had a wife and daughters. She just kept on shaking her head when the sheriff told her!' Even though Dan had their photographs, Janelle thought Macie and the little girls were his dead sister and her children. Dan told Janelle that his parents and all his family were dead."

"I can't believe Janelle even talks to you, since you turned her in to the law."

"When I went to the sheriff and reported the brown spot in the cotton patch, I suspected foul play, but I didn't suspect Janelle. I'd have never dreamed she killed her husband."

"Ole Pem would you have done everything the same way all over again, had you known the consequences?"

"Aunt Mae that's a soul-searching question, but I believe I would have."

"So, you didn't like Janelle enough to lie for her?"

"No."

"Ole Pem, I'd like to ask you another personal question. You don't have to answer it, if you don't want to."

"Aunt Mae, you want to know if I am in love with Janelle?"

She glanced at him, startled that he perceived her question so quickly. "I don't want Locket to be hurt, Ole Pem."

"I know why you're asking, Aunt Mae."

"I see how you look at Locket, Ole Pem—not too innocently, I might add," she smiled mischievously.

"I just want to help," he said.

"I thought you might be in love—" she hesitated. "Locket and Janelle both need help."

"Yes, they both do need help, but Janelle's in serious trouble—in jail for life or—"

"Don't say that word, Ole Pem."

"We have to face up to how serious this is. Her sentence will probably be death if something doesn't come up to help her soon, so there's some urgency in my trying to help Janelle before her trial. Will you allow Judge Pewter to read Macie's diary, again, with the idea of helping Janelle in her murder case—in her trial. Could you do that?"

"How could Macie's words help Janelle? Hume says anything we do with Macie's diary is hearsay."

"I was hoping Judge Pewter could find a way. He already knows about hearsay," said Ole Pem.

"You want to read Macie's writings, Ole Pem."

Ole Pem nodded. "I want to try to help Janelle. If Macie's words are what I think they are, the jury needs to know that Macie Zanderneff existed, and that she wrote a diary about Dan mistreating and beating her. The jury needs to hear her words. Somehow her diary needs to be entered as evidence. The jury needs to hear the diary read just as if Macie were standing before them a' talking."

"It's a good thought."

"If the jurors knew about Macie's existence and her death, Janelle might get a lighter sentence. Maybe, with the help of Macie's diary, and your help—she'd get life!"

"I'd like to help you."

"Sounds like Dan made Macie slit her wrists, since he tried the same thing with Janelle. Also, what makes it more believable is that Janelle did not know Macie existed when she gave her written statement to the sheriff. Therefore, she couldn't have known how Macie died. Using her diary might help Janelle."

"You really think so?"

Henny-Penny and Kackie climbed the ladder to the tree house. "We know, Aunt Mae! We know! We'll be careful!" Henny-Penny yelled.

Aunt Mae waved at Henny-Penny and Kackie, and became thoughtful. She rubbed her temples and pulled at little wisps of hair that hung around her ears and neck. "I'll give it some thought, Ole Pem."

"Thank you, Aunt Mae."

"Judge Pewter will know the law," said Aunt Mae. "And, perhaps a way to get the diary read before the court."

"I know those papers are sacred to you. I know they're important and they could become even more important. They might save a life such as it'd be. Her life is shattered, regardless, you know?"

Aunt Mae looked out into the woods—into the far distance.

Ole Pem couldn't determine what her blue eyes could see, nor what her heart felt, but he knew his words made her sad.

She stood up and stretched her back, placed her hands upon her hips and reared back. "You mentioned this to Janelle, yet?"

"No."

"Ole Pem, we need to think about it. It's imaginative. I wonder how it can be done, but—" she hesitated. "Life, you say? You really think she might get *life.*"

"I hope so," he said softly.

The sweetness of her countenance touched him. A snake doctor flitted and darted towards her snow-white hair. He shaded his eyes with his hand, and observed the snake-doctor intently as it flew high into the sky, ascending, ascending. Just as quickly as it ascended, it descended upon the water.

* * * *

"So, you say you've always liked me, huh?" Jake quizzed.

"Yes, I've loved you since I was a little girl."

"Caddie, I've always thought of you as a little ole tomboy climbing trees, throwing rocks, playing ball and riding horses. You were always putting June Bugs down the back of my shirt. I can't believe I never noticed your eyes were the color of the sky until Macie's funeral. Don't know why! You know what, Caddie? When you just looked up, I realized your eyes are not blue at all, but very green!"

"Yes, I have hazel eyes," she laughed.

"Just all of a sudden, when you looked up at me, I couldn't believe it. You've got eyes like a salamander. They have green specks and they change colors."

"Jake, I can't believe you're just now seeing the color of my eyes," she laughed. Two squirrels chased each other and ran up a tree.

He held her hand, as they forded a creek. Pebbles in the stream, all different sizes, caught the light, reflecting pastel colors of gem stones, particles of gold, izing-glass and caches of nature's wealth.

Caddie fell onto the ground, still laughing. When Jake reached down to pick her up, she pulled him down beside her.

"No! No! Caddie," he mumbled.

She drew her arms around his neck, quickly, and pulled his mouth to hers, kissed him urgently and passionately. "I love you, Jake," she murmured.

Jake sat up and began to laugh. "You're not gonna believe this, Caddie. It's sorta like déjà vu."

"Déjà vu? You dreamed this happened?" she smiled.

"Caddie, listen to me! There has to be some irony here. In this very same place, on a warm, sunny day just like today, Macie and I jumped over this creek, and we fell right next to this very same tree, and in this very same spot. Macie pulled me down and kissed me. I can't believe it!"

Caddie stood up and dusted pine needles and sweet-gum leaves off her dress. "You uncaring, good for nothing, so called friend! You don't care how bad you hurt my feelings!"

"Oh, No! Caddie, I'm sorry—so sorry. I shouldn't have told you that! Please forgive me. For a moment I thought you were—"

"Macie, of course. Oh! My God!"

"At least, I'm truthful," he said.

"And, hurtful! I can't believe you deliberately hurt me!" she yelled bitterly. His blunt words brought tears to her eyes. "Macie is not here anymore, Jake!"

"She's with us, Caddie. Don't you see?"

"Why are you trying to make me feel dirty, humiliated and embarrassed?"

"I'm not deliberately trying to hurt you. You know I want to tell you what you want to hear, Caddie, but I honestly can't tell you those words in good conscience. I guess I'll always love your sister, no matter what."

Tears trickled from her eyes and down her cheeks. She stumbled away slowly, and in a daze, and left him leaning against the tree where he and Macie once lay in each others arms.

The birds stopped chirping and the squirrels stopped scampering through the trees. The sounds in the woods became so quiet, she could hear the blood rush from her heart through her veins, through her body and to her head. The emotion of anger, almost foreign to her makeup, caused by Jake's cruel words, pulsated loudly in her temples.

She held her head tightly, and moaned. Jake's verbal cruelty opened her innocent eyes, and tore her heart, and soul. She wished she had never "pushed" to see this side of Jake.

"I'm such a fool," she whispered to the wind.

A gentle breeze touched her tear-stained face, and attempted to soothe her with its cooling balm.

* * * *

"*__________, Mississippi*
Cell Block 2B
Old Jail House # 1
___________, 19__

Dear Aunt Mae,

Thanks for writing. Ole Pem has told me how unusual and loving you are.

Jail is such a dirty place! Makes me feel so filthy inside and out.

I'm not a bad person. (I know that's hard for you to believe knowing what I've done.) I thought Dan loved me. I loved him so much!

My parents had misgivings about Dan and didn't want me to marry him. Said he had no money, and he was too old for me and not good enough for me, but they finally went ahead and gave in to my begging for their permission, and consented to our marriage. They gave us a sharecropper's house and some land and let Dan try his hand at being an overseer over a large section of the farm. He did a good job for a long period of time.

One day, he said he didn't want to work for my father anymore. He looked for another job, but he blamed me when he couldn't find work.

He started drinking excessively, and began yelling and shoving me around.

His abusive actions were like nothing I'd ever experienced.

Sometimes he finished each sentence I started to express, which wouldn't be anything like what I really wanted to say. He'd call me 'stupid' or he'd yell, 'You're such an idiot.' Sometimes I believed I was stupid—and an idiot. He accused me of being the reason he wasn't able to make good decisions.

I became his scapegoat.

My daddy found out Dan was drinking and not doing his job as an overseer of the farm, and he told Dan he was off his payroll. Daddy said I should come back home, but I loved Dan. (I know my parents thought I was a fool for staying with Dan! And, especially now that I killed him.)

I thought it'd be failure on my part, if I left Dan and went back home to live with my parents.

I told Dan that I wanted everything back the way it used to be before he started beating me—like it was when we first married.

Even though I did not go back home, my daddy made sure we had everything we needed. Dan hated that! He was so jealous every time daddy gave me something like a country ham or canned goods—anything. Dan beat me every time I received something and he became more and more abusive, physically and mentally.

I can look back and see things better in hind-sight. Even though I loved Dan, I know I didn't do anything to cause his cruelty. I did not hate him and plan his murder. It just happened. It was self-defense. He tried to kill me! He tried to make me slit my wrists! To make it look like I committed suicide! Do you think the jury will listen to my side of the story—will hear my plea?

I did not know that Macie or Henny-Penny and Kackie existed! To think he had been married and had babies and didn't let me know! How deceitful he was! Apparently, I did not know him at all! If only I had listened to my mama and daddy and gone on back home, when things did not work out for me and Dan.

Dan was so jealous! BUT, I never looked at another man! How could he have believed otherwise? He would get mad about nothing—about everything—and, then, he'd kick my little cat named Democracy. (Oh, my Democracy, Democracy, where are you now?)

I must close now. I have become so tired, my hand is shaking.

Gratefully and with love,
Janelle"

* * * *

"*__________, Mississippi*
Cell Block 2B
Old Jail House # 1
__________,19__

Dear Aunt Mae,

I still can't believe you wrote me. I am so thankful and so unworthy of your time and attention.

Oh, to go back! If only my mama had not met Dan on that train and brought him to town because he needed to work! If only! If only I'd left Dan when my daddy said, 'Come on home.' Was I crazy? Looking back now, I believe I was. Why did I not go back home? I think it was because of humiliation and embarrassment. I guess I thought I could fix our marriage, and make things the way they were when we were dating. I suppose I was in a state of denial. (That's what my lawyer tells me now.)

My head aches. I'm sorry to have to close.

More later! Love,
Janelle"

*   *   *   *

"__________, Mississippi
Cell Block 2B
Old Jail House # 1
___________,19__

Dear Aunt Mae,

Thanks for listening! I want to write and try to explain my side of things. I know I should have notified the Sheriff when I killed Dan in self-defense, but I was not thinking well. After I began destroying pieces of him and burning him, I felt it was too late to call the Sheriff. I look back and wonder how I could have done such a horrible thing?

I didn't plan it. I just did it.

My lawyer wants to ask you a favor. Could you please have someone type Macie's diary, and send a copy? He said perhaps something in her words would give him some insight into how he might help my defense. (My daddy will pay for the costs of typing and mailing.)

My lawyer said he's interested in the fact that Macie apparently died the same way that Dan tried to kill me. Dan tried to make me slit my own wrists with his straight razor, but I wasn't willing to slit my wrists and die!

My lawyer said I'd be lucky to get life, mainly because the jury will be repulsed when they hear about the way I eliminated the body. I am truly sorry for everything! My life is in shambles!

I want you to know that my horrible act bears no resemblance to my true self. My actions will be a hard cross-to-carry for the rest of my life—though, it may be short. If I could bring Dan back, I would. Only my journey of ruination continues.

Again, thanks for listening!

With love but with despair,
Janelle"

*   *   *   *

"___________, Mississippi
Cell Block 2B
Old Jail House # 1
___________,19__

Dear Aunt Mae,

Good morning, dear lady, who seems to care when no loved one or stranger does!

I look into the mirror and see a reflection of one who will probably never turn her hand for a good deed again; one who will never bear a child and never know what it's like for him to sleep at my side, my breast. I look into that mirror and see a face staring back—directly at me. I close my eyes and close heart's door, for I can not bear to think! I do not know the stranger in the mirror! I look at my hands, and say, Hands, how could you have done such a horrible thing!

I am sorry for everything! My life is over! Please pray the jury will not ask for death.

Thank you, from the bottom of my heart, for writing. Will you please write me again?

Most sincerely,
Janelle Zanders Davenport

PS: I wish there were some way I'd be free one day. I sure would like to meet a kind woman such as you, Aunt Mae. I write with much frustration, love and apologies. The wreckage of my life surrounds me!"

* * * *

Aunt Mae noticed that the last name of *Zanders* was written clearly on Janelle's letter, but marked through with a big slash. Aunt Mae removed her spectacles, leaned back in her rocking chair and rubbed her tired eyes.

Ole Pem is not going to believe how candidly and openly Janelle expresses herself. I can hardly bear to read her words they are so heartbreaking. It's like being there at that time and place, and seeing Dan's cruel treatment through this young lady's eyes.

I know that Janelle's mother was disappointed when Janelle married Dan, but what is the true story? Since she was the one who brought Dan to their hometown, and introduced him to everyone at the train station, the mother has to feel some guilt.

But, then, how much did the mother know about Janelle needing help? Did she know what was going on and turn her back on her daughter? Surely not.

I can't help but think of myself and how little we knew about Macie's circumstances. Caddie jumped right in there and sent her money the very moment Macie asked for it.

There are a lot of questions left unanswered about both these young ladies..

Dan must have persecuted Macie the same way he persecuted Janelle. If Dan was attempting to kill Janelle, she should have protected herself! But, to hit him with an ax, and to dismember him—and to burn him—she had to be extremely angry and violent!

Yes, it was a fearful place for Janelle to be in. Janelle was in a bad spot with Dan coming after her with a gun and a straight razor.

Janelle is still in a bad spot!

* * * *

Aunt Mae folded the letter, placed it in the bottom of her sewing basket, and pulled her shawl over her shoulders.

She picked up another letter from the stack of letters from Janelle, and began to read again, searching for answers to Macie's death:

"__________, Mississippi
Cell Block 2 B
Old Jail House # 1
*___________, 19_*

Dear Aunt Mae,

Thanks for trying to help me! Listening to me! I sit and wonder what went wrong? I can't believe that Dan loved me and hated me at the same time.

Sometimes, at night, I awaken at the slightest noise. Insomnia sets in. I see shadows upon the walls of the cell, and before I realize where I am, I feel as if Dan is alive and coming after me with his long arms outstretched. I am haunted by the memories of his cruelty.

At first, I dreamed a lot—terrible and disturbing dreams about Dan, but now the dreams have become scrambled and intertwined with animals attacking.

One of my scariest nightmares is about Dan. He has a shy countenance upon his face, and he walks towards me, and, then, an unexpected toughness and grotesqueness appears in his face. He bends slightly forward and places his face close to mine. Just as we come nose to nose, I awaken, screaming!

Sometimes, I'll sit on the bed in my cell and just stare. When that lawyer talks to me, I clasp and unclasp the arms of that Sheriff's office chair. It almost splinters in my grasp. I know he expects me to cry, but the tears won't fall. All of a sudden, I'll start trembling and I hold my hands to my face and say to them, Hands quit trembling!

I can't eat. I used to be an attractive person, but now, I am just skin-and bones.

My hands are trembling. I can't write. I must say 'good-night.'
With love and much hope!
Janelle"

* * * *

"__________, Mississippi
Cell Block 2 B
Old Jail House # 1
*___________, 19_*

Dear Aunt Mae,

Good morning—thanks for your letters.

I never experienced violence in my growing up. I was extremely disappointed and confused, when Dan started abusing me. I guess that's why I'm unable to comprehend what I should have done to deal with violence when it happened. I was so surprised when Dan began to mistreat me. I thought he was a gentle and kind man when I first met him.

Sometimes, I wondered what I needed to do to change myself so that Dan wouldn't be so mean, so violent. I could never tell if it was something I had done or had not done. I tried to please him. I didn't know how, really, but I tried different things. I told him constantly he was the only one in my life. But, somehow he felt that I betrayed him, that I strayed! I never strayed! I loved him!

Sometimes, Dan would beat me severely and fall into bed in a drunken stupor, and leave me to tend to my wounds. Then, the next day he acted as if nothing had happened and if I questioned him about anything he did, he'd become quiet, and say he was very, very sorry. He'd stroke *my face and hair and be very gentle and apologetic and talk softly. Then, he'd spend a lot of time with me and for days he would not drink at all. I'd think, each time, he's really straightened up. He made promises and I believed him.*

He'd whisper secretive things in my ear with his charming and resonant voice—it was like music—so captivating. I suppose I wanted to hear those romantic things. I'd decide things are better—or they will be better.

We'd go a short time and nothing extraordinary happened. Suddenly, without my doing anything to provoke him, right out of the blue—he'd start out abusing me verbally and eventually striking me. After a while it took very little to set off his anger, his assault.

He seemed proud I loved him, yet he didn't want to be bound by love. Apparently, Dan wanted to possess me, not love me.

I am very tired. I must close for now.

With gratefulness to you for your kindness, Aunt Mae, and with a searching heart for God to forgive my murderous action!

Love,
Janelle

* * * *

Aunt Mae's hands shook and her eyes misted. She removed her spectacles from her sweaty forehead, polished them and picked up the next letter from Janelle.

__________, Mississippi
Cell Block 2B
Old Jail House # 1
___________, 19__

Dear Aunt Mae,

Aren't you precious—writing me like you do!

I wanted to finish telling you what happened.

A couple of months before I killed Dan, I hesitantly told him that I thought I was pregnant. He was furious. He lashed into me and knocked me down and straddled me, and took my head in his hands and slammed my head on the floor. Then, he stood up and kicked my stomach, over and over again. I thought I would die. Afterwards he slumped down on the bed and began to cry.

I crawled to the bathroom, pulled myself up on the tub, to the sink, and looked into the mirror. I was so bruised and hurt, I didn't recognize myself.

I was in bed hardly able to move for several days. A short time later, I learned I was not pregnant.

Dan tried to hold me and begged my forgiveness, but I pushed him away. I couldn't forgive him. I said, 'I hate you, Dan, for what you've done. I thought we had such a perfect love in the beginning, but you destroyed it, and for what reason?' I hated what he'd done to me and I hated the way he destroyed the close bond—the love that I thought we had.

Dan knew it was the end of our relationship. He began to drink more, and more and more.

I told him to get out of my house, but he refused to go. How foolish I was to stay—just to hold on to my tangible possessions—my clothes—that old, old renovated sharecroppers house. As I see it now, nothing was worth my staying. I should have gone home—not even pack.

Why? Why, did I not? One of the main reasons that I stayed was because I didn't want to fail. I didn't want to hear, 'I told you so!'

I must close. I'm tired of thinking so much.

Love,
Janelle

* * * *

Aunt Mae re-read the letter. *Oh! Janelle, if only you had left that old sharecropper's house and gone on home to be with your folks!*

Her hands trembled as she replaced the letter in its envelope, and picked up another letter from Janelle.

__________, Mississippi
Cell Block 2B
Old Jail House # 1
___________, 19__

Dear Aunt Mae,

It's funny how writing all of this down seems like a purging of the soul! Do you think God hates me? Do you think I am going to hell? Aunt Mae, please let me keep writing to you—please let me write. Ole Pem said you are Healing Woman. Are you? If you are, please heal me.

The part I am about to write to you, Aunt Mae, is the very hardest part.

Dan started verbally abusing me more and more! It escalated!

I finally got up the nerve to do something for myself—to leave him. When I finally made that decision to leave, I don't think anything in the world could have changed my mind at that point. I told him I didn't love him anymore. It was over. I was ready to leave.

He yelled drunkenly, 'You'll leave over my dead body!'

I went to the bedroom to pack.

Then, later, I went to the kitchen to pack more of my things. Dan was sitting in a chair at the kitchen table, holding a gun in one hand, and a straight razor in the other. He threw the razor at me and said, "Get over to that sink and cut your wrists. Let your stinking blood drain and be gone forever and ever."

I think I screamed, but I'm not sure. I do remember that he yelled, 'Pick up that damn razor!'

I was terrified and frightened. I froze. I just stood in one spot staring at him.

He got up from the chair, walked over to me and hit me so hard on the jaw, I fell to the floor. I held my jaw and attempted to move my jaws. I could hear my ears and head ring. I could hardly see! I remember that I looked up at him from the floor, and he came down on the floor beside me. His filthy words were beyond my comprehension. His eyes were wild and his expression like an animal. It was an expression I'd never seen before in a human-being. He had the expression of what I'd imagine on a demon's face.

He cocked his gun and pointed it at me. I think I screamed, 'God, help me!'

Dan said, 'Here, take this razor, I told you, Bitch, and slit those damn wrists!'

He thrust the razor out towards me.

I think I reached for the razor, but I was thinking I could not do it. I could not kill myself. He'd have to shoot me! He'd have to kill me!

Suddenly, Dan got a bizarre look on his face and began to wretch. His hand slackened. The gun slipped from his hand. He held onto the cabinet with one hand, slid to his knees and onto the floor. He bent over, vomited and fell face-forward into his own vomit. The gun was under him and I didn't dare reach under him to get the gun!

I jumped up and ran outside to get anything—anything! I could leave now—but he would follow me and hunt me down. I saw the ax on the back porch. When I came back into the room, Dan was snoring and making loud, gurgling noises. He was asleep in his vomit.

After it first happened, I could remember every horrible moment—every detail of what I did, but, now a lot of it is vague. I remember I hit him with an ax. I know I wielded the ax, over and over again. But, now—at this time—I don't remember much more than that.

I pray for my soul to be quiet—to hush, hush and find an inner stillness! I can't concentrate.

'Thou shalt not kill!' roars in my ears. Sometimes I cover my ears to stop the roar, the sound of that violated commandment!

I violated my conscience—my personal code, and have bound myself for eternity. It has left dirty tracks indelibly gouged in my brain—seared forever. Just knowing I can not go back—I can not make amends is unbearable. I feel worthless.

I would undo it all, if I were able. Now, I must learn to live with the guilt, the despair, the grief and bitterness.

Oh! Aunt Mae, help me! Heal me!

Love,
Janelle

* * * *

__________, Mississippi
Cell Block 2B
Old Jail House # 1
___________,19__

Dear Aunt Mae,

It makes me feel better to write. Thanks for writing me back. No one but my parents associates with me.

My lawyer says I have been victimized mentally and physically. All I know is, I felt too ashamed, humiliated and embarrassed to tell my parents about my being in danger, and about Dan's abusiveness. For some reason, I felt like I needed to keep it a secret from everyone because no one would understand. I felt trapped! I know I should have told my parents about those awful encounters I was having with a devil, before it got so bad.

Writing exhausts me mentally and physically. I struggle to make myself finish each letter before I become too tired and stressed.

I have no interest in anything anymore. I don't want to ever love anyone again, even if the jurors gave me a verdict of life, but I would like to live!

Thank you, again, for the time it takes to respond to my letters.

Love,
Janelle

P. S. I'm enclosing a copy of the letter I wrote Dan last night. If I sound bitter, well then I'm bitter."

* * * *

Aunt Mae sat on the front porch, read Janelle's letter and tried to understand. She removed her bonnet and pushed the white ringlets of hair from her face and neck and wondered how this girl could give so many intimate details now, but could not tell her parents at the time that things were going wrong in her life. *I can't believe how frankly Janelle describes her life with Dan.*

She laid the letter aside.

How awful it must be to be married to someone that doesn't love you back. How awful it must be to pick a man to marry and learn too late he's cruel, mean and deadly.

Ole Pem is really in for it, if he's in love with Janelle.

She rubbed her elbow with camphor, tried to put herself in Janelle's place, and realized what a fearful series of abuse she must have endured, *at the time* she killed Dan, and, now, how fearful she must feel being locked up in jail.

She glanced at Henny-Penny and Kackie sitting under the Weeping Willow tree and playing with cut out Sears Roebuck Catalog paper dolls. They seemed happy enough.

Aunt Mae opened the pages Janelle wrote to Dan from her jail cell and continued to read the purging of her soul.

"Dear Dan,

I was a mere colorless, blank, and shapeless canvas the day I met you. I was no closer to love and friendship than I was to hate. In fact, I knew neither love nor hate before I met you. You wove yourself into my heart! How wrong I was to not be aware of the deadly road upon which you led me, that road we traveled together, yet, it was one of your making alone—not "ours." My heart drew closer and closer to you until I could feel the dynamic and hidden transformations which made me more feeling, and more aware. You purred beautiful words into my willing ear. You were as cunning as a seductive cat and as wondrous as an owl—your animal instincts drew me and haunt me even now.

As I lie upon my canvas, my cot, and close my eyes and soothe my wounds, I can still hear the hoof-beats of those horses which carried us into the unknown, to the edge of that great cosmos. My soul bleeds—my words of anguish color the canvas droplets of red. I pick up the brush of destiny and stir in the blue of anguish, yellow of disappointment, and accentuate black, uncontrollable sobs.

My canvas has changed now. Once it was smooth and slightly crinkled, calm, serene and mediocre, but, now, the canvas is cracked by the vibrations of the horrible screams that your tortuous love has inflicted. I was not aware of the treacherous journey we traveled. How could I have been so naive?

How surprising to learn you were not perfect—your allusions and delusions were continuously transforming you into the most complex.

I thought I knew you.

I cry out—I scream as I crawl in the dark bowels of hell! I have no colors to calm me! I envision you as I close my eyes and I claw my blood-streaked, ochered face in acute agony to think you betrayed me.

In deep reflection,
Janelle"

* * * *

Aunt Mae placed Janelle's dissertation to Dan on the dining room table. *Janelle's most intimate thoughts and feelings make me feel like an intruder, a peeping-tom! How can she allow someone else to read such inner-most heart-wrenching thoughts?*

I had the same feeling when I read Macie's diary.

She held her stomach, which had become bilious. *How could this young girl carry out the murder, then the burial and then the gruesome, bloody cleanup after she killed Dan?*

Aunt Mae went to the kitchen to make cornbread and tried to think of a way to help this troubled young girl.

* * * *

Aunt Mae's hand trembled when she picked up the next letter for another review.

__________, Mississippi
Cell Block 2B
Old Jail House # 1
___________, 19__

Dear Aunt Mae,

Thank you for your letter. Especially thank you for saying you think I didn't premeditate Dan's murder—because I really didn't plan to kill him!

My mom came to the jail the other day, and sat and held my hand. She said, 'What did you do to make Dan so angry with you?' It was as if she had tuned out everything I had ever told her about his physical and mental abusiveness—his hitting me, his stomping me.

I said, 'Mama, you and the preacher who come here to see me don't listen very well, do you?' The preacher told me I should have tried to have been a better wife.

He quoted scriptures and said my soul was "in danger of hell,' and that God said, 'Do no murder.' I told that preacher that I was a good wife to Dan. I was a good girl. Dan didn't need a cause or a reason to be angry. He just got angry and didn't have to have a reason. The devil came out when the whisky went in him.

I believed if I cared enough I could cure whatever the problem was. I had no idea that he didn't love me. What a very false presumption. I see that now. I told the preacher I didn't want Dan to be dead. When he was down on the floor wallowing in his vomit, I knew that if he ever got up again, he'd kill me.

I told mama and the preacher both that I don't need a lecture now. I don't need to be put down and made to feel worse than I do, if that's possible. I need understanding and kindness. I had a choice—yes—I could have left when I went outside, but instead I came back in with an ax, and that choice will probably be the reason for my death!

I was not only mentally caged and trapped as Dan's wife, but look at me now! Caged! Trapped! Alone!

Have to go now! Tired! Listless!

Love,
Janelle

* * * *

__________, Mississippi
Cell Block 2B
Old Jail House # 1
___________, 19__

Dear Aunt Mae,

One of the jailers took his turn at duty and brought my supper. He said,_'You know you might have wealthy folks, but death awaits you. Don't think about getting away with murder.' I stared at him and he stared back. I couldn't eat.

Sometimes at night when I fall asleep, I dream about a human-sized, colorful bird. It looks like an enormous, giant parrot sitting in a tree.

I dream this dream a lot, and it haunts me in the daytime.

The sun is shining when I walk up to a large tree limb, which holds the most gorgeous, colorful bird, the size of a human-being. Its feathers are the color of a rainbow.

The sun goes away and the day becomes overcast. Suddenly, it begins to snow. I look up into the giant bird's eyes and when it appears to recognize me, tears roll down its blue, feathered cheeks and the tears turn into small cubicles of ice. The snowflakes stick to the tree limb and snow piles high upon the bird's head. It appears so sad, I reach my hand toward the exquisite creature, as if to console it. When it flutters its red, green and blue wings, snow falls from the tree limb and snow covers my head.

The bird remains on the cold, cold limb and stares after me, as I stagger away dejectedly.

Isn't my dream strange? But, then, it's strange to be in this place. This jail!

Love,
Janelle

* * * *

Cell Block 2 B
Old Jail House # 1
__________, Mississippi
________, 19__

Dear Aunt Mae,

Thanks for yours and Laughing Eyes' interpretation of my dream. It is interesting that you think the colorful bird is my old self. I talked to my doctor and he said your interpretation of the dream was as good as any other—clever. He wanted to know if you were a witch? My doctor listened to my story, my complaints and said I acted compulsively, without thinking of the consequences when I killed Dan. He suggested I might have married Dan compulsively. He thinks subconsciously I knew Dan wouldn't work and subconsciously I knew other negative things about him, but I chose to ignore my instincts and married him, anyhow. I wonder?

I'm having other problems.

When I picked up my wash cloth yesterday, I suddenly gasped. I had recall of the blood-soaked rags, where I cleaned up Dan's blood off the ceiling, off the walls, off the floor, and off myself. I could still smell the stench of his blood. I washed and rinsed my hands with the hard, jail soap and water all day. My hands became withered and gnarled. (I loved Dan! How could I have done what I have done?)

With much frustration, but Love,
Janelle

P.S. Where did that colorful bird-self go? Is she gone, forever? Can one ever get one's real self back?"

* * * *

Aunt Mae laid her spectacles upon the kitchen table, and rubbed her eyes. How could Janelle have been suddenly driven to such a desperate action—to kill? She and Dan are both victims of this savage play. Janelle says she loved Dan, but, in reality, did she hate him?

Aunt Mae admired Caddie's typing, and smoothed the copies of Macie's original diary into a neat stack. She hoped it would help Janelle's lawyer understand that Dan was a wife beater as well as a child beater. I hope the diary written in Pig Latin and Caddie's typed translation can be used as evidence at Janelle's trial. Everyone says it can't be used in court because it's hearsay, but it'll be worth trying. Her father has enough money to pay for a good defense. I hope something works, because I don't want her to die—I don't want anyone to die!

She placed an affidavit, prepared by Judge Pewter, upon the top of the diary, and ran her finger across her signature. By signing the document, she swore the hand-writing on the original document was that of Macie's. She ran her finger over the embossed notary's seal imprinted upon the jurat, wrapped a brown paper around the package and tied it with a raveled flour-sack string.

Janelle was most likely "pushed" to kill in self-defense, but I don't understand the rage and make-up in Janelle that could kill Dan. I don't understand her choice to destroy his body and burn him.

Joanie Zanderneff is also in a predicament with that husband of hers beating on her. He also beat Dan when he was a little boy. Dan beat Macie. Dan beat Janelle. What does that mean? Once beaten, you have to beat another person—-especially a family member?

Well! Janelle did more than beat! She killed! And covered up!

I have to keep Joanie's secret, or Mr. Zanderneff might beat her to death. Joanie needs to leave Mr. Zanderneff, but regardless of what I think, I know that Joanie has to make up her own mind to leave her husband. It's Joanie's choice.

* * * *

Aunt Mae looked up from her sewing, when she heard Baby Jeb barking. "Why! Jake! I didn't hear you come up. How are you, darling, Chile? Where you been keeping yourself?"

"Just busy. Thought I'd come over and say hello."

"You ride?"

"No. Cut through the woods."

Henny-Penny and Kackie slammed the screen door and ran into Jake's open arms. "Jake! Where ya been?"

"Missed you, too!" He hugged them tightly. "Guess what Uncle Jake has for you? You have three guesses."

"Candy!"

"How did you guess?" he teased. He handed them small paper sacks of cherry, penny-suckers.

"Y'all okay, Aunt Mae?" he asked.

"Doing very well. I was just re-reading Janelle's last letter. I feel sorry for that poor girl."

"Dan really did a number on all of us here. His actions affected Janelle and her family, and Joanie and Mr. Zanderneff and God only knows who else."

"Dan's murder is playing with Janelle's mind," said Aunt Mae.

"Where's Caddie?"

"Working at the law office. She'll be sorry she missed you, Jake."

"I'm not so sure about that, Aunt Mae."

"Oh? Caddie always looks forward to your visits. You don't know how much," she nodded for emphasis.

"I did something I wish I could re-live and play it all over again. The last time I saw Caddie, I hurt her feelings. She tell you?"

"Why, no. She didn't." She stared into his large, solemn, blue eyes.

He looked away, and began to pick at a black speck on his thumb. "Caddie's been a faithful, loving and dear friend throughout the years." He continued to dodge her curious eyes.

"Yes—she is."

"I did something to her that I wish I could take back. Just like Janelle, we all do things that we'd like to take back, re-do and make right, but some things we can never, ever make up for." Jake sighed.

"Macie's gone, Jake. Let her go," Aunt Mae pleaded.

"Not Macie—Aunt Mae. Caddie is also gone from my life. I goofed up."

Aunt Mae looked perplexed. "Caddie?"

"Gotta be going, Aunt Mae." He bent down and kissed her on the cheek. "I love you."

"Love you too, Son." He seemed so unhappy, she didn't nag him about smelling stale alcohol on his breath. She wondered what Jake meant when he said, 'Caddie is gone?'

* * * *

Aunt Mae and Uncle Hume heard a car, long before it arrived.

"That'll be Ole Pem driving Judge Pewter's car."

When Ole Pem got out of the Cadillac, he ran towards the house. "Guess what! I'm going back to college next quarter. Starting right away!"

"That's fantastic!" They patted him on the back, and enjoyed his sharing the good news with them.

"Judge Pewter said he'd watched me struggle long enough to know I didn't mind working my way through school. But, he doesn't want to wait any longer," said Ole Pem.

"What did Judge Pewter have in mind?"

"Judge Pewter and Uncle Albert loaned me the money! I signed a promissory note today!"

"Great news!" You'll be back at Three-Mile Crossing in no time! Are those guys robbing you with their interest rate?" Uncle Hume smiled.

"You're talking about Uncle Albert Taylor? Grandmaw Taylor's brother?" asked Aunt Mae. "If Judge Pewter is involved, I know they aren't being robbed."

"Yes! He and Judge Pewter are sharing in my loan, half and half."

"I'm so happy for you, darling," Aunt Mae smiled.

"This kind of news is so good to hear, Ole Pem!"

"I wanted to tell Caddie. She around?" said Ole Pem.

"No, Caddie went to Sojo's."

"Alone?"

"I'm not sure," said Aunt Mae.

"Maybe I'll see her at Sojo's," Ole Pem grinned.

"Ole Pem, did you ever hear that Uncle Albert's and Grandmaw Taylor's paw left both of them a lot of acreage. They sold off enough land to have money in the bank, lend money and make good interest. They've helped a lot of us folks around these parts."

"Did Uncle Albert ever marry?"

"Uncle Albert was married to a friendly girl, named *Molly Bee.* She and their baby boy died in child birth," he responded sadly.

"Guess that's one reason he dotes on all his nephews and nieces," said Aunt Mae.

"Uncle Albert's a kind person!" Ole Pem beamed with happiness over his good luck.

"Yes, he is. He's self-taught and smart too. Makes money with his inheritance. He's sorta like a bank. Sometimes I wonder how some folks have business-sense and know the things they know without studying," said Uncle Hume.

"I believe it was Thomas Edison who said ideas come to a person from space," Ole Pem laughed.

"Guess that's where Uncle Albert gets his instincts—from space!" They laughed.

* * * *

"Hume, I'm taking Henny-Penny and Kackie over to Joanie's, while Mr. Zanderneff is out of town."

"Best you be careful, Mae. If he comes back early, it'll just be harder on Joanie."

"I know, Hume, but she wants to visit with Henny-Penny and Kackie. Nobody will know we went to see her except our family."

Aunt Mae guided Henny-Penny and Kackie through the woods, along the meandering of a creek to the Zanderneff 's cabin.

Three dogs ran towards them and barked loudly, when they came into the clearing at the Zanderneff's ramshackled cabin. Rusty pieces of equipment and junked cars sat in the front yard. A rusty tricycle sat near the front doorsteps, its rubber wheels long rotted. Unfinished projects were evident. Parts of the front porch were repaired with new but molded wood. Almost half of the porch had no flooring.

"Watch your step. Knock on the door, Henny-Penny and Kackie. This is Grandmother Joanie's house."

They knocked loudly.

When Joanie opened the door, she laughed and threw her hands up in the air. "Glory be! Howdy, Mae! Howdy, pretty Granddaughters!" She hugged them and smothered them with kisses.

It was the first time Aunt Mae had seen Joanie happy since Dan's death.

"I smell something that smells like vinegar, Grandmother Joanie. What is it?" Kackie prickled her nose.

"You're right. You do smell vinegar. I spilled a jar of hot peppers and vinegar in the kitchen floor this morning."

"I smell cake," Henny-Penny smiled.

"You couldn't have picked a better time to come. Mr. Zanderneff has gone to sell some cattle and will be gone a couple of days." Joanie frowned. "Or, so he said."

"So we heard, Joanie."

"So glad you came to see me."

"That's good, Joanie. Need to talk private."

"Wal, if I can, Mae," she said nervously. She knelt down, hugged and kissed Henny-Penny and Kackie. "Put your arms around Grandmaw Joanie's neck and hug her tight, babies." She removed their coats and scarves.

"Come! Come! I'll make us a cup of hot tea," she smiled tenderly. "And, Henny-Penny, you did smell pound cake!"

"That'll hit the spot," said Aunt Mae. "But let me make the tea while you play with Henny-Penny and Kackie."

"Set here on this sofa, and make yourselves to home!"

Aunt Mae glanced at the clean, but thread-bare chenille sofa.

"Henny-Penny and Kackie, here are some books that belonged to your father. You know, they belonged to Dan. You can take them home with you."

"Our Daddy's?" Kackie's eyes opened wide with curiosity.

"My Daddy's gone away," Henny-Penny murmured.

After tea, Aunt Mae cleared the cups and saucers, and wiped pound cake crumbs off the kitchen table."

"Joanie hugged and kissed Henny-Penny and Kackie, caressed their hair, examined their faces and eyes, and smoothed their dresses.

Joanie brushed the hair off their foreheads, and guided them across the room. "Come over to this corner, here, where I have a Sears catalog and some scissors. You can cut out paper dolls and clothes and have a big ole time."

"I'm being nosy, I know, Joanie, but can you pick up your story where we left off at the grave yard the other day? I'd like to know when the beatings and mistreatment started. I'm just trying to understand why anyone stays in a bad situation, when they are getting the living stuffings beat out of them."

"It's hard to talk about, Mae, but I'll try."

"Joanie, you need to talk the pain out of your heart."

"I can't talk if Mr. Zanderneff happens to come back early." Joanie tried to smile, as she brushed her curly, brown hair away from her face. She held each side of her jaws tightly and reflectively.

"If Mr. Zanderneff comes back early, we'll just talk about Henny-Penny and Kackie. Surely, he'll understand I just brought them over to visit their grandparents."

"Don't rightly know where to start." She held her temples, looked up towards the ceiling and gathered her thoughts. "Mr. Zanderneff pestered me to marry him, said he loved me and I believed he did. Know I loved him. He was fun-loving and never hit me, when we were courting. He was pretty much a gentleman." Joanie gazed out the window and searched for a long gone memory.

"You're a handsome couple now, and you were real 'lookers' when I first saw you together."

"Thanks, Mae. He was handsome. He is my first and only love! When we first married, he was good to me. I was very happy!" She held her face in her hands and shook her head. "Then one day Mr. Zanderneff started his cruelties. At first, he'd say mean and ugly things to me and it'd cut to my heart. Hurt me so bad! I'd wonder what I did to make him act so horrible. I never did like quarreling."

Aunt Mae patted Joanie on the hand. "I know."

"He got where little things would pressure him, and he'd drink.

I remember the first time he hit me, we were sitting in that swing on the front porch. I was talking about the weather—nothing really important, and he just reached over and slapped me so hard, he laid me out cold! Knocked me so hard, I thought my jaw would never work again. My eyes turned black, but, worst of all he beat Dan. He didn't have to be drunk to beat him. Mr. Zanderneff is a mean-spirited man."

"I'm so sorry," said Aunt Mae.

"I kept saying, 'Tell me what I did, so that I'll not do it again. I can change. Tell me and I won't ever do it again!' He laughed at me, held onto the side of the house to walk, and went inside the house. He was drunk, don't you see? I went to the creek and bathed my face and cried, and prayed for God to help me." Joanie wrapped and unwrapped a navy blue apron around her arms.

"At first, I thought I was doing something to make him mad, and I'd pet him and pamper him. If I was quiet, he'd hit me for not saying anything. If I was talking, he'd hit me. Could not win for losing! I did everything I could not to provoke him. Things got so bad, I packed a few things, left with Dan and went to his Mammy's house. I just needed a place to stay 'til I doctored my wounds and got where I could think good. His Mammy turned me away."

"What did she say?" Aunt Mae asked, gently.

"In hindsight, I believe she was afraid to take sides against her son, but at the time I thought she was just a mean old woman. His Mammy said, 'What did you do to make him hit you?' "I told her I didn't do nothing. Nothing. He just hits me and for no reason. I said, 'Your son hits your grandson!'"

"What did she say then," Aunt Mae asked softly.

"She told me that I couldn't stay there with her. I told her I had nowheres to go. And, Mammy said, 'You made your bed, now sleep in it'," Joanie hung her head.

"What a cruel thing to say! I am so sorry!" Aunt Mae shook her head.

"If only Mammy had reached out to me and said, 'Stay here until you're stronger, until you can figure it all out.' If only Mammy hadda said to me, 'Joanie, I'll protect you and feed you until your body is healed. I'll listen to you, Joanie, and hear. I'll listen to your silence and weigh it, as well. I'll help you get away, Joanie. I'll help you and my grandson!'

"If only she would have listened and helped me when I said, 'Mammy, I've never experienced such things. My family never beat me, nor beat anyone else.'" Joanie flailed her right hand.

Aunt Mae sat down beside her, stroked Joanie's arm, and attempted to soothe her.

"And, if only I could have said, 'Mammy, you're stronger than I am, pull me out of this pit of misery, out of the danger and the fear!'" Joanie frowned and wiped her teary eyes on her sleeve.

"But no, Mammy turned me away. So I went back to the only place I knew to go, back to Mr. Zanderneff and his beatings and his torture. This is where I've been ever since. I guess I did make my bed to lie in," she sighed.

"Joanie, do you want to stop talking now, and we'll talk more later?"

"No, let's go on with it." She poked the fire with a poker. "But, better still, best we go out in the yard. I'll build a big fire and we can take some chairs out and sit by a bonfire. Henny-Penny and Kackie would like that, wouldn't they?"

"Listen, Joanie, it's very cold outside."

"But, I need to be in the yard doing something when Mr. Zanderneff gets back. He might come in early. Oh, Lordy, what if he did?" Joanie picked up her coat off the back of a rocking chair and put it on. "Best we get in the yard, Mae."

"Okay, Joanie. I'm listening. I hear what you're saying." She patted Joanie on the hand.

Joanie went to a corner in the living room and removed a stack of newspapers from an untidy area, and continued: "Well, it started out by Mr. Zanderneff criticizing everything that I'd do and I just couldn't believe his horrible actions. When I'm in front of people, I always pretend everything is okay!"

Joanie picked up several pieces of rotted wood and began to make a pile of wood in the front yard.

"Why do you pretend everything is all right?"

"I am humiliated and embarrassed." Tears came into Joanie's eyes. "I can't believe my marriage is a failure, when other people seem so happy."

"Would it have helped if someone else had said, 'Let me help you. You don't deserve this bad treatment." Aunt Mae asked quietly.

"Not at first, because I was too embarrassed, but as time passed I'd have liked to have someone say that to me."

"At first, you would not have left?"

"Not at all. I was trying to make our life like it was originally, when we first met. When we first married. He was sweet to me when we were courting." Joanie struck a match and lit the papers.

"So, Mr. Zanderneff became more domineering?" asked Aunt Mae.

"Yes! He was so domineering that I found it was easier to stay than leave, even if he was abusive. I didn't have any money and didn't know how to make a living for me and Dan. That's when I became lucky and went to work for Judge Pewter, but I never saved enough money for Dan and me to get away. Mr. Zanderneff always took most of my money, anyhow."

"Your parents were dead at that time?"

"Yes."

"I remember one time Mr. Zanderneff beat me so bad, he knocked me down to the floor. I was in a stupor. I didn't want to come back to the present. I wanted to just die and keep on going."

"What happened when you came to yourself?"

"I was screaming at first, and then the cries stopped. I went somewhere inside my head. When I regained consciousness, Mr. Zanderneff helped me to bed and handed me a wet wash cloth. I could hear Dan screaming my name from the next room, where he was locked in."

"Did Mr. Zanderneff ever apologize?"

"No. He used to apologize after he beat me, when we first married. Told me he was awful sorry. He'd do better. He'd be extra nice and everything for a few days, but, now, he never apologizes."

"You never get used to someone beating you, Joanie. I don't see how you continue to endure the mistreatment."

"I used to love him, but he beat the love right outta me. I've never hurt anyone in my life and I can't understand why someone wants to hurt another person. It's easier said than done to get away. He doesn't want me out of his sight. It's a miracle he's gone today and I am here alone, talking to you." Joanie walked up the front stairway, stood at a window and peeped inside at the little girls. She rubbed her hands together, and then rubbed her left arm. "He's given me a lot of pain."

"I wish I could say or do something to help," said Aunt Mae.

"I've never told anyone about my fear or about my bruises before. It seems like a stranger is here talking to you right now, and not me speaking."

"I'm trying to figure it all out, Joanie."

"As time went on, I loved him less and less. His beatings became more uncontrollable!"

"I don't need to ask, do I?"

"No. I hate him. Hope God doesn't send me to hell for hating."

"Don't be too hard on yourself, Joanie."

"I think back to the days when Dan was a little boy. Mr. Zanderneff beat him for no reason, regardless of whether I interfered. Sometimes, I wished Dan had never been born, even though he was the most precious thing in my life!"

Joanie raked the trash into the bonfire so fiercely, the fire scattered and caught some leaves.

Aunt Mae grabbed dirt, poured it over the leaves and stamped the fire.

When the fire was out, she came back to where Joanie continued to fling trash and leaves with the rake, and held Joanie's arms. "Calm yourself. Calm yourself."

Joanie stood still. "When Dan and Macie moved away, I was glad he finally got away in one piece. I would have never dreamed that Dan would ever beat Macie. I never thought he'd choose to follow in his mean father's footsteps, and become a wife-beater. I am so sorry for whatever has happened to Macie and Janelle."

Aunt Mae patted her on the hand.

"Mae, I heard tell you're going to go and see Dan's wife—going to see Janelle. Is it true?"

"Yes. I want to try to figure out why she and Macie stayed with Dan when they were being beaten to death. It's for my own healing process."

"I'd like to see Janelle, but I don't think Mr. Zanderneff will allow me to talk to her by myself. But he says we're going to the trial. We need to be there for Dan."

"I understand."

"News in the holler says Dan tried to make Macie and Janelle both slit their wrists. What do you think, Mae?" Joanie avoided Aunt Mae's eyes.

"You feel up to all this stress, Joanie?" They both continued to hold onto the rake.

Joanie's voice shook. "As much as I'll ever be."

"Macie's diary says that Dan beat her," Aunt Mae spoke softly.

"I wonder what I could have done differently to make my son a better husband to Macie and Janelle. And, make him a better father to Henny-Penny and Kackie. It's very humiliating to think I failed him as a mother." Joanie lowered her head and sighed loudly. "God rest Macie's sweet soul. I pray for her, and I pray for Janelle. Such a waste! Mae, do you hate Dan?"

"At first, I hated Dan for what he did, but I can't live with hate in my heart," said Aunt Mae.

"Glad you don't hate Dan."

"Of course, I'm very upset with him, and I suppose I always will be," said Aunt Mae. "The Lord is the one that forgives."

"Mae, as close as Dan and I were, I just can't believe my son didn't write me or call me on the telephone at Judge Pewter's office after Macie died! Not a single time!" she lamented.

Aunt Mae placed her hand on Joanie's hand. "Hope I've not distressed you too much, Joanie. Thanks for helping me try to sort things out."

"Thank you, Mae. I loved playing with the children."

"Joanie, if you ever need a place to go. Please come to our house."

"I couldn't. Mr. Zanderneff would kill me."

"You don't deserve this treatment!" Aunt Mae stressed the word *deserve*. She placed her fingers on her temples and became thoughtful. "I know what you can do. Remember my quilting house? If you ever need to leave, go there and hide."

"Bless you, Mae. Bless you. Just to have you offer means a lot!"

"Joanie, you don't deserve anything but the best."

"It's too late for me. The light in my heart went out the day I learned Dan was dead. I'm too old for all this!"

"Joanie, it's not too late. Go to the quilting house—light a lamp. I'll look for a light in the quilting house every night before I go to bed. Give me a chance to help you. To help you might help put salve on my own hurt and the guilt I feel that I didn't help Macie when she needed help."

"I'll think on it. Thank you my dear, dear Mae, from the bottom of my heart! God love you!"

"I know it must be very hard for you," said Aunt Mae.

"I wonder if I could have done something to help turn this awful event around. Is it my fault?"

"Joanie, it is not your fault. I believe a person doesn't have to beat another person just because he's been beaten himself."

"I guess so."

"Joanie, have you ever hit anyone in your life?"

"No I never have. I love too much."

"You've been hit, kicked, and beaten you said, but you're not mean and vicious. It didn't make you abusive. Joanie, why do some people that have been abused end up hitting, or humiliating or beating other people?" asked Aunt Mae.

"You're asking me that question? You try and tell me the reason!" Joanie exclaimed, indignantly and began to flail the rake.

Aunt Mae held on to the rake. "I believe somehow these people have come to hate life," said Aunt Mae.

"What about that person hating himself?"

"Do they hate themselves?"

"Yes, that's my question."

"Don't rightly know. But, I believe if you loved yourself, you'd want everyone to love you. You'd try to make other people happy. Maybe the abuser—the wife beater or child beater does hate himself."

"Does anyone know the answer?" asked Joanie.

"I don't know. I best be getting on the path. Hume will be worried. Aunt Mae released the rake and held onto Joanie. "I'll get Henny-Penny and Kackie, and my medicine basket."

"I need to stay here and be busy, just in case Mr. Zanderneff comes in early."

"Looks like snow."

"Yes, cold, cold snow," said Joanie.

"Joanie, will you come home with me now? Pack a few clothes and leave everything behind. Come with me this minute. Don't put up with this treatment anymore! Please! Let me help you!"

"I can't leave, right now, Mae, but I'll always remember your kind words."

"Joanie, I'm saying everything you wanted Mammy to say. I'm offering you the help you wanted Mammy to give you."

"I've reconciled myself to this way of life so long, I don't know if I can leave now," Joanie whispered. "You can't imagine the strength I'd have to muster to get away!"

"I'm giving you the opportunity."

"The pain of loss—the pain of losing a child is greater than any physical pain," said Joanie.

"Yes, I know. I can sympathize. I lost little Mandy and I've lost Macie."

"Yes, you do know the pain," Joanie agonized. "I've had many sleepless nights."

"Joanie—"

"Sometimes I just feel like my life—my mind has conked out. I have this feeling of being caged—locked up in my own mind, and I have a great feeling of doom come over me. I want to just lie in bed and do nothing, but I have to work. I make myself work." The rake rested against her bosom, and she held her temples between both of her hands.

"I'm sorry, Joanie, so sorry," Aunt Mae spoke softly, and patted Joanie on the shoulder.

"Dan's death has sent me into an awful tailspin. I can't get the terribleness out of my mind. My heart hurts sometimes until I think it will burst."

"Oh! Joanie!"

"I have a secret part to my heart, and I keep Dan hidden in that place. He'll always be my baby boy." She touched her breast with an open hand and closed it into a fist. She walked to the window next to the fireplace, and peeped in.

"I'll get Henny-Penny and Kackie and bring them outside," said Aunt Mae.

"Thanks, Mae. It'd be best."

"Always keep Dan in that secret place where no one but you can touch him. Feel him. Think of all the happy times you had together—those very special times," said Aunt Mae. "It'll help get you through the rougher times, I'm sure."

"I have no refuge, but God!"

"You need to get away from this place, Joanie."

"I know."

"Just remember whatever your decision is, whether it's to stay here or leave, I'm behind you one-hundred percent, and I'll try to help you either way."

"Thanks, Mae."

* * * *

"Will you be back home before Christmas?"

"We'll be here in time to decorate the tree," Aunt Mae smiled.

"Will you bring us a surprise?" asked Henny-Penny.

"Of course, I will!" Aunt Mae primped the brim of the floppy black hat a little more over her left eye.

"We'll be too lonesome, when you're not here to play with us," Kackie whined.

"Wish we could go, too," Henny-Penny pouted.

"You'll have fun with Mary," said Aunt Mae.

"We'll have a good ole time," Mary Daniels laughed. "I'll cook you some teacakes. You like cookies don't you?"

"I like pound cake," said Henny-Penny.

"I like popcorn," said Kackie.

"We'll have both of those things to eat and lots more," Mary promised. "I used to have a little girl." She caressed Henny-Penny's blond hair. "I know what they like to eat, and what they like to play," she said.

"What was your little girl's name?"

"Her name was Ratchel-Robin."

"Robin? We had a bird named 'Sparkle-Sparrow,'" said Kackie.

"Yes, I remember." Mary hugged Kackie and patted her on the back.

"Mary, we appreciate you and Rob-Hunter making our trip possible."

"You're mighty welcome, Uncle Hume. Just take good care of yourselves."

Upon hearing Ole Pem on the porch, Mary opened the front door. "Morning, Ole Pem."

"Morning, Miz Daniels. Everybody ready?"

"Come in, Ole Pem! Henny-Penny, you and Kackie give Uncle Hume and me one last hug! Be good little girls for Miz Daniels."

Ole Pem walked Aunt Mae to Judge Pewter's Cadillac. "Aunt Mae, that day we talked at the spring, I never dreamed you'd want to take Macie's papers to Mississippi yourself, personally."

"Ole Pem, we'll do what we can to help Janelle, but I also have some unanswered questions about Macie. I want to talk to that girl!"

"You never cease to amaze me, Aunt Mae."

"Mae's full of surprises, all right," Uncle Hume smiled.

"Judge Pewter told me that he'll need some *legs* about the time I graduate, and pass the Bar."

"Awesome! What about Locket?"

Aunt Mae, it's early yet. Locket is just getting her divorce, and I am trying to be a friend to some girl in jail."

"Just some girl, Ole Pem?"

"Okay—I am being a friend to a most gorgeous girl, who happens to be in jail. Where does that leave me?"

"Seeking a law degree and getting on back home?" She patted him on the sleeve. "Yes, getting on back home," she repeated.

* * * *

"Came to see everybody off. Brought y'all a picnic lunch, and John got y'all some ice at the icehouse to keep the food fresh." Laughing Eyes handed Aunt Mae a split-oak basket filled to the brim.

"What'd you cook for us, Laughing Eyes?"

"Fried country cured ham, fried chicken, a lot of biscuits, muscadine jelly, strawberry preserves, pound cake and a jug of sweet tea. Enjoy! Enjoy!" she laughed.

Aunt Mae hugged her. "I know it'll taste extra good, if you cooked it."

They clung tightly to each other in their camaraderie.

"Ole Pem and Judge Pewter sure did organize this trip! We've got first-class transportation, first class food, and first class friends to see us off!" Uncle Hume said, excitedly.

Ole Pem stood with his arms around his mother and father, smiling. "Thanks, Mom and Dad, for being here. Please tell Judge Pewter, I'm going on down to the Sojo's Gas Station and get the tank topped off," said Ole Pem. "Be back shortly."

"Okay, Son."

They stood before Judge Pewter's mahogany office door and admired the Christmas wreath made of freshly cut holly leaves and red berries. Bells jingled when Uncle Hume opened the door and waited for the ladies to enter the office. A strong aroma of spiced tea filled the waiting area.

"Judge Pewter, please. He's expecting us," Aunt Mae teased Caddie.

Caddie laughed. "Please be seated. Judge Pewter has someone in his office. I saw you outside the window and went ahead and put the kettle on. How about a cup of spiced tea?" She brought a silver tray with china cups and saucers and set it on a small table in front of an antique sofa.

"My! My!" Laughing Eyes exclaimed. "To think we're having spiced tea on fine china in a lawyer's office."

"Nothing's too good for his clients," Caddie smiled.

The door to Judge Pewter's office opened.

Grandmaw Taylor and Hannah walked out of Judge Pewter's office ahead of him.

Grandmaw Taylor handed Caddie an empty china teacup and saucer. "Thank you, for the delicious tea. I enjoyed it so much."

"You're welcome." Caddie began to type, but stopped when the telephone rang.

"Thought Bessie was working for you?"

"She'll be here shortly."

"Sounds like homecoming time out here," chuckled Judge Pewter. He shook hands with everyone.

"Aunt Mae, I thought I heard you and Laughing Eyes talking out here. How in the world are y'all doing?" Grandmaw Taylor cackled.

"Fine. Fine. We're just visiting, while Caddie and Judge Pewter get ready to leave."

"I heard all about your trying to help Dan's wife. With all of you working so hard for that girl, what're her parents doing for her?"

"Her parents are supportive in every possible way.!"

"I hope everything works out for the best," Grandmaw Taylor smiled a toothless smile. "By the way, Brother Albert's really impressed with Ole Pem! He thinks it's amazing how Ole Pem has befriended that girl."

"God has greatly blessed John and me with a handsome, healthy son that cares so much for people," Laughing Eyes said appreciatively.

"Hannah, your dress is lovely!" Aunt Mae beamed. "And, so are you!"

"I heard you'd be here, Aunt Mae. I'm real glad to see you before I leave!" Hannah walked over to Caddie's desk. "See you when I get back, Caddie."

"Take good care of yourself, Hannah," said Caddie.

"Caddie, you going to Mississippi with everybody?"

"Yes, I'll probably be called as a witness."

"A witness?" Hannah asked inquisitively.

"Yes. I'll be asked about my sister's diary."

"How interesting," said Hannah. "If the place was closer, I'd like to be in the courtroom. "Good luck, in the witness seat, Caddie."

"Thanks, Hannah. We'll miss you."

Hannah touched Aunt Mae on the sleeve, and motioned towards the front door. "Will you come out on the porch with me, Aunt Mae?"

"You said you are leaving? Leaving to go where?" She peered into Hannah's blue-green eyes, clouded by a redness that made it obvious she'd been crying.

"Oh, probably to Atlanta, Aunt Mae," she became quiet, and looked towards the Blue Ridge Mountains.

"You taking Benjamin?"

"He'll be staying with Mama and Grandmaw Taylor."

"I didn't know you were leaving! How long?"

"Don't know how long. I'll try to find work."

"May I have your address?"

"I'll miss you, and I'll write you and stay in touch."

"I hope it's a good move for you, Hannah," Aunt Mae said softly. "I think about you and Benjamin, often!"

"We think about you a lot, too. Mama will take care of Benjie for a little while."

"Hannah, I wish only the best for you. You're an intelligent girl, and I believe everything is going to work out. I love you!"

"I know you do," said Hannah.

Aunt Mae picked up Hannah's wrist and tapped the Bulova watch, "Don't short-change yourself, Hannah!"

Hannah blushed and looked down, "I'm a 'needing to get away, Aunt Mae."

"Good luck, Hannah."

Aunt Mae placed her arm around Hannah's waist and walked with her to the edge of the front porch. When Hannah looked towards Pewter-Mapp's Little Store next door, Aunt Mae followed her eyes. George-West Myers leaned against a pole and stared with cold and searching eyes. When he met Aunt Mae's glance, he turned completely around with his back to her.

"Hannah, don't do anything foolish. I'll be back from Mississippi soon. We'll talk."

"I can't wait, Aunt Mae! Don't you see? I can't wait! It's not as simple as it looks—as it sounds!"

"Hannah, you're not going to Atlanta to get a job are you?"

"No!" she whispered.

"Hannah, don't go. Some quack could botch you up. You could die!" Aunt Mae cringed at the thought.

What some people would give to have the baby Hannah's giving up!

Hannah's face had changed since the last time Aunt Mae saw her. She looked tense, hard and older than her years. The troubles, the ups and downs of her love affair left premature wrinkles etched in her brow. She was still a youthful looking girl, but no longer a glowing innocent.

"No, Aunt Mae, don't say it. Grandmaw Taylor's trying to talk me out of going to Atlanta. That's one reason she brought me over here to see Judge Pewter. He's been counseling me."

"Don't do anything foolish, please, Hannah."

"Grandmaw Taylor says we all have *misery* and weather in common."

"Hannah, you're a wise young lady. Let's think happier thoughts. Will you not try?"

"I know I should, Aunt Mae, but I've learned that the relationship I have with the man that I love dearly will never be anything more than a secret. It's hard to realize I'll always be alone, and Benjamin will never have a visible father."

"I love you like you're my own daughter." Tears came into her eyes as she touched Hannah's shoulder.

"I'll let you know where I am, Aunt Mae." She turned around and walked towards Pewter-Mapp's Little Store.

Grandmaw Taylor stood nearby. "Well, goodbye, Mae. Take good care of yourself."

"You do the same Grandmaw Taylor and take care of my little Benjamin!"

"We'll take good care of him, Mae. Thanks for everything you do!" She grasped Aunt Mae's hand and held it a little longer than usual. "Mae, can I ask you a question?"

"You know you can, Grandmaw Taylor."

"You're going to Mississippi. You want to set that girl, Janelle, free?"

"Just trying to help her, that's all."

"Mae, I know it has a lot to do with Macie somehow, but this girl is a stranger and a murderer!" She hit her cane on the floor.

"Dan apparently killed Macie, and he also tried to kill Janelle. It was Dan's pattern, don't you see? Janelle needs help."

"But how can you help Janelle?"

"I believe Dan tried to kill Janelle, and I don't want her to die. I want a jury to hear the words Macie wrote in her diary."

"But how can you condone Janelle's heinous crime!"

"That's God's job, Grandmaw Taylor. Not mine."

"You don't even know this girl. She's a killer!" she whispered.

"I want to eyeball her, to see her. I don't know her, but I will know her better when I meet her."

"Good luck, Mae. You're a love! Lordy! You try to take on the world. Do a fine job too!" she cackled.

"Thank you, Grandmaw Taylor. You're a love too!"

"Naw! I'm an old grouch," she chuckled. Her face became serious. "Mae, you talked to Hannah. I saw you through the office window."

"Yes."

"You know who Benjamin's father is?"

"I think I do."

"If I threw a stone would I hit him?" She looked towards Pewter-Mapp's Little Store and stared at George-West Myers.

"I wouldn't cast the first stone."

"You think you know. You keep things close," Grandmaw Taylor sniffed.

"Yes."

"Hannah's in for a lot of heartbreak. She reminds me of myself, when I was a young girl. I had wild notions, too. Men found me attractive and it wasn't easy with me being a widow-woman."

"I'm sure of that."

"Yes, Mae, I guess that's why I understand her. Trying to get her some counseling with Judge Pewter. Want her to be somebody."

"She is somebody."

"Mae, Let's go!" Uncle Hume stood with the door open. "Come on, Caddie. Best be going, now. I see Bessie coming up the road!"

"See ya, Mae. Take care." Grandmaw Taylor squeezed her tightly.

"By the way, tell Uncle Albert thanks for loaning Ole Pem the money."

"Sure will, Mae" she nodded.

Judge Pewter ushered everyone out the door, and onto the office porch. "Ole Pem, tell your folks *bye*! You ready to handle the wheel? Everybody ready to get on the road?"

"Need to get my hat and coat, and then, I'll be all set to go," said Caddie.

"Let's go," said Ole Pem.

The Cadillac sagged under Judge Pewter's weight when he sat in the front passenger's seat.

Jake drove up in the sheriff's vehicle, got out and ran to Judge Pewter's automobile. "Hi, everybody! Say Judge, I'm glad I got to see you before you 'got away!" He bent down and looked into the window on the passenger's side. "Sheriff Olliff said give you this envelope. Said to tell you it's the picture of Macie that Buker Webster had in his possession the night he was taken to Milledgeville. Said to remind you that it shows bruises on Macie's body."

"Thanks, Jake." Judge Pewter glanced in the envelope and placed it inside his vest coat pocket.

"Hi, Jake. Where you been? We haven't seen you in ages," said Aunt Mae.

"Doing fine." He hugged her tightly, and shook hands with Uncle Hume.

"Looks like you lost weight," she said.

"Nah, I'm okay." He blushed.

"Judge Pewter, do you think Macie's diary can really be used in Janelle's case?" Jake asked, hopefully.

"It's up to the Judge to make decisions. All our maneuvering may come to nothing. We're trying to help Janelle and her father and mother—Mr. and Mrs. Davenport."

Caddie ran to the car. "Judge! Come quick! Honey Clements is on the telephone! One of her boys has been in a car wreck."

"Honey's in no condition to have to deal with this situation alone—her pregnant and all," said Judge Pewter. "Y'all might as well go on down to Pewter-Mapp's and get a coke. This telephone call might take me quite a bit of time." Judge Pewter stepped out and lightened the Cadillac.

* * * *

Caddie buttoned her black wool coat, pulled her black, felt hat over her head, picked up a stack of letters and stepped out of the office door. She scrubbed against a Christmas holly wreath, and bells jingled.

Jake stood on the front porch waiting for her. "Hi, Caddie," he said sheepishly.

"Where you been, Jake?" Caddie answered coldly. She turned away from him and started walking down the street toward the post office mail drop.

"Oh, I've been around. Mostly working." he frowned. "You okay, Caddie?" he rushed after her. "I missed ya."

"Do you think there's any reason I wouldn't or couldn't be okay, Jake?"

"I thought I'd give you a little time to cool off."

"I haven't seen you in ages and now you want to know if I'm okay?" She spoke sternly and glared at him.

"Let's start over by me asking you if you're okay, Caddie?"

"I'm in a hurry. I have to drop some mail off at the post office mail drop before we leave to go to Mississippi."

Jake followed behind her. "You seem a little put out with me today, Caddie."

"Put out with you?"

"Yes, I can't stand it when you don't smile, Caddie. You always smile."

"I have nothing to smile about."

"You've always smiled at me, but now you're testy."

"Tomboys don't smile at guys, and they don't have feelings either, or so you apparently think!"

"I'm sorry for being such a cad and saying what I did when we were at the tree, and I'm sorry I hurt your feelings about calling you a Tomboy. I think you're a perfect girl and a perfect friend."

"You're sorry that I'm not Macie, that's your number one problem, where I'm concerned."

"I'm sorry for what's happened to our friendship. I shouldn't have told you that incident about me and Macie falling down under the same tree that you and I fell under. It wasn't thoughtful of me."

"You don't have to say it, Jake. I know in my heart that you've apologized to Macie's ghost for telling me."

"No! Caddie, you're wrong!" He held his hands out apologetically. "I know I hurt you and I'm sorry. We have to make up for Aunt Mae's and Uncle Hume's sake. It's not just about you and me," he pleaded. "It's for Henny-Penny and Kackie and the rest of the family's sake, too."

She raised her voice. "Jake, I'll forgive you because you asked, and for the sake of family, but things are different now. I feel different. That incident tore my heart out and changed everything. My perspective will always be changed. I'll forgive you, but I can't forget what happened."

"Caddie," he whispered. "We need this friendship. Let's start over!"

"I have things to do, Jake." She opened the door to the post office mail drop, and walked in. She stopped at the door and looked back at him. "We'll always be together at family gatherings. We're family, regardless of what's happened."

* * * *

Caddie and Jake were unaware that Ole Pem sat at a table in Pewter-Mapp's Store, and noticed that two of his best friends appeared to be in a heated discussion.

He placed his coffee cup on its saucer and stood up. "Excuse me a moment, Mom—Dad."

Their eyes followed their tall son as he opened the door and walked outside.

He leaned his back against the wall in front of Mapp's, placed his hands in his navy blue corduroy trousers, and gazed across the street. He listened intently to the heated conversation, and felt the highly charged atmosphere between them.

For the most instantaneous moment, he caught a glimpse of an iridescent image of Macie standing between Caddie and Jake. Her left hand reached out and touched Caddie's left breast, and her right hand touched the heart of Jake. He blinked his eyes and the mirage of Macie was gone. He realized how real Macie was to them, and to all of those who knew her!

* * * *

"Caddie and Jake looked like they were having a few words." Grandmaw Taylor raised her eyebrows, and nodded towards the young couple.

"Yes—their courtship is a little shaky," said Aunt Mae.

"Sounded like Jake did something to her, but I couldn't hear what he said very good." Grandmaw Taylor leaned forward on her walking cane. "Wonder what's going on?"

"What's going on is probably what he hasn't done," said Aunt Mae. "He hasn't been around for a while."

"Does he still love Macie?"

"Yes."

"I should say it this way, Does Jake still love Macie's ghost?" Grandmaw Taylor shivered and pulled her gray, handmade crocheted shawl close to her neck. "Can't think of much of anything more terrible than being in love with a ghost!" She nodded her head in sympathy.

"Yes, Macie's ghost has a tight grip on Jake."

"Changing the subject. I hope the news isn't bad about that boy of Deaver and Honey being in a wreck, but this gives us more time to talk. Feel like walking down to the church yard, Grandmaw Taylor? We'll sit on a bench at the church."

"Yes. Believe I can walk that far. Hope it'll do me good."

"Are you warm enough?"

"I'm okay. Don't fuss. I sure do hope everything turns out okay for Honey and her young'uns." Grandmaw Taylor walked slowly. "I believe I feel like hobbling that far."

"We'll walk slow."

"Mae, listen, I was just gouging at you a little about Janelle Zanderneff just to see what you'd say. If you want to help her, I'll be the last one to say a word. I was just testing you, I suppose. It's a wonder I didn't kill my ole husband and go to jail—get the chair, or serve life, one or the other, don't yuh know? My husband almost killed me, but I got away. That could be me, don't you see? Lord, help my time! I'm lucky I never killed him."

"You did have some problems didn't you?"

"Mae, that husband of mine nearly beat me to death before I got away with the little'uns one night. 'Bout near didn't get away. I divorced him right after that."

"I recall some of the encounters you had with your husband, but you kept your personal life with him very close and I never pried into your business," Aunt Mae said gently.

"Most of the people around here think the bond of marriage is forever, regardless of what's happening in the marriage. Didn't seem to care if I escaped with my life, but the choice I made was my *life,* and I had to make my own choices, don't you see."

"No one thinks of you as divorced, Grandmaw Taylor."

"Yeah, I've called myself a pore old widow-woman till 'bout near everybody thinks I am," she cackled.

"I'm sorry you've had such a hard time. Grandmaw Taylor, Macie was apparently trying to leave Dan, when she was killed. She wrote Caddie and Hume and me that she would be home soon. Caddie was so caring to send her the money to buy train tickets for Macie, and Henny-Penny and Kackie to come home."

"Yes, I recall." Grandmaw Taylor sighed. "You still believe Dan made her slit open her wrists, Mae?"

"Sure do think so. He made her do it somehow, or he did it himself."

"Now, this girl, Janelle, she claims Dan tried to make her slit her wrists wide open too, and this girl, Janelle, refused to slit her own wrists, right?"

"Yes, Janelle told the sheriff that Dan tried to make her hold her hands over the kitchen sink and cut her wrists. She told him this without knowing about how Macie died. She didn't even know that Dan was ever married, and had two little girls!"

"Wal, I'll be jiggered. It's just awful. Awful!"

"It seems like both of Dan's wives saw him angry without cause—but others saw him as a gentle person. Always thought Dan was a sweet boy. Guess he fooled us, huh?"

"Sure did. He fooled me more than anyone else that I know."

"Except Reverend Buker Webster fooling all of us?"

"Yes, except him, but I had my suspicions about The Reverend Buker Webster all along. Feel mighty sorry for Locket! She didn't even know what a rascal that preacher husband really was!" Grandmaw Taylor exclaimed.

"Horrible!"

"Sorry to hear about y'all finding Ratchel-Robin's and Macie's pictures and all those other nude pictures of women lying on a funeral home slab that Buker Webster had on his altar. I know it was more than traumatic for you to see it! To know it!"

"It was more than horrible!"

"It's so sad," Grandmaw Taylor sympathized.

"You better believe it!" Aunt Mae uttered disgustedly. "I've never been so stunned in my life. You know that those nude pictures he took of Macie showed bruises all over her? That preacher asked the family about Macie all the time. He must have seen the bruises all over her body when he opened her coffin and unclothed her at the funeral parlor. After he saw the bruises, I suppose he had a curiosity about whether Dan beat her—and, maybe killed her. Anyway, he was puzzled about Macie's life and asked a lot of questions."

"Yes. I remember you saying the preacher asked personal questions about her."

"Yes, and those bruises helps prove to me that Dan beat her and killed her."

"Does it help you cope with Macie's death to believe she was killed—that she didn't kill herself?"

"Yes, it does. It helps me."

"Then believe Dan killed her, if it helps you feel better. Go ahead, then, believe it. Dan's dead—so believe what makes you feel better." Grandmaw Taylor insisted.

"Yeah, Dan's turned out to be a horrible person. We've had some sad times the last couple of years, haven't we?"

"Yes, real sad times," said Grandmaw Taylor.

"Now that we've learned that Buker Webster is more than a rascal, I've asked Jake to try to learn something about his upbringing, and tell us, if he can," said Aunt Mae. I remember you didn't think he was innocent enough for a preacher."

"Yeah, I told you so. They say he's got a lot of money. Probably a millionaire."

"You know a tarot card of a Hanged Man was on Buker Webster's make-shift altar propped against a crystal ball."

"He was such a rascal—such a varmint!"

"Also—they've learned his parents were fortune tellers. So, I guess that's where the money came from."

"Yes, I heard that! Doesn't it beat all? Know what, Mae?"

"What?"

"I should have read his cards!"

"What would his cards have told you, Grandmaw Taylor?" Aunt Mae smiled.

"I don't rightly know, but the cards woulda been hot and smoking from the fires of hell," she chucked.

In the distance, they noticed Ole Pem crossing the road and walking towards the meeting house.

"Guess Locket is at the meeting house," said Aunt Mae.

"Think Ole Pem and Locket Webster will get together, Mae?"

"You're the future reader. What do you think?" She laughed.

Grandmaw Taylor stopped talking, leaned on her walking cane with both hands as she stared at the meeting house. "It'll be an interesting story—a lovely story for both of them. But, the ending might not turn out like you and I might think."

"Well said—like a politician," Aunt Mae laughed. "I wonder how Janelle is going to fit in Ole Pem's life."

"How does Janelle fit?" Grandmaw Taylor frowned, squinted, and peered into Aunt Mae's eyes. "She'd have a hard time fitting, I'd say."

"Ole Pem's really does want to help Janelle. He liked her a lot or at least he did before he learned that she killed Dan."

"Love's mysterious, isn't it?"

"Yes, love is beautiful."

"For you it is beautiful, Mae. You're fortunate, and rich in blessings. Not everyone is so blessed!" Grandmaw Taylor continued to stare at the meeting house. "Believe Ole Pem will find his way successfully. He'll come back here as an outstanding, highly educated lawyer. Yes sir, he's gonna be fierce in the courtroom!" She said it loudly, but then she lowered her voice and her tone became wistful. "Wish Hannah would look towards someone like Ole Pem. She's pretty, but with her having a child and gonna have another one, she's messed up her life."

"Hannah's young. She'll do okay, Grandmaw Taylor."

"I want to wring George-West Myers' neck! Him married and all! And, that Jessie Myers is so stuck-up, she just about trips on her uppity 'ways.' I wonder if she knows her husband is having a hot and torrid affair with my granddaughter."

"I doubt it," Aunt Mae said softly.

"She has to be suspicious. Hannah meets George-West all the time. We're all worried about it."

"Suppose it'll run its course," said Aunt Mae.

"Yes. Run its course—" Grandmaw Taylor heaved a deep breath, and readjusted her gray wool shawl around her shoulders.

"Here we are, Grandmaw Taylor."

They sat on a bench, next to the little creek which ran through the churchyard.

"Good! I'm a might out of breath, Mae." The wrought iron bench shook when she sat down.

"Grandmaw Taylor, would you do something for me?" Aunt Mae untied the string and brown paper carefully that encased Macie's diary.

"If I can be of help, you know I will, Mae. What is it?"

"Please take time to read a copy of Macie's papers. Tell me what you make of them." She handed the papers to Grandmaw Taylor.

"This package is what you'll be taking to Janelle and her people? Is this what Macie wrote about Dan in code—in Pig Latin?"

"Yes. This is her diary. She wrote it in Pig Latin, but a translation is with it. Caddie translated it and typed it." Aunt Mae sighed, and offered the package to her.

Grandmaw Taylor laid the package in her lap, and reached for her spectacles. "Pig Latin—you told me this before. I suppose Macie wrote in code so as to keep Dan from being able to read it."

"Yes, I'm sure it was to keep Dan from reading it. Also, it starts out like a fairy-tale."

"Clever. You say you have a translation of the code, cause I can't read Pig Latin," she chuckled. "Seems like I might need to clean my specs. Don't see like I used to."

"Want me to read it to you?"

"That would be nice of you." She leaned forward, placed her head on her walking cane, and listened intently.

After reading the full documentation, Aunt Mae re-wrapped Macie's living and breathing words in its brown wrapping paper and retied it with the flour sack string.

"What's your interpretation of what Macie wrote to *Di-Ar-Ree,* and the answers of *Di-Ar-Ree* to *Me*?" Aunt Mae asked.

"Mae, that's just like my life before my divorce. I coulda written a diary like that, myself. Sad ain't it?"

"Grandmaw Taylor, without upsetting you too much, I need to ask you something?"

"Of course, Chile. It's okay. Makes me sad, but life is sorta sad anyhow, sometimes."

"Why did Macie not write or call and say, 'Aunt Mae or Uncle Hume, come get me! Rescue me?' Why? You said that at one time you were a beaten wife. You understand the circumstances better than I do."

"Mae, our dear Macie was struggling with anxieties, and hurt. She wrote words of pain, words of a tormented soul—a wounded soul haunted by a dying love. She was trying to hold on, trying to change herself and trying to change

Dan. It was a harsh atmosphere. She found out too late changing herself would not help the state of events. Also, Dan could not be changed. Nobody can change another person."

"But, why? Why! Why did she not leave everything and come on home?"

"You're asking me why didn't Macie come back when she first learned how cruel Dan was? She was finally on the way back, Mae. She'd had her fill of Dan's meanness. I can tell by hearing you read. She'd been persecuted and injured enough. Her babies were beaten and their pain essentially helped her make up her mind to come back to you. She was packed and ready to come back! She'd had enough—she'd had all she could take—she was full to the brim. She finally knew it was time to git while the gitting was good!"

"To think of the danger she was in!"

"The first time my ole husband hit me, I just couldn't believe he did it. I had low self-esteem and thought I'd done something to annoy him. I tried to do everything to please him. Nothing worked. Maybe Macie saw herself leaving Dan as a failure. She mentioned it in her diary—failure—fear of failure—just plain old *FEAR*."

"Yes! Fear!"

"It was a starry-eyed girl who left your home. You said her letters were always telling you she was happy—her letters were very much alike. She set herself up for a worse time—a harder time because of trying to fool other people into believing she was happy. We can't say I'm happy one day, and just leave the next without getting ourselves embarrassed and humiliated. But, apparently Macie told herself I'm happy hoping she would be or could be happy again. She wished it and hoped it would be better. Also, she hid behind I'm happy.

"She was in denial?" Aunt Mae whispered. "Grandmaw Taylor, her letters did appear to be happy, and that hurts me now. Why couldn't I read those letters and feel that something menacing was wrong?"

"You're perceptive, Mae, but she didn't give you clues in the mail. If you'd a 'seen her in person, you'd a knowed it because you're such a keen observer."

"You think I'd have known something was wrong, if I'd seen her in person?" Aunt Mae held the packaged diary tightly to her bosom. "Oh! Why did I not visit her? We were always waiting for Hume's leg to heal."

"Don't blame yourself." said Grandmaw Taylor." Judging by my own experience, I'd say she was too embarrassed to tell anyone that Dan beat her and beat the young'uns, but, mostly, I'd say it was because she was not only wounded physically but spiritually. The shrapnel in her soul was festering away and she was anguishing at the unknown—not knowing what to do. Her common sense told her she needed to get away, but being wounded physically, mentally and spiritually, she may have been semi-conscious in her decision making."

"What do you mean *semi-conscious*? She was knocked out?" Aunt Mae frowned, and tried to understand.

"Something like that. When a person is wounded physically, sometimes he goes into a state of shock, and might even lose consciousness for a time. I believe the same thing happens with the soul, when it's wounded."

"You think that the soul can be wounded physically and spiritually? You believe that?"

"Yes, I believe the soul can be physically and spiritually wounded. But, for the grace of God, Macie is not the one in jail for killing Dan. Her diary tells me she didn't have that love she once had for Dan. He hit her one time too many. She was packed and leaving the day she died. You said Miz Mitchells saw a suitcase at the door when she went inside the house the night that Macie died."

"Oh, dear God—"

"It seems like Macie was struggling to make decisions. She was on the right course, but her thinking process and acting process were not in sync—because she was wounded physically, mentally, emotionally and spiritually."

"Oh! Sweet Jesus! You believe her body and her soul were wounded! Grandmaw Taylor, this is so awful!" Aunt Mae sucked in her breath, and looked down.

"Mae I don't mean to hurt you worse than what you already are, but you're all fired bent on knowing what makes 'beat-on' wives tick. I don't have an easy way tuh tell yuh." She cleared her throat and looked into the distance.

"I know! I know! Go ahead, and tell me. I'll try to handle it!"

"My husband could be a sweet one. Especially when he allowed a lull between beatings. I'd try to cook, bake, look after the babies and push the thoughts of his meanness to the back of my mind. I wanted to forget. I'd deny to myself what was really going on. I'd pretend no *boogerman* was at my door. But, one day my ole man hit me and wrung my jaws so loud and hard, they cracked and he knocked out some teeth, right here in front. It jarred my brain and my soul." She held her index finger to her mouth and wriggled her finger on her lips, indicating she still remembered the pain of the wounds.

"Oh! Grandmaw Taylor, how awful!" Aunt Mae lowered her head, in empathy.

"Mae, later I cleansed and tended my physical wounds but how could I minister to my heart and my deflated soul? The spirit was gone out of the soul—just like a deflated balloon. My injured soul festered and bitterness set in." She cleared her throat and wiped her eyes.

"Grandmaw Taylor, I'm sorry to put you in such pain."

"It's okay, Chile. I'm fine." Grandmaw Taylor held the walking cane between her knees, and coiled the ball of gray hair at the nape of her neck and pinned it with yellowed, celluloid pins.

"But, if you were wounded, it seems like you couldn't wait to leave your husband fast enough!"

"People stay in these horrific streams of fire, these pits of hell for different reasons."

"What reasons? What could be a good reason to stay with someone who is beating you? Hitting you? Cursing you? Beating your children?" asked Aunt Mae.

"Mae, the reasoning may not make sense. At first I stayed because I thought I could fix everything and could change things back like they were before me and my ole man got married. But, that wasn't true, of course. It was a big mistake to think that could happen. I told myself getting away from my no good husband was easier said than done, and I stayed even though he criticized every little thing I did or didn't do. He cursed me, and he beat me." Grandmaw Taylor sighed aloud, and looked into the distance. "I began to have brooding thoughts of vengeance."

"So, you hassled with the decision of what to do? Was it hard to decide? It seems like you'd do what you could to get away from the pain, and you'd want to just leave!"

"Yes, I hassled with the decision! I wanted to leave, but he threatened to kill me, if I left. I believed him. I feared him."

"How horrible! I had no idea it was this bad," Aunt Mae sighed.

"Fear is a terrible thing to deal with. You know, fear is a more persuasive power than love."

"To deal with fear is nerve-wracking, and beyond comprehension. You've had an unhappy experience, Grandmaw Taylor, but, you always seem so jolly."

"I'm happy now. Very happy, Mae."

"Thank God for that, Grandmaw Taylor."

"After years of beatings, I finally got the nerve up to go to my mother-in-law." Grandmaw Taylor looked into the distance as if to search for that day in the past, and wiped her nose on a white lace handkerchief. "I told her I wanted her to speak to my ole man—you know, her son—about his beating me. I asked his mother to tell him to stop!"

"Good! She helped!"

"No! I felt so alone—so alone!"

"How cruel! It's horrible to have someone turn you away."

"Yes, it was cruel. She didn't offer a good thought or a turn of the hand. By that time, I was getting braver and speaking out and I went to my maw. Paw was dead then. She saw my teeth were knocked out and just gasped."

"She helped?"

"No! She said, 'I told you that boy was no good but you just had to marry him!' Her condemnation embarrassed and humiliated me more. I was already down. I needed words of encouragement—not a put down. She began to lecture me. Instead of asking her to let me move back with the young'uns, I just ran away from her house as fast as I could. I couldn't stand the extra mental anguish."

"But, surely, you didn't go back home to the same abuse!" Aunt Mae exclaimed.

"I went back, but then I got away, later."

"Tell me."

"I got a divorce in the days when the word *divorce* was a stigma on a woman's character and a divorcee was many times considered vile and wicked and evil by religious fanatics. Those fanatics believed only evil women divorced ... divorced women were honky-tonk women. Hot to trot, don't you know? I had to deal with that after my divorce, but that's another story—"

"Stop it, Grandmaw Taylor."

"Mae, you're naive. You're a protected person. Never been hit, never been beat. You'd never understand!"

"I'm trying, Grandmaw Taylor. Please tell me how you got away."

"Wal, the last time my old man beat me, he gave me such a tremendous whack on the side of the head, it sent me reeling against a chair, the wall and then to the floor. And then I found myself in a dark void."

"Horrible! Horrible!" Aunt Mae whispered softly.

"When I woke up, I found my old man passed out on the bed in a drunken stupor, and I got me a strong rope at the barn and tied his hands and feet to the bedstead. I 'high-tailed' it through the woods with my young'uns to brother Albert's house and beat on the door. It was about dawn when the young'uns and I got to his house. He opened the door."

"What did Albert do?"

"He was horrified to see how beat up I was. My face was bruised and cut and my eyes were swelling shut. It was awful. He got the Sheriff, and they went to the house to untie my old man. I said, 'Tell him he'll be getting the divorce papers soon, and tell him to get out of my house.' Albert was curious, like you are, and wanted to know why we stayed and didn't come to him sooner. I told him that I was embarrassed and fearful of my husband. Also, I told Albert I didn't want to give up my house."

"You got the house?"

"It was my house that I inherited from my paw. And I got custody of the young'uns. I never went back to my home to live. I started renting the place to the Donahoos. I always stayed with Albert from then on out, and as you already know, he'd never married after Molly Bee died. Didn't have anyone. He seemed happy to have me and the youngun's live with him. After the divorce, my old man pestered the daylights out of me, threatening to kill me, but later he moved to Missouri."

"Albert was happy you came to him!"

"Yes, he was. Albert gave me and the younguns money and sent us to town for a vacation. I got my teeth pulled, had dentures made, and I bought new clothes for me and the young'uns. Got a new hairdo. When I got back, I was different. I realized those licks my husband gave me weren't love-licks but hate licks. My ole husband fooled me for a while, and he apparently hated me. I guess he hates all women! I was angry he beat me, and I knew I didn't deserve the beatings and the cruelty."

"I never realized you suffered like this, Grandmaw Taylor. Did he try to kill you, after you left?"

"My old man gave us a hard time for awhile, but the Sheriff helped out with keeping that monster away from me and the young'uns. If it were not for that good ole Sheriff, I would have had a harder time. But with his and Albert's help, I made it."

"Ever hear from your husband after that?"

"Heard from him about 20 years ago. He'd fooled another girl into marrying him. God bless her—I just hope she survived his cruelties. Hope she got away before he killed her."

"Grandmaw Taylor, what really helped you to make the decision to leave?"

"Plain ole stubborn, I suppose. I wanted to live. I knew if I stayed, I'd eventually be killed. His mother turning me away didn't set well with me. I decided I'd made the choice to marry my husband but that didn't mean I had to continue to sleep in the danger. I had a choice of leaving or staying. I then made the choice to leave."

"Best thing you could have ever done!"

"Yes, it was the right decision."

"I'm trying to understand why my Macie didn't take Henny-Penny and Kackie, and just leave! With all the explanations you have just given me, I still wonder why didn't she call us, slip a note to the next door neighbor to mail for her? What reason could she have had that made her stay? Why didn't she come back to us?" Aunt Mae whispered. "I still don't understand."

"I suppose we might think of good and bad reasons, but at first us women will find a reason to stay. Some don't want to leave because their ole man makes good money. If they left, they'd have nothing to live on."

"But most women can work! Macie was able to work!"

"Women may stay for *love*, or maybe because they think they deserve what they're getting."

"Are they weak? Do you think this means these women are weak when they stay?"

"No! They're unable to think well, usually."

"Or it's like you said—because their psyche is damaged or injured?" asked Aunt Mae.

"Yes, I suppose. No one really knows—out of all the women I know and have heard their tale-of-woe—most of them can't explain the *why* of it all—the *why* they stay," said Grandmaw Taylor.

"So, I'm back to *why?*"

"Yes, Mae, you are back to *why*! A negative why?—a judgmental why? a blaming *why*."

"But, Grandmaw Taylor, I've never thought of the word *why* as being negative. I'm trying to understand by asking *why*."

"Each of us who has been abused has her own story, and it's different—yet it might also be similar. It's complicated, and I can't explain all that I felt at the time these things happened, nor exactly what took me so long to leave. I knew if I stayed I'd probably be killed and if I left I'd probably be killed, but I took that chance to leave—a long time later."

"You're remarkable, Grandmaw Taylor. I appreciate your trying to help me understand *why* Macie didn't come back home—*why* she chose to stay with Dan," Aunt Mae sighed.

"You'll probably never know the *why*," said Grandmaw Taylor.

"I'm searching for answers," Aunt Mae raised her voice with concern.

"Maybe there are no logical answers."

"You think I may *neve*r have logical answers?"

"The answer you seek might not be the same for everyone. It's hard to identify with another woman's life, which might be so different from your own, but all of us have a stronger emotion in us than 'love,' and that emotion is FEAR! FEAR, Mae, FEAR!"

"Yes, fear can defeat us!" Aunt Mae trembled with emotion, and the air was chilly. She pulled her long black coat closer to her neck.

"Yes, fear is one of our greatest emotions. Fear holds us, binds us and that same fear frees us."

"That's what Laughing Eyes told me, too. She said fear is a tool of the devil," said Aunt Mae.

"Mae, let me say this. Even though Janelle killed Dan, when you meet her and talk to her, you'll find her tale-of-woe is similar to mine and similar to Macie's. If all of the *stories* of all of us women were alike, we might figure out all this unusual behavior and place our finger on *why* people stay in abusive, horror-stricken, disappointing situations. Our psyche is different and our lives and environments are different. That's the reason why it's so hard to dissect and pinpoint why we—the abused—*stay* in the abusive pits of hell."

"Grandmaw Taylor, Janelle's letters are similar to your story, except for describing the violence. She went through hell, too."

"It's hell, all right. Pure hell! It's awful!

"Grandmaw Taylor, I appreciate your trying to help me understand the why's."

"I hope God will give you peace, Mae."

"Yes, peace," she sighed.

"The biggest answer to *why* may be fear, just like I said before. Some of us choose fear as our *why,* and that's *why* we stay. Some of us leave for the same reason. We are afraid to stay."

"That sounds logical," said Aunt Mae.

"Mae, let me try to put it another way. You know that little sparrow you found last year. I believe it was wounded?"

"Yes, that's right."

"You nursed its wounds and fed it and nurtured it."

"Yes."

"You willed it to live—to fly again."

"I surely did. That's right. And, it did fly again."

"The wounded sparrow recovered from its wounds, but it had to take its own flight. You couldn't do it for the bird."

"That's right."

"Mae, when I nursed my pains and patched my wounds, it was still up to me to take flight. If someone else had nursed my wounds and helped me, I'm still the one who had to decide it was time to fly away—to get away. It was up to me. It was my choice."

* * * *

"You may sit here." The jailer placed a chair in front of Janelle's chair. "I'll be just outside. "You've got thirty minutes."

"Uncle Hume could have stayed, you know." Janelle smiled shyly.

"Hume wanted to give us some time together. He thought you'd want to talk to me privately."

"Thanks for coming, Aunt Mae. You're so far away from your home. I just can't believe you're here. Ole Pem was right when he said you're a very special person. You really are. I wish I could have met you and Pem years and years ago.

"You're special, too, Janelle."

"I used to be a wonderful person, but not anymore. My whole life is wasted. I didn't think through any of my actions before I did what I did. I didn't even think of consequences. I just killed Dan." Tears came into her eyes and her chin trembled.

Aunt Mae looked at Janelle's sensuous, porcelain complexion and extremely slender face. *She appears no different than any other pretty girl. Maybe more nervous and fidgety. She doesn't look like a murderess.*

"Janelle, I can't cure your problems with herbs but I've brought you some herbal teas, to soothe your nerves."

"Oh! I'd love to have some. Wonder if they'll let me?"

"I had to leave my herb basket at the jailer's desk, but he said he'd make the teas for you. He's a very nice man."

"How sweet and thoughtful. The gentleman at the desk right now is a nice person."

"Sorry I had to leave my packets of herbs with him and couldn't give them to you."

"Everything reminds me I'm not free to go."

"Yes, I know."

"Thirty minutes—so short—so long—I know I need to say a lot in a short time, Aunt Mae. I understand y'all are meeting my lawyer today. Is that correct?"

"Yes. We sure are, Darling. I've already met your supportive and loving parents. They are doing everything they can for you. They have the best lawyers—everything!"

"Yes—my parents are wonderful to me and love me unconditionally. I want to thank you, Aunt Mae, so very much for trying to help me." She brushed her curly black hair from her eyes with shaking hands.

"Janelle, we brought the originals of some of Macie's writings, her diary, and some of the letters she wrote to us. We also have photographs of Macie and Dan and Henny-Penny and Kackie."

"You told me in a letter that Macie's body had bruises, too?" Janelle whispered. She sat on both of her hands.

"Yes. Judge Pewter got a statement from the coroner in Tennessee, stating that when her body was examined at autopsy, they found bruises on Macie's body. They found discolorations of what appeared to be old bruises and scars."

"Just think! Macie and I both got beaten up by the same man—by Dan."

"Remember I told you about that impostor of a preacher—that Reverend Buker Webster?"

"Yes, I do," said Janelle.

"We have an awful photograph of Macie that crazy impostor took of Macie when she was at the undertaker's place. The nude photograph also shows bruises on Macie."

"The preacher was not a preacher—just an impostor?"

"He had a degree that qualified him to preach, but he was really an awful person—a rascal."

"A rascal?"

"Yes, more than a rascal, Janelle. Buker Webster was a deceiver. Deceived the church people and he deceived his wife. He hood-winked every last one of us!"

"How terrible!"

"Janelle, come to think about it, Dan was also a deceiver."

"Yes, he deceived me in many ways. Sometimes Dan's words were like daggers. You can't imagine the hurt." She pushed the hair from her forehead with her right hand and continued to sit on her left hand.

"I'm so sorry, Janelle."

"Dan's gone and I'll never be able to lead a normal life, even if the jurors came back with a verdict of *life*." She sighed, rubbed her sallow face and pushed her black hair from her forehead. "Dan's dead, but he'll never be out of my life. Oh! The nightmares! Very few mornings I wake up rested."

"So sorry—"

"Aunt Mae, I wish Dan had gotten up, after he fell down."

"But, Janelle, would Dan not have killed you?"

"Yes, he would have killed me." Her chin trembled. "But I would be free."

"You'd be dead, Janelle, not Dan, if he had gotten up!" she whispered. "I just wish you had run away."

"Yes, I'd be dead, but, the way it is I'm paying the consequences for my actions—for killing him."

"Did you kill him out of fear?"

"Yes! Terror! Fear!"

"Do you think your parents could arrange for you to have a counselor?"

"I suppose—"

"It'd give you a better focus. Might help change your state of mind."

"The jurors might recommend death, Aunt Mae. I'll probably die."

"Let's try to pray otherwise, Janelle."

"I can't forgive myself for what I've done. I was so stupid! I wish I could undo that part of my life and walk away—run back to my parents instead of killing Dan."

"Janelle, forgiving yourself is the only way you can release your heart from the clutches of the past."

"I'm so hurt, so angry, Aunt Mae. To think that sometimes he spoke so gently with his most melodious, enticing voice. It contrasted with the mean Dan who yelled and beat me!"

"Use the anger. Scream it all out. Get it all out. Forgive yourself, Janelle."

"I want to! I want to! But, to forgive myself would be evil."

"Listen, darling. You're not evil."

"You know this about me, Aunt Mae?"

"I believe I do, Janelle. I came a long way to *eyeball* you, to see what you're really like. You're not an evil person."

"Thanks, Aunt Mae. Can you heal me? Please heal me!"

"God is the Healer, Janelle."

"Thanks, Aunt Mae, for encouraging me to feel better, but I am so alone." She held her hands tightly, in a praying position, and looked up through swollen green eyes.

"Lord knows you've had enough preaching, already, but God desires us to seek Him. The great psalmist, David, was overwhelmed by his troubles, but God brought him into a safe place in the mind." Aunt Mae held her tightly while Janelle cried on her shoulder.

"Sorry, your time is up," the jailer called.

* * * *

Uncle Hume and Ole Pem sat on each side of Aunt Mae directly behind the Defense's table. From time to time, Janelle turned and glanced at her mother and father, and stole a glance at those supportive few that sat behind her.

Joanie and Claude Zanderneff sat behind the prosecution's table. They stared at Janelle from time to time, and whispered. The Zanderneffs were true to their word and attended court for their son, Dan.

Ole Pem, the sheriff and other officials testified and graphic photographs of the deceased were entered.

The coroner gave his report.

The prosecution presented its evidence of a heinous and horrific crime committed by the wife of Daniel Zanderneff, also known as Daniel Zanders.

* * * *

"The Defense calls Kathryn Brown to the stand."

The courtroom became quiet when she entered. All eyes were drawn to the young lady dressed in a long, navy blue dress with a high white collar.

She was sworn.

Counsel for Defense: "Please be seated, and state your name for the record."

Witness: "Kathryn Andriana Brown. I'm known as *Caddie*."

Counsel for Defense: "Please state your address."

Kathryn Brown stated her address, and settled back in the witness chair.

Counsel for Defense: "Did you know the deceased, Daniel Zanderneff?"

Witness: "Yes, I did."

Counsel for Defense: "How did you come to know him?"

Witness: "He married my sister, Macie. She's deceased."

Counsel for Defense: "What is your sister's full name?"

Witness: "Macie Mariana Brown Zanderneff."

Counsel for Defense: "Did you know that your brother-in-law had remarried after your sister's death?

Witness: "No I did not."

Prosecutor: "Objection!"

Court: "Overruled!"

Several more foundation questions were laid by the Counsel for the Defense.

Counsel for Defense: "I'm handing you a thick document of several inches, wrapped in a brown paper and tied with a string. I'd like for you to tell me if you have ever seen this package before?"

Witness: "Yes, I am familiar with the package. The document inside was written by my sister, Macie."

Counsel for Defense: "How did you become familiar with this document?"

Witness: "My parents and I brought it back to Georgia from Tennessee right after Macie's funeral. We packed it in a suitcase, along with some of the other belongings of my sister, Macie. Dan asked us to take the suitcase that was full of Macie's possessions back home with us to Georgia, and we did."

Counsel for Defense: "What is this document?"

Prosecutor: "Objection!"

Court: "Overruled!"

Witness: "On the front page of this document it states the word, *Manuscript*, but it's really Macie's diary."

Prosecutor: "Objection!"

Court: "Overruled!"

Counsel for Defense: "How do you know it's Macie's Diary?"

Prosecutor: "Objection, your Honor. The title is 'Manuscript,' and not a diary," the prosecutor yelled.

Court: "Overruled. You have already stipulated to enter this document!"

Counsel for Defense: "Do you believe this is her handwriting?"

Prosecutor: "Objection, your Honor! The witness is not a handwriting expert!"

Court: "Overruled. The witness may answer. She can state only from her viewpoint. The jury knows she is not a handwriting expert. They can examine the document in the jury room, and make up their own minds about whether the document is or is not what has been stated."

Witness: "I have no doubt it's her handwriting and that she's writing about her abusive life with Dan Zanderneff. I'd recognize her handwriting anywhere."

Prosecutor: "Objection!"

Court: "Overruled."

Counsel for Defense: "Is there something at all unusual about the document referred to as a 'Manuscript?'

Witness: "It's written in code—in Pig Latin."

Prosecutor: "Objection, your Honor!"

Court: "Overruled."

Counsel for Defense: "What is Pig Latin—only if you know?"

Witness: "It's known as a child's language. Macie, my foster brother, Jake, and I spoke Pig Latin sometimes when we were little children. Most of our friends did."

Counsel for Defense: "Is this entire document written in Pig Latin?"

Witness: "No. The first page is written in regular English. And, I believe the last page, as well."

Counsel for Defense: "So, how can we interpret what the document really says?"

Prosecutor: "Objection, you Honor!"

Court: "Just tell us what you know."

Witness: "You take the first letter of a word and move it to the end and add the sound *ay*. An example for *Let's play* would be Ets-lay laypay."

Counsel for Defense: "You make an *ay* sound?"

Prosecutor: "Leading, your Honor."

Court: "Stop leading the witness."

Counsel for Defense: "Yes, Your Honor.

With the Court's permission, we'd like Miss Brown to begin reading the English interpretation of the document, beginning on page one.

Then, we'd like to have her begin reading the statements to Dear *Di-Ar-Ree* which are signed by *Me.*"

Court: "This has been stipulated between the parties."

Counsel for the Defense: "We'd also like to have one of the Clerks come forward and read the answer to *Me*, from the Manuscript/Diary of Macie Andriana Zanderneff. Then, we'd like to have Miss Brown to also read the last page of the Diary."

Counsel for the Defense took a deep breath and looked at the jury.

The jury will be furnished with the original document, and an interpretation of the Pig Latin found in Macie Zanderneff's document."

He handed copies to the jury.

Court: "Please have the Clerk come forward."

An older woman walked forward and stood in front of the witness chair. She pulled at the neck of her dark brown dress, and smoothed her short, brown hair.

She was sworn.

Counsel for Defense: "Please state your name and address."

Clerk: "My name is Miss Michelle Argo. I live at ____________.

Counsel for Defense: "Thank you, Miss Argo. You may be seated in the chair we have placed in front of the other witness chair. I will hand you a copy of the document. Please read each section to *Dear Me*, when it comes your turn."

The clerk took the document and sat down in the chair provided for her.

Counsel for Defense: "Miss Brown, I will ask you to remain seated in the witness chair, and read from Macie Mariana Brown Zanderneff's diary. Please begin on Page One."

Caddie Brown read with emotion and feeling, beginning with the introduction: A Fairy Tale.

The audience looked at each other, and many whispered under their breath.

Court: "Absolutely no talking in this court room."

Caddie Brown's voice trembled and her hands shook. She took a deep swallow and appeared to calm. And, then, she read the entire document beginning with "Dear Di-Ar-Ree,"—Signed: *"Love, Me,"* in a clear and precise manner, and only occasionally stumbling through the words when tears filled her voice.

The Clerk read the answers with feeling, meaning, and perfect diction. And, finally, Caddie Brown read the last page of Macie's Manuscript, which concluded *The Fairy Tale.*

Upon hearing the cries of Macie Zanderneff, some of the jurors wiped tears from their eyes.

Prosecution: "Your Honor, we object! This is not a regular clerk that's reading here. She's from the Drama Club at the college. She was hired to persuade the jury."

Court: "Over ruled—this clerk works for me."

Prosecutor: "But, your Honor, this is highly unusual. Your Honor—"

Court: "Counselor, you and the defense stipulated to read the whole manuscript—the first page called *Fairy Tale*, the diary, everything. That's what we're doing here."

Joanie and Claude Zanderneff were visibly shaken. They wiped their eyes and noses with their white cotton handkerchiefs and clung to each other.

The Counsel for the Defense continued his questioning, laid the foundation—and presented evidence of an abusive husband who more than likely killed Macie Mariana Brown Zanderneff, and attempted to murder his second wife, Janelle Davenport Zanders, in the same manner, and with the same Modis Operandi.

At the conclusion of his questions concerning Macie's diary, the Counsel for the Defense stated, "Your Honor, I respectfully request the Court to enter the entire Manuscript which includes the Diary of Macie Brown Mariana Zanderneff, as the Defense's Exhibit 8."

Court: "It will be so marked."

Aunt Mae stiffened, and whispered, "Hume, the Court's not keeping Macie's Manuscript—they're not keeping her diary are they?"

Hume nodded affirmatively, dreading to face her feelings of despair, those feelings of losing the living and breathing cries of anguish and the final words of Macie speaking from the grave.

Aunt Mae placed her fingers to her quivering mouth, and closed her eyes. Tears rolled down her cheeks.

* * * *

______Mississippi
Cell Block 2 B
Ole Jail House # 1
The ____ day of _____ 19 __

Dear Aunt Mae:

Can you believe it!????!!!!!!!

L I F E!

Can you believe I got Life imprisonment! It is so hard for me to believe I am in jail, but I'll take LIFE!

How the judge ever agreed to allow Macie's entire Diary into evidence is the buzz around town, daddy said.

Thank you for sharing Macie's life with the court. My lawyers said the coroner's documentation and the pictures of Macie's bruised body were terrible to look at, but they helped prove a point. I appreciate all your efforts. Mama and Papa also said tell you thank you, again and again.

You look just like I thought you would. You and Uncle Hume are a handsome couple, but most of all sweet. Uncle Hume was much taller than I thought he'd be!

It was such a long way for all of you to come and see me and be with me during my trial!

I thank God that Ole Pem brought you into my life. I just wish it were under different circumstances. He's such a caring man! I wish I could have met him before I ever met Dan. How different it all might have been!

Aunt Mae, would it be asking too much for me to ask you to continue corresponding? Please say you will.

Thank you again with all my heart! I am so very grateful to Judge Pewter for allowing Ole Pem to drive you, Caddie, and Uncle Hume to Mississippi.

At the trial, I could hardly bear to look at Dan's parents, knowing I'd taken the life of their beloved son. They were present to see that justice was done—to seek vengeance—my death!

BUT, THE JURY SAW FIT TO GIVE ME ANOTHER CHANCE! God sees me as I am and knows I am not an intentional murderess. I literally became unbalanced by Dan's cruelty. Oh! The hell I went through!

Today, I looked at my hands and remembered these hands pulled the rag rug, which held Dan's body, down the back stairway and it bumped on each rung—I remembered that the rug was full of Dan's blood. And, then, I had a flashback—a recall of one occasion when Dan beat me, and I fell on the floor. He threatened to beat me again because I bled on the rug. I shudder to think of our blood mixing together on that same rug that I drug to the cotton field, holding his body.

When I met Dan, I had the heart of a dreamer. It was full of love, excitement, and a visualization of a completed beautiful dream, full of peace.

I lived and loved in my dream-world and had no inclination that anything would ever mar my life. My reservoir was full of happy thoughts and memories, which are now shattered and depleted.

I have asked God to forgive me for my horrible crime of murdering Dan. I hold my ears and tell my brain and my soul to quieten itself—to be still!

I SIGN THIS LETTER—

With MUCH LOVE and LIFE!
Janelle

P.S. I couldn't believe you brought Macie's Manuscript/Diary in person to try and help me. I am so sorry you had to leave it behind, as a Court Exhibit, and I know how sad you must feel. I'm sure that Defense's Exhibit Eight saved my life!"

* * * *

Aunt Mae read Janelle's letter hesitantly and intently. Her hands began to shake and perspiration formed upon her forehead. *Dan! You monster! How could you have been so cruel that you forced Janelle to kill you? I can't believe she chopped you into pieces like an animal. Was Janelle also a monster just waiting for you to come along, so she could carry out her evil rage, or did you create her into a monster by your own cruel treatment? Did the cruelties of your daddy make you become a monster, Dan?*

* * * *

"Hume, do me a favor, please."

"Sure. What can I help you with, Mae?"

"Don't laugh, Hume."

"Laugh? I haven't heard what you want yet."

"You see this pink thread?"

"Sure."

"It's 19 inches long."

"Yes. I see a pink thread and it's 19 inches long. Now what?" He scratched his head.

"Promise you won't tell anyone."

"Okay, I promise." He crossed his heart with his right hand and laughed.

"You need to take this thread over to the old sweet-gum tree. You know the place where you rest when you go for a walk?"

"I need to take this thread to that old sweet-gum tree?"

"Yes. You know that rock you rest your arm on? Remember?"

"Sure."

"Well, just put this 19 inch, pink thread under that old rock. Okay?"

"What superstition is it, this time?" He twisted the pink thread around his index finger, unwound it, and pulled it through his fingers. "Is it for luck?"

"It's just something I need to do." She smiled at him sweetly. "It could be lucky."

He searched her face, as he wrapped the pink thread around his finger, and remembered the last time she went alone to carry out her superstitions. "I shake in my boots to think how you may not be here today, Mae. That day you went by yourself to Ghost Hollow still bothers me."

"It bothers me, too, Hume. Deaver sure gave me a fright!"

"I still think about that day."

"Yes! Me, too!" Aunt Mae said, as she smoothed the wrinkled collar of his blue cotton shirt.

"By the way, Mae, I've been thinking." He squeezed her hand. "When we went to see Janelle and you tried your best to help her, I know you were doing it all for Macie. I believe Macie knows you've done it all for her, don't you?"

Aunt Mae fingered the chain and gold locket around her neck, which held a sacred piece of Mandy's hair. She nodded her head. "Yes, Hume I did it for Macie and I did it for Mandy."

Uncle Hume closed one of his hands over her hand which held the locket, and kissed her on the forehead. He studied her face intently. "Mae, I never knew you did things for other people because of Mandy."

"Yes, I see Mandy each time I look into the face of every little child. Each time I help someone, I am closer to Mandy."

* * * *

AT THE QUILTING HOUSE

Bunches of dried mint, bay, basil, rosemary, lavender and thyme hung from the rafters of the Quilting House to repel moths. Its odor was comforting and soothing.

"Can you believe we're almost finished with *The Crown of Thorns!* It's lovely!" said Gossiper One.

"It was harder to do than the pattern of *The Garden of Eden*, but it's prettier," said Gossiper Two.

"We heard Janelle got life, Aunt Mae. You did her a good service letting her use Macie's diary, and all. But, then, her daddy did have a pot of money to spend on her defense, so they say," said Gossiper One.

"She needed to be punished, but I didn't want Janelle to die," said Aunt Mae.

"We can't believe the court kept Macie's original manuscript as evidence. We know it's hard on you, Mae," said Gossiper Two.

Aunt Mae sighed, and kept her eyes on her needle. "Yes, hard. Maybe it's the Lord's way of preventing me from reading it over and over again, and rehashing regrets and guilt. Hume and I were so ignorant, we didn't know they'd keep her diary as evidence, after it was read in court. I grieve for Macie's papers, but I'm glad it helped Janelle. The judge gave the Defense a lot of leniency—a lot breaks."

"Bet Judge Pewter and his brother helped her daddy pull some strings," said Gossiper One. "They say Janelle's paw has lots and lots of money and money talks, don't you know!"

"If anybody can do it, Judge Pewter can!" said Gossiper Two.

"Yes, Judge Pewter said you and Uncle Hume changed the outcome of Janelle's case by allowing them to use Macie's manuscript," said Gossiper One.

"Yes, I suppose it helped to let the court know that Macie was Dan's wife, and Macie died in the same way that Dan tried to kill Janelle. He tried to make

Janelle cut her wrists," Aunt Mae sighed. "And, remember, Macie's wrists were cut."

"How's Caddie taking all this news about Janelle's case and about that crazy preacher taking nude pictures of Macie, Ratchel Robin and all those other dead people?" asked Gossiper Three.

"Caddie's holding up as well as can be expected," said Aunt Mae. "She works everyday."

"You know everyone thinks Caddie is the spit image of you, Mae," said Gossiper One.

"And, how is that?" Aunt Mae smiled.

"She's different from most girls. She forages, and gathers herbs. She's assisting you bringing babies into this world and helping first aid the people when Doc is not around, and her being so kind and all," Gossiper One nodded, looked down at the quilt, and pushed her thimble firmly on the needle. "She's gonna be or is another you, Mae."

"How flattering!" Aunt Mae laughed.

"Haven't seen Jake at church lately. He out of town?" asked Gossiper One.

"Haven't seen Jake in a few weeks, but I suppose he's in town."

"Guess what, Mae," Gossiper Two giggled.

"I can't guess. What is it? Have you got more news about that crazy Preacher? That Buker Webster?" asked Aunt Mae.

"We know Buker Webster is still in the boobie-hatch. He's at Milledgeville. Just sits and holds his Bible close to his chest. But this news is about something else." Said Gossiper One.

"Can't guess the news—what is it? What?"

"News is probably about Honey," said Gossiper Two.

"Can't believe Honey Clement is a slut—her having that baby girl and all!" said Gossiper Three.

"Who do you think is Honey Clements' lover, being as how Deaver has run off from the revenuers, and all?" asked Gossiper One. "Aunt Mae, you delivered the baby. What do you think?"

Aunt Mae shook her head.

"Never saw her even speak to a man, myself!" said Gossiper One.

"Maybe her man is not from around here. It's a mystery to me," said Gossiper Three.

"Well, who could the daddy be?" asked Gossiper Two.

"It's a mystery," said Gossiper Three.

"Honey's baby girl is very cute. Her name is *Daisy Dee Clements,"* Aunt Mae announced with a smile. "She's 19 inches long and has a head full of dark black hair."

"'Daisy Dee Clements?' What kind of a name is that?" asked Gossiper Two.

"A pretty name," said Aunt Mae, "for a pretty baby girl."

"Guess Honey's boy finally got over that car wreck. He's pretty wild, don't you know," said Gossiper Two.

"Honey's boy is home from the hospital and doing okay," said Aunt Mae.

"Guess what else I heard? This is really a shocker, but it's kinda sweet, too!" said Gossiper One.

"You got your ears full of gossip, I'd say," said Gossiper Two.

"Is it really good news?" asked Aunt Mae

"Yes, and you'll be surprised," said Gossiper One.

"Don't keep us in suspense!" Aunt Mae insisted.

"George-West and Jessie Myers have adopted a little red-headed baby girl. She's just a few weeks old!"

"You don't say! Jessie wants children. When did they adopt her?" asked Aunt Mae.

"Judge Pewter made the arrangements for the adoption. He went with Jessie and George-West to Atlanta to get the baby. Just got back." The Gossiper laughed.

"You don't say?" Aunt Mae smiled. "Now, isn't that interesting?"

"Knew you'd be surprised and happy, too."

"Can't wait to hold that little baby girl. What's her name?" Aunt Mae asked.

"Carol Mae," Gossiper One volunteered. "Carol Mae Meyers."

"Well, if that doesn't beat all! Jessie Mae will be so proud!" Aunt Mae laughed, as she pulled a heavy thread through the three layers of material. "That does beat all!"

* * * *

Missy Taylor Williams arrived at Jessie and George-West Meyers' white two story home, shaded by tall oak trees and overlooking a well-kept grassy yard. She hesitated at the gate, took a deep breath and glanced at her watch. *On time,* she thought. She admired the green fields, the woods surrounding the back of the house, and the Blue Ridge Mountains in the distance.

She stood before a dark red door, and rang the shiny brass, doorbell.

Jessie Meyers opened the door. "Come into the front room and sit down, Missy."

"Thank you, Miz Meyers." She sat on the edge of an antique settee and observed matching red, Chinese urns setting on each end of an exquisitely carved mantel piece. "I don't know why you sent for me."

A cool breeze blew through the windows causing the white lace curtains to flap. A door in the back of the house slammed. Missy jumped.

"I'll get right to the point."

"Yes, please do," Missy responded.

"George-West and I have noticed you at church. You seem to be kind to your children and take good care of them. But with the exception of Hannah. You know how I feel about Hannah—I don't approve of her ways."

Missy's face flushed. She shifted in her seat and held her black, patent leather, out of date purse, tightly. *What does she have in mind? She's talking about my daughter. Does she want to approach me about her husband having an affair with my Hannah?* Her heart began to beat faster. *How awkward this is going to be!*

"You've heard that George-West and I adopted a perfect baby girl, I suppose?"

Missy sighed heavily, and with relief. "The whole neighborhood is excited and happy for you, Miz. Meyers."

"Missy, how would you like to take care of the baby for me? We have very few people around here that I can call on."

Missy placed her hand upon her heart, hoping its fast beat didn't show through her blouse. She smoothed her blue, cotton skirt and leaned forward. "You mean as a job? You'd pay me to keep your baby?"

"Yes, of course, we'll pay you well."

"May I see the baby?"

"But, of course! Missy, I'd like for you to come with me to the nursery and see the most beautiful baby in the world."

* * * *

Ole Pem pulled a blade of grass through his hand, as he sat on the doorsteps outside the meeting house waiting for the children's Sunday School party to be dismissed. He jumped to his feet and dusted the seat of his pants, when he heard the doorknob rattle. The first ones out of the building were Tommy and Bobby. "Hi, Ole Pem," they both yelled, as they ran past him. The other children followed in an orderly fashion.

When Locket appeared in the doorway, he rushed up to her. "Locket, I missed you!" He flashed his most enchanting smile.

"I'm so glad to see you, Ole Pem!"

"I wanted you to be one of the first people to know that I passed the Bar. I'll be working for Judge Pewter starting next week."

"Congratulations, Ole Pem. This is welcome news." Her blue eyes danced happily.

"I was worried you might have already moved to Atlanta, Locket. I'm glad you're still here."

"I plan to move when my teaching contract expires—in about a month."

"That's too bad. Are you going to renew your contract?"

"No, I'm afraid not. I can't keep staying here. It's too much pressure. Besides, Jessie Meyers is on the board, and she insisted that my contract is not to be renewed. She called me *an evil woman.*" Her sky blue eyes flashed concern.

"That's too bad, Locket."

A flock of geese flew overhead towards the lake.

"The Meyers govern everything around here, don't they?"

"Not everything, but just about everything. If you want to stay, I'll talk to Judge Pewter and see what we can do. He's on the board. Want me to speak to him?"

"No, I've talked to Judge Pewter about my contract and about my divorce and the final decree. I've decided not to fight the board. I'm going on back to Atlanta and try to start over. It's been hard to stay here, Ole Pem. A crazy husband doing crazy things is hard to overcome. I love the children at the school and they're very special, but some of the people here treat me suspiciously."

"I know it must be very hard for you." He stared into her large, round blue eyes, and wondered at their innocence. "Your contract doesn't refer to your husband's actions does it?"

"No—but you automatically become a package deal, if you're married," she said.

"I suppose."

"It'll be hard to leave Aunt Mae and Uncle Hume. Guess I'm addicted to their loving ways."

"Addicted, huh? That's a pretty good description. You heard Janelle got a life's sentence, huh?"

"Yes! How lucky she is to have you as her good friend."

"The specifics in Macie's diary about Dan mistreating Macie really helped Janelle get *Life.* The jury said it was an eye-opener. The judge told Judge Pewter the jurors told him that's mainly why they voted for life." He smiled.

"The judge in Mississippi discussed the case with Judge Pewter?"

"Yeah, they went to law school together. They go way back," said Ole Pem.

"But, you are the one who convinced Aunt Mae and Uncle Hume to go to Janelle's defense with Macie's diary."

"I've tried to be a good friend. Guess it paid off for Janelle."

"It was miraculous that Janelle had all of you to help her!"

"The court kept Macie's manuscript as evidence. I guess you know, since you board with Aunt Mae and Uncle Hume," he said, sadly. "I never figured on that taking place. I didn't think things through."

"Aunt Mae is still grieving over the court keeping Macie's original documents and photographs, as Exhibits for the Defense, but she said if it helped save Janelle's life, it was worth giving it up."

"I know she's grieving for Macie's documents, but that diary is definitely what kept Janelle from getting the death penalty. Her words backed up Janelle's daily life and experiences with Dan. Lucky, though, that the judge allowed it in," said Ole Pem.

"Uncle Hume said that even in death, Macie helped someone," said Locket.

"That's right. Even in death, she did a good work. Isn't that amazing?"

"I feel like I knew Macie."

"Macie was a good girl," said Ole Pem.

"I wish I could have met her. You know, Aunt Mae and Uncle Hume are very unselfish—"

"—caring and giving," Ole Pem completed her sentence.

"Wish I could have heard Caddie read Dear Di-Ar-Ree,—Love, Me, and hear the clerk when she read Dear Me,—Love Di-Ar-Ree. It had to be very moving."

"When Caddie read her part, and then the clerk read her part of the Manuscript/Diary, you could hear a pin drop in the courtroom.

"It must have been emotional and heart-rending," Locket smiled compassionately.

"Caddie sat in the witness chair and read the first and last pages of the Manuscript—you know, the part that sounds like a fairy tale. She also read the part to *Dear Di-Ar-Ree.* One of the clerks sat in a chair in front of the witness chair and read the answers to Dear Me," said Ole Pem. "She was an older lady, and looked kinda old-fashioned. She was the perfect one to read the parts to Dear Me." Her delivery—her voice was perfect!"

"And, what did Aunt Mae do after they read the manuscript?"

"She sat very quietly—very dignified. When the judge said, 'And let the Manuscript of Macie Mariana Brown Zanderneff be marked as the Defense's Exhibit Number Eight,' Aunt Mae was visibly shaken."

"Oh! Just hearing about what happened at the trial gives me chills."

"Like I said it was highly unusual. The way the whole thing unfolded was very dramatic. The judge gave Janelle a lot of breaks. What he did is unheard of."

"How did you feel when the Manuscript was marked as an Exhibit?"

"It tore my heart out knowing how sacred those pages were to Aunt Mae, and Uncle Hume—knowing they had to leave the original Manuscript/Diary behind."

"—and, now?"

"I feel guilty thinking that Aunt Mae could still be holding Macie's manuscript in her arms, if it had not been for my asking her to help Janelle."

"But, it saved Janelle's life."

"That's what Judge Pewter keeps reminding me," he said meekly.

"You and Macie saved Janelle's life." Locket smiled and looked into Ole Pem's eyes very earnestly. "What a dear, dear friend you are to her, and what a dear friend you've been to me," she smiled.

"Her father had the money to get her a great lawyer, and that lawyer was imaginative, intelligent and effective. That's what got her Life, but, most important of all—the judge gave her a lot of breaks. She's a lucky woman."

"Yes, and I still say she's lucky to have you," she smiled.

"May I take you home, Locket? I have Judge Pewter's car."

"I'd love it! Let me lock up!"

* * * *

It was about midnight.

A light rain fell on the tin roof.

Ole Jeb barked about the time Uncle Hume heard a loud thud—the sound of something dropping on the back porch. Ole Jeb barked again and became quiet. Uncle Hume got out of bed quickly, and retrieved a shotgun from the gunrack hanging over the bedroom door-casing.

"What is it, Hume?" Aunt Mae whispered.

"Stay here, Mae." He tiptoed out of the room, hardly making a sound. He moved slowly to the kitchen and opened the door.

Lightning flashed in the distance.

He looked all around the back porch and stepped outside.

Ole Jeb stood at the top of the stairway and looked out into the darkness. He barked again once, became very quiet, looked out into the backyard, and began to wag his tail. Baby Jeb ran into the yard, but returned immediately to the porch, and stood beside Ole Jeb.

Uncle Hume looked out into the darkness. "What is it, Ole Jeb? What's out there?"

Aunt Mae stood in the doorway, holding a coal oil lamp. "Was it a critter?"

"Don't know, Mae. Let's go back in. It's getting mighty windy—stormy."

"The wind probably knocked something over."

When Uncle Hume started to go back into the house, he noticed an apple crate leaning near the back door. "What's this inside this apple crate?" he asked. "Whatever it is—it's wet. Looks like a black tarp wrapped around something."

He handed the shotgun to Aunt Mae. She leaned against the door to hold it open.

"Put it on the kitchen table," said Aunt Mae. She placed the gun in the corner of the kitchen, and set the coal oil lamp upon the table.

They leaned over and peered inside the crate.

"What is it, Hume?"

He removed the wet, black tarp. Inside the tarp was a package wrapped in newspaper, tied with flour-sack string. He untied it carefully.

"This is curious," he said.

Inside the package lay a bundle of newspapers, also tied with flour sack string. Tucked inside the string was a note written on bluelined tablet paper.

May the persimmin (sp?) be sweeter

May Yellow-Medder be greener

This year.

Signed: Your Friend

Uncle Hume jerked the note away from the package and lying before them was Macie's Manuscript/Diary—the original manuscript:

<u>MANUSCRIPT OF MACIE ANDRIANA BROWN ZANDERNEFF,</u>
<u>DEFENDANT'S EXHIBIT NUMBER EIGHT</u>

"Oh, my Lord! My Lord!" Aunt Mae screamed.

"How in the world did this get all the way from Mississippi?" asked Uncle Hume, excitedly. He looked at the newsprint, '<u>The Daily News,</u>' ________, Mississippi.

"Oh! My!" Aunt Mae picked up the package and held it tightly to her breasts. "Somehow Deaver stole it or had it stolen. That note is from Deaver."

Uncle Hume stared at the manuscript with mixed emotions. "Yes, Deaver is in a peck of trouble."

"Yes, trouble."

"But, Mae, you can't turn the manuscript back in, the law will start looking for Deaver, hotter than ever," he said as he lovingly touched and smoothed his long and bony, fingers over Macie's diary.

"How sweet of Deaver!" Caddie whispered.

Aunt Mae and Uncle Hume jumped, and turned around.

"Caddie! You scared us to death!"

"Listen, Caddie. You can't tell Jake. You know his conscience. He'd get torn between turning Deaver in; taking the Manuscript back to the evidence room in Mississippi or us keeping the Manuscript/Diary," said Uncle Hume.

"No, we can't tell Jake," said Caddie. "No way."

"Caddie!" Aunt Mae whispered. "You can't breathe you saw this! Not to anyone—not anyone!"

"I understand. I won't tell, but this means Deaver is nearby."

"Don't pry into it. Let it be!" Aunt Mae whispered.

"Like I said, I understand. It's a good thing that Locket has already moved to Atlanta."

"Yeah! Locket would be standing right here beside us," said Uncle Hume. "Making things more difficult."

"Why are you up, Caddie. Did you hear the commotion?" asked Aunt Mae.

"Yes, I heard the noise, but I was already awake. I couldn't sleep."

"What's wrong, Chile?" Aunt Mae placed her arm around Caddie.

"I was just thinking about Jake—knowing he's drinking more and more, and destroying himself."

"I know. I know. But, what can we do?" asked Aunt Mae.

Caddie wrapped "The Yellow Star of Texas" closer to her body. "What can we do is a very good question."

"It's serious, Caddie. Remember Colonel—your father let the bottle destroy him," Uncle Hume whispered.

"Yes. Don't we all know it."

"Have you talked with Jake?"

"Not lately. One of the last times I saw him, I told him that I don't want to see him again. He loves Macie's ghost and he loves moonshine. He needs professional help, Aunt Mae."

"I'm going to bed," said Uncle Hume. "I believe this is woman talk."

"You can stay, if you want to, Uncle Hume."

"Naw. I'll check on Jake tomorrow morning—*this* morning it is now! Something must be wrong by him not coming over to see us in such a long time. I'll get to the bottom of what's going on with Jake."

"Aunt Mae, loving Jake was very challenging—very exasperating!" Caddie sighed. "When I saw him the day we went to Mississippi, I told him we'd always see each other at family gatherings."

"You said *was very challenging*, like you're talking in the past. May I ask—has Jake ever made you happy?" asked Aunt Mae.

"I used to be happy just to be with him, but something happened to change the way I feel about him."

"Will he ever love you?"

"I used to hope that he would. I don't hope anymore."

"Marriage wouldn't change him or make him love you, would it?"

"I know marriage wouldn't help. I just hate to think about what he did, and what he said. He made me feel so worthless and dirty."

"Disappointed, maybe—not worthless," said Aunt Mae.

"I'm disappointed, all right."

"Don't be like Macie. She stayed with Dan knowing that she should get away."

"Macie could have done anything she wanted to do in this world that she set her mind to do, but she made some wrong choices. I don't want to end up like her."

"You'll come to the right decision, Caddie."

Aunt Mae followed Caddie to her bedroom.

"I'm very mad at Jake! He's uncaring, insensitive, callous, mean and disappointing."

"I believe you *are mad* at him and you should be. He doesn't treat you right."

"I mean—I am really, really mad!"

"It hurts me to see you in such a dilemma."

Caddie allowed the quilt to drop from her shoulders to the floor. She looked into her bedroom mirror, smoothed her hair, and rubbed the freckles across her well shaped, cameo nose with long and tapered fingers. "Macie had smooth olive skin—no freckles." Caddie sighed.

"You are just as lovely as Macie, inside and out, only in a different way. Don't put yourself down."

"Thanks for talking, Aunt Mae. It always helps." Caddie whispered. She sat down on the edge of her bed and rubbed her tired eyes.

"I love you, Caddie. You're the most giving and caring young girl that I know. I'm so lucky you're here with me everyday as my daughter and a friend."

"Me, too! I'm the lucky one. I love you more than you'll ever know. I'm so grateful for your guidance in my life," she sighed loudly. "Glad you got Macie's diary back. Guess we all kissed it goodbye the day it became Defense's Exhibit Number Eight."

"Can you believe it? I just want to take Macie's words to bed with me now and curl up and go to sleep," said Aunt Mae.

"I understand how you feel."

"I love you very much, Caddie. We'll talk tomorrow." Aunt Mae pulled the door closed very quietly.

"Love you, too—" Caddie said softly, as she scooted herself closer to the bedside table which held a coal oil lamp. She removed a worn and torn piece of paper from her bathrobe pocket, spread it, smoothed it between her fingers, and held it to the light. She read:

Dear Caddie,

—I especially wanted to reminisce about Macie.

She thought back to the afternoon that Jake left the note at the boarding house in Atlanta. She caressed her name *C-A-D-D-I-E.* Jake's long and muscular fingers held the pen that wrote the letters of her name. She placed the note to her nose and held it close. She felt compelled to beat herself up for being so obsessive of Jake. Tears rolled down her cheeks, and blurred the black ink.

She held that very small, worn and yellowed piece of paper over the kerosene lamp that sat on her bedside table, and watched a blue flame catch and turn the note into fiery red and yellow words, Dear Caddie,—reminisce about Macie**.** The burning words irritated her nose.

She held the edge of the paper between her fingers, felt the heat and released the blazing note into the white ceramic water basin which sat upon the table beside the lamp.

Her eyes became riveted to the last burning words, Love, Jake, which gnarled brown and twisted black as they charred into grey and white ashes.

She blew out the lamp, walked to her window, fumbled with the aging, squeaking shutters and opened them.

Lightning flashed in the far distance—somewhere in the direction of Jake's cabin.

She suddenly realized that from the very beginning, Jake always said that he *wanted to reminisce about Macie.*

Macie—are you listening to me? The note is about you, and not "Dear Caddie." I agree he said he loved you, over and over again, yet he led me to believe our friendship was deeper than a casual friendship. He came to see me, wined and dined me. We went for walks, listened to the radio, and did stuff with Henny-Penny and Kackie and the family. Jake should have stayed away from me completely if he didn't want to lead me on. Even though I loved him, I can't forgive him for what he did to me. When we fell down at the tree, he laughed. It hurt to know he'd never care about me the way I cared for him. Macie, I need to ask you a very personal question: Was Jake so careless with you, so rough, so crude? I wonder? Is that why you chose Dan, and not Jake? I have been such a fool to push myself on him!

She searched her heart for a good reason why she'd become so controlled by her obsession of Jake. *Dear God, forgive me for being so foolish—I know that I shouldn't have, but I pushed myself on Jake and let him know I loved him and was ready to give him my body, freely and lovingly. Please give me the peace of heart that I need to get on with life. Thank you, Lord. May Your Will be done.*

She stood before the open window, and lifted her face to the early morning sky. A fine mist bathed her face, and a chilling dampness coiled around her neck and breasts. She clasped her hands around the neck of her nightgown, and pulled it closely around her chin. The acrid odor of the remains of the burned ashes lying in the water basin filled her nostrils. A tremor of revulsion and anger ran through her body because of the self-inflicted pain she had brought upon herself through her obsession for Jake.

* * * *

Rain pelted the tin roof of Jake's cabin. It was loud, but not loud enough to drown his drunken thoughts of Macie. He opened the door, staggered onto his front porch, down the narrow wooden steps and into the front yard.

Lightning flashed and the thunder rumbled.

He held a glass fruit jar high over his head and the raindrops blended with the moonshine.

He staggered in the direction where he heard the wind carrying the voice of Macie. She seductively whispered his name, wooed him, and touched all his instincts and yearnings: JAKE! JAKE!

He fell to his knees!

A thunderbolt rolled, boomed and cracked overhead, and lightning flashed. A giant bird with a wide wing-span flew close overhead, and its flapping wings whirred in the wind. As lightning flashed, and the thunder rumbled, he looked up as The Storey Angel landed before him. A marble covering fell from her body in large chunks, and exposed a lovely, perfect creature—a heavenly angel that hovered closely. She looked at him with warm, sympathetic eyes and he felt her love and understanding.

He looked up from the large puddle of gushing water, which engulfed him. He struggled to get up, but his intoxication hindered his thinking processes and movement. "What are you doing here?" Jake yelled loudly, hoping that he could be heard over the rumble of the thunder.

The Storey Angel smiled, and knelt down in front of him. She held his wrist, shook it, and directed him to drop his jar of moonshine. She plucked him from the rising water, wiped the rain from his head, the tears from his eyes, spread her warm, dry wings out to full capacity and covered him from the elements. Jake nuzzled his head in her bosom of down feathers, and sought the warmth and comfort he knew would be there.

* * * *

"It's after five, Caddie. Why are you working so late?" Ole Pem walked to the front door and placed the "Closed" sign on the door. He pulled on a navy blue, wool overcoat, walked over to her desk and attempted to sit on the edge of her paper strewn desk.

She stacked plats, petitions regarding land disputes, deeds, proposed agreements between disgruntled partners, Memorandums of Agreement, divorce battles, depositions and drafts of wills, transcripts of trials, and copies of subpoenas into neat little stacks on her oak desk and made room for him to sit down.

"Trying to finish typing this letter for Judge Pewter before I leave," she said.

"He's gone for the day. Want to go to Sojo's?"

"Need to go to Pewter-Mapp's Little Store and pick out an electric lamp for Aunt Mae before they close."

"Okay."

"You knew Uncle Hume had electricity strung down to the house," she giggled.

"Believe everyone around these parts has heard by now," he grinned.

"He's so happy!"

"It's thrilling to know that he finally met his goal and had the wires strung down to the house. He's saved his money forever, hasn't he?"

"Oh! Yes! Forever and ever, as Henny-Penny and Kackie would say."

He smiled and touched her lightly on the shoulder. "And, then, after you go to the store?"

"And, then, what?" she asked. She stopped typing, looked up at him and smiled.

"And, then, after you go to Mapp's?" he asked again. "Do you have plans?"

"Going home," she said.

"May I take you and the new lamp home in my new car?"

"That would be great, Ole Pem!"

"Good! Let's go now. You can finish that letter in the morning."

"Oh—okay," she covered the typewriter with a black canvas cover, stood up, and pushed the chair under the desk.

"You still think about Jake a lot?" he asked.

"But, of course."

"You still love him, don't you, Caddie?"

"I used to obsess about him. He hurt me very much. I told him I didn't want to be with him anymore, after he did everything he could to tell me, and show me that I pushed myself on him and bothered him. It was very embarrassing. He always loved Macie—not me."

"You knew that he still loved her, when you came back here from Atlanta, didn't you, Caddie?" he asked, softly.

"Yes, I knew he loved Macie. I thought he'd love me after Macie died."

"Sometimes ghosts can be more real than life, huh?"

"In this case, yes," she sighed.

"Caddie, it was hard not to interfere in your friendship with Jake. I've wanted to ask you to go out with me for a long time."

"Ole Pem, you want you and me to do things together?" She looked deeply into his hazel eyes, his handsome face and smiled.

"Is it such a surprise? Surely, you can't be surprised that I want to be with you, talk and walk with you. We've always had a lot of fun together. We have a very close friendship." He touched her shoulder lightly with his index finger and took it away.

"But, I thought you liked Locket."

"You don't see me with her, do you?

"But, I thought—"

"Locket has a goal to be a preacher's wife—a *real* preacher's wife. She's dating a preacher as we speak."

Caddie laughed and placed her hand over her mouth. "That's fabulous!"

"Don't believe I qualify, do you?" Ole Pem laughed with her. "Being a preacher, I mean."

"But, you're a very good person, Ole Pem, and one of my best friends."

"I'm okay, but I'm a lawyer, not a preacher. Also, I'm not in love with Locket."

"I always love doing things with you Ole Pem." Her eyes sparkled. "We always have a good time."

"Good—Let's start by going to Mapp's and then Sojo's." He pulled her to her feet and gave her a hug. "As Tinker Daniels would say, 'I'm gonna *whup ye* playing pool!'"

"Yeah—right!" she drawled. "Ole Pem, may I ask you a question?"

"But, of course—"

Her brow crinkled and her voice became husky and low. "Do you like Tomboys?"

"You're speaking about yourself, aren't you, Caddie. Lean forward. I want to whisper something very important in your ear." He smiled at her mischievously.

Caddie leaned her head forward.

Ole Pem stood in front of her, gazed into her wide open blue-green eyes, and smoothed her long, blond hair behind her ears. "Such awesome, gorgeous, thick hair!" He held his hands on each side of her freckled face and nuzzled her ear with his lips. He whispered, "Being a Tomboy is just one of the things I love about you, Caddie Brown."

"Thank you, Pemrick McIntosh," she smiled.

He held the lapels of his overcoat and wrapped it tightly around her body and drew her close to him.

She placed her arms under his arms beneath the overcoat, held onto his back, and snuggled close to him. The odors of pipe tobacco leaves, Old Spice and perspiration filled her mind and blended into a heady, intoxicating and comforting place.

"I fit next to your body perfectly. My head comes right under your chin," she said so softly he could hardly hear.

He nuzzled her ear, bussed her on the lips and wrapped the coat around her more tightly.

"And, your lips fit mine perfectly," he whispered in her hair.

*   *   *   *

It was late in the evening, but Aunt Mae was wide awake.

She placed a coal oil lamp on a table and sat in a rocking chair near the fireplace. The firelight and lamplight reflected in her wire-rimmed spectacles and light danced through them upon the open, well worn pages of Macie's diary, enhancing blotches of tan and yellow smears of coffee stains. She lovingly moved her index finger across the words, "Defendant's Exhibit Number 8."

Welcome back home you sacred words and thoughts of hope and those of despair—all of you belong here with us. I will touch you and soothe you and give you all the comfort that I know how.

She leaned back in her chair, closed her eyes and held the Manuscript closely to her heart. She sighed heavily and contentedly, and placed Macie's Manuscript in her sewing basket, covered it with a crocheted afghan, and removed her spectacles. She rubbed her eyes and massaged her tired and achy neck

She thought about Hannah and her baby girl. *Wonder if Jessie Mae Myers has any inkling that her little adopted baby girl's father is really George-West Myers? One-half of that baby girl is George-West's flesh and blood.*

She poked the fire in the fireplace and rested her head on the back of her chair. *My! My! Judge Pewter really pulled a slick one.* She smiled to herself. *To think Judge Pewter arranged the adoption of Hannah's baby and placed that baby girl right in the lap of its own father—George-West Meyers, but, of course, I'm only guessing, except for Grandmaw Taylor being so sure. This is kinda like the story of Moses—this little baby girl's babysitter will be Missy, her own grandmother.*

And, Hannah? How can she stand by and see someone else raise her baby—no say so—see the baby, but not be able to touch the baby, ever. Could she love George-West so much she gave him and Jessie this baby—this gift?

The chair creaked when she arose from her chair.

Hume is grieving so bad for Jake! I don't know how to comfort him because Jake was just like our own son. I'm grieving, too. Sweet, Sweet Jake! I knew the call of the bottle was strong, but, still, it's hard to believe he was so drunk that he drowned in a puddle of water. We know that Jake re-lived; re-breathed the days he spent with Macie, and re-played every word they ever spoke together! And now, he's in heaven with his beloved Macie. That's about the only thing about his death that soothes me, and when I go to the graveyard, I see the Storey Angel standing tall, looking over them. I know how much Jake loved that angel.

I'd have never believed how wonderful Caddie's life has turned around! She and Ole Pem seem perfect for each other! I am thankful she's happy at last!

* * * *

She rubbed her eyes on the corner of her white apron, opened the front door, walked out into the front yard and looked up into the stormy sky. Lightning flashed in the distance.

She sighed heavily, and stretched her tired back.

Lord, you do work things out in mysterious ways, especially with the help of Judge Pewter and the help of Deaver Clements. And, Lord, I know Deaver stole Macie's Manuscript from the property room in Mississippi and it was the wrong thing to do, but I'd be lying if I said that seeing Macie's Manuscript, and holding it again in my arms didn't make me feel powerful happy—so all I can say is thanks. Thanks a whole lot! God, you're a good God!

Suddenly, she became aware of a dim and flickering light in one of the quilting house windows. She began to run and stumbled over the river rock as she neared the quilting house.

She moved slowly up the stairway to the front door, stopped, and took a deep breath. She turned the doorknob with great anticipation, and eased the door open, quietly.

Sitting on the floor next to the unlit fireplace was a woman, covered with a pieced quilt, it's design called *Remember Me.*

Aunt Mae held her arms out, and called, "Joanie!"

A young girl turned her bruised, battered face with blackened, purple, and swollen eyes towards the coal oil lamp light.

"No, my name is Minnie." She held her jaw, and moaned through swollen and parched lips.

Aunt Mae knelt down beside the young girl and gently touched her misshapen face with her right index finger and turned her battered face towards her. "Minnie, I'm Aunt Mae."

"Oh, glory be! Thank God, that's you," the young girl whispered reverently. "I heered tell in the holler you'd help a beat girl."

THE END

978-0-595-42934-
0-595-42934-3

Printed in the United States
80014LV00001B/163-258

9 780595 429349